W9-BER-979

BLACK WATER

ALSO BY LOUISE DOUGHTY

FICTION

Apple Tree Yard

Whatever You Love

Stone Cradle

Fires in the Dark

Honey-Dew

Dance with Me

Crazy Paving

NONFICTION

A Novel in a Year

BLACK WATER

LOUISE DOUGHTY

SARAH CRICHTON BOOKS
FARRAR, STRAUS AND GIROUX NEW YORK

Sarah Crichton Books
Farrar, Straus and Giroux
18 West 18th Street, New York 10011

Printed in the United States of America
Originally published in 2016 by Faber and Faber Limited, Great Britain
Published in the United States by Sarah Crichton Books / Farrar, Straus and Giroux
First American edition, 2016

Library of Congress Cataloging-in-Publication Data
Names: Doughty, Louise, 1963– author.
Title: Black water : a novel / Louise Doughty.
Description: First American edition. | New York : Sarah Crichton Books, 2016.
Identifiers: LCCN 2016026815 | ISBN 9780374114015 (hardcover) |
ISBN 9780374713669 (e-book)
Subjects: LCSH: Mercenary troops—Fiction. | Man-woman relationships—Fiction. |
BISAC: FICTION / Literary. | GSAFD: Romantic suspense fiction.
Classification: LCC PR6054.O795 B58 2016 | DDC 823/.914—dc23
LC record available at https://lccn.loc.gov/2016026815

www.fsgbooks.com
www.twitter.com/fsgbooks • www.facebook.com/fsgbooks

1 3 5 7 9 10 8 6 4 2

For Sylvia and Keith
with love

The biggest threat to world peace? Young men between the ages of eighteen and twenty-five, especially if they are unemployed, unmarried and don't own property.

DR CLAYBORNE CARSON

He may be a son-of-a-bitch but he's our son-of-a-bitch.

FRANKLIN D. ROOSEVELT
on President Somoza of Nicaragua
(attribution disputed)

Working in the fields, we wore out our hats quickly.

PRAMOEDYA ANANTA TOER,
The Mute's Soliloquy

Contents

I

MONKEY DONKEY OWL
(1998)

He woke every night at the same time, the small hours – when it was darkest. His upper torso jerked; his eyes opened. His hand flailed for the lamp on the bedside table but met the impediment of the mosquito net. It took a moment or two to lift the net and find the switch on the base of the lamp, then he would sit upright, breathing heavily, absorbing the paradox of having woken so hot that he was damp and cold.

The electricity supply was unreliable during the day but at night the light came on immediately. The net was made of tough, opaque cotton and surrounded the bed. It was like being in a tent: outside, out there. The blood would rush in his ears so loudly that he could hear nothing else for a moment or two. He would breathe deeply, trying to still his heart and listening, then remind himself that he was not out there but in a large and comfortable hut, with ornate wooden doors and a rectangular block held in thick brackets barring them shut.

The hut was halfway up the hillside but the sounds of the rushing Ayung River filled the valley, the clamour and clamber of water over boulders. The rainy season had ended late that year and the river was still full. Night did something odd to the sounds around the hut: it was hard to tell how far or close they were – the scud and scramble of squirrels across his roof, the thump of something heavier, a monkey perhaps, also on the roof, or was it on the veranda? The veranda would creak, on occasion – it was supported by tall stilts and so impossible for anyone, or anything, to walk across it without making a noise.

Sometimes, he thought he heard a light scratching at the base of the wooden door. A river rat, perhaps? Did they come this far up the hill at night? He had seen several of them on his walks along the valley, black and quick, lolloping between the fat green leaves of undergrowth. At other times he would think, yes, there is definitely a creature on the roof. He would listen to the claw scratchings above him become more regular, and the *scrit-scrit* would turn into a *pit-pit*, pause, *pit-pit-pit*, which blossomed into the sound of rain. The clamour mounted rapidly then, until it was so deafening even the river became inaudible, water drowned beneath water.

In daylight hours, he liked to stand on the veranda and watch the rain, a wall of it so solid it seemed to fly upwards as well as down. In daylight it was beautiful – as long as you didn't have to go out in it – but during the hours of darkness the torrent closed the world down, masked all other noises: there was nothing but rain.

He had only been in the hills for a week but it felt much longer. The errors of judgement he had made still filled his head. Henrikson, that knucklehead, walking in like he owned the place. Well, at least Wahid and Amber had seen through him; and that journalist – he couldn't believe he'd let her play him – then, to cap it all, Amsterdam constantly questioning his ability. He went over and over his conversations with them in the hot dark hours when he lay awake, trapped in a maze of reasoning.

The last two nights, the fear had got worse. The noises on

the roof had begun to mutate. He would wake now, more violently each night, certain that what he could hear was the sounds of feet on floorboards, not outside on the veranda but inside the hut, creeping closer and closer to his bed. At such times, his fear would mount so rapidly that all he could do was lift the mosquito net and climb down from the bed and patrol the hut, restlessly, looking under the table, opening the cupboard in the corner, peering into all the dark corners where the lamplight could not reach. Then he would need to urinate, and he would force himself to slide the block from its wooden brackets and push one of the doors outwards. He would defy the darkness by standing there for a moment, staring out at the pitch black, the dim light behind him casting a huge shadow across the veranda, and he would step over the carved doorframe towards the rail, piss mightily out into the dark, go back inside, slide the wooden block across and check every corner of the hut all over again, as if someone or something might have sneaked past him, although this time the ritual was calmer, because he had invited an intruder by opening a door and so it was less likely to happen. He had proved to himself that he was not afraid. They only came when you were afraid.

Eventually, he would get back into bed and turn off the lamp, his heart stilled. The ritual search, the bravado of opening the door, had convinced him that his fears were groundless, nothing more than the irrationality of night. He would lie back and close his eyes, pulling the sheet over his shoulder. He would just be drifting back to sleep . . . And it would come, then, when he was at the point of sinking back into unconsciousness. Always then: the ghekko's honking cry, on the roof right above his head, only feet away, sudden and loud in its malevolence and echoing above all the other sounds. Eh-*ur!* A derisive, taunting pause. Eh-*ur!* He would be upright again, sweating again, furious and terrified at its warning. Eh-*ur!*

He would cry out then, shout out loud, and bang the sides of his hut to frighten the creature away. Wasn't it dawn soon? Where was Kadek?

That particular night, the night he knew, the ghekko's call was so loud, so inevitable, that he didn't even bother to bang against the walls of his hut, just sat up, breathing heavily, put the light on and slumped with his head in his hands, as if to say to the ghekko, okay, you win.

It came to him then, what was going to happen. They were going to kill him. *Take a break for a while*, Amsterdam had said. *Go up to the hills, we have a little place outside of town, it's been used before. Have a rest, you've earned it. When we've talked to the West Coast, we'll let you know.* He had wondered, at the time, why they had to talk to the West Coast at all. They had sent in Henrikson, after all. If Amsterdam was certain he was finished they should have recalled him immediately. Why send him up to the hills – unless they wanted him out of the picture if the press ran with that story? Well, that was what he had thought at the time. Now though, in the dark of night, the decision to send him here took on a different meaning.

So, that was it. He had become a liability. He had outlived his usefulness, even though it wasn't him that had wanted to come back out here in the first place; they had had to twist his arm. How ironic was that?

This certainty was something new; something solid at last. He lay back on the bed and, for the first time since he had arrived on the island, allowed himself to close his eyes and listen to the ghekko without fear.

The roof above him creaked, the night insects chirruped and hollered – but there was no rain. One thing he was sure about: they would wait for rain.

In the morning, he was woken by the dawn light and the cicadas' tuneless chorale. A dream had come to him in the night, just before waking, it felt like – he couldn't recall it, but was sure he had dreamt. There was an image in his head of a man in an open-necked shirt, smiling at him in greeting, and a feeling of fear and horror. The image made no sense. He shook his head to rid himself of it.

As soon as he started to walk around the hut, heavy-footed and exhausted as he was each morning, he heard the sound of Kadek on the veranda. He was never sure what time Kadek arrived but it was usually as dawn broke, in order to be there when Harper awoke.

He went to the doors and slid back the wooden block, a task that seemed so easy and natural in daylight he didn't even think about it. He pulled the doors wide open and stepped onto the veranda. Outside, it was grey and hot. The valley was flung before him: the hillside opposite his hut rose almost vertically, a vast steep wall of misted palm trees and in the distance, Gunung Agung, holy mountain, the volcano, its lower slopes wreathed in cloud so that it looked, as it often did, as if it was floating above the forest. His hut was *kaja*, it looked towards the mountain, which pleased him. Perhaps he was getting religious in his old age.

Kadek stood at the far end of the veranda as he did each

morning, keeping a respectful distance until bidden. He was holding a bucket of water.

'Good morning, Mr Harper,' he said, with the slightest of bows. And then, the expressionless statement: 'I hope you passed a peaceful night.'

Kadek's vocabulary was not wide but he spoke English with precision. His plain oval face was open and concerned and Harper had the feeling that the man knew nights were bad for him. He wondered what Kadek really thought of him. The hut belonged to the Institute and must have been used by other operatives but there was no trace of them, not so much as a few battered paperbacks in the wooden cupboard in the corner. As a result, Harper felt possessive about the hut, and about Kadek, although he was not naïve enough to imagine his feelings were reciprocated.

He wanted to say to Kadek, take a good look: do I look like a *bule* to you? He had spoken Indonesian to Kadek when he first arrived but they had soon slipped into English. It was often the same on these islands. In Europe and America, those demanding lands, he was a man required to explain himself, his thick black hair, his large black eyes. On the plane coming here, he could feel his skin colour changing mid flight: he got whiter and whiter the further east he flew.

He would have liked to discuss this with Kadek but he didn't want to embarrass the man, who probably thought that Harper looked pretty damn white to him and either way worked for a large and powerful organisation with some hard dollars to spend. Wasn't trying to befriend Kadek as insulting, in its own way, as giving him orders? So he did indeed behave like all the other white men who came to this island and all the islands on this vast archipelago. Perhaps that was why he woke in the night. It wasn't fear: it was hatred, hatred of himself. It was the knowledge that if – when – the men with machetes came, he, like all the other *bule*, would probably deserve it.

He nodded to Kadek. Kadek stepped forward with the bucket and poured water into the bowl on the small table to the right of the door, placed the bucket by the table, then lifted the towel that was hanging over his arm and folded it neatly next to the bowl, knowing that Harper liked his morning wash here, looking out over the valley. Later, he would pour more water in the *bak mandi* to the side of the hut.

'*Terima kasih*.'

'Shall I bring your breakfast, Mr Harper?' Kadek replied.

He stepped up to the bowl and splashed his face with water, then stood upright again with his face dripping. 'Thank you Kadek, if you could leave it on the desk. I'm going for a walk down to the river.'

Kadek gave another small bow, retreated. Harper pulled his T-shirt over his head, dropped it in a small crumple on the table, to the left of the bowl, and bent to finish his wash. He submerged each of his arms in turn, splashing water under his armpits, feeling, as he always did, the looseness of the muscles on the upper arms, muscles that had once been as taut as wire, or so he liked to think. He could pull his own weight up and down on a bar dozens of times in a row when he was a young man: not any more. He picked up the half coconut shell next to the bowl, filled it with a little water, rinsed it in case there were ants invisible against the dark grain of the wood and tossed the water over the balcony, filled it again and, bending his head, tipped it over his hair and the back of his neck, inhaling at the shock of it.

He dried himself with his T-shirt, then plunged it into the water, immersing it, pressing down on the blisters of air that rose in the fabric. A picture came to him, black water, long strands of hair, clinging like seaweed across his wrist: he dismissed the picture. Instead, he played the game of pressing at the bubbles of air beneath the T-shirt until they formed smaller bubbles, mobile beneath the thin material. Then he was impatient with the game and held the whole T-shirt down, crushing it between his fists. It was like drowning a kitten.

The path down to the river was narrow and steep. Black and yellow butterflies sprang amongst the foliage. It took ten minutes to descend but twice that to go back up, three times if you attempted it in the full heat of midday. After his disturbed night, it was calming to be walking in the grey, hot morning. His old boots – how many years had he had them? Expensive tan leather when new, from a shop on Oud Zuid, they were now so beaten and pale they were as comfy as slippers. The noise of the river rose to greet him, pure and deafening.

His favourite spot was a few minutes' walk from the bottom of the path, with a large rock that protruded over a pool. It was inviting enough to bathe in but he knew the ticks and parasites that lived there could be as deadly as the gangs of men who, he was convinced, would soon be roaming the countryside at night, just as before. On balance, he would prefer to face the men: and again, it came to him, just as it had in the pitch dark, his certainty, his own calmness in the face of it.

He sat down on the rock, withdrew his notebook and pencil from his pocket and in his neat but tiny scrawl, began to write. He had never needed to use code for his notes, that was how tiny and dense his writing was, but in any case, he would tear this page out later. It was only a first draft, the first draft of a letter that he would transfer onto fragile blue airmail paper when he returned to his hut.

He wrote a few lines, then stopped. *Francisca, how will she understand?* But he had to write or at least try. His wife – well, ex-wife now – it would be yet another tragedy for her. She wore tragedy well, it suited her, but he felt bad all the same because he knew in some way, she would blame herself. That was what Francisca did. Then there was his mother, *Moeder*. Ma. Anika. At this thought, he groaned aloud. She was alone now, with her bitter memories, and him the only child living. She was still drinking herself to death in the old house but the harder she drank, the longer she seemed to live. When they told her he was missing, it might not even register, so far gone was she. He watched the cool water of the pool beneath where he sat on the rock and the insects zig-zagging above its surface and thought that, when they came, the men with machetes, they would be very young; no more than boys really, skinny boys with long fingers and wide eyes, red bandanas tied round their foreheads, faces smeared with paint. The black shirts would come later, when the militias had had time to get organised. Did anyone really believe Habibie could prevent that, with the Generals pulling the strings? The boys were more haphazard in what they did but just as deadly. Young men believed in violence, after all: it was their religion, all over the world, whatever god they nominally worshipped – and this time, three decades on from the last, it would surely be no different. He could picture the procession that would come up the side of the valley in the night. They would pass this very spot. He was fairly sure they would come in this direction because the river path led directly to the edge of town.

It will be night, of course, he thought, a moonless night. They will wait for rain to mask their tracks. They will come along the path, walking in silence, the rushing of the river and the downpour on the leaves loud in their ears. Before they begin the climb up the steep side of the valley, they will pause for a *kretek*, crouching down beneath the large leaves of a tree for shelter, sharing one perhaps, because they have no money and have to steal cigarettes from their fathers and uncles, something they do without compunction. Their fathers and uncles have never spoken to them about what happened before so they believe, like all youths, that they have invented bravado. Their fathers and uncles seem like foolish old men to them. Perhaps, as they crouch and smoke, the water dripping down their necks, there will be some giggling, the kind of cold giggling that boys do before they transgress: the kind he remembered himself doing as he bullied the smaller boys at school.

And all at once, as he sat on the rock above the pool, he thought, yes, at school, I was a bully. He had thought he was defending himself but actually, he was a bully. *Black bastard from Batavia*, that ginger boy two years older had called him – the final thump landing with extra emphasis on Ba*ta*via. But it wasn't the ginger boy that Harper had beaten up, that boy had too many friends. It was a freckled kid in his own class who did no more than ask, *are you part-something?* Strange how that should come to him now.

After their cigarette, he thought, the boys will begin the climb up through the undergrowth, the steep sides of the valley. They will use their machetes to push the ferns and creepers aside.

That's something that won't be covered by the rain – it will leave a clear trail of their progress that would be appreciated by any investigator: except that there will be no investigation. Nobody investigated Joosten, after all.

As they near the hut, they will pause again, crouching down, observing the dark bulk of the construction above them, listening to the clatter of the water on the roof. And now the adrenaline will start to flow in their veins, and the smallest and youngest of them will be overwhelmed with a need to pee, and the one in charge, his big brother, will be most frightened of all, and so hiss urgent instructions to the others, hiding his fear in his commands. Perhaps the *bule* will make it easy for them, the boy in charge will be hoping: if he roars, or picks up an object to fight back, then it will be easy to cut him down, because then they will be threatened and have no choice. The big boy is hoping this is what will happen.

And he, Harper, alone in his hut, perhaps he will be awake, thanks to the ghekko – or perhaps, just for once, he will be sound asleep.

They will come through the window. The shutters will be easier to smash than the doors – it will make a racket, of course, even above the rain, but out here that won't matter. It will be too late by then. There is only one window, and one door, and both lead out onto the same veranda. He will have nowhere to hide.

Will they send boys? Harper wondered. If they want him dead, better to send an experienced man, one of the black-shirted militia who knows what he is doing, there were plenty of them around last time although, like the boys, they tended to work in groups. But boys would be easier to finesse if, back home, they were going to portray his death as part of the general disorder that was going on: that would be simplest for them. That was how he would do it, if he were them. There weren't any shopping malls to loot and burn out here in the forest, but people back home thought of whole countries as violent once they had seen a few television pictures. *Yes, poor Harper, wrong place, wrong time. Could happen to anyone*. Word would get around the office, just like it always did. *And I hear he'd got careless, the drinking, you know . . .* At this, the person talking would lift a cup-shaped hand halfway up to his or her mouth and wobble it. *Sending him back out there, after the problems he'd had, it was probably a mistake.* He had had many of those conversations himself, over the years. *Did you hear what happened to Joosten? They tied him to the wheel of his car and poured petrol over it. You don't mess with those drugs lords, you know.* Tales of bad things happening out in the field flattered those back home – look how dangerous our job can be, on occasion. It doesn't happen often, but it happens. Joosten had been known to smoke a bit. Harper had seen him do it. There was almost always some basis to the rumours. That's what they did in his line of work: took a thread of truth and wove a carpet out of it.

Once, when they were drinking together back in Amsterdam, Joosten had let slip he had a safe house: a flat somewhere in a foreign city, he wouldn't say where, not a country that their firm operated in. It was stocked with tinned food in case he needed to lie low for a while, and money and a false passport. Harper had left the bar that night shaking his head at Joosten's paranoia.

Beginning the letter to Francisca had convinced him that his calm during the night was due to more than exhaustion – he was sure, now, what was going to happen. What was it, to know you were going to die? We all carry that knowledge inside us, he thought: it is the one thing we know for certain.

The black and green water in the rock pool – how cool it appeared. How good it would feel, in the rising humidity, to slip his old boots from his feet and dabble his toes in that water. Up in the hut, Kadek would have placed his breakfast – rice and a little *sambal*, some chicken maybe and some fruit – on the desk by the window. It would have a banana leaf laid over it to protect it. Kadek would have opened the shutters, to air the room, and folded back his crumpled bed sheets, smoothing them neatly. He should go back. There was the letter he really should write, even though it would be full of untruths and he might not get the chance to send it.

He rose from the rock, stretched his arms upwards, performed a few loose movements from side to side with his hands on his hips, and turned to climb up the path.

*

It had already begun before Harper got there – that made it easier; it was well underway in fact. He was with Benni, that fat gangster. He liked his sweets, Benni, which was why he was down to three teeth, one front tooth and two incisors. Harper had spent months cultivating him when he got to Jakarta, on his first visit, back in '65. Benni was said to have good connections with the military and like all the gangster-militiamen was fervently anti-Communist. The stallholders and shopkeepers in his area were terrified of him but whether or not he dined with Generals was another matter.

They were in the small front area of a disused bar down a narrow alleyway in Pasar Senen. It was mid-afternoon and the sun blazed outside. There was a garage or storeroom of some sort out back where a man was being held. He had been there since dawn; a Chinese merchant who sold bolts of cloth from a shop next to the picture house on the edge of a nearby *kampong*, one of the cinemas the PKI had closed down recently because they showed decadent Western movies. Benni's friends had lost money because of the cinema closures. The Chinese merchant had no proven connection with what had happened next door to his shop but he hadn't paid his protection money in a month.

Harper gathered this and other details as a group of them stood together in the front room of the bar – he and Benni had been lunching nearby when Benni's driver had turned up and said they needed the boss. Six of Benni's men plus the driver were gathered round and Harper got the gist, though they were all talking quickly and at once. The men were excited, competing for their boss's attention. 'BB! BB!' they kept saying before they launched into their résumé of the story so far. The man was a Communist agitator who had been holding meetings in the back of his shop after closing hours, one of them seemed to be saying. Another mentioned a pile of chairs. The man was a liar, another interjected. He was worse than a *nekolim* . . . At the word *nekolim*, Benni clapped Harper on the shoulder and gave a gap-toothed grin and the other men looked at Harper for a moment until Harper gave a short bark of a laugh and suddenly the men were laughing too. Then they went back to talking at once. Most of them had been drinking *arak* all morning, Harper decided. They were his age, mid-twenties, or younger, apart from Benni who was maybe ten years older.

Benni's face became still as he listened further. In his meetings with Harper so far, he had been jovial and hospitable, giving him lunches and imported whisky, but when he was with his men,

Benni liked to affect an air of seriousness. Then, without saying anything, he strode towards the back of the bar, his men following anxiously. Harper decided to wait where he was, wishing the bar was still operational. It was the first time Benni had involved him in his daily activities, which was good, a sign he was beginning to trust him – but he would hang back until he was called, let Benni initiate his level of involvement. He rubbed his palms together quickly and tried to ignore the small thumping in his chest.

The others disappeared behind a door that clanged shut, leaving a metallic silence in its wake. Harper went to the front of the building, which was open to the alleyway, and looked down at the cement step to see if it was clean enough to sit on: it wasn't. The alleyway was lined with drainage ditches that smelt of shit and piss.

While he waited, a very young boy wearing nothing but a dirty T-shirt came and stood opposite him and stared, fearlessly, three fingers of one hand in his mouth and the other hand supporting his elbow, little round stomach protruding. Harper stared back at him. After a moment or two of appraisal, the boy turned and ran, kicking up dirt, shouting out something high-pitched and triumphant, as if he had fulfilled a dare.

The door behind him clanged again. One of Benni's men was standing at the back of the room, gesturing. 'Mr BB says come.'

When Harper entered the room, a filthy storage place with a low ceiling and one high, barred window, he saw in the dim light that there was a Chinese Indonesian seated on a low chair, with a table in front of him and his hands tied behind his back. It took Harper's eyes a moment or two to adjust. It was hard to tell the man's age. His face was covered in blood, and part of his scalp had been removed: what lay beneath was gleaming, wet and bare. His head was slumped a little to one side, as if he knew that he was going to be killed anyway, whatever he said – which was true – and had simply given up, resolved to endure what must be endured before his final moments.

Benni was standing in one corner. 'Come, you come stand next to me,' he said to Harper in English. 'Stand next to me, watch for a bit. He sees white man, he thinks someone. He thinks maybe, things maybe okay. Maybe he talk.' Harper understood that his presence was, in effect, to extend the man's torture. Perhaps they were hoping that by accident they had picked up a Commie after all. He might give them names. Nothing was as valuable as names, back then in '65, as Jakarta simmered higher and higher, everyone was collecting names – they were a lot more valuable than the plummeting rupiah, which was worth so little now you had to walk around with a duffel bag of the stuff on your shoulder if you wanted to buy a beer. Even he, Harper, the man with access to the hardest currency of all authorised by his organisation, even he was dealing in names.

The man had raised his head as Harper entered. He was staring at him, eyes wide in his bloodied face. Harper stared back. He tried to communicate that there was no hope, that the man should simply go back to wishing, waiting to die, make his peace with whatever god he might worship, say goodbye in his head to his family. The man lowered his head.

This seemed to enrage one of Benni's men, a small moustachioed type who stood nearest to the Chinese merchant and who was, Harper guessed, Benni's number two in these matters. He snatched a pair of bloodied scissors from the table in front of the man and began to wave them in the man's face and scream. It occurred to Harper that this was a test, that Benni had invited him in here to see how he would react – Benni was, after all, under the impression that he was recruiting Harper rather than the other way around. He glanced at the other men. They were all striking various poses around the room – two of them were mimicking the man with the moustache, staring at the merchant, teeth bared, faces gleaming with sweat. Two others were leaning against the wall, arms folded, staring, trying to look as hard as possible; one of the others was turning restlessly to and fro. The last one, the driver, who was about eighteen, Harper guessed, a tall boy with sloping shoulders, stood close to Harper and Benni, motionless but with his arms raised and his fists clenched, his gaze flitting this way and that, as if he were engaged in a high-speed race on a dangerous road and needed to be hyper-alert. Some of them had been drinking but they were all, all but Benni and himself, possessed by a kind of pseudo-sexual excitement. It came off them like a scent. Harper guessed these boys didn't get much, if any. This kind of activity had to do instead.

The man with the moustache carried on screaming, his face contorted, his voice high-pitched, and Harper found this screaming more unbearable than anything. *Just die*, Harper thought, looking at the merchant, *just close down, make your thoughts leave your body*. He wondered if it was possible to make yourself die, *in extremis*, to will it to happen but of course it wasn't. Dying was a giving up of will. You could no more will it than levitate.

He wanted to think about something other than the bloodied man in front of him so he thought about his own end. He would like to be able to see the sky, he thought. A perfect death would come in an arbour of some sort, with trees and flowers around, with a woman beside you who loved you and laid a cooling hand on your forehead. Your last thought as you slipped into unconsciousness would be that you were loved; the air full of sunshine, a blue and infinite sky.

Not somewhere like here, alone but for the people who wanted you dead. Not this darkened room, with dank walls and a stinking dirt floor and a little grey light scarcely strong enough to illuminate the faces of the people who were about to kill you. Not like this. *Not circling in water, either, unaware – how's that for fresh air, Bud?*

The thought that he pushed to the back of his mind, as he stood and watched a man in pain and did nothing because his handler at the embassy had told him to win the trust of a filthy gangster who may or may not have good contacts with the military, was that he would never know what the look on his own face was like in the minutes before he died. He would never see it mirrored in a loved one. It felt like the most profound of premonitions, that there would be no witness to his departing, or no benign witness, but it was only three decades later, sitting on a rock above a green pool on a beautiful island, with a notebook on his lap, that he remembered it.

That night, he slept better than any night since his arrival on the island. The irony of this did not escape him. He rose early and greeted Kadek, told him that he would like to go into town later, pick up a couple of things. The roads to town were so potted and poor that he could have strode along the river in the same time it would take them to bounce there together on Kadek's moped, the weight of Harper on the back flattening the tyres.

He told Kadek to finish his duties first and then get the moped and return for him later in the morning. It didn't look like rain that day. When he stared at a man across a desk or in a prison cell, he could assess with cold accuracy not only whether that person was lying but whether later he would give up the truth. When he looked up at the sky, he knew what it was hiding too, what it would yield later that day.

By the time they got to town, the sun was high. He got Kadek to drop him on the main street and told him to meet him there at five. He would walk around a bit to get his bearings, then find somewhere to drink coffee and watch the street, see what he could glean from a couple of hours observing who was in town. He would probably drink several coffees. Kadek brought a flask of hot water in the mornings so he could make it with powder but it didn't really do the trick.

*

The main street of town was scarcely wide enough for two lanes of traffic and lined with cafes, overpriced jewellery and art shops for tourists alongside fruit and veg stalls and mini-markets; the Museum, the Palace, a Chinese restaurant that blared American rock. He spent two hours in a new, Euro-style place, jazz tinkling from speakers but barely audible above the noise from the street. He ordered a coffee and a cinnamon roll and, in an impulse he felt himself regretting even as he conceded to it, a packet of *kretek* cigarettes. The cigarettes came first, on a plate, the packet opened for him and propped up on its own lid, one cigarette helpfully extended and a frangipani blossom tucked in by its side. He smoked it slowly, waiting for his coffee and his roll, then closed the packet to discourage immediate consumption of another. He sipped the coffee, tore small pieces from the roll. It was sunny, the street was teeming; small trucks, tourist vans, locals on mopeds. Even the grandmothers drove mopeds these days. He had just ordered his second coffee when, right in front of him, a white municipal truck pulled out to go round a parked car and blocked the road. There followed a brief comedy of chaos as some moped drivers tried to circumvent the truck only to meet others trying to get round the other way. These things were always conducted with an orchestra of horn tooting and calling, much as the Italians did but without the undertone of aggression. He watched and, for a moment, the traffic jam made him miss Jakarta, then it was over and the cars and trucks and mopeds flowed again in their congested, casually dangerous way.

It took a few moments for the line to clear. When it had, he saw that at the end of it was a low jeep that bumped past slowly – it was stuck behind the last moped in the build-up, a very old-looking machine with a woman and three children; a young girl on the back, a small boy standing on the foot panel in front and a baby strapped to the woman's chest – and he had time to observe the four young men in the jeep. They were dressed a bit more smartly than the local men, in white shirts and loose pants. Their faces were not as rounded as the typically Balinese face, he thought: they were sharper. One of them sitting in the back caught his gaze briefly and returned it. The truck moved on.

A very tiny, elderly woman with a tree-bark face approached the step below where he was seated, holding a woven tray on which she was carrying twenty or so offerings. She gave him a single-toothed smile as she knelt to arrange one of the offerings on the ground, to appease the demons, the rice and flower petals in the little basket made of a stapled banana leaf. He returned her smile and tried not to think what he always thought when he saw locals of that age: what were you doing, back then? Where were you? Were you out in the middle of the night, joining the hunting parties in the rice fields? Or did you simply raise your hand to point at a neighbour's house and whisper to the men in black shirts the single word that would slaughter the entire family asleep in there: *gestapu*? A young woman tourist in white shorts and a tight yellow vest stopped and watched the old woman as she placed three incense sticks at angles in the offering and lit them with a cigarette lighter. The young woman took a step back, respectfully, then lifted her camera to her face.

A newspaper seller wandered past with piles of thin broadsheets over his arm. He stopped when he saw Harper and raised one but it was the *International Herald Tribune*. Harper shook his head. That wouldn't exactly fill him in on what was going on in Jakarta. None of the local bars had televisions: how was he supposed to know what the latest was? Normally, he would check in with the Jakarta office or Amsterdam but he was officially taking a break. Taking a break, so far, meant being kept in the dark.

Smoking hard and drinking coffee was making him feel both hazy and alert: the contradiction was pleasant. There was a certain merit in doing these things infrequently. He wanted a whisky but he hadn't touched a drop since that disastrous night in Jakarta a week ago, even though he had an unopened bottle at the hut. He had bought it for himself as a kind of test, which – so far – he had passed. He wanted it now, though. That's okay, he thought. Acknowledge to yourself that you want it, and then move on.

He walked back to the meeting point with Kadek still intending to return to the hut. But as he approached and saw him waiting by the moped, chatting with the other drivers, he was filled with an overwhelming desire to stay in town, even if it meant breaking protocol and sleeping in a guesthouse room. (Did it matter any more, how many protocols he broke? Not if he was right, it didn't.) He had been going to bed early at the hut in an attempt to get some rest but however early he retired, the evenings were still long.

He handed Kadek a thin plastic bag with two shirts he had bought at a roadside stall and another with some biscuits and cans of Coke, and asked him to take them back to the hut, saying he would make his own way back later on a *taksi* moped. Kadek offered to return for him whenever he wanted but Harper was firm in his dismissal. He wanted the freedom to play the evening by ear. Then he turned and walked back along the main street. It was time to find a bar.

It was his first trip to Ubud since he had arrived in the hills, so he took his time, walking down to the bridge in the heat, where he came to a small row of food shacks: maybe I'm hungry, he thought to himself. He stopped at the second one and ate a plateful of *nasi goreng*, then thought about carrying on to the far end of the street where the road climbed upward again out of town. Every minute or so, a man with a car or a moped would call out to him, *taksi!* He could hail one and go exploring for a bar, but the coffee and the *nasi goreng* had used up his loose change and paying a fare of a few rupiah with a hundred thousand note might draw attention to himself. Maybe it was simplest just to walk back into town.

If it hadn't been so hot, if he had had some small notes in his pocket, then he would never have met her. Rita.

The bar was on Jalan Bisma, five minutes or so from the main street. It was one of those bars that doubled as the restaurant and breakfast room of a guesthouse. He noticed it because of the string of yellow lights that wound around the coconut tree at the stone archway entrance. There were seven or eight round tables and wide wooden chairs with patterned cushions. A lone barman in a leafy-patterned shirt nodded and smiled to him as he stepped up from the street.

He spotted her as soon as he entered, sitting in a far, dim corner, alone at a small table with a cocktail containing mint leaves in a long glass. Her head was bent and reading glasses balanced on the very end of her nose. She was going through some papers with a stub of pencil. The only other customers in the bar were a couple of hippie-student types nursing bottles of Bintang and a small group of local businessmen, probably the owner and his friends. Nobody looked up as Harper approached the bar.

He took in, briefly, that she was white, very white, a few years younger than him, late forties perhaps, long, light brown hair, a solidly built figure in a cotton shirt, loose trousers and flat sandals, absorbed in what she was doing. There were no bar stools but after he had been served, he stood leaning on the bar with his whisky in front of him, his back to her, to allow her to notice him. During that time, he chatted to the man behind the bar in Indonesian. The waiter smiled and chatted back, as if he could foresee the encounter to come and was happy to play his small part in the pantomime. After half an hour, Harper turned, took his almost empty whisky glass and approached the woman's corner table.

He looked down at her and said, in English, 'I'm sorry, please excuse me, you're busy I can see, but I'm new in town, could I join you, for a short while?' As he spoke, he took a small step backwards, to indicate that he wasn't going to cause any trouble if she said no, which would make it that little bit more likely she would say yes.

She looked up and gave him a sceptical smile, eyebrows slightly raised. Her rounded cheeks made her look girlish. Her eyelashes were long; no make up, good skin. 'Sure,' she said, taking the reading glasses off her nose and folding them, 'rescue me from my homework.' He couldn't quite place her accent, a hint of something north European.

He turned and lifted a hand to the man behind the bar, beckoning him over, then sat. He looked at the papers, which she gathered into a pile and lifted to tap their edges on the table, neatening them, he noted, in the manner of someone who had concluded her work for the night.

'What is it?' he asked.

'I'm in education, training,' she said with a light sigh. 'You?'

'I'm an economist, based in Jakarta, taking a break.'

'If you're an economist,' she said, leaning back in her seat, regarding him steadily with her wide-set eyes, 'can you explain why the IMF has put forty billion dollars into this region but the families of my students are still having to mix hard old corn kernels with their rice every morning, so that their stomachs won't rumble in my class?'

'I could,' he said, 'but you wouldn't believe me.'

Her smile was a yes.

Several whiskies later, he had almost forgotten his nights in the hut, and that he was on enforced leave after a catastrophic error of judgement. He had not forgotten who, or what, he was – he never did that.

'John Harper . . .' she said. 'John Harper . . .' She repeated it slowly, as if turning the words over in her mind and examining them for plausibility. 'Your sentence construction is interesting, John Harper. I'm usually pretty good at this but I can't quite place you. You sound like a European,' she said, 'but there is occasionally an Americanism.'

'Is there?' His surprise was genuine.

'There was a "gotten" a few minutes ago.'

She was on her third cocktail. She raised the glass, closed her mouth over the straw and sipped from it while flipping a look up at him through her long lashes. He found the gesture silly from a woman her age but then she stopped and laughed out loud and he suspected she was not so much flirting as taking the mickey. Taking the mickey. Where did that phrase come from?

'You're making me self-conscious,' he said.

'That I doubt.' She put her cocktail down and stirred it with the straw. The mint leaves whirled amongst the ice cubes. 'So, the Americanisms?'

'I work for a company that's owned by Americans so I deal with them a lot . . . and I spent a few years in California as a kid, when I was young, I mean.'

Her look invited him to continue.

'I went back to the Netherlands, I was sent back, after my brother died, so I spent my teenage years in Europe.' He stopped. A few whiskies and some congenial company and then this, he thought: the truth. I'm losing my touch.

She gazed at him a while, her look soft, then said, 'I think we can give each other permission to leave out the sad bits.'

He stared back at her and felt such gratitude that he wondered, for a moment, if this could be what falling in love was like. Seeing as he had never done it, he had no way of knowing.

'Are you staying here?' he asked, looking at her directly, a catch in his throat that he wanted her to note.

She shook her head, replying casually, as if she had not picked up on his change of tone, 'I live in a family compound on Monkey Forest Road,' then, without missing a beat, 'and I certainly can't take you back there. Where are you staying?'

'Out of town,' he said. 'I'll ask about a room here.'

As he rose she said, 'The rooms here are nice but pricy by local standards. It's mostly older tourists.'

'I have money.'

The room they were given was on the ground floor at the back of the compound, a short walk along a stone path turned into an alleyway by thick vegetation. Frogs croaked unseen; the air was heavy and scented. He could feel that his shirt had become glued to his back. The carved wooden doors were similar to the ones on his hut, with a solid frame that you stepped over to enter. Inside, he felt along the wall and flicked the switch for the ceiling fan. It turned slowly into life, then picked up speed until it rattled round with a *tick-tick-tick* that stirred the air above them. On a chest of drawers beside the bed, there was a table lamp. He walked over and turned it on, noting that the bed was high and wide, neatly made, with a frangipani flower on each pillow. The mosquito net around it was fine and translucent, much more delicate than the one he had in the hut.

He dropped the key to the room next to the lamp and turned to Rita and although she was a tall woman her expression seemed suddenly small and shy. She said, 'I'm just going to use the bathroom.'

He went over to the shutters and opened them to look out at the night and listen to the frogs and the insects in the greenery below the window. There came the chirrup of a ghekko, a smaller, sweeter one than the ominous animal that woke him out in the forest. He heard her flush the loo and run the tap, then return to the room. He stayed where he was, his hands on the windowsill, his head dropped slightly, the whisky swimming pleasantly inside him. Despite how long it had been, he felt empty of lust at that moment. He wanted to put the encounter on pause, to enjoy the fact that he was here and it was about to happen. This is the best bit, isn't it, he thought, just before?

The next morning, she would hold him after they had had sex for the second time and say, 'This is my favourite bit, afterwards,' and he would smile to himself thinking how that was what separated men and women, before and after: and joined them, of course, as if the act of sex was a border that cleaved them together and asunder in the same instant.

But right that moment, standing there looking out into the garden – or rather, listening – he felt no physical desire at all and wondered if she would mind if they didn't do anything, just slept. His younger self would never have believed he could reach this point but here he was, a man in his fifties, who had successfully picked up a strange woman in a bar (or she had picked him up, it didn't matter which), and what he really wanted was to stop the evening and just be in a room. No one knew where he was. No one would disturb them: but he was not alone. It was perfect.

She came up behind him, slowly. They had both removed their shoes as they had entered the room and her bare feet scarcely made a sound against the tiled floor but he could feel that she was standing right behind him, very close, without touching him. They stood like that for a moment and he listened to their breathing. They both began to breathe a little more deeply. Still, he did not turn. Their breath deepened further. They were breathing in unison, both waiting to see who would move first. He went from feeling no desire to being suddenly, painfully hard, just at the sound of her breath behind him, at the long gap between her approach and any contact between them. He and Francisca had not had sex for the last two years of their relationship. His body had forgotten what it was like to be in physical contact with that of another. She lifted both hands and placed them very gently on his upper arms, right at the top, almost on his shoulders. He could feel the heat of her palms through the cotton of his shirt. He turned.

*

There were surprises in store. In the bar, he had observed her big-boned frame, her solid torso, and during their conversation, she had laughed at her size and told jokes against herself, about her clumsiness when she was a girl. 'A great galumphing girl, I got called once, by an Englishman,' she had said. 'You know this word? Galumphing! Something that gallops along but is heavy, no? A rhinoceros, perhaps.' Horizontal and unclothed, she did not feel great and galumphing, but pillow-soft and comforting, in a way he would not have expected from her ironic way of speaking. Hers was not the kind of body he normally enjoyed. Most of his other lovers – with few exceptions, short-lived – had been slim-limbed, fragile even. And it was not the kind of sex he had had in the past. There was no battle. It was neither hurried nor teasing. They fondled each other and took it in turns to come and smiled, slightly mockingly, during it. He did not feel that he was doing it to her, or she to him, but that they were doing it together, much as they might have washed one another's backs in the bath. Her breasts were small for her overall size, low-slung, wide apart. On her abdomen, there was a caesarean scar. Her pubic hair was sparse and going grey. Afterwards, they turned the light off by mutual agreement and even kissed each other goodnight. He fell into a deep sleep.

In the morning, there was another surprise. He found that he didn't want to leave as soon as possible.

He woke first, before dawn, a slow and easy awakening, the kind that comes only when you have slept deeply. He was just in time to hear the beginning of the dawn chorus – that bird, what was that bird? There was one that acted as a kind of outlier for the others; the single, hesitant cheeping, like the lead violinist tuning up before the full orchestra began. Then would come the whole, delightful cacophony, breaking out all of a sudden, like prisoners fleeing the dark. Here in town, he could identify individual sounds a little more easily than out in the valley. In the midst of the chorus, loud and assertive, came the bird he loved most of all, the one that sounded like an old man convulsing with laughter, trying and failing to withhold it. *Cheep! Cheep!* Two loud exclamations came first – then a cascade of smaller notes, tumbling over each other in a descending scale.

Dawn: to hear dawn coming, to breathe in and feel the lift of it and know yourself to have survived another night.

He lay still, listening to the birds and Rita's breathing beside him, and watched as light began to stripe the slats of the shutters.

After a while, he needed the bathroom, slipping from the bed as quietly as he could. As he returned to the room, he stopped and stood for a moment, looking at Rita beneath the mosquito net, the fine soft-focus of it blurring her features so that she could have been any age; a face made featureless by sleep, a smudge of hair. She turned as he came around to his side of the bed and the sheet slipped, revealing the slope of one breast, and her eyelids flickered open and she half-smiled, then turned away again as he climbed back into bed, shuffling backwards towards him so that he could spoon against her.

They lay together, dozing, for some time. She rose to use the toilet, then they had sex again.

Afterwards, they lay together some more, facing each other this time, him with his arm around her shoulders and her with one arm resting across his waist. He envisaged going to breakfast with her, in the same bar they had been drinking in the night before, sitting opposite her at a table, discussing what to have. He wondered if they did black rice pudding here, thick with palm sugar. He hadn't had that in a while. They wouldn't speak much until after they had had their tangerine juice and coffee, then the conversation between them would come slowly to life. They would discuss how to spend the coming day.

Perhaps this was what marriage was like when it worked. He couldn't remember ever feeling like this with Francisca; lust, yes, an argument of some sort here and there, a hum of low-level tension between them even when they weren't arguing – but not this restfulness, not even at the weekends, not like this.

She rolled over onto her other side, away from him. He propped his head up on one elbow and, for a few moments, watched her back, the plump pale flesh, the curve of it where it creased, the doughy hillocks formed at her waist. Her shoulder blades stood out, hard nubs in the soft flesh of her back, like the buds of wings. Still turned away from him, she pushed her long hair back over her shoulder and a curl of pale brown, strung with strands of white, swung briefly between the shoulder blades then came to rest in the shape of an upside-down question mark.

She said, quietly, 'I need to go. I'd prefer it if you left first.'

He didn't reply.

'We can't leave together,' she said. 'It's a small town.'

They had walked along the path together the night before: but that was in the heat of darkness. Now, it was day.

She rose from the bed, pushing the mosquito net out of the way and standing for a moment, facing away from him, before moving towards the small desk against one wall, where she had thrown her underwear, carelessly, the night before.

He sat up in bed and watched her get dressed. He wanted

a cigarette. He couldn't remember what he had done with the packet – he thought he might have left it on the table in the bar. He watched her until it became apparent she would not speak again, then he flung the sheet back in a sudden, hurried-to-be-gone sort of gesture. The sheet flew away from him, making the mosquito net billow outwards. She did not turn round. He swung his legs off the bed and reached for his own clothes, lying in a crumpled heap on the floor.

He walked along the path, which in daylight revealed itself to be a side path that ran along some other rooms set back behind the bushes. Somewhere, out of sight behind the foliage, he heard a swimming-pool splash and a child's voice calling out in German. As he reached the reception and bar area he paused for a moment before remembering that he had paid for the room in cash the night before – it had been incredibly cheap, he had thought. He must have done that because he was anticipating having to make his excuses in the morning and perform a swift but gracious getaway. He passed beneath the stone archway and out onto the street.

The morning was underway: it was late by Indonesian standards. Opposite the guesthouse, a man in a vest was showing two young Westerners how to start their hired mopeds. Small restaurants lined the street as it dipped back down towards the main road. It would be the most natural thing in the world to stop and order himself some breakfast – he could have stayed in the guesthouse and had it there, if he'd wanted. It was probably included in the room price. She wouldn't have any right to think he was loitering for her. So determined was he to make her think herself mistaken that he went over to the tiny place opposite and asked for a coffee with the intention of sitting in full view of anyone who stepped through the archway. It would disconcert her, he thought, to see him sitting there as she emerged. The woman behind the counter smiled broadly and tried to push a laminated menu on him but he shook his head. She gestured to the table nearest the street but he sat one back from that and then, after a little pocket patting, found the cigarettes he hadn't left in the bar after all, and his sunglasses.

The moment he sat down, he wished he hadn't. If she came out while he was there, he would ignore her. Or maybe he would simply nod, then look away and light a cigarette. She would think that he was waiting for her and he could turn his head to indicate he wasn't, or, if his coffee was finished, rise and stride off in the opposite direction, up the rise and out of town. He took some small notes out of his pocket and put them on the table.

Next to the drinks shack was a concrete step with two boys sitting on it. They were looking at him and smiling, then speaking quietly to each other. He wondered if they were boys from the queue of mopeds parked diagonally at the bottom of the hill but they seemed too young and there was something in their smiles he didn't like.

His coffee arrived. The woman who placed it in front of him eyed the money on the table but didn't take it. He lifted the cup to his lips and stared back out at the street, thinking to himself, those boys are not moped drivers. He knew a hired hand when he saw one, an inexperienced young man or woman paid to do a particular job without being given any information about the significance of that job. They were always kept in the dark because they were the ones paid to trail a target and so had to get close. As a result, their chances of being spotted and caught were high, which was why they were never given any information they could divulge when the target's henchmen were burning the soles of their feet. Their inexperience meant they were rarely subtle – and in fact, the people who hired them often didn't want them to be subtle, they wanted the target to feel followed. But more than that, they had a small, excited glow to them. It was possibly the first time they had been asked to do something secret, and overpaid for it to boot. They believed it was the first step towards becoming something more than a waiter or cleaner or moped driver – they were flush with their own sense of importance.

So why were these two watching the guesthouse?

Rita emerged. She did not look left or right, or even across the road at him, but set off immediately down the hill. She had a confident walk; a slightly mannish stride. The normal thing would have been to see him – and then either acknowledge or ignore him, but she had deliberately not seen him, which made him think she had peered out of the stone doorway before she exited.

He finished his coffee and watched the youths from the corner of his eye, waiting to see if they rose and followed her down the hill, but they stayed seated. Harper gave it five minutes, then got up, and it was only then that the boys stood. Harper turned in the opposite direction to the one Rita had gone, uphill, towards the edge of town. He would stride up past the rice fields and see how far the youths stayed behind him, just to be sure. They hadn't been watching the exit to the guesthouse for Rita. They had been waiting for him.

He walked steadily up Jalan Bisma, out of town. The shacks ended and there were few people about. A pair of middle-aged tourists in khakis were walking slowly ahead of him. The

Monkey Forest was up this way, if he remembered correctly, which meant that he would be able to turn left when the road became a footpath and curve back down into town the other way. When he reached the main street, he would get a moped back to the hut. It had been an overnight adventure, nothing more, a break from his own thoughts: but his thoughts were waiting there, out in the valley above the rushing river, thoughts that turned inside his head while the water tumbled below. He realised he was dehydrated after the whisky. The coffee had been a mistake, or at least he should have had a glass of water with it. Here on the hot exposed path, with the khaki-clad tourists in front of him and the boys behind, there was no water to drink, not one drop, and like any thirsty person he suddenly starting noticing all the undrinkable water around him, the fields of brown irrigation in which the rice-plant shoots stood green and tender – the water tower in the middle of the field, tall, with an open platform at the top and a roof for shade: water towers or watchtowers – at first glance, it was hard to tell the difference.

He had started smoking again. And drinking. He might have known. Sex and smoking and drinking – the Holy Trinity. Was it possible to have one without the other two? They kicked each other off. They joined hands and danced ring-a-roses in his head. Ring-a-roses. Emma, the English girl, sang it to him when she was drunk – Emma, the girl he met in Singapore. She hit him once; he couldn't remember why.

Over the following two days, smoking was what he did mostly, although there was a certain amount of whisky involved as well. He knew that if he took the smoking seriously, did it with the kind of calm intensity it warranted after a break of several weeks, then it might forestall the booze. Forestalling the booze would be a very, very good idea. He sat on the veranda of his hut, looked out into the forest, drank whisky from a coffee cup, pictured Rita's back turned away from him in bed with her hair between her shoulder blades; and he smoked.

Christ, he thought, I survived a rioting mob in Jakarta not long ago and then began to wonder if my life could be in danger from the people who have employed me for three decades – yet one encounter with a woman and I've turned into this. He realised that he was enjoying this image of himself: the hard-bitten man on the veranda in the jungle with his whisky and his cigarettes. If you couldn't be with a woman, then this was surely the next best thing, drinking and smoking and thinking of her. Thinking about a woman was a great excuse to throw your head back as you tipped the last drops of whisky from the cup into your mouth, and then to swing the bottle as you refilled the cup. You could imagine what you might look like to her as you lit up your next cigarette, shielding the match from the wind with one hand, flicking it between two fingers so that it somersaulted into the air and extinguished itself at the same time. *Have you ever seen a match burn twice?* Ah, that was why Emma had hit him, he remembered now. He hadn't pulled that stunt on a girl again. They couldn't take it.

Kadek brought him his supplies, from time to time, and handed them over looking concerned. Harper became garrulous and started asking Kadek about his family, even once suggesting he join him in a drink, to be rewarded by a brief look of shock, a small bow, refusal.

When Kadek wasn't there, he took to mumbling to himself. He wasn't really mumbling to himself, though. He was mumbling to Rita.

He wanted to tell her how pleasant it had been and how that wasn't usual for him. He wanted to explain to her that although that sounded like a meagre compliment, it really wasn't. It hadn't felt like a first time, that was what struck him. There would be no second or third time, of course, let alone a continuing relationship – but it also hadn't felt like a first time because it had seemed so natural and inevitable, from the minute he had seen her sitting in the corner of the bar.

There had been many times in his life when he had felt the pull of a woman – and a fair few of those occasions had occurred in bars – and yet there was always a tussle to be had, an elaborate game of pursuit or persuasion, of drawing back then reasserting, of uncertainty almost up until the very moment you were entwined. A woman could pull out at any minute, of course, and some of them did. In many ways, the tussle was the point. The act itself took only a short while, after all, and when it was done it was done. There could never again be a first time with that particular woman, never again the excitement and absorption of uncertainty.

But with Rita, there had been no tussle, just calmness and pleasure, and as there had been no heightened excitement before, there had been no let-down after. The calmness and pleasure had both outlived the act.

Perhaps it was about age. The more he thought about it, rocking back in his wooden chair on the veranda until he was balancing on the two back legs of it, it wasn't so much his age as hers. Women of forty-five plus, he reflected – and after one night with Rita, he was now an expert, obviously – were endearingly like men. He thought back to some of the conversations he had had with young women when he was young himself – still young enough, that was, to be sized up as potential husband or father material. There were so many ways to disappoint a woman at that stage. You were never going to be in love enough, or committed enough even if you were in love, or solvent enough even if you were committed. And even if you were in love, committed and solvent, you were never going to help enough around the house. When he looked back on his marriage to Francisca, that was his overwhelming feeling, that he had always disappointed her, right from the start – taking so long to get around to marrying her hadn't helped. And then her quiet fortitude in the face of how he was: she always made him feel that she was being noble, good. His mistake had been to marry a woman ten years younger. Older women, he felt, with his new-found experience, had got being disappointed by men well and truly out of their system. They had had their husbands and children, if they were going to have them – they had been through the mill of family life and come out the other side. If they were available for sex then they viewed it as men had always done, as recreation.

People like himself and Rita: their attitude to sex was arguably symptomatic of their other deficiencies. They were comfortable with casual encounters at their age only because they were *un*comfortable with the conventions that discouraged them in others. They were odd or unusual in so many other ways, in fact, that sex was the least of it.

He had always had an uncomfortable feeling around men who chased after younger women and now, fresh from the comforts of Rita, he was able to say to himself precisely why. To pursue a younger woman was an act of deceit – you knew they wanted something different from what you wanted and you had to con them into not realising that until you had got your way. But with women like Rita, what made it so calm, so relaxing, was the knowledge that you were offering them nothing and they knew that, so you were not deceiving them. How had he got to his age without understanding this? If he had known it earlier, maybe he would have tried nailing the older ones years ago. Why had he been so obsessed with the women – young, pretty, or both – who reflected well on him in the eyes of other men? Had it all been about what other men would think of him, even when he was acting in private? How stupid was that?

It was early evening, suddenly, on the second day of drinking and smoking – where had two days gone? Maybe it was more. He wondered what day of the week it was, how long he had been here, on the veranda? There were blanks in his head. He couldn't remember what he had done earlier that day and he couldn't remember eating at all. The light was commencing its swift and steady slip into dusk. The wall of palm trees on the other side of the valley was growing darker and darker – soon, the gathering gloom would be upon him, then blank, ineluctable night.

Rita. He wanted her; there, at the hut, with him, as darkness fell. The thought came to him clean and unalloyed by doubt. After one encounter, he was missing her. Her absence was a kind of bodily discomfort. He ached – just a little but all over, like the very early stages of the flu.

He wanted to know everything about her. She had deflected questions about herself every bit as deftly as did he, as if they were just swatting flies together across the table. In the past, he had made a point of pressing women for facts about themselves: usually you didn't need to press. Most women wanted to tell you their most intimate tragedy within about five minutes of meeting you and those who didn't were easy to persuade; a hard stare usually did it. Rita had been happy to keep their encounter determinedly shallow, which to him implied she had something to hide, something she didn't like to talk about.

Her accent was so faint – Belgian by birth, as it turned out, she was fluent in English and probably several other languages: a teacher, but one who was now training other teachers, she had told him; a specialist in developing parts of the world. She was well-travelled, had been in the archipelago some time: a woman comfortable in almost any culture but her own, he thought. She belonged to the same nation as him, in that sense, the nation of people scattered and diffused all over the world, citizens of nowhere.

And what about that scar on her abdomen . . . ? He remembered how she had sat very still on the side of the bed the morning after, just before she had risen and pushed aside the mosquito net, in the moment before she had said, 'I need to go.' Something about that moment of stillness had stuck in his head, the image of her naked back. He had known at once that something was wrong. There was something broken there; something that needed fixing.

He remembered a young woman he had been keen on from the office, many years ago, back when he was eligible. Alida, she was called. He had liked her because he thought her unusual in the same way that he was. She had a Taiwanese grandmother, although she had been born and raised in the Netherlands and was more Dutch than the Dutch girls he knew. She also had one eye that was slightly off. Long straight hair, a slim physique – when they first met, he couldn't stop looking at her face to work out exactly what it was that was out of kilter. Later, he found out that there had been speculation round the office that they were perfect for each other, him being part-Asian too.

She was from the typists' pool, as it was called back then. The girls in the typists' pool were interested in men who had been out in the field – in those days, it was always male operatives and women office staff, although the total staff was still tiny in comparison with what it would grow to be. His line of work was still in its infancy, or rather the corporatisation of it was. Most of the operatives were young men fresh from their military service, like Harper. There were rumours their three directors were all ex-*Nefis*, although Harper thought probably only one of them was, a small, wiry man with grey hair and the relaxed air of someone so efficiently trained he had absolutely nothing to prove. The other two had a bit more bluster, threw their weight around: they were just army men.

It was 1969 and Harper had been back in the business for a year. He had returned from Indonesia at the end of '65 – via Los Angeles, his last visit there, although he didn't know that at the time – to be put on indefinite sick leave. Indefinite turned out to mean four years. When he came back to the office, no one was allowed to ask for an explanation. *You're being given a second chance because of how young you were and because of how much money we spent training you*, Gregor had said. *I hope I don't need to tell you that there won't be a third.* On his first day back after a four-year break, he had been greeted with 'Hey, welcome back,' by people who hardly lifted their heads, as if he had only been gone a fortnight. An aura of mystery clung to him, he knew, and he did nothing to dispel it – an aura of mystery made bedding women easy. Even before what happened in '65, he had had plenty of material in that respect. There was always the enjoyable moment, with a woman, when he dropped in the fact that he had been born in a camp, and the confusion in their eyes as they calculated that he certainly didn't *look* Jewish.

One of the reasons he had liked Alida was that such subterfuges had seemed unnecessary – they worked in the same business, after all. Their conversation beforehand had been mostly work-related. Their sex had been noisy and enthusiastic. Afterwards, she held him against her on her single bed in her flat-share and moved her fingertips in slow circles over his back – the sort of stroking that was ticklish before sex but calming after. He was half-dozing when she said, 'You know what they say about you, round the office, don't you?'

He thought she was about to tell him some pointless bit of

gossip: that you hate Aldemar because he earns more than you (untrue, there were lots of reasons to hate Aldemar), or you slept with Lotte in European Accounts and she took pills when you refused to marry her (true). That sort of gossip was daily currency when a group of people worked together on one floor of a building, in their case given a twist by the fact that they couldn't tell their friends about the sort of company they worked for. He was only half-listening.

'They say you were terribly tortured.'

Her fingers became still. He raised his head and looked at her face. She was smiling. She shuffled down the pillow a little and propped her head up on one hand, the arm bent at the elbow. Her fine dark hair fell down, a waterfall that flowed over her bare shoulder and upper arm. The expression on her face suggested she was not only amused by this rumour but expected him to be amused as well.

'They say when you were captured in the jungle in the Indies . . .'

'It's called Indonesia now.'

'Indonesia. They say when you were captured when you were out in the jungle that you had your back slashed to ribbons with sickles. That's why you don't speak much round the office and keep yourself to yourself. That's why you left the firm for four years. You cracked up and were in a loony bin for a bit and then tried to be a farmer, they set you up, but it didn't work out and so you came back to the firm.' That bit was true, at least. The firm had looked after him well. It was in their interests, after all. The last thing the company needed was a mentally ill ex-operative raving about his experiences to anyone who would listen. She lifted a finger and traced his shoulder. 'They say your back is covered with terrible scars.'

So that was why she had been stroking his back, only to discover it was as smooth and flawless as hers. How disappointed she must have been.

'Well,' he said, looking back at her, 'as you can see, it isn't.'

On the third day, he rose late – thanks to the booze and the cigarettes he had returned to sleeping badly – and decided he would not drink or smoke that day. It was disgusting, actually, what he had been doing, it was weak; time to get a grip. He would go to town and track down Rita.

Kadek took him into town again, silent on the journey. Kadek had grown a lot quieter during the last couple of days and Harper wondered if he was obliged to report back to the firm. Was Kadek's job to bring him breakfast or to spy on him? Probably both. But in truth, despite his doubts about the organisation, the thought of finding Rita was distracting enough for him to think that, maybe, his nighttime fears were born of simple exhaustion. Maybe Amsterdam was right – this was a new thought – maybe what he needed was rest and recreation. He was even beginning to feel a little foolish. He would not be the first operative to see shadows where none existed, along with people lurking in those shadows who were looking at him, meaning harm. Some habits became a way of life. *Is it possible that what happened before is clouding your judgement?* Amsterdam had asked him, just before he submitted his final report from Jakarta. How vehemently he had denied it.

He waited until late afternoon, changing into one of the shirts he had bought on his previous visit to town just before Kadek arrived with the moped. Rita would be working earlier in the day, he guessed, and his best chance of finding her would be around the same time as their previous encounter.

He got Kadek to drop him at the corner of Jalan Bisma and walked up to the guesthouse but the bar was completely empty, not even any staff around. He went back to the main road and took up watch in the cafe again. When that vigil proved fruitless, he walked up and down the main street, stopping off in one or two shops, where it was easy to linger by the door and watch who passed along the road. There was no point at which he despaired of seeing her. It was only a matter of persistence. Where would someone like her go if she wasn't getting some work done in a bar or cafe? Where would he himself go if he didn't want to hang out with tourists? The night market, probably.

At the entrance to the market, there were the food stalls. The first was serving yellowish chicken; a heap of them, each tied with string, sat on the counter-top. A young woman behind the counter was shredding one into a bowl, her hands flicking to and fro. In other bowls on the counter were roasted peanuts and tea-stained eggs with cracked shells, rice and *sambal*. Would Rita eat at a place like this, or did she normally eat with the family she stayed with? A gold *maneki-neko* sat upright on the end of the counter, beckoning with its lucky paw.

Although it was still early, the market was crowded. He was careful to act like any other customer, in case Rita saw him before he saw her. He moved on from the food stalls to those selling plastic plates and bowls heaped high in bright green, pink, red, orange. Then the clothing stalls with hundreds of different pairs of flip-flops. He hated flip-flops – why walk around in something that left your feet so exposed? Ugly, as well. No foot, male or female, was ever flattered by a flip-flop. The only shoppers were locals. The occasional tourist was taking photos, thrilled by how the retail goods bought by poor people were so cheap and charming and colourful. Darkness had not lifted the smothering heat and the market was lit by white arc lights that hurt his eyes when he glanced up. Stallholders shouted to each other. Children pushed insolently against his legs. The noise and the crowds were beginning to oppress him. He wouldn't find her here.

The market took a dogleg and here the crowds thinned a little. He stopped in front of a small fruit stall selling the huge apples that he liked to eat in the evenings. He bought a bag of them and, as he paid, looked to his right and saw her, two stalls down. She was leaning over at a spice stall and pointing to a bamboo basket containing pieces of twisted turmeric root. The man behind the stall was leaning forward too, with a small wooden shovel in one hand. They were in intense conversation. As he approached, he guessed that she was pretending to be annoyed at the price the stallholder wanted to charge her. She was speaking Balinese but he couldn't tell whether she was using the formal or colloquial form. The stallholder was pretending to be annoyed back but then a price was all at once agreed and they both broke into smiles.

He stood quite close to her, waiting for her to finish, so that when she turned from the stall, she gave a small start at his proximity.

He held up both hands. 'I didn't want to interrupt.'

'Nyoman and I are old friends.' She threw a smile at the stallholder and he smiled and inclined his head in return. 'What are you after?'

He was about to apologise and back off, then he realised what she meant and held up his bag of apples.

'Have you had the food here?' she asked. 'It's great, there's a great stall at the entrance.'

'I saw it.'

They walked back through the market together, slowly, with her pausing at every other stall to look over what was there. She stopped at the plastic plates and bought six green ones in the shape of leaves. 'My tutor group,' she said, by way of explanation, slipping the plates into the large cloth bag she was carrying. As they turned from the stall, he reached out, hooked a finger beneath the strap of her bag and pulled it gently from her shoulder. She stopped. He took the bag, dropped his apples in it, put it on his own shoulder. They stood facing each other. Her expression was a query. She was wearing a short-sleeved cardigan over a vest top and it had slipped when he had taken the bag, exposing a soft, freckled shoulder. He reached out a hand and pulled the edge of the cardigan back into place. She dropped her gaze. They turned and continued walking.

'It's a long time since a man has carried my bag.' She had been flustered by his gesture: she was commenting on it to diminish its power. 'As you Americans say, it's cute.'

'I'm Dutch.' They had reached a narrow gap in the crowds. He gestured for her to go through it first.

'Dutch when it suits and American when it suits, perhaps?'

'That's right,' he replied, as he drew level with her again, 'and if you don't mind me saying, you haven't been treated right.'

She spoke from the corner of her mouth as they walked side by side. 'Stop trying to make me fall in love with you.'

'No.'

They slipped into it so easily; it was so fluent and meaningless. This was what he liked about her. You could say anything to her and it wasn't freighted with significance. The gestures were important but the words meant nothing.

'I'm sorry about the other morning,' she said, as they paused by a stall selling fritters. 'About rushing off, I mean. It was a little rude of me.' *A little rude*: he liked that in her too, her precision.

'Yes it was.' Now, perhaps, would be a good moment to find out what was wrong with her, what was damaged inside. Once you knew that about a person, they were yours for the taking.

'I did wonder, at that time, what . . . ?' he started, but she spoke over him.

'What did you do after you left?' she said.

'Went for a walk,' he replied. Maybe she hadn't seen him waiting in the cafe opposite the guesthouse after all.

'I had to get home and get changed, I was already late. And I felt a little guilty, I guess.'

'For being late or for having sex with me?'

She gave a half-smile. 'Well, that's not what I'm here for, is it?'

'I don't think you should feel guilty for giving yourself a night off.' He did not add: that's what I was doing, after all.

She looked away, at the market, then gave a sigh so heavy he presumed she was about to make her excuses and leave but instead she said, 'A drink?'

'How about we go back to Jalan Bisma?'

'You are a bad man, John Harper.'

'Yes I am.'

The morning after their second night together, they had exactly the kind of breakfast he had fantasised about before. The guesthouse didn't do black rice pudding – it was a Sunday speciality only – but the tangerine juice was sharp and sweet, the coffee hot.

'The *sambal* is great here, really spicy,' Rita said, as they studied the menu.

When the young woman came with their dishes, she put the eggs and toast in front of Rita and the *nasi goreng* in front of Harper. They waited until she had turned away before exchanging plates with small smiles of collusion.

They took the same route that he had the other day, walking up Jalan Bisma out of town until the guesthouses and little *warung* fell away and the road became a track through the rice fields.

On his previous walk, the boys had fallen behind, then disappeared, and he had wondered if he was mistaken about being followed – but even so, he glanced behind them. This time, there was no sign of anything suspicious, no one on their trail. The tall wooden constructions in the middle of the field looked just like water towers. The sheen of light brown water in which the rice plants stood was nothing more than irrigation. In Rita's presence, he realised, everything was no more than it seemed. If she were in the hut with him at night, the men would not come, rain or no rain. They would not even exist.

They passed beyond the edge of the town and along the stretch of dirt road that led up to the Forest via a winding rocky path. The edges of the rice fields were dotted with construction sites, the town stretching itself to accommodate its growing number of visitors. They passed a site where the bones of a building, a small hotel or guesthouse, were in place; the concrete pillars and the horizontal beams: a bare-chested man knelt on the ground chopping fiercely at a pile of wet cement on a board. Bamboo ladders lay in rows across one of the horizontals and several men were halfway up the ladders in a row, hauling another beam upwards between them by ropes slung over the top. At the bottom of the ladders and directly underneath the bones of the building, a large concrete base had already been filled and hardened. A pack of three dogs were lounging on it, all exactly the same shape, a cardboard-cutout mongrel shape: small, skinny, with disproportionately large ears. One of the dogs was dark brown, another a sandy colour, the other dirty white. They lay on their sides in the sun as motionless as if they were dead. Harper thought how sinister that sort of dog always seemed to him, all the same shape but different colours, as if they had been made, not born, cut from paper with scissors then magicked into life like the skeletons that jerked around the animated films of his childhood.

'So many rice fields disappearing under concrete,' Rita said. 'Until recently, Jalan Bisma was a dirt track leading out of town.'

He thought, well, when a farmer probably gets the same for selling his land as he would for three decades of threshing, can you blame him?

Rita stopped and looked at the site, the fields beyond. 'You know, I have wondered . . .'

Something about her tone arrested him. 'What?'

'Oh, you know, about buying a lease, a piece of land. It would feel big, though, a big thing to do.'

'Why? You could always sell it on, couldn't you, if it was a mistake?'

She frowned. 'It would mean I was saying goodbye, to other things, other options, going back, and so on. I would be saying something, to myself I mean. Alone.'

He wasn't sure what she meant: saying something only to herself? Or buying a lease, alone? But the bit about saying goodbye to other options, that bit he could understand.

'How long have you been here?'

'Eight years. Long enough, to decide I mean. If I was going to move on, I would have done by now. Building, you know, it's saying something, no? Building something. Frightening.'

Of all the things in the world there were to be frightened of, buying land leases or building property did not strike him as particularly scary: but no sooner had he dismissed her remark than he paused for a moment. I have never built anything, he thought. How strange, at my age, to realise that only now. 'Aren't you scared of the Invisibles?'

She shook her head, smiling. 'These fields are the land of Dewi Sri, don't forget.' She paused. 'If this is your first time on Bali, how do you know about the Invisibles?'

'Look,' he said, pointing. 'What kind of bird is that?'

She lifted a hand to shade her eyes.

While she scanned the trees on the other side of the rice field for the non-existent bird, he watched the man on his knees mixing the concrete and thought how he could buy a lease here too. With the political situation so unstable, it would be dirt cheap. Local labour would be next to nothing. You could throw up a small villa in no time. He wondered what colours Rita liked. He wasn't into all that fancy folk art but he didn't feel that she was either: she was too practical. In a couple of seconds, as they stood looking out over the field, he pictured their whole lives from now on. A small villa, together. Peace. Coffee on the veranda each morning as dawn broke over the fields. The view would be less dramatic than the one over the valley but, in its own way, just as beautiful.

The sun shone through the edges of her hair where it lifted slightly. He had the idea – which he knew to be stupid – that she had just had the same fantasy.

A shadow crossed his thoughts then, as he remembered what the rice fields were like at night. How far was he from it, two hours' drive, perhaps? Two hours and thirty-two and a half years, that's how far from it he was. What was he thinking? He turned briskly. Rita looked round at his sudden movement and, as she did, the dog nearest to them on the concrete slab, the white dog, lifted its head and with no warning other than a brief, preparatory snarl, roused itself and ran at them, barking in a rusty fashion, toenails skittering in the dirt. Rita let out a small, alarmed sound and grabbed his left arm while positioning herself behind him, pulling him to one side. He flinched but at her action, not the dog. The dog ran at them but stopped just short, then began following along the path. It loped beside them for a stride or two, jumping and snapping its teeth in the air, then, happy it had seen them off, lowered its head and slunk back to its indifferent companions.

Rita was walking on the other side, close to him, clutching at his right arm. He used his left hand to detach her grip, then took her left hand in his right and squeezed it. 'If there's one thing I can protect you from, it's dogs.'

'I'm not scared of them back home,' she said quickly, 'they are trained there, but here, they are just strays. You never know what they will do.'

'They are doorbells. Wouldn't you want your dog to bark at strangers?'

'Yes, well, one of those things bites you, you have forty-eight hours to get to Jakarta for the rabies jab . . .'

'The dogs here don't have rabies, the monkeys maybe.'

'I know. I just don't like them, that's all.'

*

At the entrance to the Monkey Forest, there were two women with a small portable stall, which they had set up in front of the ticket office, selling bunches of tiny bananas and packets of peanuts.

'Want me to get some?' he asked, gesturing.

'Are you crazy?' Rita replied.

One of the women was behind the stall, the other stood at the side holding a catapult ready loaded with a stone. He queued for their tickets at the kiosk and watched as the cluster of monkeys close to the entrance gate split to form a pincer movement and began to knuckle-walk towards the stall, tails in the air, gazes flicking from the bananas to the woman with the catapult. As soon as a monkey got too close to the stall, the woman raised the catapult and, at the sight of it, all the monkeys scattered back to the gate. He wondered how many shots the woman had had to fire to teach the monkeys what a raised catapult meant: not many, he guessed.

'Can you believe I've never been here?' Rita said, as they passed through the gate and entered the green heat of the Forest.

They were only a hundred yards in when a tiny grey monkey ran at them and she flinched again. The monkey stopped a few feet away and began to groom itself, as if it had proved its point, but after that, Rita stayed close to him as they walked.

The path led upwards through the trees until it reached a central area with a pond surrounded by a low stone wall and moss-covered statues. A man in a uniform was holding a short rectangular machete and hacking at a scattering of coconuts on the ground. As soon as he moved away, a dozen monkeys lolloped towards the broken pieces – the smaller ones making a dash then retreating with a piece to a safe distance, the larger ones approaching more casually, making their selection, then sitting where they were to shred it with the defiant air of playground bullies.

'Look at that one,' Rita said. A young monkey too afraid of the other monkeys to approach the shards of coconut had hold of a small, unbroken one that had rolled some distance away and was lifting it and bashing it on the ground. He had the feeling she was trying to recover her dignity by pretending she thought the monkeys cute: they weren't. The baby monkeys had the faces of little malicious old men.

As they watched, another adult monkey approached a mother and baby sitting on the stone ledge of the pool and grabbed at the baby's tail, trying to drag it from its mother's grasp. The mother swung the baby underneath her stomach, and lolloped away on three legs. The other monkey pursued and tried to snatch the baby again. The mother moved once more, but never quite far enough to deter the other monkey from trying again.

As they stood watching, Rita said, 'Monkey, donkey, owl. You know that saying?'

'Three ages of man.'

'Donkey, or owl?'

'Thanks,' he said. 'Still donkey, although sometimes I think I'm ready for owl.'

'I don't think anyone is ever ready for owl, do you? On your deathbed maybe.'

'Isn't it wisdom rather than death? What about you?'

'Definitely still donkey,' she replied, with a sigh in her voice. 'You have no idea.'

They watched the monkeys for a little longer and he wondered how soon he could suggest they leave – there was an awful lot of forest still to walk around, not to mention the holy stone carvings. He hoped she didn't want to look at all of it.

'I don't have to work on Monday,' she said.

'Why not?'

'There's another trainer coming in. Normally I stay and watch but I've seen this one before.'

What else was there to do, while he waited for news? With Rita, he felt he had been wrong: of course no one was going to kill him. With Rita, he felt his anxieties to be mistaken, no more than the inevitable result of his work. Could he not allow himself this a little longer? Work would still be there waiting for him, after all. If he hadn't heard from Jakarta or Amsterdam by the end of next week, he would take the initiative then.

'How about we go to the Tirta Empul Temple?' she said. 'Been there yet?'

'I'm not a tourist!' He could not keep the scorn from his response.

'You're here on holiday, aren't you? Don't you want to look at places? Anyway I didn't mean as a tourist.'

'You're a practising Hindu?' Now the scorn was mingled with disbelief.

'No, I just think, well, you put on your sarong and you bathe in the Holy Waters and what you feel is . . .'

'Wet,' he interjected.

She bore him with an indulgent sigh. '. . . Inspired, really, you feel inspired. You pray for someone each time you get under a spout and after a while you run out of the obvious people to pray for and there are still a lot of spouts left and . . .' Sensing he was unimpressed, she hesitated. 'Makes you think, that's all.'

Of all the forms of faith that humans indulged in, the one he hated most was this sort of freelance spirituality – a belief that it was okay to pick 'n' mix your rituals, try a bit of this and a bit of that and feel better about yourself. At least belonging to an established religion required action and sacrifice, visit Mecca once in your life or don't cut your hair – even Protestant Christians were obliged to go to church at Easter. But this: I'll do a bit of what the locals do and feel good because I'm getting some of the insight with none of the sacrifice. All he said was, 'I don't think it's for me, thanks all the same.'

'Okay,' she said lightly. She turned away from the pond with its stone wall and they began to walk further up the path. Another man with a machete came past the other way, carrying a huge sack made of rope net and full of coconuts. There were other exits, Harper thought: he'd seen them on the map at the entrance. If they followed the curve of the path round, they could leave by the other route, head back into town. She had taken his rejection of the temple pretty well. Was it too early to suggest they go to a bar?

'The beach, then,' she said.

He was about to object to that one too, then he thought, if they went south, down to Denpasar, maybe he'd be able to find out a bit more about what was going on in Jakarta. Amsterdam wouldn't like it but then Amsterdam wouldn't know. 'There's an Intercontinental at Jimbaran Bay.'

Now it was her turn to roll her eyes. 'Only someone like you could want the Intercontinental. You'll get your scrambled eggs there. You'll probably get cornflakes if you want. I know a much better hotel, a bar on the beach, great cocktails, Balinese enough for me and international enough for you. How does that sound?'

'Our relationship in a nutshell,' he said drily and they both made ironic sounds in mutual acknowledgement that his use of the world 'relationship' was a joke.

They turned back towards the entrance and, as they did, a monkey ran from behind them and with one swift movement, leapt up and clung with its hands and feet to the bottom of a woven shoulder bag worn by a woman in front of them. The woman shrieked and let the bag fall, then ran a few paces before turning and pointing. The monkey upended the bag and another half a dozen monkeys ran forward to inspect its scattered contents. One ripped open a purse, another seized a pair of sunglasses, another snatched up a plastic water bottle and sank its teeth into the bottom while lifting it up to suck from it. Rita gave an amused exhalation and a shake of her head as they passed and Harper noted briefly that even she was entertained rather than alarmed when the monkeys' victim was someone else.

Nearby, the baby monkey sat, alone now, looking at them.

*

There had nearly been a child. That was the way he thought of it. It. How unconscionable, that small word: it. But what was the alternative? He couldn't do what Francisca did: Francisca, his wife, the fragile beauty from Friesland – the woman his mother had hated so much it was inevitable he would marry her eventually. She had started choosing names for the baby in the early stages of her pregnancy, convinced it was a boy. She had bought piles of soft cloth diapers and little knitted vests. She had the cot they would bring him home in all ready with a yellow bow tied to the handle. He would watch her sometimes, when she was sitting on the window seat in the sitting room, unaware of his gaze, reclining on a pile of fat firm cushions and staring out at the canal while running her hand over her taut belly, a small smile of knowingness on her face. He thought how perfected she seemed then, in her happiness, in the knowledge that something was coming that she would love beyond all else but for the moment was safe inside her, enclosed in the wet wall of her womb; the repository of all her hopes and dreams; entirely imagined, entirely protected.

When he saw that expression on his wife's face, what he felt was fear. Fear gripped his stomach like a fist. The helplessness of babies disturbed and disgusted him, that was why it had taken him until his middle years to consider having one. He told himself he would feel differently when it was his own, but looking at other people's he just thought, at what point do they become human?

Then he said to himself, you're fifty years old. She's forty and it's probably her last chance, which is your fault because it took you eight years to agree to marry her. This thing has come to you both at a time in life when, for most people, there are no more surprises. Be grateful. Put the past aside, let go of the convictions you have nursed ever since you came back from Indonesia as a young man, broken. Okay, so you're not sure about her, not sure at all about the baby – but she seems sure enough for both of you. Maybe her certainty will be enough.

Francisca went into labour in the middle of the night, eight weeks before her due date. It was a girl. She lived for two days. The doctor explained later: it was an aspiration problem, something to do with the baby swallowing or inhaling something in the amniotic fluid that blocked its – her – airways. It caused the pneumonia that killed her. She lived long enough for them to hold her, name her – Anika, after his mother, Francisca's suggestion. They had watched her breathe in the tiniest, most shallow of ways, her small chest labouring – but Harper still thought of her as having drowned in the womb. It made more sense, somehow. How could a baby float in fluid for nine months, anyway? When he sat next to the cot in the incubation unit, Francisca clutching his hand and weeping, he remembered his mother's story of how he had been born during a monsoon in an internment camp in the Dutch East Indies and the rain running down the sides of the hut and the dirt road turning into a brown river and wondered if this story had somehow been there inside him when he thought of his baby daughter as having drowned, as if a story like that could be passed on to his baby, like a genetic disease.

Francisca had sobbed in his arms at night for weeks afterwards, and said things like, 'I know you are suffering too but you aren't able to express it, it's okay, I understand that.' He did not tell her that when their tiny baby had died he had thought – in the moments before his own grief and disappointment had taken hold – *at least you have been spared life*.

The day started well enough. He had arranged to pick Rita up at two pm and although she had told him to park outside an electrical shop on Monkey Forest Road and wait for her there, he got out of the car and wandered up and down a few paces each way, curious to know which compound was hers. He was standing right outside it when she emerged alongside a young Balinese woman who was holding a pile of textbooks with both arms wrapped beneath.

'You are here,' she said simply. 'This is Ni Wayan.'

He nodded and the young woman nodded back, then she looked at Rita and said, '*Ibu* Rita,' with a bow and smile, before turning towards town.

'I thought today was a day off,' he said, as he led Rita to the car. It had pleased him to hear the girl call her *ibu* with such affectionate emphasis: she was a well-liked teacher, held in affection and regard. He had thought as much.

'Wayan came to me yesterday and asked for an extra lesson. It happens often. That's why I said after lunch. My days off usually start after lunch.'

'Are you good to all your students?' He opened the passenger door for her.

'They are all good to me.'

As he climbed in his side, she said quietly and seriously, 'God bless the Balinese.'

They bumped slowly down Monkey Forest Road and turned right onto the main street. Rita leant forward and opened the car's glove compartment.

'What do you want?' he asked.

She pointed at the tape deck between them. He glanced at it and said, 'I'll be really surprised if that works.'

Rita pulled out a handful of tapes, loose with no cases. She lifted a couple in turn then shrieked, 'Superman Is Dead! Suckerhead? Where did you get this car?'

Kadek had got the car for him. He had wanted a local vehicle, nothing identifiable as a foreigner's hire car. 'What's Suckerhead?'

Rita was still looking through the cassettes. 'Local death metal. Big underground scene here. Even Balinese youth need to rebel sometimes. They rioted in Jakarta when Metallica came, you know.'

It occurred to him to mention the riots in Jakarta that had recently led to the downfall of the Sustainer of the Universe, which he thought a somewhat more significant event, but it would be hard to discuss the political situation in the capital without it becoming clear that his knowledge of it was a little more detailed than your average economist; although she would know if some of the Chinese families fleeing the capital had come here, she would know what the talk was amongst her students – she could be a useful source of information. *Stop it*, he said to himself then.

Once in Sanur, they went straight to the hotel and parked in the car park at the entrance to the gardens and walked down a pretty lane to reception and Rita laughed at his irritation that there was no valet parking. He resisted her attempts to show him round the grounds; they headed straight to the beachside bar.

Two perfect seats were waiting for them, low and comfy, facing the sea, with a small table between. As they settled into them, Rita leaned forward for the cocktail menu, making a small noise of satisfaction. It was a cloudy day. Down by the water, a row of red, blue and yellow *jukung* boats were ranged in a row, painted in bright colours, with outrigger legs, raised and bent like spiders, for decorative purposes only, he presumed: the fishing and the coral harvesting on this stretch of beach must have ended many years ago. On a neighbouring terrace, a group of small boys were having their dance practice, the warrior dance – whatever it's called, nothing to do with battle, these days, he thought.

Rita lifted a hand. 'Across the bay, there, you know that's where they built the Bali Beach Hotel in the sixties, first of many, Western triumph or monstrosity depending on your point of view.'

I know, he thought, *I watched it being built*.

A waiter had materialised at his shoulder and Rita sat upright in her seat, holding the cocktail menu sideways so that he could see.

'Choose for us,' he said. Before she even spoke, he knew she would order something that included fruit.

After taking their order up to the bar, the waiter returned with some tiny glass bowls containing toasted biscuits. Rita picked up a bowl and tipped some into her hand. 'Want some?'

He shook his head, staring out at the beach where, between them and the fake fishing boats, three young women in bikinis were lying very close together on a large grass mat, like sausages in a pan. Wandering past them was a young white couple in patterned baggy trousers, the man bearded and tall, the woman skinny and short; hand-woven bags slung over their shoulders, bracelets on their wrists. They would not be sunning themselves all day long, nor would they buy cigarettes or alcohol in Duty Free on the way home. They would go home with luggage full of sarongs and woodcarvings. They would learn *please* and *thank you* in Indonesian and use them on every possible occasion, whether it was appropriate or not. They would tip as generously as their backpacking budget allowed and they would always, always, behave respectfully in temples.

But when they got home, the young couple would do exactly what the three young women would do. They would buy houses, cook food, drive cars. The fuel for those cars would come from somewhere and it would come via the pipes built by the sort of company that employed companies like his in order to ensure the safety of their investments and their staff.

He remembered first arriving on the island, November '65. It had been a relief to get off Java, the Jakarta job done. At Tuban airport, as it was called back then, he had handed over an extortionate bribe to a man in a suit and sunglasses in order to evade a queue that had built up in front of a group of soldiers whose purpose in questioning passengers disembarking from the domestic flight was unclear.

The operative doing his handover was waiting for him outside the low building, his car parked at an angle halfway up the kerb. He shook Harper's hand, said, 'Welcome to Bali. Call me Abang. You got through quickly.'

'It wasn't easy,' said Harper, pushing his glasses back up his sweating nose.

The area around the airport was surrounded by construction in the shimmering heat. No amount of political chaos ever stopped the building works. The new regime would be hoping for international flights as soon as possible, once it had defeated the Red Menace – and he had no doubt it would all flow, flow on the shiny new planes landing on the shiny new runways. First came the massacres, then the arms and the money and the economic advisers, then the runways – then, the tourists.

'Congratulations,' Abang said. 'A good start. They should make it some kind of test.' He meant the Institute.

'Well,' Harper said, 'there's a lot more people trying to get out than in.' He had passed through a huge crowd of families on their way to Departures.

They got into the car. He didn't know much about Abang at that point but later found out he was an Indo like him, mixed-race, an older man who had picked the right side in the war and, unlike Harper and his mother, hadn't had to flee back to Holland in '46 – useful to the Institute in the same way he was, for being a bit brown. He was based in Sumatra but had been touring the Eastern Islands to do an advance report while Harper had been doing Jakarta. Although they had never met before, Harper felt an instant affection for him, reciprocated by the invitation to call him Abang: big brother.

Abang nodded at Harper's observation as they joined the queue of cars trying to get in or out or go round and round the airport – in the crowd of vehicles, it was hard to tell. The smell of aeroplane fuel mingled with exhaust and cigarette smoke. Everyone had their windows rolled down, their arms hanging out – occasionally, a driver would shout or gesture in a desultory fashion. It was a slow kind of chaos.

As they sat looking straight ahead, Abang said, 'It's going to be just as bad here, you know, it's on its way. Funny how people know and don't know.' He nudged the car forward a couple of feet. 'You want to go and rest a bit? Do the briefing after?'

'No, let's get on with it.'

'Okay, good, let's go and do it with a beer.'

They drove straight to Sanur. Abang wanted Harper to see the Bali Beach Hotel, under construction for two years now. They had a beer together in a bar opposite the site while he explained how the building of the hotel had caused trouble locally ever since it started. Suteja had given the best contracts to his friends in the PKI, which had led to a lot of resentment. Control of the tourist industry was going to be as hotly contested as control of the rice harvest. 'The PKI have got it all wrong. They are putting all their effort into land reform for the peasants but the peasants aren't even grateful and the foreign dollars aren't going to come for rice, they're going to come for sand.' Abang indicated the beach in front of them with an open, palm-upwards gesture.

Harper thought of the charred corpse he had seen hanging from a tree by the side of the road at a crossroads just before Jakarta airport. The sign around the neck read: *Gerwani*. 'You really think anyone is going to want to come here, after what's going on here hits the news in Europe and America?'

Abang had given a humourless yelp. '*Hits* the news? In any case, you'll find blood sinks into sand really fast.' He lifted a copy of *Suara Indonesia* from his bag, folded to the editorial. He tossed it onto the table between them and jabbed a finger.

Harper looked at the paper and Abang translated the headline of the editorial out loud. 'Now It Is Clear Who Is Friend and Who Is Foe.'

He looked at Abang and raised his eyebrows. 'How long do you think we have?'

'You mean in general, or here?'

'Here.'

Abang wobbled his head from side to side, a small balancing movement. 'Two weeks, three at most, maybe less, maybe a lot less.'

'Really?' Harper had been assuming he had a little more time. What was the point of him coming over from Java to do reports if it was almost underway?

'Rumour has it the Brawijaya Units are due next month.'

'Who's in command?' Harper asked.

'Sarwo Edhie.'

Harper was silent for a moment.

'Yes, that's what I thought too,' Abang said. He lifted his beer bottle to his lips. Harper did the same. He felt something, then, some thrill of fear – had it been a premonition of what was to come? Or was it simply that the adrenaline of witnessing what had happened in Java had drained, just a little, with his arrival on the island, and he was now feeling a shiver of weakness at the thought of the danger that would soon be evident here? He had better get his adrenaline levels back up pretty soon, particularly if Abang moved on and he was the only one reporting back. If they closed the airport it would mean a boat to another island, dangerous enough in itself, or more likely lying low in the hills until things blew over.

'Have they started collecting names?'

Abang shook his head. 'They've been doing that for some time. Anyone in the PKI or any of the other Communist groups is out of a job, in the government sector anyway, schools, civil service, they've all gone, family members too, any association will do. They are building up the lists, village by village. Two weeks I reckon, before it starts. They may not even wait for the army.'

'The lists.'

Abang lifted his beer bottle in a dry salute. 'There's always a list.'

There was an unspoken acknowledgement between Abang and himself, Harper thought. There was always a list; often more than one. The army, the Islamists and the nationalists were all drawing up lists of Communists to kill. The Communists would have their own lists, and if the 30th September Movement had succeeded, Harper had no doubt that he and Abang and anyone else with European or American connections would have been on it. Their brown skin wouldn't have saved them, not considering who they worked for, not now it was clear who was friend and who was foe.

Blood sinks into sand really fast. The waiter arrived with their cocktails, some large red fruit-filled thing. He wished he had asked for something short and whisky-based instead of telling Rita to choose. He looked at the young women in bikinis lying just a few feet in front of them, then stared out beyond them at the sea. He could tell that Rita was watching him and sensing he had sunk into silence and after a moment or two of watchfulness, concluding it was best to leave him to it. She leaned forward for the cigarette packet that he had dropped onto the table as they sat down and he reached out and grabbed her hand, grasping it in his, pressing her soft fingers. They both looked at the hands.

'Can we get a room?' He could hear, in his own voice, a different tone from their previous encounters, something else mixed with the desire, a kind of need. He heard it without understanding it.

'No,' she said, 'I said, remember, I need to be back tonight.'

He released her hand. She shook it a little then reached for the packet and withdrew a cigarette but then sat holding it, as if she had thought better of lighting it. Her fingers were trembling. She hadn't smoked in front of him before.

He stood, took his lighter from his pocket and tossed it onto the table. 'Why don't you order some food?' he said. The cocktails were strong and they would be drinking several.

'Where are you going?'

'To talk to the concierge.'

He turned and walked back down the path to the main building. She had been right about one thing, it was a beautiful hotel. He couldn't remember it from before. It was a low, discreet collection of Balinese bungalows set amidst gardens. You could come here as a wealthy Westerner and hide in decorous seclusion from whatever was going on in the outside world.

He could have asked the waiter in the bar about what was happening on Java but the waiter would only have given him a polite answer, 'Everything is fine, sir.' The concierge would be a much better source of information.

The deputy manager was on the desk. Harper straightened himself as he approached and spoke in English.

'Can you help me? My company has closed our Jakarta office and I can't get through. What's the latest?'

The concierge turned to the pile of newspapers on his desk and reached out a hand but Harper said, 'I've got yesterday's news. Put a call through to the concierge at the Mandarin or the Four Seasons, or the Grand Hyatt, any of them.'

It took the man six calls to get through to someone he could talk to and at first, he only got bland answers: order would soon return, the army was in control, there was no need for anxiety.

After a polite interval, Harper intervened. 'Ask him if any more shopping precincts have been set on fire.'

The man spoke into the phone, returned the answer, 'No sir, no more commercial premises have been attacked.'

'Are the Americans and Europeans still evacuating their nationals?'

'I believe so, yes.'

'And what about elsewhere, Surakarta and Medan?' The conversation following this question took a little longer.

'There are no further incidents, the army is in control, sir, there is no need for alarm.'

'Ask him if there are still tanks parked on the Hotel Indonesia roundabout or Merdeka Square?'

'My friend does not have that information, sir. The streets are clear. The banks and schools are closed only as a precaution.'

'Is there a phone in the lobby I can use to make an international call?'

The deputy manager took him over to a booth with a small stool in it and a wall phone.

'Shall we charge this call to your room, sir?'

'I'll pay cash.'

It was Hannah who picked up the phone, that was good. Hannah was his boss's secretary and had worked for the company for years. Every now and then, they had a beer and exchanged notes on Jan's peculiarities. Unlike some of their colleagues, they would never use this information against each other. 'Good morning, Institute of International Economics.' Hannah wasn't particularly attractive but he loved her voice, slow and low, gravelly.

'Hannah, *lieveling,* it's your favourite brown guy. Ninety kilos of sheer muscle.'

There was a slight delay on the line. 'Well, hello stranger.'

'Is Jan in?'

After a pause, 'No, I've only just got in, haven't taken my coat off. How's Jakarta? Sounds pretty bad.'

'I'm not there any more, I'm on leave, enforced leave. Henrikson is running the show.'

'Oh, I see.'

'Hasn't there been talk?'

'News to me, my friend. Why haven't you been recalled?'

It was exactly the same question he had asked himself.

The pause before each of her answers implied she was being careful in what she said but he was fairly certain she wasn't. All the same, it was odd that his predicament had not been discussed. Hannah knew everything that happened in the Asia Department and normally Jan would be sure everyone in the company knew it too. That was what the partners did if you messed up.

'Are you sure? He hasn't said anything?'

'Not a word. I was wondering why I hadn't heard from you though. The office is still closed, Henrikson's calling in from Le Méridien. I thought you were with him. I was wondering why you hadn't called. The news reports, it's calmer, but . . .'

'I know, still in the balance, looks like. What's the word your end?' The pause this time was a little longer than the mechanical one on the line. Hannah was hesitating about how much to tell him. 'C'mon, I'm going crazy stuck on an island, being kept out of the loop. You've no idea how hard it is to get news here.'

The pause shortened again. 'More of the same. The Americans have got all non-essential personnel out but they've left staff in place. British the same. Things are much calmer on the streets but nobody's taking chances. Most of our existing clients are out now but we've got a whole load of new ones, people still panicking. Chinese families still fleeing in droves. Everyone's waiting to see if Habibie can stabilise things but who knows.' So Hannah's opinion on the way things could be heading wasn't so different from his own.

'Beijing made any pronouncements?'

'No, they're sitting on the fence. There's demonstrations outside the Indonesian Embassy there, though.'

He emerged from the booth and pulled his wallet from his pocket as he went over to the reception desk. The deputy manager had gone but a young woman took payment for the call.

As he turned back to walk through the gardens, he stopped, patted his pockets and regretted that his cigarettes were sitting on the low table next to Rita. He was right, he knew it: things could go either way, but the oddest thing of all was that his suspension wasn't official. As far as his colleagues were concerned, he was still out in the field.

As he walked back along the tiled path, back to the beach, Harper thought, the rest of the day is spoiled now. He had brought the real world into the bubble he and Rita had been in during their encounters so far. He had liked the bubble: the enclosed space of a room in a guesthouse, the car – they could exist as long as they had a wall of some sort around them. They existed best of all beneath the fine gauze of a mosquito net.

As he sat down next to her, she said, 'I've ordered.'

Summoned by her words, a plate of satay with a sticky coating arrived, some rice cakes and a bowl of water spinach.

They ate in silence. 'This satay is really good, spicy,' he said at one point but it was such an obviously small-talk remark, she ignored him. She ate the satay and the spinach but only picked at the rice.

After they had eaten, they walked along the beach. They talked about whether it was worth going for a drive around Sanur and decided it was mostly hideous and touristy. It grew greyer; the light was dull as they returned to the bar – as though the sky's heaviness matched his mood.

Without discussion, they sat down in the same seats and both ordered soft drinks: she had watermelon juice and he a Coke, then they sat in silence, looking out at the sea where the waves crested apricot, the beach almost empty. He noticed a long trail of ants that were processing up the leg of the small table between them and clustering around a speck of satay sauce. The table hadn't been wiped down properly while they were on their walk and he considered calling the waiter over.

In front of them on the sand was a pair of loungers in a reclining position. Between them was a standard lamp with a wooden stem and white lightshade of the sort you would find in any domestic sitting room. Even though they were still some way from dusk, a white-coated member of the hotel staff approached and turned the lamp on, and only then did Harper notice the cable that led from its base to the bottom of a nearby coconut palm. There was an electricity feed in the palm tree, a socket in its trunk. He glanced at Rita and saw she had noticed too and was also amused by how that small patch of beach had been transformed into a lounge. They smiled at each other. He wished he hadn't made the call to Amsterdam, or asked about Jakarta. He wished he was no more than what Rita thought him to be.

*

As they walked back to the car, Rita perfectly happy, he felt annoyed with himself, and so did what most people do when they are upset about their own behaviour – he got upset with the person he was with. In the middle of a conversation about her work training secondary-school teachers, he interrupted with, 'Of course all the good stuff here was built by the Dutch. The irrigation ditches in the fields used to be wood and bamboo but they went rotten. There's a stone aqueduct in the highlands above town, you know, transformed the villages. You should go and see it.'

Why was he provoking her? He didn't even believe it was true.

'You mean the aqueduct above Keliki,' she replied, her voice light. 'I've seen it, of course, irrigation is everything. Only us Westerners take water for granted.'

'Yes but the point I'm making is that if the Dutch hadn't . . .'

'Oh, c'mon,' she responded.

When he unlocked the car door for her and opened it, she slid herself down diagonally without looking at him.

He jammed the key in the ignition. She worked in education, so what? How about looking a little deeper? What about that caesarean scar on her abdomen, where was that child? He imagined a boy, a small boy, dying young perhaps – whatever it was, some common but excruciating tragedy that had led her to flee cold northern Europe and end up here, in a country so hot and full of flowers that sweat smelled sweet, deep greens and monsoon rains and slowly swaying people – the sort of country a white woman could run to because it was beautiful – because yeah, that's right, I'll go and live somewhere with lots of frangipani then I can convince myself the world isn't ugly after all. He thought this last thought in a high-pitched voice in his head, a mockery of a female voice, of optimism of any sort.

They drove in silence.

They continued to drive in silence for an hour, the ribbon development along the road thinning little between villages: the open shacks with people sitting on the steps selling wooden tools and carvings and beads. They were most of the way back to town when Rita spoke and when she did, all at once with no preamble, it was obvious that throughout that hour of driving she had been continuing the debate between them to herself in just the same way he had. It was the worst kind of arguing: the silent kind.

'How many killed in the Holocaust?' she came out with. 'How many? Six million, right? Everyone knows that. Even you know that.'

Thanks for that 'even', he thought. Thanks a lot.

'Want to take a guess on how many of that six million were babies? Go on, take a guess. Of course the total dead was fifty million, in total I mean, everybody on all sides I mean, biggest category probably Russian soldiers but let's stick with the babies shall we, the babies gassed and burned, out of six million people who just happened to be Jewish, no, how many babies?'

He conjured the image of a family being rounded up by the Gestapo. He watched the image in his head, like a flash of archive news footage in black and white, a sturdy father in a long black coat, a mother white-faced with fear, six or eight children, perhaps? A baby, clutched in the arms of the eldest daughter because the mother had her hands full helping the smaller children into the back of a truck with its tailgate down. The father and the eldest boy were lifting up suitcases and then turning to assist a group of elderly people who were waiting patiently behind the family. A young soldier stood next to them, holding a rifle. One baby, perhaps, in a group of twelve or fourteen?

'I have absolutely no idea,' he said, allowing – and that was a mistake – the hint of a sigh to enter his voice. Six million divided by fourteen. Did she really want him to do that particular calculation? Why was she bringing this up anyway?

'Guess,' she insisted.

'I don't know, three hundred, four hundred thousand. Are you serious?'

'One million,' Rita replied. 'In the war on our continent in the middle of the century we happen to live in right now, the continent of the Renaissance and mass industrialisation and the vote and penicillin, we killed one million babies. Not out of ignorant prejudice at all, it was perfectly knowing and industrial. We put all that *progress* we're so proud of to *very* good use. In living memory.'

Harper allowed a silence to speak the phrase, *and your point is?*

The village street was busy and he had slowed the car to a crawl because there was a man on a bicycle just ahead and to his left. The bicycle had two wooden cages of squashed chickens with dirty-white feathers slung either side of the saddle, held together by string. The man was standing up on the pedals as he cycled in his sarong and as they drew level, he glanced over his shoulder, slowed, then wobbled and fell against the side of the car. The cage scraped against the car door, sending the poor skinny chickens into a constrained flurry of panic.

'Fuck!' He braked more savagely than he needed to. He was flung against the steering wheel then back in his seat, momentarily winded.

Rita was wearing her seatbelt. She jerked forward a few inches before it caught her and pushed her back again. She sat while he recovered his breath, then said in a low, conciliatory voice, 'A million of them, John, in living memory, and with industrial efficiency. Do you really think Europeans are in any position to lecture *any* other culture about barbarism?'

He drove straight through town and out the other side. She did not question where he was going. The road remained good for twenty minutes after town and then he turned the car off onto the poor, potted track. He wouldn't be able to drive right up to the hut. The track ran beneath, and then they would have to cut up on foot along a narrow path that joined the one down to the river.

When he parked the car, she was still silent, so to break the tension he said, 'Here's where I am staying.' He was about to ask, politely, if she wanted to see it or go back to town but before he could, she had opened her door. He had parked on a steep camber and she had to lever both hands against the doorframe to clamber out.

The hut loomed above them, a dark shape visible through the trees at the top of the steep path, about to disappear into dusk. She paused for a moment, turned to the valley. He thought, she feels it too, the singing stillness, alive with so much that is invisible

After a while, she said, 'The villages are like this too. A short drive, and suddenly . . .' She was feeling the isolation of the place – and yet, for him, bringing her here had made it much less isolated. That was all you needed, one person, newer than you, to make a strange thing feel owned.

They looked at each other in a moment of truce. He gestured up the path.

As she walked ahead of him, he watched the slow side-to-side movement of her hips and wanted, very badly, to put his hands on them. He wanted no more talk.

On the veranda, he stood for a moment, looking around for any sign of Kadek, but he rarely came late afternoon or evening unless by prior arrangement. There would be a basic meal left on the desk, under a banana leaf.

The ornate doors were kept padlocked – not that that would make much difference to a determined intruder, or intruders. He took the small silver key from his trouser pocket, unlocked the padlock and placed it on the veranda table, pushed back both of the narrow doors and gestured for her to go in. She stepped over the threshold.

They were silent while she wandered around the hut, casting her gaze slowly over each object and item of furniture, looking round and seeing how it all added up to a kind of comfortable barrenness. He remembered what Francisca had said the first time she came to his bachelor flat in Amsterdam, many years ago. 'You know, you should have tidied up, don't you know what a woman thinks when they see a man's habitat, *is this the kind of life I would lead with this man?*' What was Rita gleaning about him from the few objects in the room?

'It's only a forest toilet outside I'm afraid, and a *bak mandi*, although I usually just wash with a bowl on the veranda in the mornings, to watch the sunrise. Kadek brings water from up the hill, there are streams that feed into the river.'

She looked at the ceiling. 'No fan?'

He indicated a rusty desk fan that sat in the corner. 'Only that, but the electricity is pretty poor. I have a couple of kerosene lamps if I need them.'

'I love the smell of those.'

Stay with me, he thought. Stay here tonight. We can share the food that Kadek has left. We can sit cross-legged on the bed, facing each other, and I will feed you rice balled up between my fingers.

'You know I can't stay the night,' she said, as she turned.

He thought of the possibility that he would be visited during the hours of darkness by a killing squad. This was ridiculous, this fantasy of his, that she was looking round the hut and imagining a life with him. They hardly knew each other. She knew nothing, nothing about the world and certainly nothing about him. *A million babies.* Who the fuck did she think she was? 'I wasn't going to invite you.'

'Okay, there's no need to be rude about it.'

And suddenly, it was as if they were having a full-blown marital row, facing each other full on, speaking too loudly and too quickly; as if they had, all at once, reached the stage that couples who have known each other for many years eventually reach, where the arguments are always the same argument and the victor merely the one who is most vehement on that particular occasion.

'I don't know what's wrong with you today and I don't know where your cynicism comes from,' she said, 'but most of the people who live in this country are lucky if they eat each day, and maybe we should . . .'

At that point, without any conscious decision to escalate things between them, Harper shot out his hand and grasped her upper arm and spat, '*How* can you be afraid of some dog in the street, some starved dog you could kick aside, one foot, in your strappy sandals, and he would slink off? Some mangy little monkey, who would run away backwards just if you . . . if you . . . *lifted* your hand? Do *dogs* and *monkeys* have knives or guns? You think your Ni Wayan is so charming or your driver so kind because he takes you to the water temple? How can people like you be so stupid? *Now?* At this time? Don't you know what's going on in Jakarta and the other cities? People have been burnt to death in shopping malls, beaten to death in the streets. You *live* in this country. Don't you even follow the *news*?'

This speech poured out of him and all the while he continued to grasp her upper arm, just to ensure her attention he thought, but then he realised that instead of wrenching herself away and spitting back – something like *of course I do* – she had let the arm go limp in his grasp and cast her gaze to the ground. Francisca would have been yelling at him by now, jabbing her finger in his chest – for all her mild manners, she was snarly and argumentative enough when she chose. Rita was behaving quite differently. He saw the neutral look on her face and realised it was the look of a woman who had extensive experience of a man with a temper, a woman who knew how to become perfectly still.

The scar on her belly, the absence of any mention of her past or a child dead or alive and her reaction to him now conjoined to form an image of her particular tragedy. It came to him in one piece: a man who hit her, a child taken away or left behind, the price she had to pay for her own freedom and sanity, perhaps – and he thought, *oh no*, and let her arm drop, expecting her to turn away or rub the arm but instead she stood motionless before him, still staring at the ground, as if she was waiting to see whether there was any more where that came from. He had done much worse than this, as well as witnessing worse and doing nothing – but watching this large, soft woman standing carefully in front of him, he could not have felt more ashamed.

He took a step back, to indicate that he was not going to touch her again. Please look at me, he thought. If you look, you will see it in my face. I am not like him. I think men who hit women are scum, beneath contempt.

She would not look at him and he did not want to speak until she raised her gaze. When she did, she did not look him in the face. Instead, she stared into the corner of the room behind him, then said very quietly, 'John, what happened to you?'

II

NOW IT IS CLEAR WHO IS FRIEND AND WHO IS FOE

(1942–65)

He had no memory of leaving the East Indies, going back to what his mother called the Homeland, back to Holland. It was 1946. He was three and a half years old and had only known life in a camp of one sort or another; the internment camp run by the Japanese on Sulawesi and then three displaced civilian camps run by the British and Dutch in the suburbs of Batavia.

His mother told him about it though, the journey, the perilous weeks at sea. They shared a narrow, windowless cabin with another woman and her two daughters – the daughters slept on a mat on the floor between the bunks; the youngest girl had whooping cough and gasped for breath all night. Harper slept on his mother's bunk. She pushed him against the wall and lay on the outside, to keep him away from the whooping girl. Like all the children, he had had his head shaved before embarkation to stop the lice and scabies spreading and at night, his scalp scratched his mother's arm. 'You're prickling my arm,' she would whisper to him in the dark, and they would both giggle together, then lie awake listening to the whooping child. 'Still, at least you don't have diseases,' she would say, after a while, stroking his stubble.

He remembered none of this himself, but later, when they had moved to Los Angeles and he had acquired an American stepfather and a baby half-brother, his mother would take him on one side and talk about their life together in the camp and the long journey back to Holland. She liked to do this when she had had a fight with his stepfather because it was something only she and Harper shared. 'Weeks and weeks on end,' she would say, 'just you and me, baby boy, on a boat crammed full of people who were running out on their lives so far. You slept in my arms every night, you and your prickly head.' At this, she would throw a glance at her new husband, or at the doorway through which he had recently departed, as if to say, *this important thing happened before you, it excludes you, and don't you forget it.*

He and his mother spent only eighteen months in Holland before emigrating to America – long enough to find out that she was not eligible for an army widow's pension even though his father had been decapitated by the Japanese while in the service of the Dutch Colonial Army. Harper's father had been half Dutch, half Indonesian, an Indo, which made Harper – or Nicolaas, as he was called back then – an Indo too. You needed to be all white to be white but only a small bit brown to be brown. 'Your papa wasn't Dutch enough for you and me to get the money, baby boy,' his mother said, 'but he was Dutch enough for the damn Japs to cut his head off.' She said that kind of thing when she had been drinking. The *damn Japs* had cut his father's head off and put his mother in a camp and as he had been inside his mother at the time, he'd had no choice but to go along.

He had no memory of the camp either – no direct memory, in any case. But his mother talked about it a lot when she was drunk or angry or both, which meant she talked about it for a substantial proportion of his early childhood. She told him the same stories often enough for them to form pictures in his head – they became his own memories even though he remained outside them, as if he had been there, watching his mother's life before he was born. 'It was 1942, baby boy, but the Japs made us call it 2602, can you imagine? They even said the sun rose when it did in Tokyo. You got beaten if they caught you speaking Dutch.' In the pictures in his head he saw himself as a brave toddler, asking for food in Dutch, a massive Japanese soldier taking a stick to his back. Making up memories from the seeds of his mother's stories was, after all, a lot more interesting than actually having them. Through these stories, he could remember what it was like for her to be pregnant with him in an internment camp, standing in a queue with her mess tin and homemade wooden spoon waiting for her tiny portion of all there was to eat, grey tapioca cooked over camp fires in huge vats. 'You grew anyway,' she said. 'That's how it works, the baby inside takes all the goodness it needs from the mother and the mother starves and gets sick.' He saw his mother dressed in a tattered dress and wooden clogs, her taut belly as round as a basketball, matchstick arms and legs, cheeks hollow, hair falling out, and him curled up inside her, feeding off her, eating away at her internal organs. 'And then, when I was at my biggest, when you were taking your time deciding you were ready, it was getting close to the rainy season. Man, that was the worst. I thought I would die. I thought I would just melt like an ice cream. My waters broke the same day the skies opened and the monsoon began. Water ran down my legs, baby boy, and down the sides of the buildings at the same time, and then it started pouring in through the roof where there were holes in the palm leaves. The road outside the shack flooded – I won't call it a clinic or anything, it was just a shack with six bamboo bunk beds. They put the sickest on the lowest bunk so it would be easier to take the corpse away when they died. It was the filthiest place you can imagine, cockroaches and leeches, and I was screaming and screaming as I squeezed you out and outside there was a river where the dirt road had been and then pretty soon a river inside as it was only a dirt floor. Seriously, I thought I would die, and you would die with me, and the water would wash the shack away and we'd both be carried away on that river and after what I'd been through that seemed like it would be a pretty good thing to happen to both of us.' Harper saw himself as a newborn baby, lying on his back on top of a brown river, waving his arms as he bobbed and floated and was carried away.

He and his mother had not been carried away by a flood. They had stayed in the shack with the palm-leaf roof and she had nursed him until she had fallen ill with an infection and nearly died, apparently, had come within an inch of it, 'As any girl would giving birth in those circumstances, baby boy,' and when he was badly behaved she liked to remind him how close to killing her he had come, just by arriving into the world. The ways in which he had nearly killed his mother seemed impressively various.

You had to bow to the Japanese soldiers whenever you saw them. You had to bow so low your nose was lower than your waist and you had to stay that way for a good few seconds and if you tried to straighten up too quickly, they hit you with a cane across the shoulders. 'Happened to me once when I had you in my arms, just 'cos I didn't bow quick enough on account of holding a baby. When he hit me my knees gave way but I managed to get a hand out in time to stop my fall before I fell on you. You were such a skinny little thing, you'd have snapped like a twig. Plenty of babies born in that camp didn't make it, you know, that's why you'll always be *my miracle*.' The emphasis on the words 'my' and 'miracle' was always the same. His mother, it seemed, had kept him alive by the sheer force of her love, all on her own. Perhaps that was where the mothers of those other babies, the ones that had died, had gone wrong. Maybe they just hadn't loved their babies enough.

There were competing stories about how his father had actually met his end. His mother always said that his father had disappeared into the hills to fight for the Dutch army, and that he had been decapitated during the course of a fierce battle when eight gallant officers and men had held out against a whole hundred Japs. After their return to Holland, his aunt Lies, his mother's elder sister, who featured in their lives both before and after Los Angeles, told him that his father had tried to save himself and his pregnant wife from the camps by hiding his uniform beneath the floorboards but then he had been caught out on the streets after curfew without a Rising Sun armband on. He had been beheaded right on the street corner, at the end of their road. Aunty Lies told him never to raise the subject with his mother – which seemed a little unfair as his mother brought it up herself often enough when she'd been drinking – but he obeyed the injunction, understanding you couldn't really ask for more details of the two accounts when decapitation was the common theme.

They had lost all their belongings in the war so there were no photographs, no family records. Later, he wondered if his parents had really been married or if he had even had a father at all. The evidence for his father's existence came only through stories that seemed to have a suspiciously mythic quality in both competing versions.

*

Some nights in Los Angeles, in the small bedroom he shared with his baby half-brother, he would dream about his father's head. In the dreams, it would be sitting on a shelf when he opened the linen closet in the hallway, just there on a pile of towels or, once, on one of his mother's dresses stretched across the cupboard shelf like a picnic blanket. They were not frightening dreams; the head was always smiling and friendly and would talk to him. When he woke, he muddled through to consciousness with the warm and comforted feeling that lingers after a benign reverie and, for a moment, he would feel regretful upon realising it wasn't true.

Later, when Harper had been sent back to Holland, after what happened, he would use his father's decapitation as playground capital, when the white boys picked on him. He would save it up, then announce it, and ask them what had happened to *their* fathers in the war. Everybody had war stories, of course, often involving dead or missing fathers, mothers starved or bombed, older siblings who had perished before they could be known, but other people's stories, however tragic, were rarely as good for bragging purposes as decapitation.

Sometimes it would be the heroic fighting-in-the-hills version. At other times he would claim to have witnessed it himself, in which case the streetcorner version worked a whole lot better. His accounts became so detailed, he believed for a while that he had indeed been there. In that version, his father always had time for a few last words for his beloved son before the sword swooped down. In that version, it was quick and clean.

*

Peach-coloured lipstick: that was how he learned of his stepfather-to-be. He and his mother were in her bedroom in the tiny apartment on the top floor of the building behind the laundromat – he couldn't remember the name of the street, just that there was a hot-dog stand on the corner called Hair of the Pup. They went there when his mother was pretending it was treat time but in fact there was no money for dinner. The hot dogs were pink sponges with skins so fine they were porous: if you squeezed the bun, liquid fat ran out like water.

Technically, the room they were sitting in was their bedroom rather than hers as he slept on a cot at the bottom of her bed, so poorly sprung and sagging that it slung him in a crescent-moon shape a few inches above the floor. His mother was sitting at the vanity unit in the corner next to the window. She was wearing a floral dress with a white collar and was carefully sculpting waves of her hair around her face with a fine-toothed comb and the occasional *tsk* of hairspray. When she had finished, she patted the waves gently, testing them, then opened a small drawer on the unit and dabbled her fingers amongst the lipsticks inside. She frowned. Selection made, she leaned across the vanity unit into the scalloped mirror, unwinding the lipstick slowly from a golden tube. Harper watched the lipstick emerge. He was six years old and his mother's rituals still had that power.

'Hey Mom, is your lipstick called "orange"?' They had spoken English together since arriving in California. His mother had insisted, had started teaching it to him every day even when they were still in the refugee camp in what used to be Batavia but was now called something else. English was the most important language in the world, she told him, and he could forget his street Malay and Javanese, they were good for nothing. His English wasn't bad now, although he still lapsed into Dutch from time to time. After spending his early years in the camp, his language development had been slow – Aunt Lies had said, when she first met him, 'Anika, does he speak at all or is he, you know, backwards?' Funnily enough, his language skills had caught up ferociously when there were no guards with bamboo canes around.

'Don't call me Mom like a Yank kid when we're alone, only in front of Americans. Call me *Moeder*. It's all about who's around when you're talking, always remember that. Who are you speaking to and what do you want them to think about you?' She paused with the lipstick held up to her mouth. 'How do you think my accent is coming along?' She smiled into the mirror. 'I was *awful* young when I had you, baby boy. Why, I was just a little girl.' She nodded approval at her own reflection. Nothing was more important than fitting in, she often said, although what you did inside your own head was entirely your own business. Her reflection smiled at him from the mirror and he smiled back at it.

He watched as she leaned forward, applied the lipstick in smooth arcs, rubbed her lips together, smiled at herself the way she smiled when she first met someone, frowned, turned to him.

'This lipstick is called Peach Dream,' she said. 'Do I look like a dream?'

'*Klaar*,' he replied.

'Clearly,' she corrected him. 'But that's a bit formal. *Of course* would be better. *Of* and *course*. Say it for me now.'

'Of and course.'

'Two words, you noodle!'

'Of course it is!'

She laughed obligingly. 'Very good, Nicolaas. Now, there is

something I got to tell you about my new beau. I don't want you to be shocked.'

This evening, a summer evening in 1949, was the evening he was to meet Michael, the man who would become his stepfather.

'He's black.' Anika had turned back to the mirror and was adjusting the wide straps of her dress, pulling them down a little over her shoulders, turning a little in the mirror.

'Black?'

'You know, coloured, a negro, *neger*, as they say back home. You know what black is, don't you?'

Before coming to America, Harper had believed black to be him. He had been black in Holland, that had been made very clear to him on a daily basis, in the streets, the shops, the school playground. *Neger* was one of the more polite things he had been called.

'The coloureds have had a terrible time over here,' Anika said, 'you know that too, the prejudice against them is just awful. You know what it's like in the South, don't you? Michael's father is a lawyer, gets people out of jail. Imagine, a lawyer. You any idea how unusual that is? Mind you I can't say there's much sign of Michael himself following suit.' She became still for a moment. Then brightened again. 'He was in the army you know, Michael, he was a GI. He fought for our freedom, well, in France, not our Homeland but it was the same thing. Lots of his friends were killed. He was so brave. Anyway, I have another surprise for you.'

Harper had learned over the years that surprises from his mother were not always pleasant ones. He remembered her saying before they left the Homeland, 'I have a surprise for you, baby boy, we're going to live in America and you're going to get a lot of new friends.' They had been in America for eight months now, moved four times during that period to various tiny apartments, each one a little worse than the last. Sometimes she had worked for a bit, sometimes she had taken in typing and did it on a small but very heavy typewriter that he had had to lug from one boarding house to another. He had had two different schools with a long break between and the new friends had yet to materialise.

'Maria isn't coming tonight.'

He felt a clutch of fear. 'Who's going to look after me?' Please let it not be the old man across the hallway who stank of beer and stared at him, stubble-faced and moist-lipped, whenever they passed him on the stairwell. Maria was a plump teenager downstairs who gave him some of her Junior Mints as long as he didn't tell his mother that she hung out of the window and smoked while she was out. He had neglected to mention that his mother didn't bother with the window when she smoked in case the Junior Mints dried up. He'd been wondering how many times Maria would have to babysit before he could drop a hint regarding Liquorice Laces.

'I'm not leaving you tonight, you're coming with me, you're going to meet Michael, that's why I warned you he was coloured and ironed your shirt this morning.' She pointed to where his clean shirt was hanging on the front of the wardrobe door. 'We are going on a bus and a trolley car. We are going to Michael's house and we are going to meet his father, the lawyer, and his father's, well, whatever she is, and then they are going to look after you while Michael takes me out. Now what do you think about that?'

It was a Saturday and he thought how he and his mother had been together all day – he had watched her iron the shirt on a towel spread out on the floor this morning and had asked her what she was doing. She had known this information at that time but had withheld it from him so that she could 'surprise' him. Why did adults do that? Was it something about wanting to prove they were in charge? He tried to process the list of events she had just outlined but it was too much information in one go. He was going out with his mother, that was good: he hated it when she went out without him. They were going on a trolley car together, that would be fun. He would have to put his new shirt on – that was bad. It was too big for him, he could see that just by looking at it. He was going to meet a coloured man and his parents. Would the parents be strict or nice? Would they give him any supper and if so, what would it consist of? Did they have a dog? He longed to play with a dog. His mother would leave him there, in a strange house. That was not good at all. For how long?

They caught a bus, then a Red Car, then waited for more than half an hour at another bus stop before Anika approached a man in a trilby hat who took them to a different stop around the corner and said, 'You sure this address is right, young lady?' as he looked at the piece of paper she had shown him, a crease of concern on his face. Anika patted her forehead with her embroidered hankie before tucking it back inside the edge of her glove and smiling up at the man, saying, 'Why yes, sir, I'm quite sure, but thank you so much for your assistance.' Harper wondered if that meant they were going to an area like the run-down tenement block where their boarding house was but instead, when they got off the final bus, they found themselves in the middle of a grid of streets with individual houses, the pastel-coloured paint on them a little shabby-looking, it was true, but big places with steps leading up to verandas and porches.

Black people sat on the porches, some elderly women in chairs, talking, knitting or shelling peas. Girls played skipping games in front of the houses. Nobody paid Harper or his mother any attention as they walked up the hill, but for one old lady who watched them as they passed with her fingers still flicking over her embroidery job as though they worked all on their own whether she paid attention or not.

Harper and Anika held hands as they walked up the steep incline to number 2246, set back a little and with a huge cactus plant growing in the front. A vine of some sort corkscrewed around the porch support. The front door was freshly painted in a shiny cream colour. '*Well* . . .' his mother murmured approvingly.

Michael was sitting on the top step but rose as they approached – and kept on rising. He was immensely tall it seemed, with rangy shoulders and close-cut hair. He was dressed in baggy pants with an immaculate crease and a shirt buttoned up to the neck with long points to the collar. A jacket was folded neatly over the veranda balcony.

Harper and his mother stopped at the bottom of the steps and looked up at Michael, the tall man standing above them. Harper's mother lifted her hand to shield her eyes from the sun – she had lost her sunglasses the previous week and had cried bitterly that she couldn't possibly afford another pair, not with a child to feed.

Michael looked down at Harper's mother and then he smiled, and it was the slowest smile that Harper had ever seen, beginning with the corners of his mouth rising, as they normally did when people smiled, and then suddenly the whole of his face lifted and his eyes shone and he seemed like the nicest man in the world – less handsome, perhaps, than when his face was in repose, but a whole lot nicer. Harper glanced up at his mother who was staring up at Michael and smiling too. In their locked gazes he glimpsed a future where, yes, they lived in California and were Americans and had a house and a dog.

'Hey, *May-on-naise* . . .' said Michael, and shifted his gaze to Harper. 'So this is the little guy, the one I've been hearing so much about?'

'Nicolaas,' murmured his mother.

'Pleased to meet you, sir,' said Harper, extending his hand upwards, as high and as firm as if he was reaching for cookies on a top shelf.

Inside the house, in a narrow hallway with another cactus-type plant in a pot, they met Michael's parents. Michael's father turned out to be an older version of his son – more portly, a little stooped, steel-rimmed glasses. There was a woman called Nina in a plain beige dress with hair swept up in a bun. Her status in the house wasn't immediately apparent – he was just told to call her Nina.

Michael's father did not give slow smiles like his son. He regarded Harper from his great height with a stern and steady gaze.

After the introductions were over, Anika knelt in front of Harper and smoothed his hair and said, 'Now, Nicolaas, you are to be very, very good, the best you've ever been, do you understand?'

Michael had shrugged on his jacket and turned to the mirror to shake out his sleeves and check his cuffs.

'You're going already?' Harper said quietly.

His mother gave a false little laugh. 'Of course, Michael is taking me to, well, a place where they do music, it's a kind of supper club. Now, you'll be very well looked after.' She hadn't mentioned supper for him. And there was no sign of a dog. What kind of house this size didn't have a dog?

The woman called Nina took him by the hand and they and Michael's father saw his mother and Michael off from the front step. As the two of them walked back down the incline, a black woman holding a little girl by the hand and walking on the other side of the street stared at Anika and Michael with a hot look and Anika lifted her chin, set her shoulders back and slipped her hand into the crook of Michael's arm.

As they stepped back inside the house, Michael's father said to him in a grave voice, 'Now young man, in the kitchen. There is something you and I have to discuss.'

Nina dropped Harper's hand and went into the sitting room and he and Michael's father walked together through to a small kitchen with windows that overlooked a short, steep backyard. Miraculously, at the bottom of the backyard, with a collar and a long rope lead that was tied to a stake, was a large white dog.

Nina had disappeared. Harper looked about him. Michael's father instructed him to sit at the kitchen table while he remained standing, his large arms folded and held high up above his chest.

'Now young man,' he repeated.

'Yes, sir,' Harper replied.

Michael's father lifted his finger. 'For the rest of this evening, or in fact for as long as you and I turn out to be acquainted, you will call me Poppa, you understand that?'

'Yes sir.'

'Good. Well, there is something I need explaining to me right away before you and I can be friends. Your name is Nicolaas.'

'Yes, sir.'

'Poppa.'

'Yes, Poppa.'

'Good, now is it true, can it be true, that your name is Nicolaas but when they gave it you they gave you an *extra a*?'

Harper pulled both lips inwards, the same way he would as if he was making an *mmm* . . . sound, and looked at the ceiling. Then he said, 'I believe they did, sir.'

'You *believe* they did?'

'Yes, sir, they must have done.'

Michael's father shook his head from side to side, very slowly. 'I thought as much. Well young man, there are only two rules in this house, one is that you always call me Poppa and drop that *sir* business and the other is,' he turned and opened the fridge door, 'that when Nina is out of the room, anybody who has an extra *a* gets to choose what flavour syrup we put in the milkshake. That understood?'

'Yes, sir.'

He looked back. 'Any questions?'

Harper hesitated.

'Don't be shy, young man, rule number three. I just made that up on the spot on account of how it suddenly seemed to be necessary. Speak up. I didn't get where I am without speaking up, believe me, but that's an awfully long story and it can wait until after milkshake.'

'Later, perhaps, after milkshake, after the story, would it be possible for me to go and visit the dog?'

*

Later, after he and the dog had made friends, there was a supper consisting of some sort of stew. The stew was placed on the table alongside dishes of vegetables and Harper folded his hands in his lap politely, waiting to be served, but his hosts put their elbows on the table, knitted their fingers and lowered their heads.

'Dear Lord,' Poppa began, 'thank you for the gift of good food, for family and nourishment, and please Lord bless your servant Wesley A. Brown and send him Godspeed for all his sailings on those High Seas of yours and thank you of course for new guests who come into our home. Amen.'

'Amen,' said Nina, already lifting her head and reaching for the serving spoon.

Harper sat staring at her for a minute, until she beckoned with her fingers, the spoon lifted in the other hand, 'Come now, young man, don't be shy, hand that plate over.'

The stew had lumps of meat in a dark brown gravy with a strong smell that, at first, made Harper's stomach turn. But when he put one of the lumps of meat in his mouth, it was not chewy like the meat they had had occasionally in Holland but fell apart in his mouth in soft moist pieces. Harper wondered if the strong smell and the taste of what he was chewing was what they called, over here, *flavor*. Throughout the meal, Poppa questioned him about his life in Holland and how it had been, coming to America that was, until Nina said gently, 'Michael Senior . . .'

'My apologies, Nicolaas, it's a lawyer's habit, asking people everything about their lives, drives Nina here a little crazy.'

'Spreads himself thin, sometimes,' Nina said looking down into her stew and giving a soft shake of her head. 'Always, in fact.'

'I have the same name as my son, that's quite common here,' Poppa said. 'Stick to Poppa, it makes things easier.'

'Michael Junior is certainly a chip off the block,' said Nina, as she ladled a second helping onto Harper's plate, saving him the embarrassment of asking for more. 'In some respects, that is.' She slipped the serving spoon into the dish of mashed orange vegetable on the table and looked at Harper and Harper felt confident enough to shake his head.

'Is he like you too?' Harper asked politely, congratulating himself on the grown-upness of the question.

Nina glanced at Poppa and Poppa said, 'We're not a usual household here, Nicolaas. Michael Junior's mother died when he was around your age. Nina came into our lives about a year later, and she's been the best wife and mother we could have hoped for.'

'Even though, legally speaking, I'm neither,' Nina said with a smile that seemed resigned but not particularly unhappy. 'Well, not quite yet.'

'Soon, though . . .' said Poppa firmly, looking over his glasses at her and beaming, before turning to Harper and adding, 'Nina's mother was from Salvador. She's Catholic,' as if that explained everything.

'And we weren't too sure about the father side of things when I was growing up,' added Nina, with a half-laugh that implied this was something else that was openly discussed, amusing even.

Harper looked from one of them to the other, amazed. This, then was the house he had come into – a house where people joked about not having fathers, where, for once, he wasn't the odd one out because he was too brown or not brown enough and had been born in an internment camp in a country the other side of the world, a country so distant he only had his mother's word for it that it actually existed.

'The damn Japs cut my father's head off,' Harper announced cheerfully, keen to impress upon them that no unconventional domestic arrangements could prove shocking to him.

A start passed between Poppa and Nina, as if they had given each other the small electric shock you get from shaking hands with someone when you've walked towards them across a cheap carpet. Nina raised her eyebrows at Poppa and Poppa coughed into his napkin before saying, 'Yes, we heard that story, Nicolaas, Michael Junior told us a bit about you and your mother, and what you both endured in the Pacific.' He coughed again. 'But I should say, we don't allow profanity at the kitchen table.'

After the meal, they helped Nina clear the table, then she washed up while Poppa and he went through to the sitting room so that Poppa could show Harper certificates with his name on them that were framed and ranged along one wall. Harper began to wonder when his mother might return and it seemed Poppa and Nina might be wondering the same thing as twice during their conversations Poppa went into the kitchen and closed the door behind him and he heard the murmur of their voices. It was dark by now.

Eventually, Nina came in and clapped her hands and said in a happy-sounding voice that he was going to stay the night. By then he was too tired to have the polite and grown-up conversation that would be necessary in order to extract more details and so allowed himself to be led upstairs to a small room with a narrow single bed against one wall and a table with a huge sewing machine and a basket full of large folded material that looked like curtains. Nina brought him a glass of milk and a T-shirt belonging to Michael Junior to sleep in and told him where the bathroom was. When she went out, she left the door ajar and the landing light on.

'You know where Poppa and I are, right downstairs, need anything, you holler.'

He was tired enough to fall asleep quickly, despite the strangeness of this arrangement, but later he woke and the landing light was still on and he could hear raised voices downstairs. He slipped his feet down and padded silently to his bedroom door. He couldn't see anything but heard several voices in the hallway and could feel the chill of night air. One of the voices sounded like his mother's but a little odd, high-pitched. Should he run down to her? Poppa was speaking to Michael then, and the two men had a brief, angry-sounding exchange. He caught the words, 'You think this is alright? This!' Then the front door slammed again and there was silence. He padded back to his bed and pulled the quilt over him and lay listening for a while but there were no further sounds.

The next time he woke, it was pitch dark. He lay for a moment, confused about where he was, particularly about how comfortable the small bed he was lying on was in comparison to his cot at the end of his mother's bed. A telephone was ringing, somewhere. There was a certain amount of rustling on the landing outside his room. He fell asleep again.

In the morning, he woke up to full light through thin green curtains, birdsong. The house was quiet.

Nina was in the kitchen. On the table, a place for one was laid. Outside, the dog, who had turned out to be called Jimmy, was running up and down the garden. The sun was high and bright.

Nina smiled and gestured to the table. 'I ate breakfast a while back but Poppa's sleeping late so we'll go to church this evening. He had to work in the night. It happens.'

Harper hovered by the table, assuming the place set was for Poppa's late breakfast, until Nina indicated with her hand that he should sit. As she poured a glass of milk for him, she said, 'I expect you are wondering what those youngsters are up to.' Harper nodded. Nina smiled reassuringly, but he had the feeling she wasn't too sure of her own answer. 'They had a good time last night. They'll be over later.'

He had just finished a breakfast of eggs and a bread roll when Poppa came thumping down the stairs. He burst into the kitchen, fully dressed, grabbed a roll from the basket on the table, said, 'Morning, Nicolaas,' and turned to go.

'At least have a coffee!' wailed Nina, as Poppa rushed back out without bidding either of them goodbye. The front door slammed.

'When they call, he goes,' Nina said, shaking her head. 'There's always someone in trouble somewhere.'

Harper never returned to the boarding house. That Sunday, his mother and Michael came over with a small suitcase with stiff clasps that contained his clothes, two books which he had to give straight back to them as they belonged to the local library and a new ball that Michael had bought him as a present. He was told he would be staying with Nina and Poppa for a few days while his mother and Michael 'sorted out a few things'. The few days turned into a fortnight. Then it was announced to him, with some degree of fanfare, that Anika and Michael were going to get married. They were all going to live together in the big house with Jimmy the dog. The room with the sewing machine was going to become Harper's official bedroom and he could choose which colour it was painted as long as it was blue or white. It was the first time he had ever had his own room.

The household had its own engagement party, the five of them, standing a little awkwardly in the sitting room together, while Poppa came through from the kitchen holding a bottle of something he called 'homemade elder wine' to pour into the glasses Nina fetched from the cabinet in the corner. It was the only time Harper ever saw Nina and Poppa take alcohol and he sensed even then that it was something of a momentous gesture.

Poppa held up his glass and said, 'This is to welcome Anika, and Nicolaas to our family . . .' he paused, 'and also to celebrate the fact that this is legally possible since only just over a year ago, God bless the wisdom of the California Supreme Court!' He turned to Nicolaas and looked down at him and said knowingly, 'Perez v. Sharp.' Michael groaned aloud, took Anika's hand and squeezed it, and Nina frowned at them and Poppa lifted his finger in admonition while continuing, 'And henceforth, this state, *the first since Ohio*, is no longer going to violate the Fourteenth Amendment to the Constitution of the United States, amen!'

'Amen!' said Nina, much more loudly than she did at mealtimes, and even Michael and Anika murmured it, and Harper piped it too, raising his glass of orange juice and cheering along with the others. He didn't really understand why they should toast the Supreme Court of the State of California but he did understand that the unusual collection of people that was his new family was somehow heroic, just for existing, and that the figurehead of this heroism was Poppa, who looked, as he lowered his glass, both delighted and exhausted. Nina was standing the other side of Poppa and he heard Poppa say then, from the corner of his mouth, 'You're next, baby. You in big trouble now.'

'Don't I know it,' Nina replied, and a small laugh ran around the group.

'Are you getting married too?' he asked Poppa, looking up at him.

Poppa rested his large hand on the top of Harper's head and said gently, 'Yes son, we are, not immediately though, it's been a long wait, but this time around it's Michael and your mother. Nina and I get our turn later in the year.'

Harper was silent for a minute then. There were five of them in their group, and four of them were paired off. Poppa bent down, his hand on Harper's shoulder, and it was the first of many occasions when Poppa seemed to know exactly the right thing to say. 'I guess you might be feeling like the one left out at the moment, but all you have to do is wait a while. No one is the odd one out for long.' Harper looked up at him, and as Poppa straightened, he gave him an enormous wink.

Harper's baby brother was born some months later. He was called – after some heated debate in the household – Joseph, although from the beginning, they all called him Bud.

It was Poppa and Nina who brought Bud home. Anika was in hospital for three weeks after the birth, with complications, Nina said. Michael was with her a lot. Harper was not allowed to visit her in hospital but she would be home soon, he was told. It was nothing to worry about. Sometimes ladies got sad after a baby, it was normal.

Poppa lifted Bud in his carrycot onto the kitchen table and Harper went over to have a look. He had been hoping his newborn brother would look up at him and smile and clutch his finger in his fist like babies were supposed to do, but Bud was tightly swaddled and only his fat little head was visible, moving very slightly from side to side as he began to stir from sleep. Looking down at this thing, slug-shaped in its blanket, Harper was suddenly overcome with a feeling he had never felt before, a wave of some strong emotion so sudden and welling within him that he felt dizzy and gripped the sides of the carrycot. He stared down at the baby and the baby opened his eyes and his dark-eyed gaze roved around loosely, ill-focused and helpless. Then baby Bud yawned and Harper and Poppa and Nina all looked at each other and smiled and exhaled at the same time.

Nina came and stood next to him and put her hand on his shoulder. 'He's all yours, Nicolaas, he's *your* baby brother.' And Harper realised that, for the first time in his life, he was no longer the newest addition to any group or family. Poppa and Nina would die one day because they were old and his mother and Michael would die too because they were the next oldest and he had always thought that when that happened, when his mother died, he would be alone, but here was a baby that belonged to him and he would die first, not the baby, because he was older than the baby.

Baby Bud screwed his face up in an expression that in an older child or adult might have meant a sneeze was coming but in a newborn baby, Harper quickly learned, was preparatory to a cry.

'Milk time,' Nina said, 'you'd better help me, Nicolaas, it's going to be your job sometimes, you know.' A bottle was boiling in a pan of water on the stovetop. A pile of diapers was neatly folded on the counter beside it. Not being the youngest any more was going to make Harper a certain amount of work.

He had a new school now – he went on the bus each day that stopped at the bottom of the hill. It was black kids mostly and on his second day, two of the boys in his class shoved him up against a wall in the corridor and demanded to know what he thought about Pearl Harbor, but the school secretary came along and said to the boys, hissing beneath her breath, 'Shame on you. Nicolaas isn't Japanese, he was locked up by them and has come to America to live with his grandfather.' The boys had stepped back and looked at him. 'Locked up?' said one, impressed: but Harper hadn't noticed that bit. His insides were swelling with pride at the word *grandfather*.

At the end of the school day, he would run up the hill to see his baby brother. Nina was usually in the kitchen when he got home. Harper would sit on a chair at the table and Nina would give him a drink of milk and he would demand a full account of Bud's day.

When he looked back on those few years in California from the perspective of adulthood, it was hard sometimes to remember that early part, the happy part: five years of routine and certainty for him – what happened at the end of those five years was so overwhelming and calamitous that it collapsed time, concertinaed those years into no more than a few images. It made it seem as though that early, happy period for him had been no more than the prelude to the inevitable.

Poppa's work was something that Harper only ever comprehended glancingly. What it meant to him mostly was that Poppa was out of the house a lot, including evenings and weekends, and that this was a source of tension between Poppa and Nina and sometimes Poppa and Michael. Sometimes, the people Poppa worked with would come to him. The sitting room would fill up, often so many people that some sat on the floor. There would be debates and one or two of the men would leave, shrugging their coats on as they went out and slamming the door behind them. Mostly, people filtered out quietly, often long after Harper had been sent to bed. He would be awoken by the murmurings of hallway departures.

Once, when Bud was still a baby, Harper came downstairs to see Nina standing at the front door, holding it open, looking out anxiously. She turned as she heard Harper and said, 'Go through to the kitchen, go on now.'

Harper stopped where he was, halfway down the stairs. 'Why?'

'Just go, go on, not long. Poppa's just clearing something off the front lawn.'

He couldn't see Poppa from where he stood but he could hear the hiss of the garden hose. 'What's on the lawn?' he asked.

'Nothing,' Nina replied, shutting the front door and turning to him, shooing him with her hands. 'Just some bleach, someone stupid spilt it.'

The next two meetings were held in the kitchen, until Poppa decreed it was ridiculous. The kitchen was too darn small.

People would bring things on plates for the meetings, often – there was always food in Nina and Poppa's house – and sometimes, Harper would hand round the things on plates. Once, as he was handing round some slightly undercooked cookies that collapsed as people lifted them from the plate, a plump man with large hands looked at Harper and said, 'Say, son, where you from?'

'My grandson is from Indonesia,' Poppa called across the room, where he was standing talking to two men who were both smoking. 'All the way across the world.'

'How come you . . . ?' the man began to Harper.

Poppa cut across him. 'How he got here doesn't matter. He's here now.' He gave Harper a smile.

It was only later, years later, that he realised that the whole time things were going right for him, they were going very wrong for Michael Junior and his mother: almost from the start.

They had jobs for a bit – his mother worked in a shop for a while, Michael a garage, but no job seemed to last, and sometimes they were both home for weeks at a stretch but they stayed in their room and if he asked Nina she would say, 'They're very tired, they're resting. Don't disturb them.' Then they would be gone all weekend. One day, he went into their room when they were away; he was looking for a book he had been reading on their bed and, underneath the bed, he saw a tin box and a flat-shaped bottle on its side and a row of four or five glass tumblers that all looked sticky and, without understanding, he knew that these were bad things that had been hidden. He said nothing to anyone.

Michael was kind to him, when he was around. He sat on the steps leading down to the garden wearing a white undershirt and smoking, smiling his slow smile and tossing a ball to the end of the garden so that Harper and Jimmy could run after it together. Harper always let Jimmy win.

But there were the fights between his mother and Michael that took place in that bedroom when the door was closed. Michael's voice was deep, patient mostly, until something crashed against the wall. His mother always started shrill and hysterical, right from the very beginning. They did it in the evenings after Harper had gone to bed, but he woke to hear it often.

One evening, when it was particularly noisy, Nina came into Harper's and Bud's room and sat on the edge of his bed, and stroked his hair back from his forehead. Bud was sound asleep in his cot. Harper had been lying awake for a while. Nina stroked him for a while in silence, then said, 'They saw a war, Nicolaas, try and remember that, what your mother went through, what Michael went through in a different way, those of us older, those of us younger like you, it's difficult for us to understand what they went through. They were just so young, and Michael saw some terrible things, I know, even though he doesn't talk about them. He is . . . well, it's hard to explain.'

And then, one day, Michael wasn't there any more, and Poppa stayed off work for a while – which was unheard of – and took to standing at the window in the front sitting room, just staring out into the street, his hands in his pockets, for hour after hour. Harper's mother stayed in her room and wept and there were sharp words between her and Nina on the rare occasions that she emerged.

He began to wonder if Michael had died and nobody had told him, but when he asked Nina what had happened, she sat him down on the back step, which was where the difficult things often got said in their house, and told him that Michael had been unhappy for a long time, ever since he came back from the war, unhappy in the same way that his mother was sometimes unhappy, and that she, Nina, guessed they had got married hoping that their unhappiness would cancel each other's out but instead it just made it multiply. Did he know that his mother sometimes took a few too many alcoholic beverages? He nodded. That much he had worked out. Well, Michael did too sometimes and they had sort of encouraged each other, which was obviously a bad thing. They both should have been with people who would have done the opposite. There had been a big argument when he had been at school one day and Michael had gone off to another city and it would probably be a very long time before they saw him again and it was making everyone very sad. It was particularly hard for Poppa, Nina said, because he saved people all day long and yet he couldn't save his own son.

At this point, they heard, behind them, 'Dubba! Dubba!'

They turned. Bud had crawled out of the open kitchen door and wanted them to watch as he stood unsteadily, a feat he had only just learned, before dropping to all fours again and crawling the small space over to Harper. Once he reached him, he levered himself to his feet again by grasping at Harper's shirt, standing unsteadily for a moment like a tiny, genial drunk and then splaying both fat hands and bashing them on Harper's head, a kind of fierce patting.

'Hey Bud, cut it out,' said Harper, smiling and remaining motionless to allow Bud to continue, and Bud laughed his throaty chuckle as if what he was doing was the funniest thing in the world.

Nina looked at them both and shook her head and said, 'You two brothers got a lot more sense than the whole of the adults in this house put together. People say things are complicated but you two know they aren't, they're really simple.'

It was a Sunday afternoon when his mother told him she was going back to Holland for a bit, to see Aunty Lies. His first thought was that she was going to say he had to go with her – she had told him often enough that he was the centre of her world. The thought of being separated from Bud and Jimmy the dog, even for a few weeks, was more than he could bear.

But instead, Anika pressed him to her bony chest and said, 'I know you'll miss me so much, Nicolaas, but I need you to be braver than you've ever been. Things here have been really hard for me since Michael left and I need to go back home for a bit. Can you manage without me for a little while? It's something I just have to do, things have been so mixed up here lately and you know how much I miss our Homeland.' Did he? 'I'm just going back to sort out a few things. Bud is still little and he'd get seasick if I took you both now, you wouldn't I know because you're really good about that kind of thing. You know, you're the only man who has never let me down.'

With Michael and his mother gone – and neither absence given a definite end date – the house was calmer, although as Bud grew, that livened things up a bit. He was a toddler who ran up and down, everywhere, from the minute he could, both furious and amused at the same time: tight curls, light brown skin with a throw of dark brown freckles across his nose, as if he had been playing with a very fine paintbrush, a high piping voice that called Harper, 'Nick-er-lus.' Three syllables at least. Once he had learned to pronounce it, he would jump his small bottom up and down in his high chair at mealtimes, repeating it again and again if he did not have Harper's full attention for one minute of the meal. 'Nick-er-lus, Nick-er-lus, Nick. Er. *Lus*!'

'You know, Nicolaas,' Nina said once, when she was getting him to help her fold laundry. 'That little boy thinks all the good things in the world come from you, like you're a god or something. You should hear him when it's time for you to come home from school.'

He was not a god. Nor was Poppa, the great lawyer who everyone admired so. If either of them had been a god, it would never have happened, that dreadful day three years later, in the bright sunshine, with the sun sparking off water clear as glass.

So many times, in the aftermath, he found himself reliving that afternoon and holding back or running forward, insisting that they took the other fork in the path, being ill that morning, or pushing Bud off a step so that he would twist an ankle – anything, anything that would mean that day could not progress until the moment when time stopped altogether, in bright light, the thunder of white water in the air.

Other families had holidays, that was the truth. But other families were not like theirs: Poppa, Nina, Nicolaas and Bud. It wasn't just their ages or their different skin tones, no one of the four of them alike, it was Poppa's work too. Nina explained it to them one evening, when Poppa was, as usual, late for dinner. 'Think of it like this, boys. Your Poppa is out there fighting this giant monster. It's a great big monster that eats people. And he knows full well he can't defeat it all on his own and that it's going to take years and years but even when he works really hard that monster keeps on eating. But if he stops work for a bit, the monster eats harder and faster.' She paused and looked at each of them sternly. 'And so what's Poppa to say to the people who get eaten if he takes a break? Sorry, I'll be back tomorrow?'

Harper looked at Bud, across the table from him, five years old, wide-eyed, knife and fork clutched in the wrong hands. He thought maybe that comparison was a little much for his small brother.

The front door slammed and Poppa ambled, shoulders down, into the kitchen, loosening his tie. Bud dropped the knife and fork onto the table with a clatter, jumped down from his seat and flung himself against Poppa's legs, burying his face in them. Poppa put his hand absently on Bud's head and looked up and

Nina said, 'I was just explaining to the boys how you were out slaying the dragon.'

'Oh,' said Poppa, gently detaching Bud from his trousers and giving him a small shove back towards the table, glancing at the food, 'that dragon.'

That night, Harper lay awake in his room after bedtime, as he often did, using his new torch to make hand puppets on the wall. He and Bud still shared the same small room – he didn't really see why he couldn't have the one that his mother and Michael had used. It had been kept just as it was three years ago, except cleaner, and was now called 'the guest room'. It annoyed Harper that he got sent to bed at the same time as Bud. He was *more* than *twice* his age, after all. Nina said it was okay for him to read for a bit while Bud went to sleep but often he lay awake with his hands behind his head for some time. Since he got his new torch, last birthday, he had taken to making finger puppet shows on the walls, the stories of princes and warriors that his mother used to tell him about, from the place she always called 'the Indies'. It was the only time he missed his mother, at bedtime; something about telling himself the stories made him hear her voice, occasionally. His shadow shows were always an amalgam of his mother's tales and events from the cartoons he and Bud were allowed to go to on Saturdays at the Variety picture house for nine cents apiece, although he didn't think the original Arjuna had had a space rocket.

That particular evening, Harper was doing a puppet show for himself with the torch laid horizontally on top of books piled on his bedside table. Across the room, Bud was asleep, curled up turned away from him, the small hillock of his back exposed where his quilt had slipped down. Then Harper heard voices from across the landing.

Bored of his own puppet show – Arjuna always won, of course – he crept out of bed and went out onto the landing. The door to Poppa and Nina's room was not quite closed.

'C'mon,' he heard Nina say. 'They're growing boys, especially Nicolaas, a few days is all I'm asking.'

'I can see they're growing.' Poppa sounded disgruntled but not annoyed. He sounded like a man who had already lost the argument. 'Seems like they're doing just fine to me.'

'He just wants to feel like a normal boy, you know, in a family, doing things that families do.'

'That's true enough, honey, but how many black families do you know get out in all that "fresh air" you talk about?'

'You saying fresh air is just for white people?'

'I'm saying fresh air costs money. How many families you know . . .'

Nina's voice rose. 'I'm not talking about the families we know, I'm talking about ours. You telling me you're scared of the looks we going to get from whitefolks on a path through a forest? After you stand up in front of judges?'

'You know that's not true.' The way Nina and Poppa talked when they were alone was different from the way they talked in front of Harper and Bud, less proper, a kind of in-joke, as if they were about to start laughing and thumping each other any minute.

'You scared of *bears*!'

'No . . .'

'You *are*, Michael Senior! Shame on you, big man like you and he's scared of *bears*!'

He loved that laughing tone they had when they talked to

each other like this. He loved nothing better than overhearing it. Eavesdropping was a habit he had got into when Michael and his mother were around and it had proved a habit hard to break – but when he eavesdropped on Nina and Poppa, what he heard mostly was them teasing each other.

The door to his room creaked. He looked round. Bud stood there in his pyjamas. Harper lifted a finger to his lips and gave him a stern look to be quiet.

'I need to pee,' whispered Bud.

'Ssshh . . .' said Harper, 'they're talking about taking us on holiday.'

Bud's eyes widened. He crept up behind Harper, shuffling his bare feet silently along the boards so as not to lift them, then stood very close, leaning his head on Bud's arm.

'You know, the boys would probably go somewhere for a bit of fun . . .' Poppa's voice was the tone of a man negotiating the terms of his capitulation. 'Like the beach, or amusements, you know, throw balls at coconuts, eat sticky stuff. There's a great big ocean over thataway, you know, goes by the name of the Pacific. You saying you want to go the other direction?'

'Fresh air, and some education, somewhere they can climb up a mountain and use up some of that energy, camping maybe.'

'I couldn't put up a tent, woman, not if my life depended on it.'

'Bet you those boys could.'

'I'm just not sure about people like us going to a National Park.'

'*People like us*, huh? *People like us?*' It sounded like Nina had thrown a pillow at Poppa's head and Poppa had batted it away. 'The Martins are *people like us* and they went to see the Carlsbad Caverns.'

'That's New Mexico. That's different.'

'People down there worse than California.'

'Well, that's true.'

It had been Nina's idea, but when they got to the National Park she discovered that walking uphill all day was not really her thing. And the superintendent of the campsite stuck them in the canvas cabin furthest away from the amenities because, they were all convinced, they were the only non-white family in the whole damn village and Poppa had said, 'I told you so,' which had wounded Nina's pride. And then some Mexican nuns arrived and were put in the canvas cabin next to them and that cheered Nina up no end because, she said, at least she had some women to talk some sense to. And so it happened that that day, it was just the three of them, Poppa, him and Bud, that set off up the mountain path to see the waterfall.

They were all in something of a bad mood, having argued about which way to go at the bottom of the path: it was early and not many people were about. It was incredibly hot. Poppa had said that it was cooler the higher up you got, that the hot air settled in the valley and that all you needed to do was walk up a little bit and then the breezes would blow, but Harper and Bud were unconvinced. 'I'm only *five*,' Bud moaned, as they stood studying the wooden sign at the bottom of the path. 'I'm smaller than *you* and *you*.' He was drawing a shape in the dirt with the toe of his shoe. Harper tried to be the good one, lifting his head, breathing in the scented air from the pine trees, but Poppa didn't notice, just grumbled, 'Come on boys, Nina says you need fresh air and it's fresh air you're going to get. Whether you like it or not.'

The dirt track was steep right from the very beginning and hard work. Harper's feet slipped on the loose scree. They didn't have proper leather boots like they had seen some of the serious climbers wearing – he and Bud were in the cloth shoes they wore for physical education at school. The thin rubber soles did nothing to protect them from the pebbles and sharp stones on the path.

Poppa went ahead, his long legs taking a stride that equalled four small steps of theirs. He and Bud began to play a desultory game, hanging back, kicking at loose stones on the path, kicking them forward, running up to them, kicking them forward again. He noticed how unpredictable the trajectory of each stone was. A smooth one could shoot far ahead even if it was small and light. An awkward-shaped, multiple-sided one would sometimes tumble twice then lodge in the dirt, however hard you kicked it. Some went in a straight line. Some somersaulted off the edge of the path into the gully below: the path was bordered by a steep, wooded rise on one side and a plummet down to the riverbed on the other.

After a short while, Poppa stopped, withdrew a handkerchief and mopped his brow, then turned and said, 'C'mon you two, you're idling. We want to make that waterfall before we need to stop and eat.' He was carrying a knapsack with a metal water bottle and three small sandwiches. The thought of a sandwich, Harper realised, was the only thing that would get him up the mountain.

At that point, a middle-aged couple came down the path. They must have risen early if they had been up to the fall and were on the descent already. They stared at Poppa as they approached, slowing their pace. They both had those leather boots on, with stripy laces, thick socks, long shorts and walking sticks. The man was white-haired, wearing glasses; the woman had her hair in a headscarf. Poppa moved to one side on the narrow path, politely, to let them pass. They stared at him, then their gazes shifted to Harper and Bud, and Harper saw on their faces the calculation that people often made when they were out as a family: Poppa black, Bud black but light-skinned – and him, something hard to guess at. Part-something.

Even though Poppa had moved to one side to let them pass, they didn't say thank you or smile at him. Instead, the woman said lightly, to her husband, as they passed Bud who was trailing third, 'Well, I can't say I realised this was the coloured path.'

The three of them stood still for a while after the couple disappeared down the path, around the bend, then he walked up to Poppa and said, 'There wasn't a sign.'

Poppa's face was set. 'No, son,' he said, 'there's no sign because there isn't any coloured path and there isn't any whites-only path here either, that woman just thought there should be. Take no notice, she's just ignorant.' He looked up the path and passed his hand over his face, then muttered, 'As if this mountain isn't steep enough.'

Then Bud ran up to them, his hand outstretched, calling, 'Poppa!' and Poppa turned and took his hand firmly, his large one enfolding Bud's small one, and said softly, 'Come along, son.'

They all set off again, Bud and Poppa walking ahead of him, holding hands, and Harper found himself hanging back. He kicked at stones on his own. After a few more paces, Poppa turned his head to the side and without looking round properly, said over his shoulder, still walking, 'You too, Slim Jim, you too,' and he ran ahead and took Poppa's other hand, and they walked like that for a few minutes more until the path narrowed too much for them to walk side by side and he and Bud ran ahead gleefully, jumping and shouting, 'Who's behind now, Poppa!'

and the moment with the couple, the looks, was gone.

All three of them were panting as they neared the top of the path, and then they stopped for a while and sat on a plain plank bench by the side and looked out through the dense cover of trees where the sun struck through in brilliant beams. They took it in turn to drink from the water bottle. Ahead of them, they could see that the path forked. To the right, it widened out – the left-hand fork was steep and narrow.

Poppa was studying the pencil-drawn map he had made after looking at the visitors' information in the lodge at the bottom of the hill.

'We can go that way,' he said, pointing to the right-hand fork, 'which is easier but takes a little longer, and goes up to the official viewing point, or we can go that way. Steeper but shorter I think.'

'Shorter! Shorter!' said Bud.

'Shorter doesn't mean easier, son.'

In Bud's world it did.

Poppa looked down at his map and frowned at his own handwriting, turned it upside down and back again, the full three hundred and sixty degrees.

There were voices then, and a moment later, a group of eight or nine white people, two families with older children, came down the wider, easier path. Poppa nodded at them as they passed. One of the men nodded back. The rest of the group ignored him. 'Okay,' Poppa said after they had gone, 'let's try that way.' He pointed to the narrow, steep path, the left-hand path.

By the time they were halfway up, they were bad-tempered with each other again. The terrain was steep and at intervals involved clambering over boulders that blocked the narrow path: Poppa hauled Bud up by his arm a couple of times – Harper refused help. The trees and undergrowth of ferns and bushes were so dense that they heard the thunder of the fall before they could see it: and then at a point about halfway up, there was a space where there was a gap in the trees and, yes – there it was, as if suspended mid-air, the magnificent crash of brilliant water, frothing and foaming as it fell.

All three of them stopped to look: the relentlessness of it, the continuous descent of all that water. It carried the eye down as a passing train carries the eye along but just kept falling and falling, so densely white in the centre it seemed blue, the fine mist of spray all around, hanging in the air: and most miraculous of all – the air full of small rainbows, faint small rainbows flung in all directions in the mist.

'Whoa . . .' breathed Bud. He was not a boy who was easily impressed by natural wonders.

Harper looked up, to where the top of the fall was just visible high above them, where the water shot out horizontally, foaming ferociously, such was its force and power. 'We really going all the way to the top?'

'You bet,' Poppa replied, mopping his brow. 'There'll be somewhere up there we can sit down, have the sandwiches. We should have brought Nina, what do you reckon?'

Harper pulled a face. 'It's going to get slippy up top, the rocks will be wet.'

'Well, you two take care.'

The path became steeper and steeper: their pace became slower and slower. At times he doubted it was really a path at all, just a scramble through the trees over boulders made treacherous with spray water and rotting brown ferns. We should have taken the longer path, he thought, never mind how many looks we got, but he didn't share this thought with Poppa or Bud.

It must have been an hour before they reached the top, and then they emerged into a clearing that was a little way upriver from the edge of the fall. At this point, the river turned just before it fell: he was disappointed you couldn't see the edge. Bet you can from the official viewing point, he thought.

You couldn't see it but you could hear it, the thunder of it – and feel it too; the air in the clearing was hung with fine spray. A large, wet stone made a natural platform that went up to the river's edge and here the river was so wide the water was very shallow – it would be easy to wade across to the other side: it would come only partway up your calves, he thought. The widening of the river meant it slipped more slowly at this point. There was no frothing or foaming here; the water was completely calm: you could see the gleaming brown and grey rocks on the bed. Right by the edge closest to them, there was a natural pool made by a dip in the riverbed. And here, miraculously, the water was still. Around the edge of the pool, it flowed in small eddies downstream towards the fall, but inside the pool, the water was motionless and clear as glass.

'Well, look at that,' said Poppa. 'Perfect.'

From somewhere upriver, they could hear voices, the people at the official viewing point, out of sight amongst the trees: but here, they had their own private spot, a clear pool and total privacy. It had been worth climbing that more difficult path.

'Can we get our clothes wet?' Harper asked. It was going to be difficult not to if they stopped for their sandwiches here.

'Sure,' Poppa said, 'let's take our shoes off. It'll all dry soon enough back at the camp.'

It was strange to think how hot it was down in the valley below, with the cool damp air up here: the relief of it. Odd to think they would be descending into such heat on the way back. He thought about how, when you were hot, you couldn't imagine ever being cold again: and vice versa. Some things could only be felt, not imagined.

The rock was too wet to sit on so they perched on boulders at the edge, each on their separate one, grinning at each other while they ate their sandwiches. Bud finished first, as usual, leaving his crusts; Poppa wheeled a large hand, 'Bring them on over here, Bud.' When he had handed his crusts over, Bud said, 'Can I go paddle in that pool?'

'You crazy?' scoffed Harper. 'That water will be freezing. That's ice melt, Bud.'

Poppa frowned.

'*Please!*' said Bud, putting his head on one side, smiling. It annoyed the hell out of Harper when Bud did that. Bud was five, he wasn't a baby any more – but he sure knew how to behave like one when he wanted his own way. He could twist Poppa round his little finger with that look.

'You'll have to take everything off excepting your underpants,' Poppa said.

Bud jumped up and down a couple of times, then began to undress.

'He's crazy,' Harper commented, although in fact, the thought of dabbling his feet in that glassy water had already occurred to him. He couldn't do it now, though, or Bud would say, 'You're copying me.'

Bud passed Poppa his T-shirt and his shorts and Poppa hung them on the twig of a bush behind him. Then he put on his stern voice, 'Now listen, *no swimming*, I mean it. You get in that pool and paddle, stay close to the bank here, that's it, okay? Two minutes.' In the distance, through the trees, Harper could hear some people on the official viewing platform laughing and calling out to each other, taking photographs, perhaps.

Bud dipped a toe in the water and then shrieked, pulling his elbows into his torso and screwing up his face. 'It's *cold*!'

'Told ya,' Harper said. He was still sitting on his rock, wishing there was another sandwich and thinking how the littlest one in a family got to do all the cute stuff, while he had to be grown-up and responsible. 'Chicken!' he called out, as Bud hopped from foot to foot.

'Am not!' Bud called back.

'I'd get in before you fall in dancing round like that,' Poppa said, laughing.

Gingerly, Bud stepped in. The pool was very shallow – when he stood upright it only came halfway up his thighs. He kept his arms bent and elbows tucked in tight.

'Come on out, Bud,' said Poppa, smiling, 'it's too cold. Let's dry you off with my handkerchief.'

'You can't do much in that,' said Harper, and heard in his own voice a mean edge. 'It's too shallow to float in even.'

Goaded, Bud dropped down, bending his knees, and leant back, and then there he was in the pool, arms and legs extended, floating on the surface in a starfish shape, and Poppa called, 'Whoo-hoo!' and clapped a couple of times and Harper waited for Bud to jump up shivering but he stayed in the starfish shape, eyes clenched tight shut, face turned up to the sky, and said, 'Whoa . . .' in satisfaction at his own bravery.

Show-off, Harper thought. *I give him ten seconds maximum*.

Still lying flat, Bud began to turn. He was on his back in the water, spread out, eyes closed, arms and legs motionless: but even though he wasn't moving any part of his body, he began to wheel in the water. Beneath the still surface of the shallow pool, there was a current, an invisible force turning Bud's small floating body. As his brother began to spin, Harper jumped to his feet at the same time as Poppa and they both called out and Bud opened his eyes, raised his head and looked at them, just as the eddy at the edge of the pool took him, tumbled him, pulled him to the left. He made one attempt to stand, getting to his feet so quickly that he slipped immediately on the wet rocks. He was down again, then gone.

In the terrible and silent months that followed, the pictures that came into Harper's head when he lay awake in his bed at night, eyes wide open in the dark, were this: the sunlight striking the water, how it was clear as glass; Bud's arms and legs outstretched in a starfish pose and how it seemed that he began to turn and spin in the river so very slowly at first, even though everything had happened so quickly; the dreamy look on his face as he turned and drifted and then, all at once, went from a slow turn to spinning in the water as he lifted his small, questioning face at the sound of their cries. The water beyond the pool was still so shallow, no more than thigh height on him, but the current beneath the surface so strong that when he tried to stand it took his feet from under him in an instant.

As Bud disappeared around the corner towards the fall, pulled from sight, Harper looked at Poppa for confirmation that what he thought was happening was not happening, and that was the worst moment of all: the look on Poppa's face as he stared after Bud, the knowledge that the fissure that had opened in his head had opened in Poppa's head too. Something so horrible it could not even be imagined had actually happened, right before their eyes. The edge of the fall was a few feet away, just out of sight. While they were still trying to believe the unbelievable, Bud was already dead.

It was four months on from that afternoon, when their house was still cloaked in grief, that the letter came from Holland, the pale blue envelope with the blue and red flashes on the edge, wafer-thin like an old man's skin, his mother's spidery and precise hand, addressed to Michael Luther Senior.

It was a Saturday so he was home – he didn't go to the cartoon shows at the Variety any more, not on his own. He had collected the letter from the mailbox himself. When he handed it to Nina, she put it on the kitchen counter and said lightly, 'Let's wait till your grandfather is home, shall we?'

'Why is it to him?' he asked, looking past Nina at the letter where it lay.

'I really need some help with these greens.' It was only later that he realised she had been playing for time.

Poppa arrived back about an hour later, carrying some fresh rolls from Balian's. He had been calling in on a neighbour who needed some advice: lots of people wanted free advice from Poppa. The neighbour lived in a big house in Sugar Hill and while they had lunch Poppa talked about how this neighbour had not one but two white maids and how a famous musician lived next to him – the conversation was low-key, as it always was since that day. Harper felt much older, these days – old enough, in any case, to recognise that normality was effortful for all of them. It was only as Poppa was patting his lips with his napkin that Nina, who had scarcely spoken a word throughout the meal, rose, turned to the counter-top where the letter lay and held it up.

Poppa stared at the letter in Nina's hand, and then he stared at Nina, and Nina stared right back.

'It's from my mother . . .' Harper announced, unnecessarily. 'We haven't opened it.'

Poppa said, calmly, his gaze still locked with Nina's, 'Nicolaas, if you've finished, you can go and play with Jimmy.'

Harper rose and picked up his plate and Poppa said, 'You don't need to clear the table today, Nicolaas, go play.' Harper began to feel sick. Clearing the table was a rigid duty. He looked at Nina but she was still staring at Poppa, the letter in her hand.

Poppa repeated, in a light tone of voice, 'Nicolaas. Go kick a ball around the garden.'

As Harper closed the back door behind him, slowly because he wanted to hear what would come next, Poppa said, 'We don't know for sure.'

He sat down. A long silence came then.

Then Nina's voice, a strangled kind of shriek. 'That selfish . . . selfish . . . *trash* . . . that's all she is.'

He had never heard Poppa raise his voice to Nina before now – Michael, when he was here, him occasionally, but not Nina.

'*Never* use a phrase like that of our boy's mother! It isn't right.'

'Is it right what she's doing? Is it? How can you defend her? Everything went wrong the minute she came along. Michael.'

'Michael wasn't her fault, you know that.'

'She didn't help.'

A concession, then. 'No, she didn't. But . . .' Poppa's voice was softer now.

He had descended two of the steps before he sat down to make sure his head wasn't visible in the glass panel in the top half of the door. All the same, all they had to do was glance out of the kitchen window to see that he hadn't made it as far as the backyard.

Nina was crying now. 'Haven't we lost enough?' she sobbed. 'Haven't we?' Poppa was soothing her.

The most frightening thing was that, whatever the contents of the letter, things were bad enough for them to have forgotten him. Normally, Poppa was sharp enough to realise if he was hovering around. He sat on the step, listening to Nina's sobs. At the end of the garden, Jimmy was snuffling in the border, the fluffy swoop of his tail a crescent-moon shape, batting to and fro.

He still expected his brother to show up at any minute – still caught himself wondering why Bud did not come jumping down the stairs, two at a time, like always, or appear running around the corner of the house just as Harper had picked up a ball or a bat, claiming it was his. In the mornings, he woke up alone in the box room and looked over at Bud's empty bed, the quilt neat and smoothed. If he closed his eyes again immediately, he could hear Bud's voice in his head. He still thought to himself, some mornings, *When I open my eyes again, Bud will be there. If I believe in it strongly enough, then that will make it so.* Arjuna the warrior could have made that happen, somehow. Reverend Wilson had organised a memorial service and the whole of the district had come – people still left pies and casseroles on the veranda with chequered cloths over them – but there had been no funeral. His body had yet to be found.

Later that day, Poppa called him into the sitting room and asked him to sit down. It reminded him of the first time he had come to the house, when Poppa had asked him into the kitchen and enquired, with a lawyer's solemnity, whether it could really be true that he had an *extra a* in his name; and for the first few minutes of the conversation, even as it became clear how serious this matter was, he wondered whether Poppa was about to turn the whole thing into a joke.

'Nicolaas, son, tell me, how much do you remember about your mother?' Poppa continued without waiting for him to answer. 'Do you remember how, when she left, your mother said she would either come back or send for you and Bud? Do you remember that?'

He didn't remember the conversation quite like that, but that didn't seem important right now. It was more than three years since his mother had left. There had been letters occasionally, a birthday card each year. There had been a Christmas present that had arrived one February, three small hardback books he couldn't read with a note saying he mustn't forget his Dutch.

'Well, even though Bud is gone, has been taken away from us, that time has come,' Poppa said.

They were going to Holland? He remembered so little about having lived there. The bread they ate was stale. They had to wear three coats inside the house because it was so cold. His mother had wailed every day that without his father's army pension, they would starve. They were going back to mud and cold? Did you still have to wear three coats inside the house?

'When are we going?'

Poppa paused. 'Nina and I aren't going, son. Our lives are here, in Los Angeles. My work is here. We would keep you here with us forever, if it was possible, I want you to know that. We think of you as ours. But your mother is your mother and she wants you back.' It finally became clear: no Nina, no Poppa, no Jimmy either. He had lost Bud and now he was losing the rest of them.

It was very simple. 'I'm not going.'

'Nicolaas, your mother wrote us some time ago, after – after Bud was taken from us. We didn't tell you because we didn't want to worry you in case it wasn't going to happen. We wrote back saying how we very much wanted you to stay with us but she has written us again and she is insistent and she is your mother, after all. She wants you back.'

'I hate her.'

'No, you don't. Your mother loves you and that's why she wants you back.'

'She knows I like it here.'

'Yes, she does but her need is greater than yours, in her head.'

'Then she is a bad person. How can you let me go and live with a bad person?' He suddenly felt very grown up, like a lawyer. It was simple. He just had to win the argument, then everything would be okay.

Poppa had been standing up in front of him, but now he sat down next to him, reached out and, very gently, took hold of his upper arm, as if he needed to hold on to it for support. 'Nicolaas, I can see how it seems like the same thing to you, from your point of view I mean, but she isn't a bad person.'

'Then what is she?' At that moment, the immediate calamity was less pressing in his head than his appreciation of the struggle his Poppa was undergoing, the great lawyer, so used to dealing in certainty, now facing his toughest challenge yet: the moral reasoning of a twelve-year-old boy.

Poppa pursed his lips, taking the question very seriously. 'She is rather a person who believes that because of the bad things that have happened to her, she can never be blamed for the bad things she does herself. Nothing is ever Anika's fault, we realised that after a while. When a person believes themselves to be unaccountable for their actions then there is nothing you can do. You can't argue with them, you can't reason. You might as well bang your head against the wall over there.'

'It's the same thing, isn't it?'

Poppa hesitated. 'No, I don't believe it is the same thing. The harm and hurt from your point of view may be just as great, but being unaccountable is not the same as being bad even though the unaccountable person may do as much harm as the bad person.'

He was unconvinced. What did motivation matter if the end effect was the same? There was a long silence between them then, while he struggled with the idea that this argument was more than theoretical.

'I'm sorry, Nicolaas, truly I am, because you've had so much moving around, and we had really hoped that your moving around was done, that you were here for good. Now, son, I know how you are feeling but I think we need to go and see Nina now and be brave for her because . . .' And suddenly, Poppa stopped in the middle of this speech, and took a great heaving breath, as if he had been underwater for the whole conversation, had only just surfaced and had the chance to gulp at air. 'Because we need to try and make her feel better, okay? Can you do that? Can you, Nicolaas?'

Reverend Wilson's brother took them to the Union Passenger Terminal in his Packard sedan. Jimmy came with them in the car, then was being delivered to neighbours to be looked after while Harper, Nina and Poppa undertook the long journey cross-country. Harper watched the car pull away with Jimmy looking at him out of the back window, his ears high, head on one side slightly, panting a little as it was a hot day. But even then, he did not really feel the weight of his departure, not with Poppa and Nina with him and a long ride on an Interstate to look forward to.

They were standing on the sidewalk in front of the station. They had just waved Jimmy off. Nina was checking their belongings: small travel cases for her and Poppa, his large one; a wicker basket with a lid that was piled high with luncheon-meat sandwiches. When he had asked why she was making so many, she replied, 'The rest of America isn't like West Adams. We might not feel too comfortable in some of the restaurants.'

Poppa frowned and scratched his neck. Nina had persuaded him to wear his heavy coat. 'I'm a little warm in this thing,' he grumbled.

Just then, a police officer in a peaked cap with a badge wandered up, a leather strap diagonal across his chest, attached to his belt, just above his gun holster. Harper stared at the holster and the heavy-looking black gun: a real gun. He looked up at the officer, a man with a puffy white face and cheery smile, and grinned at him. The officer grinned back.

'You folks travelling today?' he asked them, looking at all three of them.

'I have our tickets here,' Poppa replied, patting the pockets of his heavy coat.

The officer was looking at Harper, then said, 'That's okay, I don't need to see them. This your child, boy?'

Harper looked at the officer, confused, but Poppa, who had

stopped patting his pockets and was standing very still, replied quietly, 'My grandson.'

The officer reached out a hand and placed it on Harper's shoulder, giving him a small pat. 'Nice-looking kid. You look after your grandparents now, son.'

Harper glanced at Poppa, who was staring straight ahead, looked back at the officer and said quickly, 'Yes, sir.'

And the long journey and the passing countryside led eventually to this: another embarkation shed, a huge thing with a vaulted roof and sawdust floor and great, high windows through which vast shafts of light lit the crowds of passengers below and made travelling clothes, travelling crates, boxes and suitcases all shades of brown and grey, the flat colours of transience. After they had got to the head of a very long queue and put his name on the passenger list, the woman at the desk gave them a sheet of paper with the rules for Unaccompanied Young Persons and handed over a label on a piece of string. He had to wear it around his neck at all times. It had *Holland-Amerika Lijn* printed on one side and *HAL* in big capitals on the other with his name, date of birth and his destination written in a sloping hand. Beneath was the name of the person who was meeting him at the port in Rotterdam: *Mrs Anika Aaltink*.

He was mortified. He had to wear a label like a tiny child would? He was going to be thirteen soon.

'Just like a parcel,' Nina said, as she tucked the label inside his jacket, kneeling in front of him, even though that made him taller than her now. All at once, she grabbed him and held her to him. Harper glanced around, over her head. In the corner of the departure shed was a group of teenage boys in school uniform.

'The most precious parcel in the world,' Nina said brokenly into his chest. Poppa put his hand gently on her shoulder and patted it until she released him and stood up.

His last sight of Nina and Poppa for eight years came as he exited the departure shed at the far end, on his way to the jetty. When he turned around, they were standing holding on to each other and smiling at him: Poppa tall and bulky in his winter coat and hat, Nina, petite and smiling bravely, both with their hands raised. Nina waved hard and Harper, who had attached himself to the end of the group of boys, lifted his hand in an awkward little half-wave, glancing from one of them to the other quickly, worried that whichever of them was the last one he smiled at, the other might be upset – but at the same time not wanting to embarrass himself in front of the group of big boys just ahead of him.

It was a relief to get out onto the concrete jetty, where the ship loomed and the air smelled of smoke and fuel and a soft rain fell and the business of goodbye was over. Right at that particular moment, the adventure to come seemed adequate compensation for leaving his grandparents behind. The missing them would come later.

*

Travelling the Atlantic Ocean alone, the label round his neck at all times as he had been instructed, even when he was washing – surely it must have made some impression on him? When he tried to remember that voyage, there was something in his head about an ice cream, an ice cream sandwich made with thick soggy slabs of some sort of cookie mixture. A sailor who played cards with him? A little girl in a pinafore? Without his mother there to make the pictures of the voyage, that Atlantic journey at the age of twelve seemed vaguer when he thought back to it than the one he had undertaken with his mother when he was three. Saying goodbye to Poppa and Nina must have been hard but, as far as he remembered, the voyage itself didn't bother him – being in a state of transition was too familiar to his bones.

The arrival – that was different. Like all the passengers, he hung over the side, watching the coast appear. He joined the melee processing clumsily down the gangplank, bumping his case on the wooden ridges and losing control of it at one point, tripping a young woman in heels just ahead of him. She turned her head back to him, scowling over her shoulder, then stopped, blocking the way for everybody, to adjust her stockings. Then he was on the quay and trapped in a huge crowd of adults who grouped and gathered in greetings before moving off, people clinging to each other. When a clearing opened, he turned to his left and saw, first of all, a barrel-chested man in a tweed coat and black hat who was shouting, '*Indié verloren, rampspoed geboren!*' with his arms wide open. His ruddy face was contorted and open-mouthed, as if he had made a tremendous joke. On her knees next to him, kneeling right there on the wooden planks of the arrivals jetty, was a woman with her hair scraped back in a ponytail that revealed harsh lines leading down from her nostrils to the corners of her mouth. She had tears pouring down her cheeks. She, too, had her arms open and she was crying, 'Come here! Oh come here, baby boy!'

The power of transience: in motion, you could be whoever you wanted to be. When had he learned this? On that solo Atlantic journey, with the label round his neck? Or earlier, at the age of three, watching his mother cadge cigarettes from different passengers or sailors, varying the details of who she was according to whether she was talking to a man or a woman, a sailor or a fellow passenger? Whatever lessons were learned then, chief amongst them was this: if you don't want people to know who you are, keep moving.

If you kept moving fast enough, you could be several selves in quick succession. If someone struck up a conversation with you on a plane, you could pretend to be from Macau and single and a brain surgeon – after you had assessed that the person you were talking to was neither from Macau nor a brain surgeon themselves, of course. In the taxi queue outside the airport, you could be a Spanish businessman, widowed with six adorable children. Later that same day, in a hotel bar perhaps, you could say you were psychic and that your mother had been mistress to a Persian king – you could claim you had a fatal disease and only months to live. The possibilities were endless.

He was recruited by the Institute straight out of his military service and for the first couple of years, after his basic training was done, was sent on jobs that involved a lot of transience. It was mostly delivering packages to embassies or organisations, although he was too junior to know the contents. New recruits often spent a year as delivery boys before they returned to be based behind a desk in Amsterdam and learn more about the Institute's work – they weren't going to trust you immediately, after all. This suited him fine: he was in no hurry to get his feet beneath a desk.

Travel of any sort was terrific training. Officials, for instance: there was a certain look that got you past those people – immigration or customs officers, ticket collectors; the people who wore uniforms that denoted status without any real power. This look could best be described as politeness tinged with boredom – a look that implied there was absolutely nothing at stake. That was the mistake that illegal immigrants or drug traffickers always made; either their rank fear showed or they were excessively friendly. The answer lay somewhere between the two: but a hint of boredom, that was essential. The person behind the desk in front of you was almost certainly bored as well, after all. You were in it together.

Once he was settled in a seat in a departure lounge or railway station waiting room, he liked to do his homework. How readily people gave themselves up to his gaze. The families were straightforward, the women and men clutching children, exhausted by the endlessness of it all but mostly by their offspring's obliviousness to their sacrifice. The businessmen always liked to sit a little apart, to indicate that *they* were only there because they were being paid to be there. Then there were the young couples, usually having stupid arguments, because all arguments were stupid between a couple at that age, everything freighted by the lifetime of disappointment that lay ahead. 'So much for *Things go better with Coke*,' he once saw a beautiful young woman wail at her unfortunate beau, who had trailed halfway round San Diego airport in search of a vending machine and then brought the bottle back without opening it. She meant, *are you the one? Am I having children with you? Is this it?* What she meant was, *when you're having trouble at work at the age of forty-five, will you be the kind of guy who lets his boss walk all over him and doesn't get his bonus and can't look after me and the kids? Because if you don't have the initiative to open a bottle of Coke on the opener attached to the vending machine before you bring it back to me then how do I know you have the initiative to hold a good job down and to anticipate what I need when I need it?* She didn't know it, the beautiful young woman, but that was what she was asking. And the young man's soft sigh – he didn't snap back, just accepted the admonition – said, *yeah, well, all that's probably true but I'm easy-going at least and maybe that's more important than you think and this is the guy I am so take it or leave it, hon.* The helplessness of other men never ceased to amaze him.

These were the times when he gave a shudder of gratitude at his observer status. Who would want to be part of that? The truth was, even though he was the same age as the young couple, his courier work made him feel a world apart from them, mature and powerful.

When did he ever see anyone in any of these transitory places that he would have liked to trade lives with? Rarely, although it wasn't unusual for large groups of people in motion to include one or two oddities like him. At an airport in Ceylon, on his way back from delivering a report for a British firm, he had seen one, another oddity, sitting amongst the people waiting to board one of the newly established flights. The airport had been an RAF station during the war and was only just being developed for commercial purposes. The cost of flights was prohibitive for anyone but government officials or the wealthiest of local families so the people waiting were all well dressed, many of them Indians returning home. Amongst them, clearly happy to stand out, was a white man, small, ginger-haired, tough as a little terrier, Harper guessed – he could always spot them. Ordinary people thought that the men to be afraid of were the obvious ones, the big men who shouted aggressively, the ones with uniforms and guns. Harper knew better by then. This man sat quietly in the departure lounge like him, dressed in slacks and an open-necked shirt, his frame coiled and dense, his eyes watchful. He was playing the game too. CIA, Harper guessed – definitely American, in any case, on his way back from something, technically off duty but unable to relax. He must have been doing something in conjunction with the British as well, the Americans didn't have that many interests in Ceylon. He was scanning each passenger in turn, just as Harper had. When his gaze reached him, Harper looked back, keeping his expression a professional blank as he and the other man took in everything about each other and moved on. Anyone watching them would assume they hadn't noticed each other at all, whereas he knew this man had surmised in a second that he was a fellow professional, albeit not exactly his sort.

In the far corner was an Indian couple in late middle age, sitting next to each other but staring straight ahead. The woman was wearing a knitted brown cardigan over her sari. Her husband had his hands resting on the top of his walking cane, which was upright in front of him. His mouth was slightly open.

Harper knew that this couple, each in their own way, would do almost anything rather than spend another minute together. Two British girls sat opposite the middle-aged couple, embassy secretaries perhaps, fanning themselves against the exhausting humidity with magazines, prim in their chairs, legs tucked underneath and crossed at the ankles, exchanging glances from time to time. He guessed they had been sharing an apartment for a while. They were returning home with heads full of secrets about each other. One had flat, chunky-heeled lace-up shoes and the other, the one with money in the family somewhere, was in delicate blue pumps. Even though they hadn't known each other before they came out here and had little in common, they were bound together now. Nearly everyone waiting for the plane was fed up or impatient. The travelling world was full of people who wanted to arrive so badly that that imperative stopped them observing their journey. If you didn't want that, you were at a distinct advantage.

If a flight was delayed long enough, then by the end of the wait, he felt he could write the biography of almost everyone on the aeroplane.

As the group rose to board, the American in the open-necked shirt walked past where he was sitting. Their glances met again but they did not exchange a word, or even a nod. In that instant, Harper, new to his line of work, felt that although he was a man excluded from civilian life, with no real nationality or home, he was part of something else: a kind of brotherhood, an understanding that would only be acknowledged in the briefest of looks. There was a community of shadow men out there, around the world, in airports and railway stations – on the streets, hidden in hotel rooms, disguised as ordinary people and indistinguishable to everyone but others of their kind, all ghosts, all invisible, all playing the same game. He had been inducted.

Lots of training, lots of games, lots of sex: that was how he remembered those years in Amsterdam leading up to '65. He was a young man in his twenties and apart from a multiply-divorced mother who drank so much she didn't know who he was sometimes, he had no ties, no obligations. He didn't look like the people around him but he didn't look definitively like anyone else either. *Part-something.*

The trick to being unusual was learning how to milk it. He liked to use the geography of his birth to wrong-foot people, especially women he was trying to bed. He liked to choose exactly the right moment to reveal a little about himself – after a few drinks together, when their gazes had locked once or twice. Maybe there had been a light touch or two, a brushing of a sleeve, a hand resting briefly on a knee, although that would have been quite forward in those days. In the early sixties, as he remembered, a woman's favourite way of inviting physical contact was to pick a bit of fluff off your suit jacket, often with a brusque, maternal swipe of the hand. After a certain amount of this, a certain amount of her batting him around like a small boy, came the point when he could start taking the initiative. These small physical gestures were only indicators, though. The real movement forward came when the talking started, when they began exchanging stories. That was when he knew he was home and dry.

One of his favourite gambits was to ask her where she was born: always so much more tactful than asking a woman how old she was. You could get tripped up that way if you weren't careful:

they had a tendency to ask you to guess, a question which was surprisingly hard to answer to your own advantage. If you stuck to where rather than when, it was a neat and simple way into intimacy. You couldn't say to a woman, 'Tell me your unhappiest childhood memory,' straight off, but when they told you where they were born, the conversation automatically became more intimate. The tragic detail from her childhood would be lying in wait at the end of that simple, factual answer. Sometimes there wasn't one, of course – sometimes the story of her birthplace was routine, told with a self-deprecating laugh in acknowledgement of its ordinariness. And then, because she was a nice woman – he only went for nice women – she would ask back.

The pause. The downward look. The soft voice that indicated this was not something that he usually confided in a person he had only just met.

'I was born in a concentration camp.'

The best bit was the steady gaze he received, tinged with confusion, as the woman he was talking to recalibrated what little she knew of him, this tall young man with brown but not-dark skin and thick but straight black hair, who looked definitively un-Dutch but not definitively anything else.

Once, but only once, one of them said it out loud, sceptically, 'You don't *look* Jewish.'

Was it Alida who had said that? No, Alida came later. Alida came after '65. Alida was the one who looked for the scars on his back: the scars that weren't there.

Once, in a bar on Gravenstraat, a pale freckled woman with large breasts but unfortunate teeth came up to him while he was sitting on a high stool and stood next to him, waiting to be served.

He wasn't really out for the night, just having a beer after work, making the same one last until he was ready to go: Frankenmuth, *brewed for modern American tastes.* She stood a little closer than was necessary, considering the bar wasn't all that crowded, she staggered a little – she was quite drunk, he thought – and put her hand on his thigh to steady herself, before saying, 'Oh, I'm sorry,' and then snatching the hand away, as if his thigh was hot.

The bartender came up to them and rested his wrists on the bar, looking at them expectantly, and the woman said, 'Oh, it's me now, thank you darling. Can you do a Pink Squirrel? Two of them.' She held her fingers up in a V-for-victory sign.

The bartender looked at them with such disdain that Harper wanted to say, *please, the second one isn't for me*.

'Oh, okay,' she said then. 'Two Old-fashioneds.' She looked at Harper. 'My friend's in the corner there. She's really nice.'

They made small talk while the bartender mixed the drinks. Behind the rows of bottles on the wooden shelves, there was a mirrored surface that reflected the jewelled golds and browns and oranges of the various liquors. When he moved his head, he could glimpse different shards of their reflections; her hairline, an eye or ear, his nose. She turned her back to the bar, placing both elbows on it, and surveyed the room as if they were spies, before talking from the side of her mouth.

'I've never met a *neger* before,' she said. 'Me and my friend are going to a party later, want to come along, meet my friends? They're really nice people, they'd be interested to meet you.'

Up until that point, he had been giving it some serious thought. 'Thanks,' he said, picking up the change he had left on the bar and pocketing it. 'But I've already met more than enough white people.'

*

'Choose an Anglo name,' his trainer at the Institute had told him, as they sat with clipboards in the meeting room and worked their way through the details of his new identity for travel purposes. 'Something that's easy for anyone to understand, something nice and neutral. Not Smith, for heaven's sake. Barnhardt actually *chose* Smith.'

Nicolaas Den Herder, born on the island of Sulawesi in the Dutch East Indies, to a white Dutch mother and an Indo officer in the Dutch Colonial Army, had already changed his surname to Luther, then to Aaltink, then back to Den Herder.

He thought about it.

'Favourite film star? Childhood pet?' the trainer said helpfully.

'My mind's gone blank.' How was it possible to name yourself?

The trainer sighed, lifted a sheet of paper on his clipboard, looked down and said, 'Walton, Fullerton, Jamieson, Johnson, Harper, Headley . . .'

'Harper,' he said to his trainer. Then, firmly, as if he had just put on a pair of shoes that fitted well, 'John Harper.'

Once his probationary year was over and he had Stage One security clearance, he was based in Amsterdam at the Institute's head office. His training was twofold; the training for what he would tell people he did for a living and the training for what he would really do. Officially, John Harper was a researcher for the Institute of International Economics, Amsterdam. His job was to read the newspapers and make economic forecasts and write reports. The international companies that retained the Institute then used those reports to decide upon the wisdom of sending in staff or building factories or digging holes in whichever particular country they were interested in.

Unofficially, there were the games. Maybe that was why he got into his line of work. Maybe that was why anyone got into it, because they liked playing games: well, that was why men did it, he presumed. Women didn't seem all that bothered about playing games, let alone winning them. It was the watching – yes, that was it. Maybe women just weren't voyeurs: too used to being the observed rather than the observer.

During this secondary induction period, his trainer told him to go and sit in a doctor's waiting room and stay there until he had worked out what was wrong with every single patient.

'Why?' Harper had asked. 'And how will you know if I'm right?'

'That's not the point of the exercise,' his trainer had sighed. 'The point of the exercise is to get you used to looking at people and working out what their story is. I don't want to know whether you are right or not. I want you to come back and tell me how you came to your conclusions.'

In years to come, when his line of work turned into big business – it really took off in the eighties – there would be whole manuals on this stuff, training weekends, presentations on whiteboards with handouts in folders to take away and read at your leisure; graphs, statistics. Back then, in the sixties, the people who trained you more or less made it up as they went along: a little amateur psychology mixed with a whole bucket of intuition. Maybe it was easier, back then, when it was clear who the enemy was – and it was very clear.

Despite what was going on in Saigon, Harper's department, the Asia Department, wasn't really where it was at in 1964 –

President Johnson wasn't listening to de Gaulle, so what was new there? No, the best people were all in the Soviet Section, a whole separate unit staffed by people who had Russian or Eastern Bloc language skills: bunch of comedians they became round the office, once the guy with the eyebrows took over in Moscow, those Groucho jokes wore thin pretty fast. Other than that, there were certain countries that were hot for a while for one reason or another; the small South American desk got very excited about the coup in Brazil. There was Panama, Zanzibar, Cuba of course. The focus tended to change emphasis according to the State Department's priorities. Even though the Institute was independent and nominally Dutch, the Americans were their most important clients – nearly three quarters of the contracts were coming from them. Company offices were going to open up in Los Angeles and New York as a result and they were already in partnership with a West Coast firm like theirs – later, there would be a merger. Harper was one of the operatives who applied for transfer there but the jobs all went to people with experience in the Soviet Section.

Everybody wanted to be in America if they could, not Europe with its old, cold, bombed-out cities, their cheap concrete buildings flung up like dentures in a ruined mouth. There was going to be this big new skyscraper in New York, the world's tallest building it would be. They'd been arguing about it over there for years but now it was going to be designed by some Japanese guy – how ironic was that. Harper had a debate about it with Joosten who said that the guy wasn't a Jap, he was just an American with a Jap name, and Harper said he didn't care, he thought maybe the guys who gave him the job had memories that were pretty short, like, er, Pearl Harbor, a load of aeroplanes came out of the sky one sunny day without warning, remember? He didn't really mean it and Joosten knew he didn't, being anti-Japanese was something he made a show of to remind his colleagues that not all brown guys were the same. It was just something to say while they sat in a bar after work. A moment later they were arguing about whether the A-11 would burn to a crisp at seventy thousand feet.

One day, Harper's boss Gregor came to the door of his office and leaned casually against the doorpost, arms folded. Harper had his head bent over his desk but the moment he became aware of a figure blocking the light, he knew who it was. Gregor never announced himself with a 'good morning' or a 'hi'. He announced himself with silence.

Harper's head was down over a list of figures. He was muttering the figures out loud and twirling ticks and crosses on the list with a pencil, so he had a small but satisfying excuse to take a moment or two before he looked up. While he took advantage of that moment, Gregor waited. Gregor continued to wait when Harper lifted his head. Gregor met Harper's gaze and waited long enough for their mutual stare to become odd, expectant.

Gregor dropped his gaze, lifted it again, pushed his glasses further up his nose and sniffed – only then did he say to Harper, 'Got a minute?'

Harper sat back in his chair to indicate that he had. He did not put the pencil down.

Gregor used his weight to lever himself upright from the doorframe, looked behind him at the open-plan office, quiet but for the discordant clacking of several typewriters at different distances from where he stood, and only at that point did he uncross his arms, take a step into Harper's office and close the door behind him.

'It's raining,' Gregor said, lifting an arm to indicate the view from Harper's office window, which included the brown water of the canal and the blank brick wall of a warehouse building that dropped straight into the water. Harper liked the fact that there were no other windows looking into his office. The rain was invisible against the brick but when he looked at the brown canal he saw tiny pits on its surface, disappearing and reappearing in a pattern.

'So, our Asia Department.' It was a statement rather than a question so Harper remained silent.

'Well,' said Gregor with a sigh, as if Harper was being particularly truculent that afternoon. 'We need someone on the ground. Jakarta, land of your birth, it was Jakarta, wasn't it? Six months, a year maybe, maybe longer.'

'Long time.'

'He speaks! The enigmatic one speaks!'

Harper did not return Gregor's smile. 'Have they asked for me?'

'I'm asking for you.'

He frowned, leaned forward, dropped his pencil on his desk. 'Why me?'

Gregor actually shrugged. 'Look, it's up to you. I know it's a big deal, it would be your first big job and you'll need Stage Three clearance, and some physicals. To be honest, seeing how new you are I'm not sure but you know the region.' He sniffed and rubbed at the side of his nose with one extended finger. 'It's your background rather than experience.'

'Joosten knows the region better than me. He's been.'

'This one isn't for Joosten. This one needs the time to develop contacts on the ground and we need to send someone as soon as possible, now the guy in the black hat has pulled them out of the UN. You'll be taking a crate on delivery so instead of an aeroplane through Karachi, you get to go on a cruise, pretty good I would think, lots of deckchair time to do your homework . . . and,' this next point a concession to the obvious, 'Joosten can't pass for a local if he has to. Things are getting a little hot for us palefaces out there.'

'Why not use the local operatives?'

'Client doesn't trust them, wants someone we're sure of here, who we can move swiftly to another island as soon as job done, but it also has to be someone who can do the local thing, which, my friend, narrows it down to you. Pronto.'

Gregor watches too many movies, Harper thought. 'Why the hurry?'

'I can't tell you until you've said yes.'

He'd been waiting for an overseas assignment ever since he joined the Institute. He had always been curious to visit the country where he spent his first three years, even though, especially though, he had no memory of those years and only his mother's dubious stories to go on. True, it was something of a backwater, but that would give him more autonomy too.

Gregor was waiting. His patience irritated Harper so much that he was on the verge of saying he wasn't sure he was ready and didn't want to be told any more details, just to be difficult, but then Gregor lifted both hands, splaying his fingers in an *okay, hands up* motion, as if Harper had opened a drawer of his desk and extracted a pistol. 'Look, there will be bonuses involved. Quite a few of them, in fact. And an opportunity to move sideways, which is presumably what you've been waiting for. It's what all you new young guys want, isn't it?'

'Sideways in which direction?'

'You don't look all that happy behind a desk.'

Did anyone look happy behind a desk?

The following week, Gregor summoned him to his office and introduced him to a middle-aged American who called himself Johnson. Johnson had dull, pitted skin on his cheeks, the remnant of some childhood disease, and a very bald, very shiny head – it was adulthood that had done that bit. He kept running a hand over his shiny head while he spoke, as if he liked to keep it polished that way.

After things were agreed, Harper shook hands with both men and Johnson said, 'Gregor here speaks very highly of you. I must admit I was a little concerned you were inexperienced, on paper, I mean, but now I've met you I can see why he does.'

Now you've seen my skin, Harper thought.

Gregor intervened. 'I told him you got the Cadet Lion Honourable Mention in your year. And you scored ninety-eight per cent on our induction programme. There's a few physicals but that won't take long.'

'Thank you, sir,' Harper replied.

Later that day, Gregor said, 'I also told him you spoke all the languages out there. You can get up to speed, can't you, once you're on the ground? It's not going to take you that long to pass.' He wondered if the Malay he had learned as a child might help with his Indonesian, whether it was buried there somewhere. He was quick at languages, he'd get conversational faster than most, but the sort of fluency Gregor was talking about took years – and Javanese was another thing altogether. Javanese was fiendish. Gregor's optimism about Harper's language skills was based on no more than his own colossal ignorance. He pulled a face to indicate it wasn't that simple and Gregor said, 'Oh c'mon, you half-castes have a real facility for languages, you're gifted at it, you guys, you'll be fluent within weeks, accent and everything.'

Harper felt the drip, drip, drip of all the remarks they made around the office, about how good his sun tan was, how much he must like spicy food. Such remarks were always phrased as compliments. He had been permanently resident in Holland since the age of twelve but people often remarked on the flawlessness of his Dutch.

*

His pain threshold was fairly high but he had a secret weakness: a great and pressing fear of any situation where breathing might be difficult. It wasn't the same as claustrophobia: lifts and cars were fine. If the situation demanded it, he could have happily spent hours hiding in a wardrobe as long as there were holes in it – but suffocating, drowning, these were the fates he dreaded. It was the totality of them, he sometimes thought. Pain belonged to the location where the pain was situated – a broken arm was a broken arm, however agonising. Even a stomach ache or backache, those most internal of pains, could be ring-fenced from the rest of your body, your consciousness, if only you were strong enough: but being unable to breathe, for whatever reason, was a state that possessed the whole of you.

So when the hood came down over his head, he panicked, sucking in a great breath that pulled the rough fabric into his mouth. The two men holding either arm threw him to the ground and he landed on his back with a thump that made his head snap backwards and expelled what little breath there was left in his lungs out into the hood – he sucked in again, more violently this time. As he rolled to one side, he forced himself to do an inventory: whiplash, perhaps, some bruising to his back no doubt. No broken coccyx at least – he would have felt that immediately. He tucked his chin down and braced himself, expecting one or both of the men to kick him now he was on the floor: with his hands tied behind his back he couldn't roll into a ball – his head was very vulnerable. But it wasn't that that was worrying him most, it was his breathing. He had a moment to observe his own efficiency in noting this.

Instead of laying into him, the men left the room. At least, he thought they had left – there were the sounds of their feet scuffing on the dirt floor, the slam of the door.

He lay very still but his own breath was ragged against the cloth and too harsh for him to listen to the room. He was still hyperventilating and each time he did, he sucked the hood back into his mouth, shortening the breath and making him hyperventilate more. It came to him that if he did not control his breathing, then without the men doing anything more, the end would be suffocation. That was what happened. You shortened your own breath millilitre by millilitre, a bit like someone with a rope around their neck struggling so much they pulled the noose tight. Would they use the water trick? He had heard stories of people choking on their own vomit when they did that.

It would be really stupid to suffocate himself when they

weren't even trying to kill him. He lay trying to steady his lungs, interrogating the pain in his shoulders where his arms were pulled back. He found that if he rolled his shoulders back in tiny movements, like a minute version of a limbering-up exercise, it eased the pain.

He managed to slow his breathing a little, but only a little. Each time he inhaled, he still sucked the cloth into his mouth, like a tiny billowing sail, shortening the breath that followed. When he exhaled, he blew the cloth back out with more force than was wise, filling the interior of the hood with his own CO_2. *I must stop this*.

The door opened again, slammed back against the wall. The light in the room changed – he could tell through the hood. Sounds were muffled but he felt sure that several men had entered the room. A pair of hands scrabbled against his neck and the drawstring around the bottom of the hood. For a moment he thought, if they aren't careful, they'll asphyxiate me instead of getting me free. The string pulled against his windpipe, released, and the hood was yanked away. As his eyes adjusted he caught the blurred form of a figure in front of him and then another two against a wall, more distant, to one side, but before he had time to configure what he was seeing a hand grabbed a handful of his hair and shook his head from side to side and Joosten's round face was in his and his voice was booming in his ears, 'Wakey wakey Nic old man, you've passed!'

'Fuck you, Joosten,' Harper gasped, his breath still painfully laboured in his chest, 'fuck you.'

The two trainers, leaning back against the wall of the cell with their arms folded, burst into appreciative laughter; Joosten clapped him on the shoulder; and for a moment or two, as the breath that heaved in his throat still felt as heavy as sand and his chest pressed painfully inwards, it occurred to Harper that when he got out in the field, it would not, after all, be one big game.

There was a pleasing symmetry to his arriving in Jakarta by ship. He had left on a long sea journey at the age of three from this very port, perhaps even this very jetty, and here he was, returning the same way, nearly two decades later. Last time he had stood on this spot he was an undersized boy, head shaved to keep the lice at bay. Now, he was a man. He had done his national service; he had – as Gregor had pointed out to Johnson – received the Cadet Lion Honourable Mention in his group; he was fit and trained.

He imagined his younger self, big-eyed and malnourished, a refugee child clinging to his mother's skirts, looking up at his grown self in awe. I'm *back*, he thought, as he stood on the dock long after the other passengers had disembarked, waiting for the crate he was accompanying to be unloaded, looking around at the vast sheds and the gangs of shirtless men, a foreman yelling at them in a high-pitched voice. The jetty he was standing on was for deep-sea ships, the passenger liners, and his boat was the only arrival in port at present, but stretching far in the distance, to his right, was the long strip of docking bays for the smaller freight boats, old wooden things, hardly seaworthy they looked, with peeling paintwork on their high bows. These were the boats that would sail to and from Sumatra, Borneo, the smaller islands perhaps, carrying everything from cement powder to coconut husks for animal feed, coffee, spices. He could get on one of those freight vessels and be almost anywhere, nowhere as far as anyone else was concerned. What a fine thought. The further you travelled, the more you faded from view, until nobody knew where you were or if you even existed. Were it not for the seriousness of his mission, he would be tempted to stroll down to one of those boats now, deserting his crate and his tin trunk full of research, shedding everything Dutch or American about himself, bribe the captain with cash, stow away – and disappear.

The port was undergoing expansion; skeletons of new sheds were ranged in different stages of construction and beneath the mechanical chunter of boat engines and the shouts of men was the grind and spin of machinery at work: a cumulative noise that made the port seem like a living thing, a monster needing to be fed. A row of open trucks loaded with sandbags and coils of rope lined the edge of the concrete jetty to his left – parked perilously close to the water, he thought. As he watched, a man standing on top of the bags raised a hand in which there was the steel question mark of a hook. He jabbed the hook into one of the bags then pulled, slitting the bag open. Sand ran out in a torrent, down the side of the truck and into a wheelbarrow held by another man waiting below. Indonesia: always a work in progress – he had followed the recent history of the land of his birth enough to know that. But now what? Where was that progress heading now the great *Bung Karno* was drifting ever closer to Peking?

He had bought a packet of *kreteks* on board ship and he paused to light one now, ceremoniously – he had made himself wait until he was standing on Javanese soil. It wasn't much to mark his return but it was small and private, which suited him just fine: the only other person who would appreciate the significance of this arrival was his mother and she didn't know where he was, only that he had left Amsterdam 'on another one of your stupid trips', as she called them. Lately, she had taken to accusing him of not being abroad at all, just avoiding her. 'When are you going to find a nice girl and settle down? What's wrong with you? I'd been married twice by your age.' That wasn't strictly accurate but then Anika rarely was.

He flicked the match away, inhaled deeply on the cigarette, blew out, then flapped his hand at the young man who had darted forward from the crowd in the hope of picking up his tin trunk or one of the cases that sat on top of it. '*Tidak, tidak* . . .' he said, then added, '*Terima kasih, tak usah* . . .' He passed his tongue over his lips – the sweet taste of cloves; the *kretek* was a honeyed hint of delirium, temporary and addictive. The ground beneath his feet felt pliant after three weeks at sea.

He was being met by a driver – the local office had organised it. The ship had docked early but it would take some time for him to locate his crate once the ship had been emptied. The driver would be late. There was no hurry. Above him, to the right, some of the crates from the cargo hold were already swinging on ropes, the men waiting below, the foreman shouting.

The Institute's operations were in their infancy here: there was no physical office, just two local staff who both operated from their homes and they were out of town in Central Java, assessing the situation there. There would be no briefing for a while and even afterwards, he would be running his own operation, more or less, under Johnson's instruction. The local staff were there to help with his language skills and advise on customs and etiquette, they weren't trained men. There would be a chance to orientate himself, walk around, get used to the humidity, practise his Indonesian in shops and restaurants in districts of the city away from the ones where he would be working – and to buy more *kreteks*. Gregor may have been over-optimistic about his language skills but soon he would be smoking just like a local.

His instructions were to go with the driver to an area north of Glodok. The driver would know where to go, which street to wait in. Afterwards, he would be taken to a guesthouse in the Menteng district – but first he had to hand over the crate to the Americans. As they drove, a light rain began to fall, misting row after row of low-rise buildings, the warehouses giving way to long strips of open-fronted shops. Harper glanced at the driver from time to time, a silent man with a small, triangular face. More than just a driver, he guessed. He tried a little of his Indonesian on him but the man spoke so quickly and briefly in reply that he couldn't catch what he was saying.

The main roads were broad in Old Jakarta but behind them were multiple smaller roads and alleyways – although he'd been told to take a walk through the *kampong* if he wanted to understand the meaning of the word narrow. Most of Jakarta was *kampong*, Joosten had said, vast shanty towns of slums, divided and subdivided, with streets so small, so densely lined with open shacks that you walked through people's living rooms as you strolled along. At the height of the dry monsoon, in August, a load of them would burn down. Then they sprang up again. And later, when the weather broke and the wet monsoon rolled in, they would be flooded. Fire and water: the alternate hazards of Jakarta.

They parked in a road behind Kota railway station. There, they waited in silence. Harper offered the driver a *kretek* and he took one with a terse nod. Eventually, another car pulled up behind and a white man around Harper's age got out with two Indonesian men. Harper saw them emerge in the rear-view mirror and opened his door. By the time he had climbed out, the white man was standing there, extending a hand. 'I'm Michael, welcome to Jakarta.' He had an American accent and a short crowbar leaning at a diagonal out of his jacket pocket.

'John.' They shook hands.

Michael turned to where the other men were already lifting the crate out of the boot of Harper's car. It was heavy – they both carried it, two-handed and shuffling, to the boot of the American's car and placed it inside. Harper waited while the American went round to the rear of the car, gestured for the men to get back in, then bent his head into the boot. There was a crack and a splintering sound as he prised the crate open. He stayed bent into the boot for a few moments, counting, perhaps, moving straw aside? M1 Garands? The Heckler & Koch? Or it could be ammo, more likely with a small delivery – or something specialist, perhaps. After a moment, Michael straightened, lifted his hand to Harper in salute.

First job done. That was pretty easy. Harper got into the passenger seat of his car.

'Guesthouse now, sir?' asked his driver, cracking a smile for the first time.

Harper nodded. 'Guesthouse now.'

For the next few months, he acclimatised. He got used to the blanket of heat that lay over the city at all times of the day and night, the way the closeness of the air made him feel a little nauseous first thing in the morning. He toured the city on a moped, weaving in and out of the traffic on the wide superhighways that carved their way through the shanty towns like a lawnmower scything grass: the Great Leader Soekarno was on a massive building programme, to prove to the world that Jakarta was a modern city, the Paris of the East. He wrote reports for Johnson and Amsterdam on the grip the PKI was exerting in certain districts: anti-Western graffiti was everywhere: *KILL CAPITALIST SKUM*. He befriended Benni the gangster – and saw his first but not last incident of a man being tortured.

As the antagonism towards foreigners in Jakarta grew, more and more of them left the city, particularly the Americans and the Brits, and he began to understand why Gregor had chosen him. He bought his clothes at a store next to the guesthouse and let his hair grow for a bit then went to a barber on Jalan Gondangdia who cut it like the local men's – he had arrived with it too short and neat around his ears, he realised. He worked on his language skills and his mannerisms. When he wasn't hanging out with Benni's gang, he took to wandering the streets in a white shirt and sarong. Sometimes, he would spend time squatting by the road alongside other men with mopeds but nothing to do because petrol was so scarce. He joined a couple of demonstrations where he wore a red bandana and shouted slogans but his instructions were clear: observe, join in a bit but don't get actively involved. Only once did he overstep the mark, caught up in the excitement of one march, when he observed an Australian television crew filming the gang he was with. As they passed, he shook his fist at them and shouted, 'Lackeys of the British!' and the young men either side of him took up the shout. The film crew followed them for a few minutes, until two of the young men in Harper's group detached themselves and went up to the

Australians and started shoving them backwards. Harper kept going but glanced back: it was frustrating, always being on the fringe of the action.

At other times, he dressed in his beige slacks and a shirt, combed his hair with pomade and pressed a panama on top and went hanging out in the bars frequented by the foreign press. Once, he even encountered a man he was sure had been amongst the Australian television crew – but with Harper in Western clothes and speaking immaculate English, there was no flicker of recognition from the Australian, to whom all Indonesian protestors no doubt looked the same. The man was called Gibson and they got drunk together on Tjap Tikus, high-end *arak*, round a small table in a side-street bar off Jalan Thamrin.

'Soekarno's started eating his own,' Gibson confided. 'You know lots of the ministers have taken to sleeping away from their homes at night? The Father of the Nation's getting careless. When you start making your own people that nervous, you know . . .' He made a short stabbing notion at Harper's ribs.

Later, after Harper had moved on to fruit juice but Gibson had stayed on the *arak*, the Australian became loquacious. 'Indonesia isn't a nation, it's an *imagin*ation,' he said, then looked around, pleased with himself. 'S'karno made it up! Made it up, the speeches, and, take it from me, when they push'm out, the whole lot will just evaporate . . . like a *dream* . . .' At this, Gibson splayed his fingers and moved his hand in a semi-circular motion in front of Harper's face. 'S'all going to fall apart. Easy to sneer at him, in his hat, with his girlfriends, but you look at what will happen if he goes. Jus' wait. Holds it all together.' He clenched his fist.

Harper made a note of the man's sympathies – perhaps the

Americans should look into him – and could not resist adding, 'Well, maybe we should wait and see what happens if this region becomes the next Communist bloc. I wonder what the Indonesian for *gulag* is.'

The bar was dark, the fan above them inefficient, the crowd large even though a lot of Westerners had left: there were so few places in the city where Westerners felt comfortable any more, they had a tendency to congregate. Gibson withdrew a handkerchief from his pocket and mopped his face. 'God knows why they call it the Cold War, it's fucking hot in Jakarta.' And Harper rewarded him with a clap on the shoulder and a convincing laugh.

Then came the abrupt command from Johnson: forget the gangsters. Four months of careful, nauseating and sometimes dangerous sucking up to Benni and it was all down the drain.

'Why?' Harper asked. He and Johnson were in the same bar where he had drunk Gibson beneath a table, but this time it was daytime and they were sipping green tea. The curfew had made nighttime excursions increasingly difficult, the journalists all stuck to the hotel bar now, and the power shortages meant many places closed at night anyway. The Merdeka Day celebrations had been and gone and Soekarno had declared a new stage in the revolution, which for most people meant that the rice shortages had reached epidemic proportions. No one was paid in rupiah any more, there was no point: people were demanding to be paid in rice and there wasn't enough rice to pay them. Some were simply marching into stores in mobs and helping themselves.

They were sitting at the front, by the windows, where the shutters were pulled back and Johnson's car was parked on the kerb. Harper had noticed that Johnson never went anywhere on foot any more – he was always in a car with a couple of minders in it. The People's Youth had taken to beating up foreigners.

Johnson was in his usual taciturn mood, sipping carefully at his tea, glancing out of the window from time to time. 'Things are moving fast,' he said. 'We need to speed things up a bit.'

Johnson insisted that Harper move into Hotel Indonesia, which was full of foreign journalists like Gibson and the businessmen who were prepared to overlook the rising political tensions while Jakarta was an opportunity: Soekarno was still building freeways, after all. 'We can't guarantee your safety if you stay in that guesthouse,' Johnson told Harper and Harper wanted to reply, when have you ever guaranteed my safety? Johnson would stay concerned for his well-being right up until the point when he was compromised in any way, upon which he would deny that he or any other American official had ever met or known him. Surely the visibility of being in a place like Hotel Indonesia, full of foreigners, constantly spied upon, had its own dangers?

And so, he changed identity again. He folded his sarong neatly and put it away and checked into the hotel wearing slacks and his panama, carrying a newspaper, walking with his shoulders thrown back.

'Welcome to Hotel Indonesia, sir,' said the doorman, with a deep bow.

He acknowledged the courtesy by touching his newspaper to the side of his forehead and toyed with the idea of saying, '*Ciao*.' Maybe he should learn some Italian. He'd passed for Italian before now. He knew Jews, Arabs and Asians who had pretended to be Italian. Everyone liked Italians – the food was great, the women beautiful, and they were hopeless at invading other countries.

He disliked being in a smart hotel, which almost certainly had eavesdroppers on the end of the telephone lines and apparatchiks of the government security services amongst the staff. Okay, so the air conditioning and comfortable bed were good but from a professional point of view, he felt too exposed to do his job. He couldn't operate underground now – there could be no more strolling the streets in a sarong. He began to wonder if Johnson had parked him here in such a stupidly expensive place because he had decided he didn't really have any use for him. Not for the first time, he wondered how much operations like this cost, and how the American taxpayers who funded CIA guys like Johnson would feel about it if they knew.

Then came the night Harper went down to the lobby and found that the doorman standing on the inside did not, for once, open the door wide onto the hotel driveway with a smile and a deep bow. He stood still and straight, with his arms folded and a serious expression on his face.

The assistant general manager was standing next to him with a smile. He stepped forward as Harper approached and said, 'Good evening, sir, perhaps you would like to avail yourself of the dining room or the club lounge this evening?' He indicated across the lobby with his arm wide.

'Is there anything wrong?' Harper asked, looking out onto the driveway, where sleek cars were still pulling in and disgorging smiling passengers for the nightclub on the top floor. The streets looked normal to him.

'No, not at all,' the assistant general manager replied quickly, still smiling. 'Shall we obtain you a taxi?'

It was nothing he could put his finger on, just a feeling. 'No, thank you,' he said.

Back in his room, he rotated the dial on the bedside radio receiver but only got the hotel's piped music or a blur of white noise. The white noise was odd. Soekarno's speeches were usually broadcast more or less continuously and there had been one at Senayan Stadium earlier that evening. He turned the radio off and went to the window. The huge round pond that filled the centre of the roundabout outside the hotel was in darkness, the floodlights dimmed. A few lone cars were circling it. It was as if the city was holding its breath.

In the morning, he woke to the same sensation. He went and looked out of the window. The roundabout was quiet. Normally, by this time, you would hear the stirrings of hotel staff outside in the corridor; was he imagining it or was the corridor quiet as well? After months of almost daily demonstrations, there seemed a strange absence – that crackle in the air, was it gone? Perhaps he was just tired of waiting. Nothing was more exhausting than doing nothing, after all.

The only place to find out more was the bar.

The journalists were all drinking and eating bowls of nuts for breakfast. That was when he knew. Those who monitored Radio Republik Indonesia had heard the announcement of the Communist takeover when they rose. Most of the hacks were there, apart from those who were still asleep: there was a rumour that a New Zealand correspondent known for his lunatic risk-taking in pursuit of a story had set off for Merdeka Square, where soldiers were already setting up roadblocks around the presidential palace.

He ordered a drink himself and sat on a bar stool next to a group of Australians. 'This is it boys, I tell you,' one was saying, 'the Commies are taking power and we might as well get drunk because it's bullets in the back of the head before sunset.'

'Let's wait and see,' drawled one of the others, while lifting his glass.

There was a note of hysteria amongst the hacks, Harper thought – a hysteria he did not share. After a while, he went upstairs and smoked ferociously while waiting for the phone to ring with his instructions. It didn't.

Within three days, the same journalists from that morning were in the bar celebrating. The Communist takeover had been defeated. The military were back in power. Two days later, the Generals who had been killed by the Communists during the attempted coup, or putsch, or whatever it was, were being buried with all due pomp and ceremony at Kalibata Heroes Cemetery.

Still no word from Johnson.

That afternoon, he decided to see if he could get an international line: they had been closed for some days but it was worth trying intermittently. More than once, one of the hacks had wandered into the bar crowing about his success in getting through and started an exit stampede, only for everyone to return disconsolate because the connections were down again.

Harper tried the phone in the lobby rather than the one in his room, although it was probably also bugged. There would be a low-ceilinged basement somewhere beneath the hotel, rows of desks staffed by young men with neatly combed hair and headphones pressed to one ear and a pencil in the other hand.

However often the regime changed, the same staff would be there, still taking notes. The junior apparatus of government always stayed the same, at least for a while: the notes might be delivered to a different boss, that was all. Small cogs still turned even though the big wheel above them was slowing, halting, then – without ever being entirely motionless it seemed – beginning to grind in a different direction.

'Sit tight,' said the operative who manned the Institute's phone – this was long before the days of the twenty-four-hour hotline and computerised information: the operative back home would be sitting at a desk with a list of handwritten instructions to pass on if Harper called in. 'When the situation has stabilised, we will want your analysis of how the economy will recover.'

'I would welcome the chance to gather more information on that as soon as I can,' Harper replied.

A few days later, Harper went for a walk around the side streets, just for a few minutes, to taste the air. It was a relief to be out, even briefly, away from the claustrophobic world of the hotel. As he rounded a corner on the way back, he saw a group of young men ripping down a set of handwritten posters from a wall. As they did, he glimpsed a Communist slogan. The young men were tearing the posters into shreds and jumping on them.

What surprised him was not that the young men were ripping down the posters but that the posters had been put up at all – a pointless act of provocation on the part of the PKI, he thought, if anti-Communist feeling was now at boiling point. It didn't make sense.

Daily, the radio broadcast detailed reports of the terrible things the Communist traitors had done before the brave, loyal army had succeeded in restoring order and saving the nation. After the heroic Generals had been abducted on that night, the wicked Gerwani women had cut off their testicles and danced naked in front of them, to torment them. Women Communists were even worse than the men, it would appear.

Death to the Communist traitors, the newscasters urged.

*

The following week, Johnson finally made contact. They met in a street behind the hotel, walking towards each other for a long time along an uneven sidewalk with the road on one side and a high, fissured wall made of concrete on the other. The wall was defaced with graffiti and torn posters, litter gathered around the base of the palm trees that lined the road and there was an unnatural silence in the cloudy air. Johnson nodded to him as he approached, casually, as if they had seen each other only the day before. As they drew near, they both stopped, facing each other. They folded their arms.

'Pak Parno,' Johnson said, looking from side to side as they talked.

'Who's he?'

'You don't need to know. He's well connected, that's all you need to know. Here's the address.' He handed Harper a small, folded piece of paper.

Harper opened it: Pejompongan, a street called Jalan Danau Maninjau, not far from the Naval Hospital. Harper knew the area a little, a mosque, a Catholic church, middle-class bungalows: a lot of civil servants lived round there. A naval attaché of some sort, perhaps? The navy had been heavily infiltrated by the

Communists, though, and this man was presumably on the side of the military so maybe an army or air force connection more likely?

'Go and see him this afternoon, visiting hour, get a feel for him and let him get a feel for you. If it goes okay, you'll deliver a list of names to a general who will be at his house some time next week.'

'What's the point of this visit?'

'Nothing, it's a social call, oil the wheels, you know how people here are. Buddy up to him a bit. Act like you're honoured to meet him.'

The street was empty. It seemed to be making Johnson nervous. On the other side of the road, there was a parked car with his minders in it, but he glanced around as he talked. Then he looked at his watch, said, 'Be there five pm,' and turned away.

Later that day, Harper got a *betjak* from outside the hotel. He leaned forward with his forearms resting on the bar in front of him as the driver began to pedal.

'Pejompongan long place, sir,' the driver said over his shoulder. He was an older man, wrinkled face, thinning hair, still out plying his trade, despite what was going on – if you didn't ply your trade, you didn't eat. Most of the *betjak* drivers were young men but this one had an air of being both aged and ageless.

'Just head that way, I'll tell you where to stop,' Harper said. He never told the *betjak* driver the exact address.

It was the densest, hottest part of the day; the air close, the sky hazy. The *betjak* driver had large bony knees that seemed disproportionate to his skinny legs: as he pedalled, they rose up and down alternately, like shiny balls in an arcade. Harper felt exhausted just sitting there. That man must be three times my age and half my weight, he thought, but look at him. Darkness wouldn't fall for hours, yet it already felt as if the buildings and the ground were exhaling the heat they had been absorbing all day. Even the swift pedalling of the driver couldn't rustle up a breeze.

With the streets still quiet, the journey was a lot quicker than he had anticipated. He got the driver to drop him by the river and decided to take a look around, get a feel for the area. The water was high, the colour of milky coffee; a few pieces of refuse floated in it. The monsoon season was upon them and the rain was getting heavier every day now. This river would flood soon, as most of the rivers in Jakarta did, the colonial drainage systems having long fallen into disrepair.

He hadn't been into a *kampong* since the coup and counter-coup. He crossed the rise of a precarious bridge made of bamboo and old planks, towards the slum where tumbledown shacks lined the bank, overhanging the water in places as if they might fall in at any minute. The cement wall of the river was broken in one place and a soil bank led down to the water, where women were washing clothes. Laundry was strung up everywhere around the shacks: an inside-out way of living, he always thought, in these tiny little houses, everything done communally – privacy just one in a long list of things denied the poor.

He strolled round a few squares of the *kampong*, nodding to the women sitting on steps with their children. In between the shacks and the dirt paths were small ditches intended to forestall the floodwater, with concrete slabs to allow people to cross into the shacks. The ditches were only half full now but as the daily downpours increased in intensity, the inhabitants would be first ankle-deep, then knee-deep in the brown water. A few people stared back at him, mildly, without hostility. Despite the city in ferment – the tortured Generals, the fear, the persistent tension in Merdeka Square and on the wide boulevards of central Jakarta, there seemed to be no changed atmosphere here. No one rose from a doorstep and went inside at his approach; people nodded and smiled.

A coup only happened to the people it happened to, that was what struck him then: that was what the likes of Johnson forgot. The grand events were Johnson's whole world, and his, to a certain extent, and yet to the people here, those events were a mere backdrop against the perpetual problem of where to find rice that day, how to pay for it, where to put your belongings when the river rose.

At the end of his circuit, on his way back to the bridge, he came across a group of elderly people, milky-eyed and skeletal, who stretched out their hands but were either too weak to mutter entreaties or too pessimistic to think him worth the effort. He brushed past them. A man like him giving out coins would be the talk of the *kampong*. At the sound of calling and chattering behind him, he glanced back to see he had acquired a posse of small boys, jumping and smiling. He smiled back, shook his head. They followed him, nonetheless, until he reached the bridge. As he mounted it, he looked behind to see that they had stopped on the *kampong* side, as if the river was an invisible wall that they could not pass through, although they carried on jumping and smiling and calling.

On the other side of the bridge he was immediately in the area of middle-class bungalows where this Parno man lived. He was hot and thirsty now, regretting his walk around. He hoped Parno would serve something cold.

Only two minutes from the river, the streets were quiet. The bungalows were long and low with the same terracotta-tiled roof running the length of the *blok*. Parno's building was at the end, tucked into a corner. As he approached it, he could hear the distant, hypnotic gongs of gamelan, fading – it was a sound that filled him with a strange calm. He must have heard it as a child, he thought. This had been a quirk of his few months on Java: new sights, new sounds, new smells, but so many of them tugged at something in him, some unconscious memory, or maybe he just felt as though they should.

As he pushed through a little wrought-iron gate and stepped into the courtyard, the door swung open. A young man in a beige shirt, a civil service clerk, possibly, stood behind it, head bowed. As Harper stepped over the threshold, the young man held out his hand for his hat.

He handed the young man the panama he wore when he wasn't trying to 'pass', as Gregor would have put it, and turned to see that behind the door was a stuffed tiger fastened to a wooden plinth, a whole tiger, somewhat battered, in an unnatural position, sitting up with its teeth bared and glass eyes staring in the way that only glass eyes can, motionless but somehow not entirely inanimate.

'Is there anything more sad than a stuffed tiger?'

Harper turned to see a light-skinned mixed-race woman in a Western cocktail dress, oiled black hair drawn back from carved features and gold drop earrings hanging from her earlobes.

'All that power, now just sand inside,' she said, and turned away from him. He followed her into the room to their left. As they entered she turned to him and said, 'My husband is here,' then went through a door on the other side of the room.

Pak Parno was seated behind a large desk wearing a batik shirt in purple and gold. He stayed seated as Harper walked towards the desk and gestured at his wife as she left the room. 'My wife is very beautiful,' he said casually. Harper watched Parno's wife as she walked out of the room. From behind, she was as skinny as a garden rake; no arse to her at all. 'She's from a good family, too.'

This observation seemed to amuse him and he chuckled to himself, rose and came round to Harper's side of the desk, extending his hand. He was as rotund as Harper had expected, although not as short. 'A wife is a great blessing, Mr Harper, although I understand you are as yet unmarried.' He smiled broadly.

Harper gave a small bow. 'That is true.'

'Perhaps you will find a nice Javanese wife.'

Parno gestured to a three-piece suite arranged Western-style. They seated themselves and Parno's wife returned with a silver tray on which were two heavy crystal glasses and a carafe. When she had placed it on the coffee table, she poured for them both, then turned to the mantelpiece above the fireplace where there was a cigar box.

He knew this routine: whisky, cigars, a little manly talk. Parno was the kind of bureaucrat who prided himself on living a westernised lifestyle but a reasonably modest one – there would be no gold taps in the bathroom. It was his relative modesty that would allow him to do deals to the benefit of friends and relatives. You didn't hand a man like Parno a briefcase full of cash; he would be insulted. You offered a job opportunity to his nephew. That way, he got to feel munificent, not corrupt. There were always ways of corrupting those who didn't want to feel corrupt. In many ways, they were the easiest to corrupt of all.

'So, Mr Harper,' Parno said as they sipped their drinks. 'What do you think? If it comes to a fight with Malaysia, what is your view?' Parno had already done two things: let Harper know he knew some personal information about him and indicated that they would not be discussing recent events in Jakarta. He was sticking to a safe subject. *Konfrontasi*: the political classes here liked to discuss it in the same way the Brits discussed the weather, as a polite opener.

Harper's view was that the sabre-rattling across the Malacca Strait would come to nothing. 'I wouldn't like to say . . .' he replied politely, raising his hands. 'The British are famously stubborn. The only thing they really understand is when other people are stubborn to them in return.'

'That is true, Mr Harper, very true.'

He let Parno lead the conversation but hoped that the point would soon come when he would move things forward, and eventually, Parno leaned towards him and lowered his voice, a little melodramatically Harper thought, and said, 'So, how soon can your friends provide us with the list?'

He paused. He had learned a thing or two from Gregor. 'The list is already prepared.'

Parno's face gave nothing away. 'How many, Mr Harper?'

'Eight hundred. Individuals, not families.' The Americans had been working on the lists of Communists and their sympathisers for years – eventually the names would run to thousands, from the top down. Aiding the provision of such a list would ensure Parno a secure position in the new regime. He imagined that however calm the man's exterior, he must be quite excited. But then Parno surprised him.

'And how accurate, do you suppose, is this list?'

Who would think a man like Parno would concern himself with accuracy? Surely it was quantity, not quality, that mattered here.

'That isn't my concern,' Harper replied. *Nor yours.*

Parno paused. His face became heavy. He was, after all, a man who allowed shadows to cross his heart, Harper thought. Perhaps I have misjudged him.

'When?'

'The end of next week.'

'And who will bring it?'

'I'll bring the list myself. But the handover has to be personal, to the General. My employers want an assurance from me about that. I am here today to receive that assurance from you so we can proceed.'

Parno raised his eyebrows very slightly. Officially, Harper had come as supplicant: unofficially, they both knew that the power in this conversation worked the other way around. Harper sensed in Parno a keenness that their transaction should be about more than the practicalities. He was a conviction bureaucrat, it would appear, not just a man on the make.

'You're an American. How did you learn Indonesian?' Parno said.

'I was born on Sulawesi, in forty-two.' Harper offered. 'Spent a bit of time here in Jakarta after the war, then my parents and I emigrated to the US. My father had relatives who sponsored us. Chicago.'

'Ah, great pity, great misfortune not to be Javanese.' Parno was chuckling again. The Javanese thought the only island worth being born on was Java: on other islands, the Javanese got blamed for everything. 'Your parents did well to get out, considering what the Dutch did to us after.' There was some none-too-subtle point-scoring in this remark: Parno would be wondering why Harper's parents hadn't stayed and fought for independence but it would have been risky for Harper to invent a cover story like that. Parno had probably fought himself, been imprisoned. If Harper claimed his parents had too, Parno would want to know all the details of what they had done, where they had done it and with whom.

'You know how backward Dutch thinking is? A few of them get locked up by the Japanese and afterwards they think that means it's justified to take our lands all over again . . .' There was genuine hatred in Parno's tone, as there so often was when Indonesian conversation turned to the Dutch. Harper's cover story never went near his Dutch roots. He would have had a bullet to the back of the head down some alleyway long before now if it had. Parno tossed back his whisky. 'They got off pretty lightly.'

Harper wondered if his father felt he was getting off lightly as he was forced to kneel on the dusty ground by a screaming Japanese soldier – or his mother, for that matter, who had been a starving young widow when she gave birth to him in a flooded shack full of cockroaches.

'But tell me something . . .'

If he uses the phrase *we are both men of the world*, Harper thought to himself, I will get up and leave right now.

'Tell me, is it true that there are people still out there hunting Nazis, after all these years? There is always something bad happening in the world. And yet there are men hunting down those Germans all over the world twenty years later, is that true? Even in South America, I believe?'

'I believe so,' Harper said.

Parno shook his head. 'The Jews, you can bet they won't ever forget. Hasn't it been proved half those stories were made up?'

'Well,' said Harper, mildly, 'the documented evidence is that it was pretty bad.'

A look of scorn crossed Parno's face. 'Why is it Westerners think a Jew child being murdered is worse than a child of ours, ha?' He lifted his fingers and rubbed them together.

Harper looked at Parno's face, which was a mask of certainty – and then it came to him what this conversation was really about. Parno was thinking of what would happen to the people whose names were on that list, them and their children. That was what was behind all this; the man had a conscience and he, Harper, was supposed to relieve it in order that they should get the deal done. Perhaps he should mention another name to Parno: Stalin. Maybe they could talk about what might happen in the Soviet Bloc now they'd kicked out Khrushchev. Perhaps if they discussed the people trying to scramble over the bloody great wall that had sliced Berlin in half, then Parno wouldn't feel so bad about handing over a list of Commies to the military. While he was at it, Parno could usefully dwell on what would have happened to him and his family if the Communists had pulled off their coup – whatever his official post, his connections to the Generals would be well known; the army and the civil service were full of PKI informants from top to bottom. It was easy to have moral qualms about people who were going to be arrested when you were on the side that was in power. Such qualms were a luxury allowed only to the winners. If Parno was in a football stadium now, on his knees with his hands tied behind his back, would he be worrying about the health of the youth in the red bandana who had the pistol pressed against his temple? He'd be lucky if a pistol was how they did it.

He felt weary. He hadn't eaten much that day, it was too sweltering, and the whisky – quite good whisky – was swimming in his head, and he had smoked a cigar even though he didn't particularly like them. Parno wanted to inveigle him into a discussion that would make himself feel better: he felt like grabbing Parno by the lapels and bringing his face up to his, nose to nose, holding him there and saying, *don't you understand, it's not my job to make you feel better and it's not your job to feel bad in the first place? It isn't our job to think or feel anything. Haven't you got it?*

They talked for a little more, then he began yawning conspicuously. He knew it might cause offence but the afternoon was getting late. He didn't want to end up here as dusk fell, curfew – the last thing he wanted was to be stuck here for the night.

Parno said, 'You are welcome to stay, have dinner with us, stay the night.'

'Regrettably, I must decline. I am expected elsewhere.'

Parno smiled broadly, as if they were old friends. 'My wife will be disappointed. Say goodbye to her at least,' he said, clapping him on the shoulder as they rose.

They went out into the hallway: across it was another sitting room. Through the doorway, they could see Parno's wife, waiting in a chair. Her forearms were resting along the arms of the chair in a pose that he guessed she had adopted when she heard the door to the sitting room open. She looked at them but did not rise. Her gaze was as glassy as that of the tiger. He looked back at her but she showed no sign of recognising him as the man she had greeted just over an hour ago. She opened her mouth, and from her wide, glossy lips, a small but dense cloud of white smoke came, an exhaled haze. Then he saw that between two fingers of her right hand, a hand-rolled cigarette of some sort was resting, drooping a little, the ash at its tip in a perilous downward curve.

Her vulnerability at that moment inspired a brief flush of desire, but he had indicated he wanted to leave and, in any case, needed to report back as soon as possible. He and Parno had arranged a handover. He bowed to her, a little, and turned back to the ornate wooden hallway, where Parno was smiling broadly and pointing at the stuffed tiger, on top of whose head Parno's wife had rested his slightly battered panama hat.

He took another *betjak* back and got it to drop him on the other side of the Hotel Indonesia roundabout. The traffic had picked up again and he walked alongside the slow procession of cars wheeling round the roundabout and past the ruined bulk of the British Embassy, now boarded up and deserted, the graffiti on the walls, *CRUSH BRITISH IMPERIALISTS,* scrawled and faded. He wondered how long it would be before that was scrubbed off and the embassy reopened, now the military were back in power.

In the lobby, two German businessmen were smoking and talking loudly – from their gestures he guessed they were arguing about whether or not it was safe to leave the hotel that evening.

As he walked down the corridor to his room, where, he knew, the air that was waiting for him would taste as though it had been breathed in and out again by a hundred previous occupants, he thought of Parno's wife and wondered, briefly, if he should try ordering up a working girl, like so many of the journalists and businessmen did. In the bar downstairs, they bragged about which antibiotics they preferred. But then he thought of the glassy, stuffed-tiger look in those girls' eyes, looks that were undisguised by their toothy smiles and chatter, and what was the point of having something that was handed to you on a plate? The whole point was the chase, wasn't it? The act was fifteen minutes, tops. Prostitutes were for middle-aged men, fat men, men who couldn't get a woman any other way. Surely it was demeaning to pay? He'd rather sort himself out: at least you didn't have to worry about making stilted conversation with the handkerchief.

He could go down to the bar, perhaps, but at this time of the evening it would be rammed with journalists. They had become unbearable recently, full of self-congratulation: they were the right men in the right place at the right time, war heroes for just being in Jakarta even though they had spent the days of the coup stuck in the hotel like Harper and the worst hardship that had befallen them was the temporary failure of the air conditioning. Luckily for them, the hotel had its own generator and things had been fixed in a jiffy. Crisis over. Now it looked like the situation might stabilise here, they were all desperate to get to Vietnam, talked gleamingly of how dangerous it was, as if there weren't enough danger in Jakarta still, as if the Indonesians being rounded up on the streets and loaded into trucks weren't newsworthy in comparison with the next large political event elsewhere. He pitied their wives when they got back home. He would rather spend an evening with Parno than with the hacks, any day. For all his vanities and prejudices, Parno was at least a man living in his own country and making his decisions, good or bad, within that context. Parno would rise or fall by those decisions. While Parno was facing the consequences of his chosen allegiances, one way or another, the hacks would be in another bar somewhere in another international hotel, visiting another country's tragedy. In fact, weren't all men repellent, really? That was why they went to prostitutes. It wasn't just physical relief they were after – it was relief from the company of their own kind, from themselves.

He stood in the corridor and felt around the doorframe to his room, checking that the small piece of paper he always left in different positions between the door and the frame was still in place. So, he thought, as he located it, after all these months, I'm actually getting something done, maybe even meeting a General.

Inside the room, he went over to the dial and turned on the air conditioning, then did what he always did, went to the bed, flopped on his back and closed his eyes; breathing, waiting for the clinking, clunking air-conditioning box to stir the air and quell his claustrophobia.

It was Johnson who gave him the list, the last time he would see that strange blank of a man. The handover took place in a cemetery.

Harper had his canvas holdall with him. He had checked out of Hotel Indonesia and bought a moped so small he had to bend his long legs high like a cricket. In the shimmering air, the stink of gas was intensified – whenever he kicked down on the ignition, he did so gingerly, as if the hot metal he was perched on might burst into flames. Considering how much danger there was on the streets, it would be damn stupid to be immolated by your own motorcycle.

After delivering the list to Parno's house, he was going straight to the airport – they were posting him to Bali so that he could take over from the operative there, who was being sent to check out the smaller islands. He would have to make a phone call before he left to ensure the road was safe – he might need to ditch the moped and go in an army jeep: an Indo in Western clothes on his own on a moped would be a little too intriguing for the militiamen who had set up checkpoints all the way along the road. Officially, the airport was still closed but there was rumoured to be a flight some time in the afternoon and he had enough dollars on him to bribe his way onto it if he ever got there. His instructions were clear. The Americans wanted him off Java when this job was done – that was the whole point of the embassy using a middleman. The next list would be someone else's problem. He was just one of many middlemen.

His holdall was slung diagonally across his chest and the strap was rubbing his shoulder where he was sweating through his thin shirt. He drove down the lane that ran alongside the cemetery wall – scrubby fields with bushes and trees on the other side. The lane was deserted at this hour. As he turned the corner along the path to the cemetery entrance, he saw a battered Borgward van parked at the far end, close to the junction with the main road. That would be Johnson's minders.

Harper bumped the moped into the cemetery, a little way down the path, so he could park it where he could keep an eye on it. On the far side, there was a small family group around a grave, some women with covered heads, but they took no notice of him. He dismounted and sat on a nearby bench, lit a cigarette and waited. The cemetery was walled on all sides – there was a gate in the middle of each side and the wall was no more than head height. The wall gave the illusion of seclusion from the rest of the city and here, amongst the graves and the palm trees lining the wide paths, he experienced a moment of calm, a chance to draw breath from the tension of journeying the streets.

Johnson appeared in the gateway before Harper had finished his cigarette: he had a canvas bag slung over his shoulder and his bald head gleamed in the heat. He glanced around, saw the moped first, then Harper, acknowledged him with a brief nod as he walked towards him and sat down next to him on the bench. Harper offered his cigarette packet. Johnson declined by pulling a face. Harper wondered what Johnson's vices were. He was suspicious of men who made a show of not drinking or smoking or womanising – the ones who wanted everyone to observe how clean-cut they were. What secret desires was Johnson suppressing beneath that shiny skull? What sort of heart beat beneath that shirt, cleaner and less crumpled than any shirt should be in this heat (apart from his bald head, the man didn't even break a sweat)? Boys, perhaps? Maybe he liked to be whipped while wearing women's underwear. Whatever it is, Harper thought, I bet he prays afterwards.

Johnson reached into his bag and brought out a small leather case, like a satchel without a strap, and handed it over. 'Don't look inside.' It was said genially enough. 'You're getting out this afternoon?' Johnson added.

'Yes,' Harper said, 'that's the plan, depends on how long the handover takes, maybe tomorrow or the day after, it'll be tight. You?'

'They're keeping me here till things are stabilised.' Johnson sighed. 'It's bad out there.' He was looking towards the cemetery gate but he meant out there in the world, in the backstreets of Jakarta, out in the towns and the villages in Central and East Java where people were being rounded up, anyone who was or who had ever been a Communist, anyone connected with anyone who was or who had ever been. Harper didn't think about it. It wasn't his job to think about it.

It occurred to him that Johnson and Parno had a great deal in common. He wondered if Johnson was about to launch into a man-to-man chat with him in the same way Parno had, if the thought of the men and women kneeling next to ditches by the sides of the roads with their hands tied behind their backs was bothering his conscience in the same way the thought of them bothered Parno.

Johnson rose from the bench. 'Don't fuck up,' he said, then turned and walked down the path.

Later, when he was being debriefed back in Holland, they asked him about Jakarta. They asked him about the things he had witnessed, how he had had to abandon the moped, the chaos and danger of getting across town and the delay in the handover and leaving Java. Two of them came to visit him at the Rest Home in the country, the big house with light, airy rooms that had floor-to-ceiling windows and views across the fields. They sat holding clipboards and filled in sheets of paper as they asked him for a detailed account of everything that had happened, first on Java, then on Bali. They understood, they said, that he didn't feel up to writing the report himself.

'Why did it take you two days to get to the airport?' one said.

He looked at them blankly, trying to keep the disdain from his face. 'The purge had begun by then. Two days was a miracle. I was lucky to get there at all and even luckier to get on a plane.'

Then they asked him about what had happened in the rice fields on Bali and he told them what they needed to know.

'And why did you disappear, then?' one of them said softly. 'You were off the radar for weeks, then came home via California. Why not the usual route? Why not contact us and let us get you out via Karachi?'

He had had to lie low in the highlands for two months, after what had happened at Komang's house – and it was true, in all that time, he had made no effort to contact the Institute, not even to let them know he was still alive. 'I had business in Los Angeles, personal business.' They hadn't pushed him on that one.

The men from the Institute were mostly interested in the facts, what he had done when. The doctors were interested in the pictures. The doctors asked him about the severed heads he had seen by the side of the road as he passed through Balinese villages. They asked him about the charred corpses hanging from trees with signs around their necks that decorated crossroads everywhere in Jakarta. On his way to the airport, he had seen one such corpse being beaten by a young man holding a collapsible chair. The doctors, so urbane: each of them had an air of practicality that, at times, bordered on scepticism, especially that bearded one, what was his name? In the middle of Harper's businesslike description of a row of shops that had human hands on strings dangling from the front of the overhanging roof, the bearded doctor had looked at him and said, 'Hands on *strings*? How is that possible?'

Later, Harper was to pretend that was what it was, the body parts; that was what was troubling him, that was where *they* had come from, the images that made him wake in the night, snapping from sleep to full consciousness in a split second, as he did for two years after his return home: lying there, his eyes wide open in the dark.

He decided to take the backstreets to Pejompongan. The sun was high, the air close, a storm was brewing for later that day: the stink of sewage from the canals stirred up by the monsoon rain and the burning rubbish from the backs of shops and houses, the humidity, all created a miasma that slowed traffic, slowed movement. Jakarta's daily thunderstorm was gathering. If it broke before he made it out to Parno's, his chances of getting to the airport later were slim, even in an army jeep.

He had only been riding for fifteen minutes or so since he

had left the cemetery, not exactly sure in which direction he was headed, following his nose down the twists and turns of side streets. At the end of a narrow road, he eased the moped to a halt and left the engine running while he lifted the edge of his shirt and wiped his face.

He dropped the shirt and looked up – and it was then that he saw them, four young men at the end of the road, no more than fifty metres away, facing him, staring at him, in positions of aggressive query. One of them, a tall one on the left, was holding a club; another was holding what looked like a table leg. Behind their tableau, at the end of the street, people were running past, a group of young women, a mixed group of men and women, two men – all his age and younger, and from somewhere in the streets out of sight came the unmistakeable sound of panic, the murmur of a crowd in danger, the occasional pop of gunfire, a shout or a scream. In the second or two it took to absorb all this, he was also making a calculation: in the time it would take him to kick the moped into action and turn in the narrow dirt road, which was covered in loose scree – the scree would make it impossible to do it too quickly without the risk of falling off – the young men, poised, tipped forward, could reach him.

And then it was happening. They were running at him – and he had no idea who they were or who they thought he was, only that they were a pack and if he hesitated for a second, they would be upon him.

He was still taking the decision to abandon the moped as he swung his leg over and ran back down the alley, still thinking maybe he should stay on it while his long legs sped to and fro with the satisfying speed endowed by adrenaline – and despite the sudden and apparent danger, there was a kind of joy in that run. He had spent two years in the Dutch army, he was a trained man with a long stride, these were just boys. He was nearly back at the other end of the narrow road, nearly out into the crowded main street, when one of the boys was on his heels and must have grabbed at the holdall on his back because he was flying backwards, turning as he did, landing on his side in the dirt and in the same moment, a blow – it was so sudden and ferocious he could not tell what or who from – landed on the side of his head and slammed the other side of it into the dirt. There was a moment of blackness, and when that had passed, he was curled in a ball on the ground, his arms crossed over his head to protect it, and they were beating him with the clubs and kicking him and shouting.

'*Ampun-ampun!*' he shouted, and for another moment or two, they did not hear him and continued – one landed an excruciating blow in the middle of his back that made him snap back, reversing the arc of his body in one swift movement.

Then they stopped and were shouting at each other, speaking with such speed he couldn't understand what they were saying, and when he opened his eyes he saw that one of them, the tall one, had his arm across the chest of the one next to him, holding him back – they were having a ferocious argument of some sort. Harper rolled gingerly onto his knees but he knew that if he tried to rise, they would beat him to the ground. He tried to think of a whole sentence, *brothers I am with you, I am your cousin*, but his mouth wasn't working. He lifted a hand and touched his chin, which was swollen and covered in dirt. He spat and there were strings of blood amidst the spittle.

Then they were gone. They had run off down the alley, back the way they had come. As he watched them go, he saw one of them stop by the moped and lift it from where it lay on its side, the engine still grumbling. It was the smallest youth – thirteen or fourteen years of age, perhaps. He sat on the moped and tried to kick it into life and was shouting at the others to come back and help. Harper hauled himself to his feet and loped off in the other direction, the holdall bumping against his back. He didn't look back.

The main street was still busy with fleeing people but nobody stopped him as he walked against the tide, head down. When he glanced up, he was careful not to make eye contact with anyone. He glimpsed a huge pall of smoke rising from a few streets away. Any building with Communist associations was being set on fire, and sometimes just any building. There was the stink of burnt rubber from somewhere: then as he was looking at the smoke, a herd of young men similar to the ones who had attacked him ran down the street – they were slightly older than the others; students, he guessed, dressed in trousers with white shirts, waving objects in the air, sticks and batons, and shouting gleefully to each other, shoving each other. Driving behind them was an army jeep with six soldiers in the back, waving and smiling. It was a hunting party and their prey was PKI. Such a group became more than the sum of its parts. They wouldn't care about any list.

Harper moved closer to the wall but kept walking, looking at the ground. He could smell paraffin. Buildings set alight almost always meant people set alight too.

The moped didn't matter. He could find some other way of getting out to Parno's. He had the holdall, covered in dirt and battered, but intact, and with the leather case still inside it, that was all that mattered. His bruises would heal. And he didn't think his back was broken – but every time he moved his left leg, arrows of pain shot up his side, torn ligaments perhaps? With each stab of pain, a wave of nausea and dizziness gripped him.

He needed to get off the streets. A man who looked as though he had barely escaped with his life from a beating was offering himself up to the next lot who wanted to finish the job.

He turned a corner: a side street, a small mosque on the corner, an administrative building next to it, at the end of it another corner, and at once he was in a quieter district, on the edge of a *kampong* but still adjacent to the main roads. Safe for a moment, he paused at the end of a street that was, when life was normal, a small, local market. It was closed and unnaturally deserted. The stalls were boarded with whatever might have been to hand: some with properly constructed wooden shutters or doors. Other families had made makeshift attempts to protect what little they had by nailing broken boards and bamboo poles in criss-cross patterns across the front. Yet others, who could not protect the open area of their stalls, had simply stripped every object from the shelves. In the back rooms, plastic buckets and wooden carvings and boxes of fruit would be piled high and, amongst them, he guessed, families cowering, waiting for things to become calm again. The stink of burnt rubber and paraffin drifted over this area too. Amidst the chaos, though, lives still had to be led, children calmed and fed. Somewhere further along the market street, someone was cooking: beneath the stench he could smell coconut oil and dried fish, smoke and spices.

Without warning, rain dropped from the sky, falling in a sudden solid waterfall. He tipped his head back and opened his mouth to catch the water, letting the hard fat drops wash the dirt and blood from his face. He would have liked to stay there until he was soaked but couldn't risk the rain seeping through the tough canvas of his holdall and into the leather case.

At the end of the market street was a ragged shack, sloping and derelict. Through the empty porch area, there was a broken door that wasn't even boarded – it opened easily, half on its hinges. Behind the door was a small square room of the sort a large family would sleep in, head to toe; a dirt floor, an empty wooden crate and a single broken plastic sandal in one corner – recently abandoned, he guessed. Given how overcrowded the *kampong* were, it was unusual to find anything empty. He wondered why the family had fled.

At the other side of the room was a narrow open doorway for ventilation, with no covering. He went and looked out. The room backed onto a canal, not one of the grand ones built for the smarter areas of town or even the river that delineated Parno's area from the *kampong* but a small, shallow one, little better than a drainage ditch. To the left, it stretched back along the length of the market street: to the right, it bent away, the view blocked by other shacks. He wondered how many men, women and children had slept here unprotected from the mosquitoes, the bad odours from the still water, the diseases it harboured.

As he stepped back, he felt his knees start to shake. It was kicking in. It had been an elementary part of training, both when he did his national service and at the Institute. One of the most dangerous parts of danger comes when you think you are safe again: that is the point where the adrenaline will drain away and you will feel hungry, thirsty and completely exhausted. He had thought he was just finding somewhere to shelter from the rain, but he realised he had crawled like a wounded animal into a hole.

He pulled the holdall over his head, dropped to his knees. He was beginning to shiver. He opened the holdall and found the few balls of *klepon*, wrapped in paper, that he had taken from the hotel restaurant that morning. They were already collapsing and had leaked through the paper. He unwrapped them as best he could and crammed two of them into his mouth, the sweet stickiness of them dissolving into glue. He pulled out a cotton jacket and put it on: it was clean but could be sacrificed. There was the thin towel he had taken from his room, too small for his purposes but better than nothing. He put the towel down on the dirt floor and lay stretched out, tucking the holdall underneath his head as a pillow, closing his eyes.

When he stirred again, it was dusk. Everything hurt. He moved his left leg, carefully, but it was so stiff he felt he might break a bone trying to shift it. His arms both ached – why his arms? He couldn't even remember being struck there. When he arched his back, he could almost feel the vertebrae cracking. His head throbbed. The thought that he had to raise himself and complete his mission made him want to throw up. It was still raining. Darkness would fall soon. There was no chance he could make it to Parno's now. He would have to shelter until dawn broke. The delay wouldn't cause alarm at Parno's end; with the streets in chaos, it was touch and go whether the General himself would have been there today, or at all. He might have got to Parno's only to find he had to wait there for a week.

The dirt floor of the shack was slightly raised from the street, otherwise he would have woken in a mud bath. When he went to the opening in the back, the rain was still falling onto the brown water of the canal, but it was easing. It would stop soon, then there would be a little dull light before darkness fell and the huge yellow moon of Jakarta rose in the sky: it always stayed low it seemed, like a mother keeping a close eye on her children.

He went back into the shack, ate the rest of the *klepon*, then sat on his backside and did a slow inventory of his body, starting with his left foot and working his way up each of his legs in turn, checking for swelling and bruising. He kept a tiny round mirror in his toilet bag, half of a woman's powder compact that he had detached from the other half after one of his short-lived liaisons had left it behind at his apartment in Amsterdam. He remembered snapping it in two, after she'd gone, tossing the powder half into a wastepaper basket and thinking, a tiny mirror, that could be useful. He cleaned it with the edge of his shirt, which made it more dirty, spat on it, cleaned it again, and then, in the indistinct smear of his own spittle, examined his face. His chin was misshapen. There was a long graze on one side, near his hairline – but he didn't look nearly as bad as he felt. He probed his left cheekbone in an exploratory manner, decided it wasn't smashed. He would wash his face properly the next morning, when dawn broke, in the canal. There was a clean shirt in the holdall. He would change into that before he set out.

Once his inventory of himself was done, he checked through each of his belongings, then, perhaps because he was feeling scornful about Johnson and Parno and all those men he dealt with who did most of their business sitting in the safety of houses or offices, he did something unprofessional. He pulled the leather case out of the canvas holdall and unzipped it, and took out the list of names.

He had expected it to be handwritten – you wouldn't think there were any typists left holed up in the American Embassy with its rolls of barbed wire outside. Instead, the list was typed on lined paper torn from a large notepad, the sort of very thin paper where the dot on the 'i' key had made pinprick holes. There were around thirty sheets, held together on the left-hand side by two small bulldog clips. He unfastened them and held up one of the sheets of paper: the tiny holes in it created minuscule white beams. There were twenty-five to thirty names on each sheet. The names were on the left, then underneath them was a one-word note. *Member* for a PKI party member. *Official* for someone they thought was higher up in the party. The names didn't appear to be in any sort of order. The officials might be conviction Communists, Harper thought, but most of the members were probably peasants and workers who thought it might get them a few hours off *corvée* labour. A couple of names had *PRIORITY* typed in capitals underneath – they would be the ones the military really wanted. *Priority* could mean, to be shot immediately, or to be kept alive for questioning. After the names were numbers in brackets, *(4)* or *(2)* or *(9)*. Sometimes, there was just a question mark, *(?)*.

In the middle of the page was a list of addresses or sometimes just the single word for a street or district. After the addresses, there was a third column that had handwritten annotations in fine pencil. Harper peered at them but couldn't decipher the tight scrawl. Eight hundred names, on this list alone: eight hundred people.

It was only after he had clipped the sheaf of paper back into place, brushed at a little dirt that had transferred onto it from his hands and replaced it in the leather case, that he realised what the numbers in brackets probably meant: family members, wives, children, cousins or servants, anyone else in the household who might be of interest.

He stood and walked towards the opening, the leather case still in his hands. Outside, the rain had stopped and darkness had fallen. The moon would rise soon.

He crouched down on his haunches and rested his back, wincing as he did, against the precarious wall of the shack. He wrapped his arms around the leather case and clutched it to his chest. He closed his eyes.

The sheaf of paper he was holding against his heart, his beating heart, the list of names: he was holding death. He was death.

He kept his eyes closed. It was still unnaturally quiet for early evening in Jakarta but around him, he could hear people stirring in the shacks; a woman called out and then was silent, a baby or toddler let out a half-hearted, old-sounding cry.

He thought of Parno, waiting in his bungalow, with his wife and his stuffed tiger. He thought of the people on the list, who were somewhere eating a meal or sleeping or talking to their children. He thought of the secretary who had typed it, the one whose fingers had come down so firmly on the clacketty typewriter that the 'i' key had made those holes in the paper. He thought of a room full of men in suits, all seated around a big oval table, with coffee and ashtrays on it, clipboards, an expensive watch that the man in charge had detached from his wrist and placed in front of him in order to keep an eye on the time because he didn't quite trust the wall clock, which was no way near as expensive as his watch. He thought of a soldier, somewhere in a barrack, here in Jakarta, cleaning a gun. Someone, somewhere, was checking the oil on the engine of the jeep that would transport that soldier to the addresses now in Harper's possession.

He opened his eyes. The moon had risen. Its glow lit the surface of the canal. If he leaned out over the water, he would be able to see a version of himself, reflected.

Of all the people he had just thought of, he was, as far as he knew, the only one in possession of the list. Perhaps there was a copy somewhere, perhaps there wasn't. It would be egotistical to think of himself as the sole possessor of it, surely? He was nothing more than a courier. He wasn't going to kill anyone. But put all the people he had just thought about – and him – together, and collectively they were going to kill all eight hundred people on this list, and their families: (4) or (2) or (9).

Those people were going to be killed anyway. The list might speed things up a bit, that's all – and think of all the people who would have been killed if the Communists had succeeded in taking power. A man like him wasn't a policy-maker. The big decisions could only be made by people who had all the facts. He, Harper, only knew a tiny percentage of the story – you had to look at the big picture, after all. He had been hired to pick up a leather case and deliver it somewhere else. If he hadn't been hired to do that job, then someone else would have been.

He stared at the surface of the canal, flat and black as oil, glossy in the moonlight, and it came to him that he did, after all, have a choice. He could stand up and with one swing of his arm, using hardly any force at all, toss the leather case into the water in front of him, where it would float for no more than a second. In the chaos of Jakarta, it was easy for a man to fail in what he set out to do. In the time it would take for another list to be drawn up or copied, another handover to be arranged, perhaps a handful of people would be warned and disappear, escape to the country – who knew?

Further down the canal, there came the laughter of some girls. They would have slipped out under the cover of darkness to protect their modesty, now the mobs had quietened and the smell of burning had been dampened by the rain. They would be bathing and washing their hair in the black water where everyone urinated and rubbish was thrown, where the canal was opaque enough to hide all manner of secrets.

He stared at the water. The only secret the canal would hide that night would be that he had realised he had a choice. He went back inside the shack. He put the leather case back into his holdall and then bunched the holdall up so that it formed a pillow. He laid his head on it and slept for some time, opening his eyes later while it was still dark, then lying there, waiting for dawn.

Two days later, handover done, he was having a beer with Abang by the Bali Beach Hotel and thinking that it was the best beer of his life. *Blood sinks into sand really fast.*

Afterwards, Abang drove him to his bungalow in Denpasar, only ten minutes from the centre of town but in a wide, tree-lined street behind some of the old buildings, now closed and boarded. Few people were out and about: two elderly men, shirtless and wiry, in bamboo hats and sarongs, digging at something in one of the ditches by the side of the road; a woman walking with a huge cloth bundle balanced on her head, her compact figure swaying a little with the effort, her hands loose by her side. As they drove past, he glanced back, to see if she was beautiful, but she was older than she looked from behind. Denpasar struck him as unnaturally quiet.

Abang had stayed with a family in the Chinese district for a bit – it was a good way of finding out what was happening on the ground, he said, but it got too dangerous after a while. 'The British have this phrase, you know this one? A bird in a coal mine. The little yellow birds.'

'Canary. Canary in a coal mine.'

'That's it.'

Abang made a point of moving lodgings every three months. People forgot their suspicions about you once you moved – even if they remembered you, your absence rendered you innocuous.

The bungalow was set back from the road, hidden behind a head-height wall in its turn obscured by tall bushes. The doors in the narrow stone entranceway were thick carved wood – the hinges creaked as they pushed their way through. Never oil the hinges, always scatter gravel beneath your doors and windows: these were the ways you made yourself secure without anyone knowing that was what you were doing. As they crossed the small lush garden and approached the front porch, he saw there was a young woman kneeling on the step preparing an offering. She smiled at Abang and Abang smiled back, then said something to her in a language Harper didn't know. The young woman bent over the offering, eyes closed, for a moment, then rose from the step and, in a bowed position, backed away down the path.

Inside, the bungalow was clean and plain. Abang extended his arm and Harper sat on a low, wooden two-seater with woven cushions. Abang went out back and returned with two bottles of beer – he handed one to Harper, they gestured *cheers!* at each other, then Abang went over to an old filing cabinet against one wall that had a wide, shallow bowl on top full of incense sticks and limp petals with curled brown edges. He tilted the bowl and from underneath it withdrew a thin notebook, which he tossed over to Harper. 'Back inside page.'

There was a name and the description of a village, a diagram sketched lightly in pencil.

'That's the village, Komang lives just outside it,' Abang said, walking over to and sitting next to him. He pointed at the page. 'He's our contact in the district. He's very well connected with the neighbouring villages, sits on the Irrigation Committee and his cousin is Big Man in the next village. His brother-in-law is a civil servant over in Klungkung Town.'

'Why's he working for us? What's in it for him?' Harper asked.

Abang shrugged. 'Decent type, family man, worried about PKI land grabs. The peasants are worried too because they are loyal to the old landowners. They don't really get the idea of parcelling up the land even though they are going to get some. Komang isn't a peasant though, far from it, and he should have been fine, he has status, but trouble is, his brother joined the PKI last year, it's widely known. Once the round-ups of Communists start here, that whole family is in trouble.'

'Can't we get a message to the military? Leave him alone?'

Abang shook his head. 'Doesn't work like that here. It'll be the local militia comes for him. Once that lot get going, they work pretty much on their own initiative.'

'Ah.' Harper took his own small, leather-bound notebook from his back pocket and a stub of pencil and, holding Abang's notebook open with one hand on one knee and his own on the other, began to copy down the details in the tiny, illegible scrawl he had developed for himself, a personal mix of English, Dutch, Indonesian, some Javanese he knew and a few words and abbreviations of his personal invention. If his notebook fell into the wrong hands – well, good luck to the man who had to try and decipher it.

When he looked up, he saw that Abang had gone to the open door that led out to the front porch and was leaning against the doorpost, looking out, silhouetted in the light from the garden, a bulky man with something of a paunch, a half-distracted air. He gave the impression of solidity, trustworthiness – even geniality in different circumstances, Harper thought: a favourite-uncle type. Abang lit a *kretek* and then stood staring out towards the street, smoking. Harper had a feeling he was thinking about the young woman who had beaten such a hasty retreat as they arrived, wondering what would happen to her once he had left, perhaps? Then Abang glanced back and caught Harper looking at him.

'Sorry.' He patted a pocket.

'It's okay,' Harper said. 'In a bit.'

Abang drew on the cigarette. 'I'm not sorry to be getting out of Denpasar before it all kicks off here, you know.'

'I'll be up country by then.'

'Yeah, I wouldn't count on it being much better up there, you know. Once you've warned Komang, it's up to you, take whichever route you like, scout out the highlands, observe and take notes, just make sure you don't stay more than two nights in any one place. I would say you'll be here for a few weeks at least, unless Amsterdam in its wisdom changes its mind. What are your contact arrangements?'

'I'll have to come back to Denpasar. They know I'll be out of contact for a bit.'

'Good one,' Abang inclined his head.

It was every operative's favourite kind of job; freedom of movement and using his own initiative.

Abang smiled. 'You're not a romantic, are you?'

Harper looked at him, a query.

'I mean, you're not the kind of person who is taken in by the landscape? Sorry, of course you're not.' He tipped his head back and exhaled smoke in a sharp, upward stream. 'You're not like Joosten and the others.'

What Abang meant was, you're not a fool. You won't think that because a field is green and has a pretty woman with sleek black hair bending to harvest it that that means you can let your guard down. You're not so stupid as to believe – like all those operatives back home – that ugly things can't happen in beautiful places. What Abang meant was, you're not white.

'No,' said Harper, bending his head back to the notebooks, 'I'm not.'

The next morning, he woke after sunrise on the low day bed in the corner of Abang's sitting room. From the back porch, there was a clanking sound and the tuneful murmur of Abang singing a low, indistinguishable song.

He had slept deeply: the light striped through the shutter slats in bright white. He threw back the sarong Abang had given him, sitting and stretching: both arms, bending them at the elbows, arching his back, then circling his head first one way then the other. He looked down at his torso, examining a livid bruise on his ribcage – the swelling had gone down and the deep red edge of it was spreading into purple and yellow tracery, like lace. His cock rested small and limp against his left thigh and he thought, not for the first time, *it could have been a lot worse*. On more than one occasion in the years to come, as an older man, he was to remember the speed of his recovery after the Jakarta incident and how much he had taken it for granted: the easy belief he had back then in his own powers of survival, the rapidity with which bruises faded and the confidence, the elasticity of youth.

He stood and wrapped the sarong round his waist, pulled on the T-shirt he had left at the end of the day bed. He hadn't told Abang about the beating. He was planning on not mentioning that in his reports. Gregor's first question would be, *why didn't you take better evasive action if there was a riot going on?* Whatever happened to any operative in the field, Gregor always liked to let them, and everyone else, know that it was their own fault.

Abang was frying rice in a wok on the stone stove at the far end of the porch. As Harper wandered out, running both hands through his hair and scratching at his scalp, Abang saluted him with the wooden spatula, then scraped the rice onto two tin plates. He took the cloth from his shoulder and used it to pick up one of the plates and hand it to Harper.

'Here, *adik*,' he said with a smile. 'Careful, it's hot.'

'Thank you.'

He sat down on the step, the plate balanced on his knees on top of the cloth, and began to eat, pinching the rice with his fingers. Abang took the skillet out into the garden and turned it upside down, banging it with the wooden spatula so that the scraps would fall in the yard for the two chickens pecking in the dirt. Then he brought his own plate over and sat down next to Harper. In the small scrubby garden beyond the yard, through some bushes, Harper could see a vast and muddy pig lying asleep on its side in a makeshift wooden corral, motionless but for the long hairy curve of its stomach inflating and deflating.

'Your pig?' he asked, nodding at it.

Abang shook his head. 'Next door's pig. Can't believe it's still alive, not much longer I don't think. Want to know how much I had to pay, for that bag of rice, I mean?' He tossed his head backwards to wherever the bag of rice was hidden. 'A thousand rupiah, last me a couple of weeks maybe, just me, no family, although I'm a big eater, it's true. I guess a local family would spin it out the month.'

Harper nodded, balling the rice neatly before lifting it to his mouth. Abang had thrown in some lime leaves and chopped chilli with seeds: all it needed was a bit of fried fish, an egg on top, perhaps. Didn't Abang's chickens lay eggs? Still, he wasn't going to complain: in comparison with the claustrophobic Hotel Indonesia and the burnt-rubber smell of Jakarta, this was like being on holiday with an old friend.

'Want to know what the schoolteachers here get paid a month?'

Harper nodded again.

'Five hundred rupiah.'

Next to the stone oven, Abang's bag lay, a large cloth bag with outside pockets. He was already packed.

They both shook their heads as they ate, sitting on the step next to each other looking out at the garden and the pig sleeping pantingly; dreaming, perhaps, of kitchen scraps and unaware of its impending fate. We are like that pig, Harper thought, tucking into our rice for breakfast. Isn't that all anyone really thinks about, where the next meal is coming from? And if you know it's coming, isn't it easy to believe that it is all you need? But if you don't know when or where your next meal is coming from, then it is the only thought to possess you. One thousand rupiah for a bag of rice, when a teacher earns half that much? How did anybody stay alive? No wonder the country is falling apart, he thought. When rice is that expensive, human beings are cheap.

Now it is clear who is friend and who is foe. He travelled up country on the back of a motorbike with a driver, Wayan. He had wanted to go on his own but Abang had persuaded him that Wayan was trustworthy and knew the countryside. 'Once you are up there, you will see,' Abang said, 'the paths and lanes, it's much easier with someone who knows it. Wayan grew up round there. After you've seen Komang, you can go off on your own, there's no hurry then.'

Once outside Denpasar, Harper told Wayan, a thin young man his age, to take it slowly. He didn't want to risk an accident on the potted road but, in addition, he wanted to get the feel of how things were in the countryside. Mostly, the villages seemed quiet. There were no charred corpses swinging from trees as there had been on Java, not yet. Occasionally, he would see groups of youths sitting on steps – once a group of four older men who looked like a more organised militia, but there was none of the humming tension of Jakarta. Who knew what was happening in the more remote villages, though, up in the hills? It might have started already but they just didn't know.

They had set off from Denpasar in the morning but were less than halfway when the rain fell. They took shelter in the porch of a shop selling woven baskets in every size from tiny to bath-shaped. The owner of the shop brought them tea in small cups and sat down next to them and they made idle chat while they waited out the rain. Opposite, there was a terraced rice field rising up in swooping green curves, deep green now it was drenched, now the soil and the plants were sucking in the deluge – the earth seemed animate when the rain fell this heavily, as if it was breathing in the water: you could imagine the field's gentle rise and fall, as if the whole island was a sleeping giant.

The rain was solid for more than two hours. After a while, he leant against a palm tree at the edge of the step and slept, the comforting patter of water around him lulling him, the low voices of Wayan and the shopkeeper nearby.

Eventually, the rain stopped; the sun came out. Wayan smiled at him as he wiped down the motorbike – they had pulled it under the porch of palm leaves but water had dripped through onto the seat. 'You sleep a long time, boss. You tired.'

Harper grimaced back. He felt not so much tired as calm; a job to be done, the means to do it.

They were around half an hour from their destination, passing through another small village, when Harper leaned forward and tapped Wayan on the shoulder. Wayan braked, killed the engine so that conversation was possible. 'Let's get something to eat here,' Harper said. He didn't want to spend time looking around for supplies when they got to their destination – such a process would only advertise their presence before they had a chance to speak to Komang and if the farmer was in as much danger as Abang thought then that might not be a good idea. They dismounted from the bike and Harper gave Wayan some rupiah, telling him to be as quick as he could without raising suspicion. He withdrew to a tree trunk at the far end of the street that was close to the undergrowth, somewhat back from the passing trade. This time, he didn't want to be sitting on a shop step right by the bike, where any villager would be bound to stop for a chat.

He could see the motorbike from where he was sitting and, beyond it, the small row of shops into which Wayan had disappeared. He heard a shout from the other end of the street and turned to see three men, two of them arguing with the third. He glanced back towards the shops and noticed that an elderly couple and two other women had come out onto their steps at the sound of the man's shout. Then the man who was being confronted stopped and leaned in towards the two others. All at once, the three suddenly had their heads together in conference.

Harper looked round. The four people who had come out to watch the argument had disappeared: the street was now empty but for a scabby grey dog who was moving to and fro across it, nose to the ground.

Of course, he thought. That man has just named someone. *Now it is clear who is friend and who is foe*. Well, it's far from clear in fact, but if you want to be a friend, you have to name a foe. Neutrality is not an option. When the militiamen turn up at your door at night, eight or ten of them, in their black clothing with their sickle-shaped machetes, fleeing is not an option – you have what, four or five children? Even if you climb out of the back window and even if the leader of the group hasn't already stationed a man there to cut you down – a swift chop to the legs, usually below the knee – then you won't get far before they hunt you down through the rice fields. So, as you cower in the far corner of your home, watching your door shake against the blows, knowing it will hold for a few seconds more, your choice is this: you can wait until the door flies open. You can wait until the men burst into the hut and drag you and your wife and your screaming, terrified children out into the open. Or you can stand, and you can approach the door and call out, 'Brothers!'

You call out, loud enough to make them pause for a second. 'Brothers!' Then, you speak to them urgently. You give them a name.

Tanu. It is your neighbour's name. He lives in a house just down the hill – a larger house than yours, a bit better than your one-room shack. And now comes the really difficult bit. You have to open the door. You have to smile at the men, greet them. You have to act as though you are pleased they have arrived in your village – if you are afraid of them, they will assume you have something to hide. So, summoning every shred of courage in your bones, you slide back the block. You gesture into the hut with your hand, then turn and bark over your shoulder at your wife to stop crying like an idiot, because these men are friends and might want something to eat and drink, and you smile out into the dark and say, 'Tanu, my friends. It's true what I say. I hear his wife is in Gerwani.' And it *is* true, now you come to think of it. His wife has always been talking to your wife about the importance of educating the girls, of them being productive workers for the good of the whole village, and she may not have tried to recruit her to the PKI but it's a bit odd, isn't it, if she isn't a Communist, that she's so keen on the girls going to school?

The men don't come into the hut. You can't even see them clearly because the flare from the burning torches is so bright – they are just dark shapes lit by an orange glow. They talk amongst themselves and leave. You bar the door again and return to the corner with your wife and children.

And, after a while, you hear the screaming down the hill. It is the kind of screaming you have never heard before: the kind that pierces your ears. Your neighbour Tanu and his family are being dragged out of their beds. You stay huddled in the corner, your arms around your whimpering children, while the screaming goes on and on, and you know that when you see the charred bodies strung up in the village square in the dawn light you will feel horror and revulsion but what you feel right now, as the screams continue, is relief that they came to your house first, for it is only thanks to that good fortune that you had the chance to name Tanu before he named you.

The three men turned and walked off together, away from the shops. The road curved and they were soon out of sight. It could be that the two aggressors were simply taking the third man somewhere to kill him, or it could be that they were now all plotting together, the best of friends. Harper looked back down the street and saw that an elderly woman had come out of her shop with a broom and was sweeping her step, looking around, but other than her, the street remained empty.

After a while, Wayan appeared at the far end, beyond the shops, carrying two banana-leaf-wrapped food parcels. He rose.

It took longer than he had anticipated to reach the village up in the hills where Komang lived. The rain had been heavy enough to turn the tracks soggy and the route became muddy and impassable. When they dismounted to turn the bike, fat droplets of water fell from the trees above.

It was late afternoon by the time they reached their destination and he was already thinking they might end up stuck there for the night, not ideal but safer than travelling after dark. Following Abang's instructions, he told Wayan to park the moped just off the village square. They stood by the motorbike for a few minutes, drinking from a water bottle, while Harper orientated himself. Komang's farm was close to the village up a steep rise that led north.

As he walked up the rise, three boys began following him, calling out, 'Hallo! Hallo!' Soon, they were joined by four or five others, like yappy dogs, grinning and jumping, keen to announce his arrival. They fell away as he approached the house and ran shrieking back down the rise.

The house was a grand construction for a rice farmer, long and low. Three dogs ran out to greet him, snarling half-heartedly. A cockerel in the front yard lifted its head, stretched its neck upwards and flapped its wings. A girl of about twelve rounded the corner of the house, saw him, stopped dead, then turned and ran back the way she had come.

Harper waited in front of the house. He wondered if it would be impolite to light a cigarette.

A man in a shirt and sarong came round the corner of the house. He stopped a few feet away, so that they could appraise each other: from his bearing, Harper had no doubt that this was the man of the household, Komang. He was a thin man, in his thirties Harper guessed, with the dense build of someone who had worked the land since childhood: at first glance rather small but then, on closer examination, with taut calf muscles and shoulders hard as steel: not a weakling, certainly. If you needed to lift a tree trunk, you would want him to help.

Komang gave him a slow look. There was no aggression in it, no challenge, but instead, a kind of knowledge, devoid of apprehension it seemed, as if Komang had been expecting him. Harper watched Komang looking at him, taking in his open-necked shirt and his slacks, acknowledging that this stranger had come for a reason.

Harper called out, 'How close to harvest time?'

Komang replied, 'As usual, brother.' It was called an *identifier*, in the trade.

'Abang says hello,' Harper added.

Komang bowed his head. 'Welcome,' he said, and came forward.

Komang's wife appeared on the veranda. She was thin too, older-looking than her husband, more wary. Her face was open but strained. She and her husband exchanged a few words. He guessed she was being given instructions about hospitality.

Komang lifted a hand towards the fields and said, 'While the light is good, shall we walk?'

Harper nodded. The light had that particular quality that came in late afternoon after a heavy rain, a dewiness still in the air, lit by gold.

They walked and, first of all, Harper asked questions. What was the latest on PKI activity in the area? How was land reform proceeding? What did the locals think? How much news of what was happening on Java had reached them here? The answers were as he had expected. On Java, both the Muslim and Christian generals portrayed the Communists as atheist barbarians; here on Hindu Bali, the anti-PKI groups said the Communists were not only against God but would destroy all the local customs, the delicate balances that had been built up over centuries, the ceremonies and worship so integral to Balinese village life. People were worried, Komang said, the omens were bad. Gunung Agung had shown anger, lava had flowed, although the gods had spared the Mother Temple.

And a teacher earns enough money in a month to buy two weeks' supply of rice, Harper thought. No wonder people were angry; no wonder they wanted someone to blame.

They had reached the end of the field: the rice plants were a flowing expanse, rippling in the breeze like the surface of a green sea. On the far side of the field was a dense wall of palm trees. If you ran across the field, it would take you a good ten minutes to reach the row of trees, he reckoned: the field was not a solid thing. The plants stood in water. If you were light-footed, barefoot, a child perhaps, you might be quicker, but if you were normal weight and wearing shoes, your feet would stick. The mud would cling to your feet. Your only chance would be if the people pursuing you were slowed by it too. He wondered how long it was until dark.

They were standing next to each other, facing out across the fields. 'Komang,' Harper said, 'Abang has told me, you must know, your brother's political activities, you must know what they could mean for you, your family. Everything that has been happening on Java could happen here . . .' He paused, to let Komang fill in the gaps.

They stood looking out over the field, the low sun still lighting it with green and gold. At moments like this, you could believe that it was worth dying on this spot, Harper thought, because heaven was here, in this soil, in the green rice plants, the light. How would a man like Komang leave all this, give up a lifetime of work?

They walked back up to the compound. Komang's wife emerged as they approached, holding a tray with two glasses on it. She stared at her husband.

While they sat on the back porch and drank tea, children ran in and out of the house. There seemed to be at least eight of them. Komang's wife brought out some chopped fruit, banana and *salak* in a china bowl with a curled blue pattern, the glaze a little cracked, kept only for guests, probably. She smiled shyly, bowed to Harper and her husband, then retreated into the kitchen to continue the preparations for the evening meal, shooing the children in front of her. A few minutes later, an elderly woman poked her head out of the back door, looked at them and then immediately disappeared. Harper wondered how many people lived in the compound in total. As well as Komang's family there might be a younger sibling or two around, his family, elderly relatives – some of the children were probably nieces and nephews. Too large a group to flee in a hurry; too many who couldn't run all that fast.

Komang leaned forward in his seat, keeping his voice low. 'I've been fortunate, Mr Harper, blessed, you might say. Tell me, how does a man like me stay fortunate?'

The madness would come to this village. It was only a matter of time. He knew it, and Komang knew it, but did he know how bad it would be?

He looked at Komang, then said, quietly, 'What will they say in the village, about my visit?'

Komang said, 'I am a farmer but, you see . . .' He glanced over Harper's shoulder to the house. 'It is a bigger house than most farmers'. There is talk, yes, of course.'

Harper could imagine the scenario all too clearly: the envy and resentment in the village, the whispers. Komang was probably using part of what he earned by giving information to the Institute to pay protection money to a local militia of some sort, but if that arrangement collapsed there would be nobody to protect him.

'My brother is not a bad man,' Komang said. 'He wants to give people who have nothing their own piece of land, so that the hours they work feed their families and are not given to a landowner who does nothing for them. The PKI are going too far, I don't agree with Communism, but the people themselves, they are not all bad people.'

'I know that. Not everybody else sees things that way.'

Komang kept his face very still. Harper admired the man's composure, considering that the rapid calculations he must be making would have such consequences for his family.

He was silent for a while then and Harper thought, he is adding up all he has to lose. His family will have farmed this land for generations: it is almost inconceivable that he could leave. Should he stay in the hope that he will be able to protect it, or pack a few things and take his wife and his children to Denpasar? What will he be in the city? A street cleaner? He has friends in this village. How could he imagine, as he sat here on his own veranda, with the golden light in the fields that his friends and neighbours down the road might advance up the rise with sickles and machetes in their hands?

He looked at Komang and could see the struggle going on behind the man's quiet face. When you belonged to a community, you felt at home, you felt safe. If he was Komang, he would hide at night at least. He would have a place out in the rice fields, a culvert of some sort, overgrown, somewhere that looked like a disused store perhaps, and as soon as it got dark each night, he would take his wife and children out there and tell them to stay there until well after daybreak. They would have to be sworn to secrecy – but the children might gab to their friends. What then? And he wasn't Komang, of course. Komang would never leave his home empty and unprotected.

Eventually, all Komang said was, 'My house . . . this village . . .' He fell silent again.

'I know,' Harper replied quietly, after a while. 'I am sorry.

Komang, you must not talk to anyone, even your family members, and especially not your brother. You must make your own decision and then act. Do it soon.'

'How soon, in your opinion?'

'Days, not weeks. I don't like the feel of things round here. If it was me, I'd leave immediately.'

Komang looked at him then; stared.

He walked back down the rise and turned into the lane that led to the village square. Two elderly women were in front of him carrying long bundles of branches on their heads, swaying in unison. Wayan was waiting at the end of the lane, next to the motorbike, squatting on his heels. A couple of local men were standing over him. 'Where are you from?' – the questions would be light enough. A few bats flitted in the trees. The gold light had diminished to grey: dusk was falling swiftly. Harper considered attempting the roads in the dark but it would make more sense to stay local – the other villages he needed to visit were north of here. Komang had offered him his home for the night but Harper knew it was best to leave the man to make the necessary decision and preparations.

As the local men saw Harper approach, they smiled but didn't stay to speak to him, turning and wandering off. Wayan got to his feet, brushed at his trousers.

They took lodgings in the home of a local elderly woman: Wayan had asked around and found them a house with some food in it. They ate with the family, cross-legged on the floor, the children rendered silent by their presence. They drank sweet tea, then retired. Harper and Wayan were sharing the day bed in the open area of the compound, partially screened by a large cloth hanging from a line while a black pig snuffled around their feet. The elderly lady handed them each a sarong and doused the single paraffin lamp hanging from the line. It was pitch dark.

He was woken by a short shout – and was instantly, fully awake, the kind of sharp awakening a person has when something inside them has apprehended threat even though the conscious part of the brain is slow to catch up. It was completely black. He sat upright and then moved into a crouching position on the bed. Next to him, Wayan was awake too. He whispered the question, 'Sir?'

Harper held up his hand for Wayan to be silent even though it was too dark for him to see. He blinked a couple of times and, as his eyes adjusted, saw there was an orange gleam to the left of his vision, through the stone entranceway that led out of the compound and onto the street. 'Stay here,' he whispered, then rose from the day bed – he had slept fully dressed this time and with his money belt still strapped inside his shirt – and crept to the doorway.

There was a large group of men in the street. Some of them had flaming torches, a couple were holding paraffin lamps aloft. Here and there, he could glimpse a disembodied face looming in the dark, appearing out of nowhere and disappearing again as the light swung away. Then the group was gone, melting into the dark. Harper stood for a minute, listening in the direction in which the group had departed: north, up the rise. There was the sudden, brief barking of dogs from a compound further up the hill, a whimper, then silence.

They could take another route to Komang's house: Abang had told him, 'You can either approach through the village, that's the short way, you can do it on foot, or you can ride on the moped on a track through the fields, but then you'll have to leave Wayan with the moped in the middle of the fields and he won't like that.' Many Balinese thought spirits lived in the water, the Invisibles. Tonight, he thought, they are probably right.

He stepped back into the compound and hissed to Wayan, 'Start the moped.' Abang had drawn a sketch of the paths and tracks around the village in Harper's notebook and Harper's visual memory was good, but he wasn't sure whether he would be able to find his way in the dark.

As he returned to the day bed to pick up his bag, he fumbled in his pocket for his cigarette lighter, flicking it and holding it up so that he could see Wayan's face, both rictus and blank. 'We should stay here, sir?' he said.

'We can't,' Harper replied. 'It's not safe.' This was not true. He doubted very much the men would come for him and Wayan, they would be too anxious that his status was unconfirmed, that he might be too important to kill.

Wayan would not start the moped for him unless he thought it was more dangerous to stay in the compound than go out into the night, so Harper repeated, 'It's not safe here, the men will come here. We have to go round a back route. I will direct you.'

The noise of a moped engine: so ubiquitous in the day you hardly registered it, yet a cacophony in the dark. It would alert the men to the fact that someone else was on the move – but he and Wayan would be riding on a different path, a circuitous route. Wayan's hand shook as he tried to turn the key and for a moment Harper wondered if he should have left the man behind and taken the moped on his own. Then the engine let loose with its small ascending growl, Wayan kicked the machine into life and Harper swung his leg over. 'To the end of the road, then left,' he said in a low voice, in Wayan's ear. 'Be careful, go slow, stay in the middle.' They couldn't afford to end up in a ditch in the dark.

They turned left up the track that wound round the village. Gripping the seat with his knees, he held his cigarette lighter out and flicked it once in a while to illuminate the track, letting it die, then flick, die then flick. Each time, he saw no more than a few feet ahead, the mud track, the bushes either side, the shadow that the motorbike and its two riders cast, like that of a strange beast.

After what seemed like a very long time, they had crested the rise and bumped slowly along another track until it narrowed and disappeared. This, if he had calculated correctly in the dark, was the edge of Komang's far field. Harper whispered in Wayan's ear, 'Kill the engine.'

There was an odd aural illusion then, as the engine died: he thought for a minute or two that there was total silence around them, only to find that as his hearing adjusted to the lack of engine sound, the night noises of the open fields rose up from the water, the click and sing of insects, the hum and shimmer of it.

'Sir?' asked Wayan and Harper put his hand on his shoulder to quiet him.

For a few minutes, they listened. The darkness was complete out here and he dared not flick the lighter now they were out in the open. Perhaps when he skirted the trees on foot, he would be able to see if there was a little moonlight, enough for him to get his bearings. He estimated it would be another ten minutes or so to walk along the edge of the field and pass the treeline, using the route he had walked with Komang that afternoon – if his guesses about the path had been correct.

He dismounted the moped, removed his bag from across his chest and gave it to Wayan, then said to him, 'Turn the moped round but don't restart the engine. Stay right here so I can find you. Don't move from this spot, and don't light a cigarette or use your lighter. Listen, Wayan, there is great danger, okay? So it's important you listen to me, only listen to me and you will be okay. Stay here. Right here. I'll be back in a short while.'

Harper turned and set off before Wayan could argue with him. Wayan would be worried about the spirits of the night, how they could approach him from behind, or any direction, all at once perhaps, if he was not allowed to use a light. But there was no argument Harper could have advanced that would have allayed that particular fear, and there was no time. And as he skirted the edge of the field, his feet sinking a little deeper each time into the soft mud, he thought that perhaps Wayan was right: perhaps the group of men approaching Komang's house now with paraffin lamps and machetes were spirits. Wasn't it easier to think of them, or even yourself, in that way, rather than to look at your neighbour's face in daylight and know the truth?

The insects hummed and sang, his feet made sucking noises in the mud, but other than that, it was silent as he approached the end of the field. As the treeline ended, he knew he should be able to see across the next field to Komang's house.

He paused for a moment to listen – and then, sailing across the field through the black night, came a single, lengthy, agonised scream.

He was frozen, a sick, light sensation overwhelming him, and then he was running forward, the mud clinging to the soles of his shoes, impeding the lifting of his feet by just fractions of a second but enough to feel as though his feet were being sucked at, pulled down.

At the end of the treeline, he ducked down, although he knew there was no danger of the men looking his way, and in a crouching position, he ran back a little then crossed the next field, towards the patch of orange light he could see at the back of Komang's house. From this distance, it was impossible to see what was happening. Where there was light at all, it was too bright and where it was dark, too dark. He could just make out a group of men, gathered close together and illuminated by a bare bulb hanging from the veranda and the orange light from their flares. Silhouetted against the glow from the house were black shapes, rising and falling. There were no more screams.

Then there were shouts as the group of men broke apart and Harper thought he saw the flit and flicker of someone fleeing the house at running pace. He crept a little closer, wading knee-deep in muddy water now. Some of the men were pointing in the direction in which the shape had fled.

A child of around six, a girl with plaited hair, appeared on the veranda – perhaps the fleeing shape had been one of the older children making a terrified dash for it, and the girl had followed but not run. *Go back*, Harper thought desperately, staring at the girl through the dark, *go back inside*, but the men nearest the veranda had seen her and only then did the child seem to realise her own folly. She turned and ran back inside the house. The door slammed shut but the men were already swarming onto the veranda and Harper had no need to stay to see what would happen next.

He made his way back across the rice field, knee-deep again, wretched at his own failure – he had been sent to do one simple thing, and he had failed. Had he been vehement enough, as he had sat on that veranda only a few hours ago, watching the golden light across the fields and drinking sweetened tea? Back towards the house, he heard the children's screams, high and shrill.

It was only when a man's shout came from behind him, sounding closer than it should be, that Harper turned and saw the silhouettes of men at the edge of his field. He had been spotted.

Caution was pointless then. He began to crash through the water, lifting his feet higher and higher with each step. How had he been spotted, out here in the dark? They must be scouting around for the figure that had fled the house. He rounded the treeline and then forced himself to pause for a moment behind a tree trunk, his back pressed up against it while he steadied his breath. He could hear the men moving across the field of water towards him, see the sway of one, two, three paraffin lanterns, but they were moving slowly, spread out, hunting him. They thought he was hiding in the water and they didn't want to step past him. That was what he should have done but panic had made him run further than they thought.

Slowly, he crept back along the treeline, which was solid enough to hide his movements, although he could still see the glimmer of their lanterns, flickering now and then through the trees. He was only five minutes away from safety now. At the rate they were moving, he would be back at the top of the rise before they had reached the trees. By the time they heard the small roar of the motorcycle engine and worked out where it was coming from, he and Wayan would be halfway down the track that led back into town, then away altogether.

He was three, maybe four minutes from where he had left

Wayan, approaching silently – he could not risk calling out – when he heard it. It was a tiny roar, sudden in the night, both distant and near. Wayan's nerve had cracked and he had kicked down on the starter pedal and brought the moped to life. *No.* And as he lifted his feet to run towards Wayan, he saw the red tail light of the motorcycle, descending the sloping path as that poor man, having waited as long as he was able to without going mad, fled the horrors that were happening around him.

One single red light, that was all that was visible, leaving him behind as it descended, dropping into the earth, it seemed, as if the earth closed up over it as it dived into safety, and in that moment, Harper knew that he was more alone than he had ever been, unprotected, no weapon, in a rice field in the middle of nowhere, with a gang of men with machetes in pursuit, their blood up, the killers of children with nothing left to lose.

When the men from the Institute said to him, 'And how did you survive the night, do you think? How come you were spared?' he paused for a long while, then replied, slowly, as if they were a little stupid, 'I hid. I hid in an irrigation ditch.' He was leaning back in an easy chair. He had one leg bent and the ankle resting on the other knee. At no point in the interview did he sit up straight or lean forward.

One of the men from the Institute wrote it down on his clipboard but the other did not move. He was sitting in his chair with his arms crossed. He had round, steel-rimmed glasses that made his eyes glint and he looked at Harper and said calmly, in a non-judgemental tone of voice, 'That's a lie, isn't it, Nicolaas?' He had no evidence either way, of course. He was just smarter than the other one. He could read a pause.

'No,' Harper replied, looking straight at the man, which he could do with impunity because he had, much later that night, hidden in a ditch. 'It isn't. That's what I did.' It wasn't a lie, as such, just not the whole truth. Later that night, he had found a place to hide an hour or two before dawn, an irrigation ditch. There had been two moments: the red tail light disappearing, and the grey light of breaking dawn – the space between those two moments, and what had happened in that space, how he had saved his own skin, that was none of their concern.

Dawn is a promise. Daylight comes softly – so softly, in fact, it is impossible to pinpoint the exact moment when it comes. *There . . . ? And, there . . . ?* It is infinitesimally slow yet comes at once: that is the mystery of it. You are lying in an irrigation ditch, stretched flat in order to submerge yourself as much as possible, with only half your face turned upwards so that you can breathe, keeping your breath as shallow as possible while still keeping yourself alive, knowing that each second of being alive may be your last because the men with flares and machetes are only a few metres away and discovery is possible at any moment. Your muscles cramp repeatedly in water that isn't freezing but has frozen your limbs nonetheless. Your shoulder is pressed against a stone – but even shifting a little to relieve that pain might create a small ripple that would be spotted. Mud has soaked your clothing and an insect of some sort is inside your trouser leg, burrowing for a new home, but the worst of the pain is in your neck, as you hold your head turned to one side in order to breathe. Worst of all is what your mind is doing. It is thinking so hard about what you must do and not do in order to avoid being discovered that it is as if you are screaming aloud. You cannot believe the clamour of your thoughts will not betray you, bring the men to you; now, and now. And it goes on for hours.

And then, softly, it comes. It comes with the birds: the outlier birds, *cheep, cheep*, such a tiny, hopeful sound. The first hint of grey appears at the edges of the sky – you think it does, you can't be sure – and, then, after a bit of tuning up, the whole chorus breaks out, the birds' triumphant orchestra, the musical holler of it all, because however black the night has been they are still there and they cry out and then comes distant cock-crowing, dog-barking, and all at once, yes, the sky is grey and lightening by the minute, and you turn in the ditch, stiff and frozen to the core, and lever yourself up slowly on one elbow, in pain, covered in mud, and you are still afraid but now it is light enough to see across the rice field, growing greener by the minute. The men with machetes have gone and, unbelievably – there are no words to describe it – you are still alive.

III

BLACK WATER
(1998)

He was sitting on the veranda of his hut, smoking, and watching dawn break across the valley above the Ayung River. The steep wall of palm trees emerged from the dark, grey at first, then lighter and lighter but still monochrome, then magically green. The call of birds in the trees; the humming stillness of the air; it was there. It had always been there. And here was the thing both mysterious and obvious, he thought: the relentlessness of dawn, the fact that whatever had occurred in the hours of darkness, the light came and illuminated it all.

After they had killed him, it would be silent inside the hut. His corpse would lie in the pitch black for a while. There he would be; motionless, unbreathing, alone. As dawn broke, the scene inside the hut would become colourised. The light would reveal that his skin had been rendered ashen by death. There would be a pool of blood, already oxidising, dark against the wooden floor – or more livid, perhaps, if he was lying on the white sheets of his bed. He thought of Kadek arriving that morning, finding the shutters smashed and heavy doors ajar and entering, slowly and carefully, surveying the scene. They would mutilate him, the boys. They would feel the need to kill him more than once. A gaping neck, limbs detached: he didn't want Kadek to have images like that in his head. Kadek wasn't even born when the massacres happened in 1965.

It was the pictures, the pictures in your head – you never escaped them. He knew that now.

He finished the *kretek* and held the stub for a while between his fingers, then rose and took the two steps to the edge of the veranda, leaning his elbows on it and looking out over the valley.

'Smoking first thing?'

Rita stood in the doorway behind him, dressed only in her underwear and one of his shirts, unbuttoned to her waist and crumpled. Her face was pale and tired, a little puffy from sleep. She smiled and stepped over the threshold.

He glanced to the left. There was no sign of Kadek as yet. He reached out an arm and drew her to him, positioning her so she faced outwards to look at the valley, then standing behind her with his arms wrapped round her, pressing her against the wooden rail. They stood like that for a while, then he lifted his hand, cleared her hair from where it was tangled with the shirt collar, kissed the back of her neck.

'Thank you for telling me,' she said, softly. 'It was a gift, from you, I think.'

He didn't reply. The previous night, he had told her about '65: I was a young man; I was a courier; I delivered a list of names. The Americans drew up lists of thousands of Communists or suspected Communists and then they gave those lists to the Indonesian military command and those people were taken out of their homes with their families and they were tortured and killed. I was one of the people who facilitated that process. I was just doing my job, you could say, but unlike a lot of people, I had an opportunity to not do my job. I spent a night in a shack by the black water of a Jakarta canal and in the chaos of that time it would have been easy to lose the particular list I was carrying; I had been caught up in a riot, after all. I would have returned home a failure but nobody would have known that I had lost it deliberately, no real harm would have come to me. Maybe it would have made a difference; maybe not. But I didn't throw the list into the canal. I delivered it as I had been told to do, and those people were almost certainly rounded up the following day, while I was sitting having a beer with a man called Abang and watching the Bali Beach Hotel being built and feeling grateful to be off Java.

'You were a spy?' she had asked.

'No, spies work for governments. People like me get hired to do the jobs that governments don't want to give their spies, or don't want to get caught giving them. We work for anyone, mostly, we work for oil companies, mining companies, banks.'

'Mercenaries, then.'

'My firm would be *very* offended if you called them that. It's a lot more sophisticated than that, well it is now, back then, it was the Wild West.'

He had not told her about his visit to Komang, or what had happened in the night that followed.

He had told her about going home to Holland afterwards and having a breakdown, about leaving his company and living in the countryside for a while. He had not told her that, four years later, he went back to work for the same firm, that he had worked for them at a desk job ever since. Once you were in, you were in. He was hardly going to retrain as a schoolteacher or dentist.

He had told her about his years in Los Angeles, the time with Poppa and Nina and Michael and his mother. He had told her that his little brother had drowned – he had not told her that Bud had only been floating in the pool of icy water because he had dared him to do it.

He had told her his mother had been an alcoholic: he had not told her she was still alive. He had told her about his short-lived marriage to Francisca but not how recent it was or that they had had a baby – and, somehow, all these half-truths had combined in his head to form something coherent, whole, something he could maintain, if he stayed with this woman – the trick was to forget that you were lying.

'Why did you come back?' she had asked.

People talked about the past as if it was a thing, an object: *the past*, like *the box* or *the house* or *the tree* – as if it was solid and singular. But the past wasn't an object with boundaries but something fluid and continuous, like a river. Nobody had one past. In 1965 he remembered 1950 in a certain way, and now in 1998, he remembered 1965 differently from how it was and 1950 differently from how he had remembered it in 1965. It was like standing in a box of mirrors and turning to see your reflection multiplied back and forth at you in endless iterations – except, in his case, each reflection was slightly different.

The last time he had seen his mother was a year ago, the summer of 1997. He had called in on a Sunday morning – Francisca made him go. 'I'm going to see Aunty Lies, I'm going all that way, the least you can do is call in on your mother.' Francisca, his wife, had adopted his elderly mother and aunt – in Harper's view, they were poor substitutes for the children he and Francisca had been unable to have. Children got less time-consuming the older they became: with the parental generation, it seemed to work the other way around.

His mother lived in a huge and gloomy house on Noorderstraat; a mausoleum, he thought, full of the relics of a dead husband, a long-dead marriage. All her life Anika had been short of money, until the point when she was beyond having use for it. Now she lived in a house she could have sold for a fortune, bought herself a new apartment and had plenty to spare, easily enough for the clothes and make-up and nights out she had craved all her life. But she was in no fit state to make that sort of choice by then. She put her clothes on anyhow, in whatever mismatched form came most readily to hand. Her make-up frequently migrated from the part of the face to which it had been applied. She rarely left her home. She smelled.

It was a light morning, the sun still pale, the air fresh. He trotted up the stone steps, lifted and dropped the heavy knocker, stepped back. His mother was easily alarmed if she thought someone was trying to shoulder their way into the house – she had slammed the door shut in his face before now. The door opened a few inches and he glimpsed a straggle of grey hair before Anika turned and ambled back inside, leaving the door ajar. Harper stepped over the threshold slowly, pushing at the door, then closing it behind him with a small shove that, however gentle, thudded with the resonance of fifty years of accumulated filial guilt. His mother had wandered back into the sitting room. It was eleven o'clock on a Sunday morning and, yes, she was drunk.

The hallway was dark but the sitting room darker still. It took a while for his eyes to adjust, then he saw the small figure of his mother, collapsed into the sagging chair in the corner, her tiny form swathed in a purple dress with a silver thread through it, once one of her favourites, and a huge green wool cardigan on top. She was barefoot and her gnarled ankles protruded from the bottom of the dress, like a wizened child dressed in adult's clothing. She was only in her mid-seventies but at a glance seemed so shrunken, with thinning grey hair and bald patches, that she looked nearer ninety. Aunty Lies, ten years older, bulky, in a nursing home on account of her gout, was much more robust.

'Let's open the shutters,' Harper said, walking over to them. 'It is summer, after all.'

'Don't forget to leave the cake, you know, on the table, don't forget, last time you forgot.' Harper realised that in that particular moment – it could change at any time – she thought he was one of the home helps he hired to visit his mother, cook meals she rarely ate, keep her company for a bit. Wine and cake. He wondered what a diet of wine and cake did to your digestive system. He decided not to dwell on the thought.

The light from the tall windows illuminated the chaos of the room – the jars with rotting flowers glued into viscous brown liquid that sat in rows on top of the piano, the piles of yellowing newspapers on the sofa – she had yet to cancel her last husband's subscription to a fishing magazine although he had been dead for nine years – the dirty plates and cutlery poking from beneath the chairs. Harper wondered briefly whether he should close the shutters again. His mother would forget to do it later and leave them open all night – but the thought of sitting in dusty darkness with her on a summer day made him feel as though he might suffocate.

'Shall I make you a cup of coffee, Ma?' he asked.

'Don't come *here* with your moaning and crying,' his mother muttered, and Harper guessed that now she was referring to the occasion, many years ago, when the wife of one of her married lovers had turned up on the doorstep with two children and wept and begged Anika to leave their family alone. Anika had slammed the door in her face, then turned to Harper – fifteen years old, standing in the hallway – and said, 'You should hear what he says about her, she nags at him all the time. She deserves to lose her husband if she behaves like that.'

He thought about going into the kitchen but the state it would be in would be even more depressing than the sitting room and his mother wouldn't drink the coffee anyway. He sat and talked to her for a while but it became clear she wasn't coherent and it would be a brief visit. Perhaps that was why he asked, that day.

'Ma, do you remember Bud?'

Anika didn't answer. She moistened her lips, clutching at the small glass tumbler that looked like it had recently held some sticky liqueur.

'Bud, Ma,' he repeated. 'He was christened Joseph but we all called him Bud. Michael's son.' He wasn't going to help her out by adding, *your son too*.

'Michael . . .' she said slowly, savouring the word, the ghost of a smile on her face. 'Michael . . .' She roused herself in her chair, using her elbows on the armrests to lever herself more upright, smiling openly now, looking at him, then lifting a bony finger.

'You know, baby boy,' she said. She hadn't called him baby boy in a while. 'The only one I ever *really* loved was Michael.'

Harper looked at her.

'It's true,' she said, a little indignantly, suddenly lucid and seeing him, seeing his look. She pushed a few strands of grey hair back from her face, then patted at it, as if it was still bouffant. 'He was the one, the one for me. Michael. Handsomest man ever, and so tall.' Her face darkened again. 'I was broken-hearted when he ran out on me. The Tatum Pole Boogie, now *that* was something.

You think these old farmer types ever even *heard* anything like that?' She waved her hand towards the window to encompass the various men since Michael, or the whole male population of Amsterdam, perhaps – possibly the European continent.

'California . . .' she said in a singsong voice. 'Now that was where we should have stayed. We only came back for your education. We should have stayed. I was happy there.'

Harper closed his eyes briefly, then opened them again to fix an expression on his face that would hide his despair. Was it possible that his mother, in her alcohol-induced dementia, had rewritten the history of their lives so comprehensively that she really believed they had come back to the Netherlands for *his* welfare? *The thing about your mother is*, Poppa had said, *nothing is ever her fault*. And he knew then that it was truer than it had ever been, that his mother, in her relentless quest for love, had gone crashing around the world wreaking havoc in other people's lives and never once paused to consider that any other person had a right to happiness but herself. That included her own son. He was fifty-four years old. Maybe it was time to divorce his mother.

Bud had been a tall, solid boy, a little tank, Nina used to say. He liked sucking lemons, of all things. Nina would slice one in two for him and put one half face-down on a saucer to stop it drying out, then give him the other to chew on. He would wander around all day with it pressed against his mouth, eyes twinkling. 'Nicolaath,' he would say – he had a slight lisp as a toddler, he had already grown out of it when he died – 'Nicolaath, why don't you like lemonth?' When he said this, he would beam, as if the existence of *lemonth* meant that all was right with the world.

'But Bud, Ma, do you remember Bud?'

His mother stared at him, pursing her lips, frown lines two

deep tracks on her brow, tipping her head to one side with a slightly coquettish air, rifling her memories of husbands and ex-husbands and other women's husbands . . . And he knew that the only thing he wanted to do was to run away from her as far and as fast as possible, and to be on the other side of the world when she died.

He walked slowly back down Noorderstraat after his visit to his mother – not because he was reluctant to leave her behind, alone in the mausoleum, but because he was unwilling to arrive back home. Francisca wouldn't be there until later but once he got back, there was a small job he had promised he would do while she was out: fix the top drawer of the chest of drawers. It was sticking: it annoyed her every morning. 'When will you fix this thing?'

The summer air was still light, not too hot, the sky still pale and fresh. It occurred to him that the most enjoyable part of this Sunday would be the walk from one obligation to another – that neither his mother's large dark house or his wife's small bright one held any sense of comfort for him, that the place he felt most at home was in the transition between the two.

His boss had been asking him for some time how he would feel about returning to Indonesia, given his background knowledge of the archipelago. They had just widened the currency trading band from eight per cent to twelve per cent: the rupiah was heading down and given what was happening elsewhere in the region, their clients were getting twitchy. He had been prevaricating – he hadn't discussed the possibility with Francisca – and at one point his boss had said, 'Is it because of what happened before, in sixty-five?'

'No,' he said, with a small smile. 'That was thirty-two years ago.'

He liked his current boss; Gregor was long gone, Jan was solid and decent, had said to him once, 'You know, I'm horrified what we exposed young operatives to back then, wouldn't happen now, not on my watch.'

He had not thought about Jan's suggestion too much at the time. He was an old man now; he had his commitment to Francisca. The Asia Department was huge in comparison with the sixties and in the intervening three decades the company had gone from a score of operatives plus back-up staff to hundreds of employees in Amsterdam alone – that was before you counted the offices in most capital cities in the world. There were plenty of other people they could send. Now though, as he walked back home, it came to him clear and clean. If he went to Indonesia, he would get away from . . . everything.

He did a small inventory of his life. It was 1997 and he was fifty-four years old: fifty-five later that year: a middle-aged man, married with no children, who had had a disrupted childhood and a dramatic youth but had spent the last three decades behind a desk. His mother hardly knew who he was any more. His marriage was not in a good state: he had known it for some time but this was the first occasion he thought it out loud to himself. Interesting, that, how you could know something and yet take so long to acknowledge it in so many words.

As he walked, he also acknowledged to himself that he had known it wasn't a good idea at the time. He had married for the novelty value: it was one of the few mistakes he hadn't made yet, after all. And still, they had tried for the baby, and then after the baby had died, they had had their grief to nurse instead, to wean and to raise, until it became old enough for them to have a little more time to themselves. That was four years ago. The grief should be a bit less dependent by now, he thought, play on its own sometimes, sleep through the night. Why was it still giving them broken nights? What were they getting wrong?

As he walked back to the small house he shared with his wife, he thought about Jan's offer to send him back to Indonesia. Francisca, brave and delicate and throwing herself into caring for his elderly relatives in the absence of a child to care for; their pleasant home, very much to her taste; their occasional dinners with friends, all Francisca's; his one-sided conversations with his mother . . . that was the inventory, that was the sum of it.

After they had lost the baby, his mother had gone through a short period of sobriety and, despite her dislike of Francisca, the two of them had come to some kind of accommodation. It was an accommodation that filled Harper with disgust. His mother's love of tragedy was well established. When Francisca had been his pretty, happy girlfriend, then wife, Anika couldn't have been less interested. Then Francisca became a weeping stick with a lost child and all at once his mother couldn't wait to claim her as her daughter-in-law, to have a piece of all that drama. They even went shopping together a couple of times, met up for hot chocolate, until his mother's relapse back into drunkenness.

Francisca's response was, as ever, less cynical. 'Oh Nicolaas,' she sighed to him, when he expressed his exasperation at his mother's sudden interest in their lives, 'hasn't it occurred to you, she lost her granddaughter? It was probably her only chance at a grandchild. Of course she has a right to grieve with us.' His frank opinion was that Francisca was being far too generous.

*

Francisca returned from visiting Aunt Lies at the end of the afternoon and they cooked pasta together in the kitchen, him slicing garlic and tomatoes, her making the salad. They made companionable conversation about the relative states of health of the two old women and Francisca said, 'You know, for some reason Aunty Lies got on to how your father first came to the house, in Leiden, and how crazy your mother was, how handsome he was, this army officer, it was really sweet. I didn't know the rest of the family never spoke to her again, because she went back to Indonesia with him. Imagine. Her stepfather gave permission then cut her off without a penny. Crazy, huh? Did you know all that?'

'Yeah . . .' he murmured, rinsing a tomato beneath the tap and placing it on a wooden chopping board.

'You've never talked about it much, don't you think that's a bit . . . well . . .'

He had his back to her. He rolled his eyes, knowing she couldn't see him do it, and brought the knife down on the tomato, which was pale, unripe. The knife was blunt and the skin resisted the pressure of the blade, then parted. 'I hope she didn't tell you he was the love of Anika's life and she's never recovered. Anika was saying the same thing about Michael this morning. Michael was the love of her life, apparently. Next week, she'll be saying it about Jan.' Jan Aaltink was the barrel-chested farmer Anika had married on her return to the Netherlands in 1952, the second of four stepfathers she offered her son over the decades.

Francisca didn't reply. She was standing over the salad bowl and turning lettuce over with her fine, pale hands. Harper knew that silence – it was the one that descended when Francisca was deciding how to phrase a criticism in the most non-confrontational manner possible. 'Why are you *so* hard on your mother?' she said eventually. 'It was a brave thing to do, don't you think? Marrying a mixed-race officer, in that day and age, going to the other side of the world with him, then a war breaking out, stuck there. Don't you think you could forgive her for once? Everything she went through?'

He wasn't in the mood for this. He slammed the knife down on its side on the chopping board, exhaling with a derisive *ugh* sound, turning.

'Okay okay!' Francisca said quickly, lifting her hands.

'No, no,' he said. 'I've heard about everything she went through all my life, over and over again, I've heard about how awful it was, giving birth to me in the camp, her endless suffering . . . Everyone, everywhere, has always let her down . . .' He glared at Francisca. 'Funny, though, I've never once heard her say anything about how it might have been quite hard for me, her behaviour.'

Francisca's voice became calm and measured then, with that placating wheedle that annoyed him so much. She would wheedle for the first half hour of an argument, then snap. It was always a relief when she snapped. 'I know it was hard for you too. I'm able to see that because in comparison with you, I've had an easy life, but the things that happened to your mother . . .'

'Yes, yes, don't you think I've had this conversation?'

'She saw it, Nicolaas.'

They stared at each other across the small kitchen. Malachi, their thin grey cat, slunk through the small gap in the kitchen door, which was ajar, walked across the room with her tail in the air, leapt up onto the counter-top and then looked at them both, unblinking, waiting to be picked up and dropped back down onto the floor.

Francisca turned, reached out an absent-minded hand and stroked Malachi's head. 'She saw it, you know. I don't think either of us can imagine what it must be like to see something so horrible at such a young age, how it must affect you.'

He looked at her.

'Aunty Lies told me today. I didn't know whether to tell you or not. I was thinking about it all the way home. I don't know why she started talking about it now but she did. I think maybe she was upset. You never go.'

Francisca had always been much better at visiting Aunt Lies than Harper, or Anika for that matter.

'I said something about how I wished that you and your mother got on a bit better, and we were talking about how angry you always are with your mother.'

He thought, you know, sometimes I get really sick of women talking about me behind my back.

'And she said how your mum had always told you the heroic version of your father being killed in order to protect you, so that you would remember him as a heroic soldier, holding out in battle in the hills. She thought it was important for a boy to feel that way about his father, particularly one who died in the war, you know, that time, all the boys who lost fathers, they all had to believe they were heroes, died saving comrades or something, not real, not how things really were.' Francisca stopped stroking Malachi, bent and kissed the top of the cat's head, picked her up and put her gently on the floor.

Harper returned to chopping tomatoes. 'Yes, well, Lies is forgetting she told me the real version. The end of the street, just because he was caught out after curfew. She told me when I was very young. And actually, I think it's stupid to make out he was a hero. He was entitled to be terrified, in those circumstances, to try and save his own life and his wife's life too, anyone was.' He had always wondered why Aunt Lies had told him the real version of his father's death. She had told him in great secrecy one day when his mother was out, and made him promise never to ask his mother about it.

'She didn't forget that actually. She remembered, she was halfway through telling you the whole story but you were only small and she stopped short. She remembered the whole conversation. What she didn't go on to tell you was that your mother saw it.'

'Saw what?' he said, stupidly.

They were facing each other now, him still holding the blunt knife and Francisca's fine, narrow features stretched, open-eyed, in an expression that swam with pity, but whether the pity was for him or his mother or simply all the suffering in the world, he couldn't surmise.

'Oh Nicolaas, your mother saw your father beheaded. She heard a commotion at the end of the street. Pregnant with you, just a girl, imagine that. She ran down the street and she saw her husband beheaded in front of her. She had no one but him. And you wonder why she has been drunk half her life and spent the other half trying to steal other women's husbands?'

Harper turned violently then and stared down at the chopping board, so angry that he couldn't speak. Malachi the cat had been winding round his legs while Francisca had been speaking but now slunk swiftly towards the door.

Francisca returned to the salad. 'You think anyone ever really recovers? Seeing something like that?'

There was a moment then – he saw it briefly, like a narrowing shaft of light through a door that is swinging shut – when he could have told Francisca about some of the things he had seen when he was a young man, and some of the things he had done, but all he said was a soft, low, 'No,' and the door closed.

Jan asked him again the following week. The economic crisis was precipitating unrest across the region, the office in Jakarta could use someone who had experience in analysis and that was what he had been doing the last thirty years, after all.

This time, he didn't even pause – he remembered that later; he didn't ask for more details or wonder aloud what the package was. He just said, 'Yes, sure. I'll go.'

When he told Francisca that he was going to Indonesia and he didn't know how long he would be gone, she stared at him for a while, then said in a voice scarcely above a whisper, 'You can't run from the sadness inside you all your life, Nicolaas. Don't you realise you just take it with you?'

Later that night, when the debate had become more shrieky, she jabbed him in the middle of the chest with her finger and snapped, 'So you're running out on everything, on me, your mother, your responsibilities, well go then, let's see how happy you are when the only responsibility you have is to stare at your reflection in the mirror.'

That night, as he lay on the sofa with the soft bulk of the spare blanket over him, thick and woollen and pale blue, he thought, I'll sign the house over to her, that's only fair. How soon can I start packing? Not tomorrow, that would be unkind. I'll leave it to the weekend.

In the departure lounge at Schiphol airport, he stared at the other passengers and tried not to enjoy it too much: that feeling, transience, as if three decades of settled life had been nothing more than the waiting room between one journey and the next. My life can be divided into threes, he thought. There was the first part of his life, before 1965, with its disrupted phases, its ocean crossings: Indonesia, Los Angeles, Holland. There was what came after '65, the quiet decades, three of them, mostly sat behind a desk in Amsterdam. Then there was this third and final phase; his return. Indonesia was the three-legged stool on which his life was balanced.

Then, with one brief change of planes at Singapore, he was hauling his briefcase from the overhead locker and arching his back to ease its stiffness, shuffling behind an elderly woman in the aeroplane aisle and descending the steel steps of the plane onto the tarmac of Jakarta Soekarno-Hatta airport. *Then shall a boat fly in the sky.* The ancient prophecy had come true.

The Jakarta office had offered to pick him up but he said he'd get a cab from the rank at the airport: he wanted to arrive alone, to absorb his first impressions. As they hit the flyover, the driver began to drift inattentively from lane to lane at speed, and he remembered what it was like, the feeling that he was in a place where anything could happen at any moment. He stared out of the window with a small engine of adrenaline in his stomach. This was fun. The six-lane highways were still there, cutting a swathe through the city – pedestrian walkways had been built over them, that was an improvement, although they looked a little on the rickety side. And everywhere, the skyscrapers, the international banks, the hotels – yes, thirty years of human rights suppression had brought the foreign investment flooding in. He wondered what had happened to the huge expanses of *kampong*, crammed together, the rivulets of small canals and irrigation ditches, shacks and market places – later, he would discover they were just intersected by the freeways, squeezed between the twenty-eight or thirty-two or forty-seven storeys of the steel and glass buildings that stood like knives pointing upwards in the new Central Business District, stretching high to the white and clouded, dust-filled, sagging sky.

Each building seemed an oddity, as his car sped by. They passed one block where every floor had a balcony jutting out at a different angle and each balcony and roof above it had greenery in profusion, creepers and climbers and palms. He supposed it was intended to beautify the concrete beneath, but instead it looked as though the building was a remnant in a post-apocalyptic landscape where the humans had all fled, a jungle was reclaiming the city and it would not be surprising if pumas stalked the streets.

Then they were pulling up at the hotel he was booked into for the first few days of his stay, while an apartment was got ready, and a liveried doorman opened his door with a white-gloved hand, bestowing a smile. A porter hastened to lift his bag from the boot and as he got out of the car he was momentarily dazzled by the light striking the silent spin of the glass revolving door that swept him through to an air-conditioned lobby. Inside, a young woman glided towards him with a tray on which there was a damp towel rolled tightly in a cylinder shape and a perspiring glass of mango juice. He thought of the airless guesthouse he had stayed in as a young man, thirty years ago, and reflected that there were a few benefits to being middle-aged and a desk-based senior economic analyst rather than a young undercover operative.

The Institute's Jakarta office was in a modern slab of a building in Setiabudi. He got a cab there to start off with, when he was staying at the hotel, but at the end of his first week he moved to an apartment that was walking distance from the office. He spent a lot of time in the apartment at first: it was a relief to be in a calm white box; silent, entirely his. His job was to acclimatise, read a lot of reports, make contact with the local clients and with government officials: he would be befriending civil servants rather than gangsters this time around. President Soeharto, Father of Development, had been in power for thirty-two years, but there was no sign that he, or the many relatives of his who held one office or another, would be vacating their seats any time soon.

He didn't rush to prowl the streets in the way he had done on his last visit. He was an old man now. Instead of running with the youths or hanging out in expat bars talking to journalists, he worked at the Institute's office or stayed at home in the white apartment, where a cleaner came daily and the brown leather sofa was cracked but pliant. For the first few weeks, he spent almost every evening there, doing his homework, watching the news and studying reports of how the Asian economic crash had come about. He brushed up his Indonesian, which came back to him with pleasing clarity. He continued to plough his way through a Dutch study of *Prelambang Jayabaya*: ancient prophecies had their uses at a time like this, in a country like this. He learned the Pancasila principles, which the politicians quoted endlessly. He took the paperwork part of his job very seriously. That was what he was, now.

Two weeks after his arrival, one Saturday, when he was reading on the brown leather sofa in the white apartment with the air conditioning on full, the telephone rang. It was Francisca. It was breakfast time in Amsterdam and he guessed, as soon as she spoke, that she had not slept well.

'Hi . . .' she said, her voice still slurred with sleep. He pictured her standing in the kitchen in her lemon-yellow robe, waiting for the coffee to brew – she drank it black and piping hot, pouring small amounts each time into her favourite blue demitasse. He felt certain she had decided to call him on impulse.

'Hi . . .' he replied, thinking of her thin frame and the belt on the robe pulled tight, the tumble of curls on her head. He felt the tug of familiarity. He had liked to hold her head against his chest in bed – or was it simply that she had liked to rest her head on him and he had put his hand there, on the back of her head, instinctively, because it was expected? All he knew was that in that moment, he felt the allure of that – the picture and feeling of it seemed suddenly clear across the thousands of miles that separated them. A relationship as long as theirs could not help but have a half-life, however certain they both were that it was over.

'How's it going . . . ?' she asked, softly, and they talked of nothing for a while. She had woken lonely and had rung to comfort herself with the sound of his voice. 'How's work?' she asked, but he could hear her moving around the kitchen and knew she wasn't really listening to what he was saying any more than she had done when they were together, any more than he had done to her. That was what it was like, after a few years: you could conduct a relationship on automatic pilot, thank God.

'Local firms are really suffering now,' he said, just making conversation. 'The devaluation's showing up in their balance sheets, can't get rid of their own currency fast enough, buying what few dollars they can while they can buy any. It's bad.'

'Mmmm . . .' replied Francisca. She had, over the years, perfected the art of the non-committal, encouraging noise that kept him talking while her mind was elsewhere. 'Always is, though, isn't it?' He heard her take a sip of coffee.

'This one's different,' he replied. 'Nobody can buy anything imported any more, think what that means.'

'Mmmm, really?'

Francisca worked as a personnel manager for a medium-sized clothing import business out at Muiderpoort. She knew plenty about how currency rates affected businesses, but he had never been able to persuade her to debate the wider picture with him. It had always annoyed him that a woman as intelligent as her didn't take more interest in global affairs, but then people who lived in countries with hard currencies couldn't grasp it: the idea that your job, your home, your life could be as vulnerable to currency changes as they would be to a tidal wave that engulfed your house in water.

'It's Christmas soon. I miss you,' she said then, a catch in her throat, and he knew that was a lie, and that he didn't miss her either. It was just the ghosts of their former selves on the phone to each other, mimicking the past.

It wasn't Christmas in Jakarta, and by January, you needed more than eleven thousand rupiah to buy yourself one single dollar.

Each morning, Harper rose with the dawn and set off early – the hot walk to the office was infinitely preferable to the claustrophobia of being stuck in a car. It was either wet or dusty, rarely sunny. The anti-government or pro-government protest demos were mostly further north, on the Hotel Indonesia roundabout or Merdeka Square. The old Hotel Indonesia was showing its age and era; it had been declared a national heritage site. Sixties architecture wasn't chic and modern these days but a relic in need of preservation. What it really needed was a big multinational to come in and modernise and restore it, but who was going to do that now, with everything so unstable?

There was a six-lane dual carriageway just before his office. Before he crossed it, he would stop by a food stall on the corner, outside a blue shopping mall, and eat standing up, then buy all the newspapers from the stand next to it. He was often first in at their unlovely, grey stone building, sandwiched between two much more glamorous, gleaming towers. He would unlock, open the shutters in his office, the only one that had any natural light. There were six local staff now – the three Harper worked with were a man the same age as him, Wahid, and two young women who acted mostly as translators and administrators, well-educated young people who were hoping that if they worked all hours then one day this Western firm might actually start paying them properly. Wahid reminded Harper a little of his old colleague from before, Abang, a phlegmatic type, did his job, fed his family, rarely passed judgement. What had happened to Abang? He must be in his seventies now, or dead.

Amber and Wahid would arrive not long after him and Amber would make them all coffee while Harper spread the papers across his desk and turned his computer on to this thing called email that he still didn't like, messages that took forever to fill the screen, line by line. It was, in his opinion, a lot less efficient than picking up the phone.

The local client base still worked mostly by phone and every day Amber was fielding more and more calls from companies wanting to know what was going to happen, what should they do? In February, the government announced a twenty-five-day ban on all street protest. Such bans always led to an increase in whatever activity they were trying to prevent. Amsterdam started to get twitchy: well, the clients started getting twitchy and that communicated itself to Harper and his team via Amsterdam. Harper advised that the large-scale companies, the important international clients, should sit tight. This kind of instability had been going on and off for years – Soeharto would never allow chaos on his watch.

'Are you sure?' Jan in Amsterdam kept asking. 'Our credibility is at stake here. If things are going to go belly up out there, our clients want to be warned, they don't want to get caught out.' Nobody knew what was going to happen in Jakarta well in advance, least of all people who lived in Jakarta.

Then in May, something did happen: a protest at Trisakti University, four students shot dead. Later, they would call it the Trisakti Incident – but it wasn't an incident when it happened, it was the army shooters getting trigger-happy after months of unrest and, possibly, just the beginning. Jakarta exploded.

That was when Amsterdam sent in Henrikson.

When it all kicked off, Harper was in his apartment, watching the riots on a small TV sheltered by the doors of a walnut cabinet opposite the brown leather sofa. He had been at home writing a report all day and only turned on the television that evening. The commentary complained of forces conspiring against the people as the camera showed a street where young men were aiming sideways kicks at shop fronts, flying it seemed, their bodies at improbable horizontals, and then suddenly, at the front of the screen, two women were laughing and rushing toward the camera, carrying something heavy between them. Harper sat upright, thinking for a moment they were carrying a human torso, then realised that they were struggling with a huge, frozen joint of meat, heavy enough to bend them double and threatening to slip from their grasp as they ran. They passed behind the cameraman and beyond them was revealed a man who lifted something and shook it in the air triumphantly. It looked like a plastic mop handle. Beyond him, there were the hurrying figures of a crowd criss-crossing the street, each person carrying something, and, dimly, beyond them, black smoke pouring out of a shop. This was what happened when you made people's lives harder and harder: eventually, things got so hard there was nothing to lose. Why fear retribution when your life is a punishment already?

He picked up the phone and tried to get through to Wahid: he tried the office line but there was no answer, then tried him at home but his line was engaged. All this was going to make a nervous client base very unhappy – there had been stories of people fleeing to the airport and getting carjacked by looters on the flyover. Failing to reach Wahid, he wondered if he should check in with Amsterdam. Then he had another beer and went to bed.

He knew, as he turned off his light, that that was not what he should be doing: but he told himself that what was going to happen would happen, and the best thing was to get a good night's sleep, then call Wahid for an update as soon as he woke up.

His pager went off before dawn. As soon as he heard the beep, he knew he had made the wrong call the night before. He called the office back home, as the message demanded. Jan – solid, unflappable Jan – was not happy. He wanted to know what the hell Harper was doing in his apartment, why hadn't he gone straight to the office as soon as word of the riots got out? Why hadn't he spent the night at the office on the phone? There had been an emergency meeting of the Asia Department, he told him. They were sending in an extraction team for the clients. It would be led by an Extraction Specialist, Henrikson.

Harper sat on the side of his bed, the room very dark and stuffy and the sheet clinging to his thighs. He was still sweating from the sudden awakening. 'If there's an extraction plan, I can arrange it,' he said firmly. 'We've got the contacts.' Perhaps if he was adamant enough he could convince his boss the clients were being melodramatic and he had it all under control.

'It's a long time since you've had to organise anything like that.'

Why not just say it, Harper thought. I'm old. I'm unreliable. You don't trust me to manage an emergency. 'I'm on the ground, and I have Wahid to help.' He wasn't going to lose this battle without arguing back.

'Henrikson will be on the ground too, later today. Wahid has booked the car from the airport, he's going to check into Le Méridien first and he'll be at the office for a briefing early afternoon. We've told the clients to prepare their staff.'

'We're going to need SUVs, lots of them, there's no point in trying to be discreet, people are getting carjacked, that's why I haven't . . .'

Jan was in no mood to acknowledge Harper's expertise. 'Wahid is on the case with transport. Henrikson will do security. Your job is to liaise between them.'

'But this . . .' Harper began.

'Give him all the assistance he needs,' his boss snarled then, dropping any pretence that this was a collaborative discussion. 'Don't get in his way. You've been telling us for weeks to sit tight, well the clients won't sit tight any longer and now we're having to extract them in an emergency situation. They're not happy and neither am I.'

Henrikson showed up at the office later that day, in chinos and a polo shirt, fresh from his power shower at Le Méridien. He was medium-height and medium-build, white, brown-haired – everything about him was medium. He looked like a man designed by a committee whose specification was someone who would never, ever stand out in a crowd. The committee had got one thing wrong though: the directness in his grey-eyed gaze. When he greeted you, it was obvious he was just a little too well trained to be real.

'Henrikson,' Henrikson announced, to each staff member in turn, shaking their hand and looking them right in the eye.

'Henrikson,' Henrikson said to Harper, and when he shook his hand, he placed the other hand on top, to demonstrate a special affection – but only briefly. He didn't want to come across as creepy. Harper imagined his boss telling Henrikson, 'Harper might be a little funny about you taking over there, he's old-school, so just go in slow and get him on side.'

'Well,' Henrikson said, after he had greeted them all, lifting his hands a little either side of his body in an expansive gesture and letting them drop, 'it's so good to meet you all. I hear you've all been doing terrific work out here.' Harper was reassured by the certain knowledge that every other person in the room had taken an instant dislike to Henrikson as well.

In Harper's office, Henrikson sat the other side of Harper's desk and nodded very sincerely while Harper went through their client list, telling him which ones had already left. When it came to diplomatic staff, each government's special forces had dealt with their own people, of course, immediately after Trisakti. The remaining clients were all commercial. Priority was getting families out. They debated whether spouses should be discouraged from giving press interviews when they arrived at their airports in London or Sydney or New York. Nothing made a better news item than an attractive and distressed wife clutching a child in her arms and talking about burning buildings. The media adored a white, articulate refugee.

Harper's view was, let them talk. 'You can hardly suppress the news coverage of what's happening here. There's nothing we can do about that.'

Henrikson placed the fingers of both hands to form a pyramid shape and nodded very sincerely. 'Well, you're the local expert,' he said. *Oh fuck off*, Harper thought. 'But I have to say that we had this discussion back in Amsterdam and company policy now is firm discouragement of anybody talking to the press; staff, clients, families. The potential for misrepresentation is just too high. We don't want our client base thinking we let this become an emergency.' The criticism of Harper's *sit tight* policy was clear.

He chose to ignore it, thinking, he even talks like a training manual. I can't believe I have to play these games at my age. 'Well, the press can be very useful too.'

'Agreed, agreed . . .' Henrikson nodded, firmly and repeatedly, quite dogged in his insistence on how much he agreed. 'You're quite right there. Well, I guess I'd better find me a desk and a phone so I can get going calling the clients.' He clapped both of his hands on his knees, clamping down firmly. Harper noticed how muscled Henrikson's legs were beneath his trousers. On one side of his neck, a thick vein pulsed and the purposefulness in his grey-eyed gaze was touched with the smallest hint of psychosis. God help us, Harper thought. This is what the Institute produces these days.

There was a light tap at the door and Wahid opened it. 'Boss?' he said to Harper.

'What is it?' Henrikson asked.

Wahid said to Harper, 'Amber says we should go and take a look from the roof.'

Amber stayed in the office fielding calls while Harper, Henrikson, Wahid and two staff from the other team traipsed up the interior staircase until they reached the top floor. Wahid pushed open a blank door to the service corridor, where the pretence of the building's painted walls and tiled floors fell away to reveal breezeblocks and a short iron staircase leading up to the roof. The light was bright white as they emerged, blinking. Wahid pointed and Harper saw immediately, looking north, the palls of black smoke rising from Old Jakarta, four columns, huge and black and billowing. To the right, further in the distance, was the blur of many more.

'Amber took two calls at once,' Wahid said. 'Doesn't sound all that spontaneous.'

'Doesn't look it either,' Harper replied. 'More than yesterday, you think?'

'Lot more.'

Henrikson hitched his trousers, clapped his hands together, leaned towards them, then actually said, 'Right, team.'

It was a week after the students had been shot. The shopping centre riots had died down, it seemed, but rumours were rife that soldiers were going round in plain clothes killing Chinese and raping women in gangs. They were saying hundreds dead – Harper's staff thought it was far greater. Most of the families of their clients had been extracted and only essential personnel were left: even they were on standby. The Institute was taking the precaution of closing the office and moving ops to Le Méridien, a move that Harper thought a colossal waste of money. They were all working round the clock now.

As Harper came into Wahid's office that morning, closing the door behind him, Wahid was standing by his desk, holding a claw hammer. He waved it at Harper.

Harper pulled a face. 'As personal protection goes, that looks a little basic.'

'It's strong enough for a skull – but in fact, it's for these.' Wahid gestured with the hammer at his desk, which was scattered with floppy disks in blue plastic cases.

'Is that necessary?' Harper asked. They weren't very big. Surely they could be hidden somewhere?

'Henrikson's orders,' Wahid replied, tipping his head on one side and pursing his lips.

'Where is that lump of meat this morning?'

'One of the embassies or banks, he wouldn't say.'

Harper and Wahid looked at each other then and both tapped the sides of their noses – a gesture Henrikson used when he didn't answer a question.

'Amber said he left some instructions for me, with you?'

'Oh yes, this.'

Wahid put the hammer down and unlocked a small drawer in his desk. He withdrew a black, hardback notebook. 'Client list, handwritten, did it last night. We've wiped the computers and the floppies are going.' He gestured at the floppy disks with his hammer. 'You've to take charge of this, Henrikson wants you to keep it at your apartment and take it to the hotel tomorrow, where he will personally place it in the safe inside his room.'

Harper groaned. 'Why didn't he just take it with him?'

'He said he wants to interview hotel security before he lets the notebook into the building.'

'You are joking, aren't you?'

'I'm afraid not.' Wahid tapped the side of his nose again.

As Harper turned to go, the notebook in his jacket pocket, Wahid added, 'By the way, there's an Englishman here. He's been waiting for you over an hour. Amber made the mistake of saying you'd be in at some point. He asked for you by name.'

'What sort of Englishman?'

'A client-type sort. But local commerce, small.'

'Extractive industries or import and export?'

Wahid frowned down at the floppy disks. 'Do you think this will damage my desk?'

'Well, you aren't going to damage the disks if you don't.'

Wahid lifted a finger. 'Good point,' then picked up a handful of the disks, bent to put them in a neat pile on the floor and knelt beside them. 'Extractive,' he said, 'but small-time and nearing his pay-off, I would say, I'm not even sure if he's still paying subs.' He brought the hammer down on the disks and the top one skidded across the room and smacked into a wall where it span and came to rest, undamaged.

'Good luck with that,' Harper said, as he reached for the door.

The Englishman was waiting in the small, empty room they used for meetings and interviews. The only decoration was a crispy-looking cactus plant in a red bowl on the windowsill – the window was frosted; it looked out over the internal corridor of the building – and a tattered, bleached map of Indonesia hanging from two bamboo poles and a piece of string slung over a nail on a wall.

In the middle of the room was a rectangular table with four chairs and the Englishman, whose stomach put his suit jacket under a certain degree of strain, was leaning back on one chair with his feet up on another. He had his eyes closed. On the table was a bottle of cheap whisky and two glasses, one half full.

'Have you been waiting long?' Harper asked politely. Damn, what was the man's name?

The Englishman sat up quickly, put his feet down and shook his head as if he had been asleep. 'Oh Harper, there you are, what took you?' His voice was very slightly slurred.

'Small matter of the city in uproar,' said Harper, sitting down on a chair opposite, pouring himself a whisky and topping up the Englishman's glass. 'You want some coffee with that?'

'Terrible habit,' the Englishman replied, 'very bad for you. Only drink green tea now.'

Harper half-turned back towards the door but the Englishman said, 'Don't bother your young ladies, they have enough to do tearing all those papers up.'

'What can I do for you?' Harper asked. They had met three or four times, he remembered now. He was a local vice president of some company or other, did he export sandalwood?

'I'm just here informally,' the man said, sipping his whisky. 'Just informally, as, you know, just wondering what your opinion is on the way things are . . . going, you know,' he waved a hand in the air, 'going.'

Ah, free information. That was why the man had brought a bottle of whisky, a gesture from one chum to another.

'Well, let's just hope that whatever the outcome is, it leads to improved stability for the Indonesian people,' Harper said, in a tone formal enough to indicate that he had no intention of giving anything for nothing. If this man wanted a report, his company could pay for it.

The Englishman groaned. 'C'mon Harper, you're an experienced man, don't go sentimental on me, I have decisions to make. You like fishing?'

He's more drunk than I realised, Harper thought. Ten minutes of politeness, no more, then he would have to lever him out of the door. 'Yes, don't get much time for it, but yes.' He had never fished in his life.

'Well, you have a bag of big fish, I don't know, some large trout or something, and there's one fish you want to let go, maybe it's small or sickly, but even so, you're hardly going to make a hole in your net, are you? Next thing you know, all the damn fish are going to wriggle out of it.'

'I'm not sure I follow you.'

'Well, the big man is hardly going to let the protestors have their way. You've heard Kopassus is involved?'

'What makes you think that?'

'Oh c'mon, Harper, there's a few too many "students" with military haircuts milling round, don't you think?'

The Englishman suddenly bent forward and clapped his hands on his knees. 'Right! Right you are!' as if he was replying to something Harper had said, rather than just agreeing with himself, as if he had got the information he came for. He stood, a little unsteadily, his centre of gravity shifting over one foot so that he tipped into a slight diagonal before righting himself. He turned, and Harper thought, great, but instead of heading for the door, the Englishman wheeled round to the wall to face the faded map and stood there, waving his glass at it.

'It looks as if God just took a few rocks and a load of pebbles and went . . .' The Englishman made a sweeping gesture with the glass. 'But beautiful. A whole country made of islands. Fifteen thousand . . . can't exactly . . . *push* them all . . . together I mean.' He turned to Harper and gestured with his hands, holding both palms apart then pushing the air between them, as if Harper was personally responsible for making sure that the islands of the archipelago did not drift apart in different directions, floating off irresponsibly to join other continents. His tone was a little accusatory. 'How do you expect to hold it all together?'

It was seventeen thousand islands, actually. Harper wasn't sure if the man was just stupendously drunk or discovering his mystical side. He must hide his drinking from his firm back home – not hard to do when you were thousands of miles away – but even British firms were getting better at sacking drunks these days. Harper made a mental note, just in case the information should prove useful. He would have to check what the man's name was when he was gone, what relationship, if any, Harper's firm still had with his.

'I thought God had abandoned me back then . . .' the man mumbled, looking down into his glass, '. . . they believe in so much here, you know, sure not what we believe but at least . . .'

Next he was going to start telling Harper how Timor was created by two small boys and a crocodile.

Instead, the Englishman took a vicious swig of whisky, turned and glared at Harper, his voice becoming harsh. 'Now the great Soeharto, Sustainer of the Universe, is on his way out, they are all at it.' He coughed heartily. 'Face it, Harper, these people just *like* killing each other.'

It occurred to Harper to remark that, in actual fact, they weren't killing each other, not really. The people being burned alive in shopping malls in the north of the city weren't burning anyone back. When an elderly woman got lynched for being a witch in East Java, she didn't lynch another person in return. This was the way killing worked: there were perpetrators, and there were victims. It wasn't a two-way process.

'You think he is on the way out?' Harper asked politely. 'Then who is giving Kopassus their orders?'

The man looked down. 'No you're right, he'll never go, not without a fight anyway, not without a few more thousand bodies piling up in the streets.'

Harper stood up. The man's voice had lost its energy. Harper needed to get him out of the office before he sat down again otherwise they might never get him up. 'I have to agree with you there,' he said, moving to the man's side and gently placing one hand beneath his elbow, to edge him towards the door.

'You think so, really?' the man said, looking at Harper earnestly. He looked down again. 'You're the expert. Well, thanks for the drink.' He put his glass down then unbuttoned his jacket and used both hands to hitch his trousers before buttoning his jacket again.

Harper got the man to the corridor and administered a small shove. The man paused, swayed, then gave a farewell salute by touching his own forehead and flicking his hand upwards.

Back in the office, Harper raised his eyebrows at Amber. She was on the phone and mouthed, 'Sorry' over the receiver.

Harper went to his own office, sat behind his desk, unlocked his drawer and took out his large notepad and a pencil. Even a drunk Englishman could see President Soeharto was never going to go of his own accord. He leaned forward in his chair, over the notepad, but when he put the sharpened pencil to the pad, the point snapped off. Suddenly, his breath was short in his chest. He sat in the chair, staring at the pencil, and realised he had pressed it down on the pad with such force that his hand was shaking. He put the pencil down, carefully, then gripped his shuddering right arm with his left hand. He squeezed lightly. That only seemed to make the shaking worse. He relinquished his own arm, then leaned back in his seat, closed his eyes and made himself breathe deeply . . . one, two, three, in . . . one, two, three, out . . . His left leg was shaking too, juddering beneath the table.

Henrikson was absent all day, a fact that Harper was grateful for. Outside, a three-hour downpour saturated the city but when it lifted Harper went into Wahid's office and said he was going to get a car to take him round some of the bars, just have a drink in each, see which expat communities were still around, talk to a few people. People became loquacious at a time like this – that much he certainly remembered from '65, they closed ranks but amongst those ranks, they talked. At least, he told himself that was why he was doing it.

Wahid looked at him and Harper saw concern behind the man's small round glasses. 'Is that a good idea?'

Harper shrugged. 'Well, we've been sitting in the office for days while Henrikson runs around the city like he's James Bond.'

'Going to check with him first?'

'Of course not. If he asks where I am, say I tried to call him and couldn't get through.'

He was woken by the bleep of his pager. *Shit*, he thought, reeling in bed, his hand outstretched, simultaneously registering that it was bright daylight at the edge of his blinds. What time was it? The apartment seemed unnaturally quiet. Normally, the traffic noise from outside was a blur of sound. Even though he was only half awake as his hand scrabbled amongst the keys, phone, water bottle and tissues on his bedside table, he knew that the streets outside were deserted. He hadn't a clue where he was, though, or what time it was. Then he thought, *the apartment*. But how come it was so bright? Oh, he hadn't closed the blinds when he got in last night.

Last night?

The pager had gone silent. He sat up and looked around. It wasn't on his bedside table. Damn, he couldn't afford to miss an emergency. Then it bleeped again and he located it on the floor. His trousers lay in a crumpled heap next to the bed – the pager must have fallen out of a pocket. *Call Motorola*. He called the office message system but instead of Henrikson or Wahid there was a female voice he didn't recognise. 'Hi, it's Alison from the *FT*, hey, thanks for the mojitos, give me a call when you're awake, super-discreet as promised. *Ciao*, buddy!' The last two words were said with a friendly flourish.

Why was a journalist sending him messages on his emergency pager? Perhaps she was a client and keeping the tone light. He grabbed the trousers from the floor and pushed his hands into the pockets until he found a business card: *Alison Rutgers, Asia Correspondent, Financial Times*, and a local number.

When she answered the phone, she didn't sound like a client about to request an emergency evacuation.

'Hey, great to hear from you, how's the head?'

He mimicked her tone. 'Hmmm, well, let's say it's been better, how's yours?'

She gave a little laugh. 'It was pretty hard getting up this morning.' And he knew instantly that she was not hungover at all – that however many mojitos they had drunk together the night before, she had been on a non-alcoholic variety, probably by saying quietly to the waiter, *skip the rum in mine*. He'd been caught out like that before. 'Café Batavia mix them pretty strong when the owner's having one of his party nights,' she continued, 'he's an Aussie, think I told you? The real place is the Tanamur, though, can't believe you haven't been there yet.' He was well aware of the Tanamur's reputation, which was why he had steered clear. But he had confided in her last night that he'd never been? Who the hell was she and what did she want? 'Listen,' she said, 'sadly this isn't just a call to check you're still alive.'

'How did you get my pager number?' he asked, cutting her off.

There was the briefest of pauses. 'You gave it to me last night.' He felt hot, and sick. 'But listen . . .'

'I have nothing to say to you.' He hung up.

Five minutes later, the pager, the highly confidential one reserved specifically for work emergencies, bleeped again. He called the Motorola number. This time, Alison's tone was very different. 'Hi John, me again, sorry if I disturbed you, look, I'll call your head office in Amsterdam and do this officially. I'm just looking for a quote, attributable or otherwise, on the Institute's evacuation plans, it's the major banks we're interested in, but I understand what you told me last night was off the record.' Her sign-off was unmistakeably spiteful. 'If you're all tied up today, I'll take it through official channels.'

Shit shit shit. He put his head in his hands. He could call her back. She would probably leave it an hour or so to see if he did. Then she would promise him anonymity in return for the information she needed. But the information would be traceable back to him: she knew that and she knew he knew it too. The Amsterdam office would be closed at this hour but the twenty-four-hour hotline monitored the regular office answering machine and if she left a message they might call her back straight away, head her off at the pass. Damage limitation. Did the bosses have any contacts at the *FT* that would kill the piece? His head reeled with solutions. Was she working on a feature or a news story?

He had no idea. He couldn't remember her at all: a vague image, perhaps, a swoop of dark hair? A hand on his knee, at one point? He thought hard and a little came back to him, but only a little. He had hailed a car and gone to some of the hotel bars first, then headed to Kota. There were still curfews and cordons everywhere, but to his surprise Café Batavia with its photos of Hollywood stars in dark wooden frames covering the walls was still open and quite busy with an influx of journalists and operatives new to Jakarta. There was some kind of party night going on. Someone nudging his elbow, apologising . . . He had turned . . . A smile, that swoop of hair . . .

He could just about remember her now: brown-eyed, small, vulnerable-looking. He couldn't remember how long he had stayed or what he had said. He couldn't remember how he had got home.

He had told Wahid he was going out on the streets, against protocol, to ask a few questions. Instead, it would appear that he had done the talking. If he had broken client confidentiality, the Institute would sack him on the spot: he was finished.

And then he thought to check his jacket pocket. The jacket was slung over the foot of the bed. The pockets were empty.

The taxi didn't get much beyond Glodok – they were still several streets from Fatahillah Square – when they were forced to stop at a police cordon; official barriers, officers in white helmets. The one who approached the driver's window had a whistle in his mouth and his hand already resting on the gun in his holster. He and the taxi driver had a hurried conversation.

'Tell him I'm a journalist,' Harper said from the back seat. 'Tell him I just need to get through to the square, I left something at Café Batavia last night, it isn't important but tell him, obviously, I'd be very grateful.' If he wanted to try getting a bribe into the policeman's hand, he would have to wind down the rear window.

The taxi driver was already putting the car into reverse as he shook his head. 'Sorry, sir, no further.'

'Okay, go back, then right, the end of the street and around.'

The driver reversed slowly back down the street.

After two more right turns, Harper said, 'Pull up here.'

The driver did as he was bid but then sat with his hand on the gearstick, looking straight ahead, clearly not wanting to offend a customer. 'Sir, I think good if I take you back to where you came from. Sir?'

'I'll get out here,' Harper replied, lifting his backside so he could reach inside his trouser pocket for some money.

'I don't think that is good, sir,' the driver replied, as he took the money, but Harper was already reaching for the door handle.

He took the backstreets, deserted but not cordoned: the roadblocks were to stop vehicles and large assemblies, not individuals. On foot, it was not hard to get to the square. Down one street, there was even an elderly lady calmly sweeping dried leaves and twigs into the ditch outside a crumbling, deserted-looking building, as if nobody had told her the city was in chaos. Most of the buildings were shuttered, though. People were still staying at home.

Fatahillah Square was deserted but for a single jeep outside the Jakarta History Museum. A few men lounged in it, smoking. Harper could see from across the square that Café Batavia was closed but he went up to it anyway, lifted a hand and pressed his nose against the glass. In the gloom at the back of the ground floor, he thought he saw movement, although it could just have been a reflection of some sort, but he banged on the glass anyway and rattled the doorknob. When he glanced behind him, he could see he had caught the attention of the young men in the jeep, who were watching him.

If any staff were inside Café Batavia, then they had no intention of opening up – but Harper knew in his bones he had come on a wild goose chase. What were the chances of the notebook being on the floor somewhere? Alison Rutgers was probably studying it right now, running a manicured finger down the list.

As he turned away from Café Batavia, one of the young men jumped down from the jeep, landing neatly with both feet together and bending at the knees, and began to walk casually across the square towards him. He turned left and walked swiftly but calmly towards the opposite corner. It was too far to walk all the way back and the sky was heavy and dark; another rainstorm was on its way. He would head south and hope for a cab somewhere beyond the cordons.

He was half an hour's walk south of the square when he heard it, the unmistakeable clamour of a crowd with its blood up: it was a collective sound, both ancient and familiar, a mixture of shouts and calls, the clatter of things breaking, chanting. He stopped to listen: it sounded as though it was coming from the road parallel to the one he was on. He turned down a side street that linked the roads. He hadn't eaten anything before he left the apartment and not a single stall or shop was open. His stomach was hollow. The gathering storm made the air close and humid. It was like breathing in soup.

The parallel street was full, a big crowd gathered, milling, a denser patch towards a small shopping centre located to his right, on the other side of the road, on a corner. No one paid him any attention. As he pushed through, he could see that there was a thick swarm of people in front of the mall. Most of the people had their backs to him, a group intent upon something in their midst.

Foreboding clutched at him, but only briefly. There was a note of hysteria in the shouts of the men and women, a rising inflection in their voices.

As he approached the group, three men on the edge of it turned. One started shouting and gesturing but the other next to him laughed and Harper laughed back, so they turned away from him again. He was tall enough to see over their heads but because the crowd was mobile, he had to shoulder his way into the midst of it. It was mostly young men, two or three young women – they didn't look like students, though, shop assistants or factory workers, perhaps, in plastic shoes and loose, plain shirts. Above their heads, the sky was now very dark.

There was a young man sitting on the ground, in the middle of the group. He had thick straight hair that hung down over his forehead and he was light-skinned, possibly Chinese Indonesian or possibly someone who just had the bad luck to look like one. His hair was matted with blood, and blood ran down his face. His shirt was torn and he was naked from the waist down. A pair of dirty trousers lay scuffed and ripped beside him. He had his arms raised and bent above his head as if to ward off blows and one forearm was gashed and grazed. As the men around Harper fell back a little, the young man on the ground lifted his face. He looked up at Harper and his wide eyes recognised him, with a glimmer of hope and fear, as a figure of authority.

The crowd pulled back a little, looking at him, waiting for him to react. Harper knew that all he had to do was nod, and draw back, and the crowd would beat the young man to death. He estimated him to be around seventeen.

'He's the shop owner's son!' said a man on Harper's left, defensively, angrily, although Harper had not asked for any explanation.

'You know what they are like! This one insulted my sister!' The man drew his foot back and aimed a kick at the young man on the ground but misjudged it and his foot swung in the air.

Harper stepped forward into the crowd in three bold, wide strides – the two people pressed either side of him fell back. He grabbed the young man by his injured arm and pulled him roughly to his feet. The young man called out in fear and pain, a high, whimpering cry. He was small and thin and as soon as Harper hauled him up, he slumped in his grasp. As he did, an older man in the crowd lifted his foot high, to thigh level, and aimed a vicious, hammer-like kick that connected with the young man's torso just above his hip. The kick nearly knocked the young man from Harper's hands.

He knew he had seconds. He pulled the limp young man round, away from the man who had kicked him, shouting, '*Ayo! Nèk̨ wani!*'

The young man then did the right thing for the wrong reason – out of sheer panic, he started to kick at Harper, feebly. This meant Harper could pull roughly at his arm and shout at him in fury, which got the crowd's support. A couple of them cheered.

He dragged the young man back the way he had come as fast as he could but several of the crowd followed and the road ahead was wide and clear, a row of concrete shop fronts with their shutters smashed and household goods spilling from them; plastic buckets, towels, shoes and sandals. Lying on its side in the middle of the street was a white metal object that might have been a storage chest or fridge. Broken glass surrounded it. It was a few minutes' walk back to the side street that Harper had emerged from and there were no alleyways or small turnings down which they could escape. Harper felt the first fat drops of rain on his arms and looked up just as the grey skies above crashed open and the downpour began.

The crowd of young people shrieked and laughed at each other. The two young men on Harper's left, who had been following them closely, ran into a looted shop for shelter, where they discovered a pile of tea trays they snatched up and held above their heads, calling out to their friends – and in the minutes this took, Harper watched until he was sure the crowd was sufficiently distracted before pulling at the unwilling young man and saying, '*Ayo!*' again but this time hissing rather than shouting.

Still, the young man did not understand he was being saved. Harper had to clench his upper arm in his fist with all his strength as he dragged him along until, finally, at the end of the street he was able to turn right and shove him up against a wall and hold him there for a minute, by the shoulders, looking into his face. 'Go home. Don't go back that way. Do you understand?' he said in Indonesian, but the young man seemed too shocked to comprehend and the minute Harper took his hands away from his shoulders, he reeled from him, back the way they had come.

Harper called out as the young man turned the corner – he was damned if he was going to have gone to all that effort only for him to endanger them both by running back to the crowd – and the young man stopped, staring back down the main street, then finally understood, reeled round again and, half bent double and with no acknowledgement to Harper, staggered off down the side street.

It was pouring with rain now. Harper stood for a moment, the adrenaline of the incident draining from him. Already, a small muddy river was flowing down the drain on the other side of the street. He lifted his shirt, untucked from his trousers in the chaos, and wiped his face. People would be taking shelter in the looted shops now, all but the most determined rioters that was. It should be safe to find his way back to his apartment but it would be a good idea to avoid the main streets until he was well clear of the old quarter and could find a cab. He lifted his face to the heavens, closed his eyes and opened his mouth, letting the hard raindrops fall on his tongue and sting his face. They were right to send in Henrikson, he thought, I'm too old for this.

His apartment was on the fifth floor and the lift had broken down several months ago – the maintenance company couldn't afford the replacement parts, which were German, so it had stayed broken. He climbed the stairs slowly and by the third floor, his legs had started to shake. He paused for a moment, thinking, how hopeless. Then he thought, no, it isn't just stairs, you've climbed these stairs many times without difficulty. It isn't just the heat or humidity either – it's the draining of the adrenaline, come on, you know this one.

His hand shook as he put the key into his apartment door. He closed it behind him and leant against it. The maid had been while he was out and the apartment was tidy, swept. The pile of books and papers he had left on the small dining table was neatened, the pens next to it laid out in a row. His legs were still trembling. How odd. And then, he was shuddering from head to foot, so much it was shaking his lungs, and he began breathing in great gulps. He had saved a boy. Without any part of his body alerting him to what was about to happen, apart from the trembling that seemed to come from everywhere and nowhere, he sank down onto the polished wooden floor, crashing onto his knees. He had saved a boy. It was a fissure. It was enough.

He crawled across the floor, ruffling the thin rug, to the cabinet – dark polished wood – where he kept the whisky. As he extracted a tumbler it slipped from his grasp and then rolled in a semi-circle by his knee. He grabbed it and threw it to one side, meaning only to remove it from his immediate vicinity because he didn't want it but it flew across the room and smashed against a wall. He unscrewed the bottle and threw the lid in the same direction, where it landed with a tinny clatter. He drank from the bottle, long and hard, and once he had started he did not stop. It was the closeness of everything. Here he was, and the floor was polished and clean because the maid had been in while he had been out in a city in which people were being beaten, killed, and there was a television and a sofa and a fridge with food in it, and all the normal business of a normal life, and a few minutes ago he had watched a boy come close to having his life snuffed out, beaten from him – and that could happen or nearly happen, and he, Harper, could then go home and put his key in his door and have a beer, or perhaps something to eat, just like all the other people who were doing things just like that, and minutes away, the world was ending for a boy, or for another boy like him, in the most horrible way. And it wasn't long ago or in the middle of nowhere: it was now, in one of the modern cities of the world. And all at once, he realised that what he could not stand was the closeness of everything. Yes, that was it. There would always be horrors, perhaps. Perhaps there would never be a time in human history when they would not exist because it would take so long for *Homo sapiens* to develop to that stage that a meteor would have wiped them all out by then, like the dinosaurs, or a freak tidal wave would have washed them all away – darkness upon earth, cold and dark, before this sick soft race worked out how to live without huge numbers of it suffering cold and hunger and humiliation in order for the lucky few to live in something approaching peace and comfort. But the closeness of it: the fact that he could walk out of his clean, white apartment again right now if he wanted and a few streets away . . . and it rippled out, everywhere, beyond Jakarta, beyond Java – on Borneo the Dayaks hated the Madurese and the Madurese hated them back and why stop with these islands? They were far from unique. The Middle East – let's not even go there – and the Pakistanis had tested those missiles and had India in their sights. And then Poppa and Nina, and Nina saying, 'Go back upstairs, Poppa's just clearing something off the lawn.' And why was there something on the lawn? Oh, because Poppa's skin was black, that was why. And then they couldn't even walk up a path up a mountain without people staring at them and why not, not for anything you've done or even want to do, just because of what you are. And his mother, his mother as a slim girl, running down the road, and his father, who he had never met, killed for not wearing an armband. He saw Francisca weeping and weeping in the hospital: the face of their drowned baby, perfect in repose, mouth a little open – there had never been anything more perfect. He saw Bud's face, lifted upwards, dreamily, skyward, and heard his own voice shouting, '*Bud!*' as loud as it was possible to shout, at the same moment Bud's eyes opened.

He crawled around the polished floor: everyone, all over the world, knew these things happened and looked the other way and got the bus to work and collected children from school and at least those sickening soft ordinary sorts of people in Holland or England or America had the benefit of distance to blanket their ignorance. But him, and people like him. They knew how close it all was. They knew what burned flesh smelled like. He heard Komang's children, screaming.

And then the creatures started climbing out of the walls. He rang the twenty-four-hour emergency hotline at the Institute in Amsterdam, the one that was reserved for operatives or clients in imminent danger, and told them that cannibals were eating his legs while he was still alive. Soeharto would never resign. He would send out the cannibals. And they would slice the flesh off him and men like him and they would cook it over fires while they watched and everyone should get out get out get out now. He screamed it down the phone. Then he hung up and fell asleep on the floor.

The next morning, he was woken by a tapping sound, the more intrusive for its lightness, on the apartment door. He opened his eyes. He was not in a bed. He was lying on a hard wooden floor. He lay very still. The tapping continued, lightly. He felt very calm.

He sat up, propping himself up on one elbow. It was full daylight, the shutters open, the air in the room light and smoky. He hauled himself up to his feet, staggered a little, reeled towards the door, but before he reached it there was the small clatter of a key and Wahid let himself in along with two men Harper didn't know. Wahid stopped when he saw him and with a look on his face said, 'The old man has gone, John. Soeharto's resigned. You've got to call Amsterdam now, then we are here to take you to the airport. You're going on holiday.'

He stared back at Wahid. The two other men stepped past him and began moving around the apartment. One bent and straightened the rug in front of him. The other began using the side of his foot to sweep some broken glass to the edge of the floor, against the wall. Only then did Harper look around the room and see that the small dining table was pushed at an angle, a chair overturned, papers and books and pencils on the floor.

'I'll get your things,' Wahid said, and walked into the bedroom.

Harper went into the bathroom and locked the door behind him. He bent over the sink and splashed his face with cold water. His hand slipped on the tap as he shut the water off – it was made of mottled brown plastic that was supposed to look like marble. In the mirror above the sink he saw his ravaged face, his hair damp at the edges, thinning. His eyes were large and watery like those of any man of his age – the tear ducts were not working properly any more. Of all the irritations of ageing, he had not expected that one to bother him so much. Even though he had not vomited, there was the taste of something bitter in his throat. He bent and ran the cold tap and tried to rinse his mouth, swilling and spitting, but the bitter taste was too far down his throat to be dislodged. Enough, he thought, his hands against the edge of the sink, letting his head drop, like a beaten dog, the bitter taste in his mouth, and the knowledge that would not be dislodged from his head stuck there, inside, like a growth of some sort. Enough. He would do whatever they said.

Wahid tapped gently on the bathroom door. 'John,' he called, 'John, you need to come out and talk to Amsterdam. They're on the phone now.'

It was daybreak now, all greyness gone, the sun was full and the valley glowing as if it had been sprayed with very fine gold paint. Still Kadek had not come. Harper wondered if he had observed him and Rita on the veranda together and was discreetly delaying his arrival, waiting in the lane until the coast was clear. Or – and here was a thought – returning to the village after spying on them, to report back that Harper had had an overnight guest at the hut?

Back in Amsterdam, there had, no doubt, been a meeting about him. He had cracked up before and they had brought him back into the fold – but that was when he was in his twenties, newly trained, with decades of useful life in him. What was he now?

He had probably frightened the young woman on the end of the twenty-four-hour hotline. The call would have been recorded. He imagined Jan and some of the other partners gathered in the office at the end of the building, the one with the curved glass wall and the bare brick. There were fourteen partners now – but not all of them would have been called in to deal with a personnel issue. There would be five or six of them in the room, perhaps, and the head of personnel, and the specialist personnel secretary to take the minutes – Hannah would have been kept out of the loop because they were friends, he thought: it was clear she had known nothing when he called her from the hotel in Sanur. He imagined the head of personnel reaching out and pressing the 'on' button on the tape recorder with a hard click, and the men around the table all listening to him shouting about cannibals, the young woman operative taking the call staying very calm and saying, 'Would you repeat that for me, please?' He imagined the head of personnel leaning forward and turning off the tape, the small silence that would follow that second click and the glances that would go from man to man around the table, the faces they would pull. The senior partner in charge of Asia, a plump half-Japanese half-German who he liked a lot, would take off his glasses and rub at the bridge of his nose before replacing them, inflating his cheeks as he blew air out of his mouth, saying, with a sigh, 'Well . . . this is an interesting one . . .'

'So . . .' he said to Rita, 'here I am. Not on holiday, not exactly. Enforced leave. If you can call it that.'

He was still holding her from behind, speaking into the back of her hair.

'That tickles,' she said, a smile in her voice. 'I didn't think you were really on holiday, you know. You didn't show a great deal of interest in sightseeing. Have you been sacked?'

'I don't know, probably, they just haven't told me yet. They are working out how to get rid of me discreetly.' He had made the Institute sound harmless enough.

'Give me a cigarette,' she said.

He leaned over to the packet, which sat on the edge of the rail, lit a *kretek* for her, passed it forward. She stayed where she was, looking out over the valley. 'I don't really understand why you're in so much trouble.'

'I was sent out here to draw up a report on the devaluation of the rupiah, the unrest it might lead to. I said things would stay stable, I said Soeharto would never resign. Badly wrong on both counts. Then the students were shot, and the riots.'

'Terrible . . .'

'I guess at that point I went to the other extreme, after before, I mean, once it got going, I thought it was all going to kick off like it did before.'

'In sixty-five, you mean?' She shook her head, leaned it back a little against him. 'The world is different now.'

He rested his chin on her shoulder. 'They thought the world was different then.'

She drew on the *kretek*, exhaled. 'Smoking this early is making me dizzy.'

'And I got drunk and broke client confidentiality to a journalist.'

'Oh,' she said. 'I'm guessing that isn't very cool.'

He sighed, lifted both hands and began to massage her shoulders. 'Truth is, I'm old.'

'You're not old, Donkey.'

'In my business, I'm old. And my boss will hate me now, my fuck-up will reflect badly on him. Makes his judgement look poor. If my intuition is shot to bits I'm no use to anyone.'

'Intuition is nothing more than experience, surely, just guess-work, anyway?'

He shook his head. 'If you're an oil company who pays tens of thousands of dollars for a report, you expect a little more than that.'

She shrugged. 'So, you've been sacked. Or you're going to be. It happens.' And he felt the small ache of loneliness he knew he would feel when he told her only a part of the truth.

She turned then, offered him the cigarette. 'It's making me dizzy . . .' she repeated, wobbling her head and rolling her eyes.

He took the cigarette, stepped back a little and smiled at her, drew on it, tossed it over the railing. They faced each other for a while, both smiling, and then the memory of his bad behaviour the night before returned to him and he reached out a hand, and, very gently, stroked her upper arm with the back of his fingers.

She lifted her chin a little then, gave him a cool look.

He exhaled.

'It's okay, you're sorry, I know,' she said softly, and stepped towards him at the same time as he moved against her, pressed his mouth to hers, lifted both hands and put them in her hair, holding her head still, his fingers entwined. Her mouth opened wide, their tongues mingled; smoke, sleep, familiarity. He pressed his groin to hers and ached with the desire to lift her knees, slip into the soft comfort of her right there on the veranda, with only the thin protection of a wooden railing stopping them from plunging, conjoined, into the lush thick valley below.

After a long while, he drew back, gave her a small smile of regret. Her gaze flicked to her right to make sure there was no sign of Kadek and she returned his smile. It was understood between them: their mutual need was enough.

He thought how short a time it was since they had first met, how few encounters they'd had, and he remembered how she had sat on the edge of the bed after their first night together at the guesthouse. He had looked at her then, had read her stillness – and concluded that there was something damaged about her, something that made mornings difficult. There was some knowledge in her life that she didn't like to wake up to, he had felt quite sure of it.

He stared at her and, self-conscious beneath his gaze, she dropped her head, turned back to look at the valley.

How much could he trust his own judgement, any more? Perhaps he was wrong about her. Perhaps she had just been thinking of everything she had to do that day, whether she needed to go back to the family compound she stayed in and get changed before work. Perhaps she had just been thinking about the textbook she had promised to lend one of her students.

And all at once, looking out over the valley with his body leaning against Rita's soft back, he was awash with hope, as clean as the dawn before him. If he was mistaken about Rita, then maybe he was mistaken about everything else. Maybe nobody was coming to kill him. Maybe there was no gathering of men in a glass-walled office, debating how to deal with the tricky problem he had become. Perhaps he could just say to her, 'We'd better get dressed before Kadek comes,' and Kadek could come and find them both on his balcony and he, Harper, would be nothing more than a man on extended leave from his job who had got lucky.

He thought of the rice fields beyond Jalan Bisma, where small plots of land were being divided up for villas. She could speak Balinese, she could negotiate for a lease. There was the matter of what they would use for a down payment as he'd signed the Amsterdam house over to Francisca and he doubted Rita had any resources behind her, but he had some savings in a dollar account. He wondered what the local bureaucracy was like, sometimes these things could take a while, but a bit of financing usually oiled the wheels and she would have good contacts with the local councils, they would be full of the parents of her students or perhaps some of her former students. She could walk to work from Jalan Bisma, even if they built a little way out of town. He could make shelves for her books: he bet she had a lot of books. He liked making shelves, had never done enough of it, in fact, he decided. In Amsterdam, their house had been too small for him to build anything, and too perfect, in a way. Francisca had made sure it was perfect.

He allowed these thoughts to dwell in his mind for a bit, to brew. Bali was peaceful. Soeharto had fallen, Habibie had taken over and the country was stabilising. Perhaps he had just been wrong about everything. Perhaps a life was possible here, with her. Now he had confided in her – to a certain extent – he had transformed so many difficult things; he had made them into stories. Stories could be put in boxes.

'It's so beautiful . . .' Rita said softly, her voice a murmur, as if she was thinking out loud. 'Isn't it? Don't you think, you could look at this, the trees and everything, and for a bit forget everything? If I could wake up to this every morning, maybe mornings would not be so hard.'

There was something in her tone of voice. He was still. 'Why are mornings so hard?'

She didn't answer for a long time. Then she said, her voice low but even, 'I have a son.'

He didn't respond.

'I don't know why, mornings are worst. I wake up, and it's just normal, but then I think of him, you know, that strange time when you are awake but not thinking? Only a few seconds, but it's my only relief. Then I think, and I think about how I haven't seen him since he was eight years old. He's a teenager now. I think about him all the time. But for some reason, in the mornings, he's in Belgium, I don't know. It doesn't seem so far when

I'm busy, during the day, but in the morning, when I wake up and remember it, it's so far it hurts. Every single morning.'

He rested his chin on her shoulder, leaned his head against hers.

She gave a little, false laugh. 'Any idea what some people think about you if you admit you have a child you don't live with, as a woman, I mean? I once made the mistake of telling a woman on an aeroplane and she spent the rest of the flight telling me how unnatural I was. We'd got talking during take-off. It was a seven-hour flight.'

She dropped her effortful facetiousness, then, and spoke plainly, with the tone of someone telling somebody else something they thought they ought to know, unembellished by anecdote. 'I had some real problems, after he was born. Head problems, you know?' She tapped the side of her head with one finger. 'I was in hospital for a while. A lot of drugs. Then I was okay. Then when he was four I had some more problems. I didn't get help when I should have done, you know. I was hospitalised again, eighteen months that time, nearer two years in fact. His father thought it was good I didn't see him until I was better and then I didn't get better for a long time and the longer it got, the easier it was to believe what his father said, that he was doing well without me, that it was disruptive for him, me coming and going. He's got a stepmother now, Lucia. She's Italian. I think about her cooking bacon for him because you know, he really liked bacon. But then I think, maybe she hates him, tells him his mother left him because he was no good. His father would back her up on that, that's for sure. Maybe he cries at night when he's alone, he won't in front of his friends I suppose. Maybe he's having a horrible life, and I'm not there.'

He was still holding her from behind. He rested his head against hers. He did not know how else to comfort her. He had no idea what it must be like, as a mother, to be separated from a child, but he knew enough to know that anything he said at that moment would sound crass. Touch was what she needed: closeness, him being close. At the same time, even as he comforted her, he could not help thinking a self-centred thought. *You were right, there is something broken here. And if you were right about that, then maybe you were right about everything else.*

'Anyway,' she said, a note of briskness entering her voice. 'I just wanted you to know, when I was a little rude on that first morning, it wasn't your fault. I had enjoyed our time together. If I hadn't had to go to work, I wouldn't have rushed off, but when I wouldn't talk and didn't even say goodbye properly, it wasn't your fault. I was thinking about my son. Thinking how he gets up every morning and knows nothing about me except I live abroad. I don't know if he even reads the letters I send. I have to send them to his father. I never get anything back. I tried calling last year, it got too much. He refused to come to the phone, he was angry I'd called, his father said.' She shrugged, then turned round to face him. 'You've never had children?'

He shook his head.

'Well, it's hard to describe but when you wake up and you are without your child, it's like you've woken up and remembered that your arm or leg is missing. That's what it's like. So,' she said, kissing him lightly on the mouth. 'So we got each other's sad stories after all. Serves you right, John Harper.'

They kissed then, but not as deeply as before: now, he was just kissing her.

After a while, he stepped back and said, 'I want to take you back to bed but Kadek could show up any minute.'

She smiled her ironic smile. 'You're worried what the man who looks after you will think about you having had a woman for the night? They are used to the funny ways of foreigners, you know.'

'Come on,' he said. 'Let's get dressed.'

She was light-hearted on the drive back to town, happy to have unburdened herself a little. Everyone has their own parcel of unhappiness, he thought, like the bundles people carry on their heads, each person has their own bundle in its own particular shape and size – but if you talk to someone, you give them your bundle to carry for a bit. It was only temporary, though, that feeling. He pitied her, as she chatted to him about being hungry and about how she couldn't believe she had to work that day and she really shouldn't have stayed the night, she hadn't meant to. She was cheerful because of the temporary relief, because she had handed him her bundle for a short while. But, he knew – and if she thought about it for a moment, she would know too – the next morning, alone in her room in the family compound, she would wake feeling just the same as she always did.

He'd better not see her again. It wasn't safe. If Kadek had come while they were at the hut together, she might have been linked with him, in the eyes of the organisation. What if they had come for him last night? He had endangered her already.

As they pulled up outside her compound, she said, her hand already reaching for the car door to open it, 'You know, you haven't told me the really bad thing in your life yet, don't think I didn't notice.'

He looked at her.

'You really think I couldn't tell when you were skipping bits?' She gave a throaty laugh, her eyes shone with amusement. 'Just because you are mister well travelled and live in big cities? You think I am some village schoolteacher? Well, you underestimate me.' She leaned over and kissed him. 'I'm going to ask later, you know.'

'Go and get your things,' he said, 'I'll take you to the school gates.'

He watched her as she ran into the family compound – her solid figure graceful in its haste. An outside observer would think of her as a self-contained, competent sort of person, not beautiful but handsome in a Nordic kind of way, the kind of person you would want to look after you if you had a cold. How hard was that air of briskness won? How different it was, when she sat on the edge of her bed each morning, a few moments after waking up, awash with grief for her lost child and wondering how she would find the strength to rise, to face the coming day?

She emerged from the compound within minutes, dressed in clean clothing and wearing a hat – the sun was bright that day – beaming at him as she walked back to the car, a large wicker bag over her shoulder. She opened the car door and slid into her seat. He gunned the engine as they drove off, even though they went a few yards and then were stuck behind a delivery truck.

'You'll have to give me directions,' he said.

'Back to the main street then up Jalan Hanoman,' she replied.

She got him to drive past the school and then pull up at the far end of the road, away from town, so her students wouldn't see her getting out of a strange man's car. He climbed out of his side as she was lifting her bag from the footwell and went round the car to open her door. As she climbed out, she gave him the same small smile she had given when he insisted on carrying her bag in the night market. How long ago that seemed. It was as if they had had a whole life together.

They kissed politely, on the cheek, as they were in public, and as he turned to go she said, 'You know . . .' then petered out. He heard in her tone a desire to arrest his departure. How often that impulse came, he thought. Even when we want to leave or want someone else to go, that moment just before the separation, when you or the other person can't help saying, *pause a while*. When he had been a young man, he had always thought that the one who asked for the pause was the one in a position of weakness. He had always made sure it wasn't him. Now, though, he wondered. The folly and pride of youth: that was all those power games had been? Rita was asking for a moment more with him before he got back in the car and drove away. That didn't make her weak or subservient; on the contrary.

He turned. 'What?' he asked, hearing the softness in his own voice and hoping she would hear it too, so that if this was the last time they saw each other, she would remember it and know that this had meant something to him.

'You know, I know there's lots more you haven't told me, not just your little brother, lots. It's up to you, I didn't mean what I said then, I'm not going to press you, it's up to you. I just wanted you to know I know.'

He looked at her. 'I told you lots of things,' he said.

'I know you did,' she replied.

There was a look in her eyes that might have been pain were it not for her smile, and then she broke his gaze for a second by glancing back into the car to check she hadn't left anything and he took advantage of that second, that brief snapping of the thread of spider-silk that held them, to turn away.

He watched her in the rear-view mirror as he drove away, a large woman with an oversized wicker bag on her shoulder, walking slowly in the same direction as him but growing ever more distant, her floppy hat hiding most of her face.

Back at the hut, he found Kadek on the veranda shaking out a pillowcase. The bed sheets were hung over the rail. He wondered if he and Rita had left traces of her overnight stay but then remembered that Kadek changed the bed linen once a week anyway.

'Morning, Mr Harper,' Kadek said with a small bow and a broad smile. 'It is a good morning, yes?'

'Yes, Kadek,' Harper replied, stopping at the top of the veranda steps and casting his gaze across the valley. There was no trace of haze in the sky today: it was a perfect blue, the valley full of light. It was the sort of day that people from all over the world paid thousands of dollars to come to Bali and experience. 'A fine day.'

'A fine day,' Kadek repeated, as if he was experimenting with the word 'fine', trying it out for size in that particular context. *Fine*, as in beautiful; fine as in good; fine as in delicate, perhaps: certainly not 'fine' as in just about okay, *oh alright, that's fine*: and not fine as in *payment due*, penalty. Ever since he had arrived at the hut, Harper had been waiting for his fine day.

Kadek moved to let Harper pass. Harper saw that beyond the billowing linen was a young woman in a sarong and sash kneeling on the wooden planks at the far end of the veranda. She was lighting the incense sticks protruding from the offering in front of her. Beside her on the wooden planks was a bamboo basket. She did not look up.

Kadek glanced at her and said, 'The ghekko, Mr Harper.'

Of course. He had forgotten that, a few days ago, he had mentioned being woken by the ghekko every night, its relentless chant. Kadek would have arranged for the young woman to come and place offerings on the veranda, to appease the gods and demons. It was all about signs and portents: everything signified. If you believed that, he thought, then didn't it become a self-fulfilling prophecy? Whenever anything happened, good or bad, you could always look backwards for the sign.

He watched the woman bend over the offering, the care and attention with which she arranged the flowers. At first, he thought he was watching sceptically, but then the image came into his head of Rita in the rear-view mirror of the car that morning as he pulled away from her, her floppy hat, the way she had smiled when she had said, 'I'm not going to press you,' as if to undercut the sincerity of her own words: and from somewhere inside him came a sonorous, rattling sigh, the kind that comes involuntarily. He felt it in his ribcage and thought, now where did that come from? Kadek was folding the pillowcase, the young woman intent upon her duties – neither of them looked at him.

What should I say to this young woman arranging flowers on my porch? he thought then. There is nothing? No one cares? Your diligence is pointless? Go home and worry about all the other things there are to worry about because that's all there is? No, the woman's offering was valid, just not in the way she thought. He did not believe in the Invisibles: there were no ghosts or demons. He believed in men with machetes. But Kadek arranging for the woman to come, and the woman making the trek up here, was a way of them saying, *we are concerned for you*. He wouldn't have noticed if she hadn't come, after all, wouldn't have remarked on it – what was he to them, a rich *bule*? They would be paid the same wage whether the offering was made or not. The offering was made because they believed they had a duty of care to the stranger in their land. The spirits were their spirits, just as the gods were their gods. And he thought of Rita saying, as she got into his car on the day they went to Sanur, 'God bless the Balinese,' and he thought, for all my travelling and my knowledge and my world-weariness, I am the fool, perhaps, yes.

Inside the hut, he ate the breakfast that Kadek had left for him, thought briefly that Rita hadn't eaten before she went to work, then opened the drawer of his desk and found the half-written letter to Francisca. He placed the letter on his desk and smoothed it out.

At the back of his desk, there was a metal ashtray, a copper-coloured one with semi-circular indents all around its edge, as if there was any chance a dozen people might want to rest a cigarette on it at the same time. Using that ashtray on his own had always struck him as a little poignant. There were two cigarette stubs in the tray, both bent and broken, nestling amongst the fine grey ash, very faintly *kretek*-scented. He wished there was a blush of lipstick on one of them, even though Rita didn't wear lipstick. They would have looked touching, nestled together, if there was. In fact, they were both his. He had risen from bed after she had gone to sleep the previous night, very late, and sat at the desk and smoked two in a row, thinking that to go out onto the veranda might disturb her: and for the pleasure of sitting on the chair at the desk and hearing her breathing in the darkness as he smoked. He had thought the smell of smoke might wake her, even though he was in the far corner of the hut, but it didn't. She sleeps so well, so deeply, he had thought. She's really good at it.

He patted his pockets, located his lighter. He leaned forward and drew the ashtray towards him, then carefully shredded the letter to Francisca. He held the lighter downwards and set light to the shreds. The paper was so fragile the small flame made it dissolve into powder and smoke: one second a blue butterfly's wing with blackened edges and the finest glowing orange rim, then nothing.

Outside, on the sun-struck veranda, he could hear Kadek and the young woman talking softly to one another. The door was wide open but because they were at either end of the veranda, he couldn't see them. He heard the low murmur of their voices cease.

Then he heard Kadek say in English, loudly and firmly, 'If you will excuse me, sir, I will see if Mr Harper is available.' There was something protective in his tone.

Harper looked up as Kadek's silhouette, dark against the bright blue of the sky, filled the doorway and he said, with no inflection in his voice, 'There is a gentleman here to see you, Mr Harper.'

Harper stepped over the doorframe and out onto the veranda. Kadek did not return to folding sheets but stood a few feet back, respectfully. The young woman had disappeared. The offering she had left was glowing on the far end of the veranda, the scent of incense drifting out over the valley.

A white man of around forty stood at the top of the wooden steps that led up to the veranda from the path. He was dressed in slacks and an open-necked shirt and holding a black briefcase with steel clasps. There was something familiar about him.

Harper gave him a slow look.

He smiled at Harper but did not advance towards him or hold out his hand. '*Goedemorgen*,' he said. '*Hoe gaat het met je?*'

Harper turned to Kadek and said, 'Kadek, do you need to return the car or can I use it today?'

Kadek stood nearby. 'That will be fine, Mr Harper.'

Harper looked at the stranger and then said in Dutch, '*Goedemorgen*, I don't have any decent coffee, or anything in fact, out here. Did you get a taxi from the village?'

'I've come straight from the airport,' the stranger replied, mildly.

Harper thought, at least they've sent someone businesslike, polite. At least we won't have the bluster and false bonhomie of Henrikson.

'Well, if you've come straight from the airport then at least I can take you to a decent restaurant,' Harper said. His Dutch sounded odd and guttural to him now, as if he was speaking through a mouthful of small stones. 'I'll come down to the lane and tell your driver where to go, then I'll follow.'

He could have taken the man to the cafe on the main street or the guesthouse bar on Jalan Bisma but he wanted to keep him away from anywhere that he associated with Rita. She had mentioned a new restaurant she hadn't tried yet, a smart one, on the other side of town over the bridge. He couldn't remember what it was called but he described the location to the man's driver, then followed in the car Kadek had borrowed for him.

At that hour of the morning, the restaurant was deserted. They walked straight through to where a huge stone balcony overlooked the valley on the edge of the town, a broader view than the one Harper had from his veranda; the valley split wider here. Birds flew in the bright light as the greenery plunged beneath them, the river hidden by a density of banana trees and palms. They sat down at a table with a pink tablecloth, already laid for lunchtime later in the day, and a young woman brought them menus. Harper didn't look at his, just put it down on the table and said to the young woman in English, 'Black coffee, please.'

'I'll have the same,' the man said, also putting his menu down on the table and leaning back in his seat. The young woman picked both menus up and turned away.

'Fabulous view,' the man said. He had put on sunglasses in his car but removed them now, leaned forward in his seat again and extended his hand. 'I'm sorry, I haven't introduced myself properly. Johan.'

They shook hands across the table.

'You don't need to wait for the coffee,' Harper said, glancing at the floor to the side of Johan's chair and nodding towards the briefcase.

Johan pressed his lips together, moved his head to the side in a cheery little *right you are* gesture and pushed his chair back, grimacing at the scraping sound it made. He lifted the case onto his lap, flipped open the clasps with two loud hard clicks, then extracted a manila envelope.

'Well,' he said, as he took a sheaf of papers out of the envelope, 'obviously, the main thing we need to address in the light of recent events is the confidentiality clause in your contract of employment. I'm sure you don't need reminding but I've brought a copy along just in case. There's the confidentiality, ah, issue . . . and of course the non-competition clause. And this piece of paper here . . .' he laid another sheet on top, 'is just an additional clause. It specifies new media, world-wide web, and so on.' He gave a small laugh. 'Of course none of all that existed when your contract of employment was drawn up!'

The young woman returned with their coffees. Harper withdrew a packet of *kreteks* from his pocket and held it out to Johan but Johan shook his head and said, 'Ah, no, thanks, I don't smoke.'

I bet you don't, Harper thought. He did not look down at the bit of paper. He looked at Johan. After a moment or two, he turned his head to one side to exhale away from Johan, then took a sip of coffee. Johan lifted his cup at the same time.

Harper let the silence between them continue for long enough to force Johan to speak.

'Look . . .' Johan began and Harper interrupted immediately, 'Just tell me what the deal is.'

'If you sign, and stay away, we mean completely away, from the business, including but not exclusively our competitors in the field, then we are calling it redundancy. With all the benefits that accrue, including this.' The briefcase was still on his lap. The envelope he extracted this time was long and white and unsealed. He handed it over and gestured to Harper that he should look inside. Harper pushed a finger in to widen it and saw that there was a cheque, a more generous one than the Institute was obliged to offer, under the circumstances.

Harper put the white envelope down on the table. 'Do you have a pen?'

Johan gave a terse, grateful smile. Harper wondered if this young man had expected more trouble. If so, he had been inadequately briefed.

'Oh, the Institute does have one more request,' Johan added as he lifted the lid of the briefcase for the third time. 'We would like you to vacate the company accommodation facilities within three days. Is that reasonable?'

For a moment, Harper was unsure what the man meant, then he snorted, 'You mean the hut?'

Johan gave a wry smile. 'It's a little rudimentary, having seen it this morning, I must agree.'

Harper felt a sudden wash of nostalgia for the hut, a feeling that by not imposing his personality on it, he had made it his. Three days? How had time slipped? He felt as though he had been there forever – and he knew, in that moment, that a return to what was euphemistically referred to as real life was impossible: Jakarta, Amsterdam, Los Angeles – it didn't matter. He had withdrawn from all these places, and from the transitional places that led from one to the other; planes, taxis, waiting lounges. He could no more imagine re-entering that world than he could growing wings and flying over the crater of Gunung Agung. If you come to a place to die, then what are you supposed to do if, somehow, you carry on living?

Johan passed over a pen. As Harper signed the addendum to the confidentiality clause he said, 'Three days will be no problem. As you probably saw, I don't have many possessions.'

Johan mistook his meaning. 'I'm afraid that the papers and reports, well anything in fact, that you left in the Jakarta apartment belongs to the Institute.'

Harper put the pen down on the confidentiality agreement then slid them both across the table. 'Fine by me. Just out of interest . . .' He nodded towards the agreement. 'What would the Institute have done if I had refused to sign?'

Johan shrugged, reached to pick up the agreement and smiled. 'Well that's the catch with signing, you never get to find out.'

Harper leaned back in his chair as Johan slipped the signed agreement into the envelope. 'Have you ever thought, Johan, that we work for the kind of organisation that has people killed?'

He saw the look of shock on Johan's face. 'Surely, even in your department, you think through the consequences, now and then? We get involved with governments, we get involved with coups.'

Johan glanced around, and then gave a hearty, vocal smile – less than a laugh but more than a facial expression. 'I thought you meant us, for a minute there!' He was embarrassed to have momentarily believed Harper to be suggesting something so absurd.

Harper looked at him and let the question hang between them.

'I'm a lawyer, you're an economist. We provide advice, that's what we do. People like us will always exist,' Johan said, closing his briefcase. 'If we didn't exist, someone else like us would, and the someone else would probably be worse, you seem like a decent enough fellow to me. Agreed?'

Harper looked to one side, at the view, and smiled.

He took the risk of parking outside the school. It was a long wait until the lunchtime break. When Rita emerged, she was surrounded by students and set off down Jalan Hanoman without seeing him. He was momentarily affronted. Shouldn't she have been looking? Then he was amused at himself; of course she wasn't looking. Why should she? He remembered how she had strode away from the guesthouse on Jalan Bisma after their first night together without seeing him sitting in plain view in the cafe right opposite. Head in the clouds, he thought, with affection. Or maybe just . . . normal. Maybe she wasn't looking because there was nothing to look for. Maybe the boys waiting by the cafe opposite the guesthouse that morning were just boys sitting on a tree trunk, the young men passing through town in a jeep just young men in a jeep. His heart sang, then. That could be him. If he was with her, he could be like her.

The car was parked awkwardly, as close to the drainage ditch on the side of the road as he could risk without losing a wheel down it, but cars and mopeds had still been forced to pull out to get past him. He restarted the engine and followed at a distance, slowly. The street was full of students streaming from the low building. It was only when she turned onto the main street, still with a student either side, that he was able to overtake, pull in in front of a shop and toot the horn as she approached from behind. He watched her in the rear-view mirror and saw her head lift, the wide brim of her hat rising to reveal her face, her smile of surprise.

She stopped and said goodbye to the students, then lifted one hand and splayed her fingers in a *five minutes* gesture. He nodded. She went into a shop just behind where he was parked, a mini-market, and emerged a few minutes later with a plastic bag. He leaned over to open the passenger door for her.

As she got in the car she leaned across and gave him a brief kiss on the cheek. The smile she gave him was an ordinary smile because, of course, she did not know that when he dropped her off at the school that morning, he was thinking it might be the last time they saw each other. She had never known what was at stake.

'To what do I owe this honour?' she asked.

'I've something to show you,' he said, pushing his hand into his pocket. 'Remember how I told you I was being fired?' He pulled out the long white envelope, which he had folded neatly, concertinaed, and put into his trouser pocket. He rested it on the dashboard and smoothed it out. Then he extracted the cheque and held it up in front of his chest, as if it was a certificate he had just won at a sports day.

She looked at the cheque, then up at his face. 'What is it?'

'It's a cheque,' he said.

She lifted her eyebrows and said drily, 'I can see it's a cheque but I can't see how big it is, I don't have my reading glasses on. Is it enough for you? I mean, are you a free man?'

'Enough for me to do a deal with the landowner who owns the fields beyond Jalan Bisma, and enough for me to stay in one of those guesthouse rooms in the meantime, if that's easier that is, while I decide which plot of land to lease, on the edge of the rice field, on the way to the Monkey Forest, although I guess it would be a good idea if we asked around about other plots as well. You know this town a lot better than I do. And you'll have to do the negotiating with the builders, *Ibu Rita*. You're the one who speaks Balinese.'

When she spoke, her voice was uninflected. 'Aren't you scared of the Invisibles?'

'It's the land of Dewi Sri, remember.'

She said nothing, just stared, and he stared right back: and this was the best thing of all, staring at her, watching the progress of her thoughts play out on her face. He saw, first of all, her slow understanding of his seriousness; then he saw how she questioned that understanding, wondering if she had got it right. When she decided she had, a small amount of joy came into her features, a flattered look, manifest in a slight widening of her gaze, a minute lifting of her eyebrows. Then, briefly, a shadow of doubt, not at her understanding but at her own desires: the hint of a frown as the eyebrows lowered. He saw her think to herself that there were many things he had not told her and many she had not told him, two whole lives lived that needed explaining. The cloud of these omissions misted her pleasure for a moment: her gaze lost focus. Then, finally, a kind of light, a kind of recklessness in her smile: if she was younger she would not contemplate this; if he was younger, he would not have asked. Their separate tragedies had brought them both to this: a point where they had nothing much to lose by taking a chance on someone as damaged as they were.

All he was doing was watching her face. Its motions were minute. He had no way of knowing if he had interpreted the panorama of her thoughts correctly – but still, in that moment, it felt enough.

They went to the guesthouse on Jalan Bisma together and Rita asked to speak to the owner. The three of them sat around one of the small round tables in the bar while Rita and the owner chatted in Balinese and she negotiated a long-term rental for one of the rooms – a corner room on the first floor: Balinese people didn't like sleeping upstairs, she told him, so the first-floor rooms were slightly cheaper. They went to see the room together but while Rita checked it out, opening the wardrobe, turning on the taps in the bathroom, tightening them efficiently, Harper just stood smiling at the bed, wondering if he could persuade her to stay with him there that night. Johan would be back in Denpasar by now, at the airport. Perhaps he would take a domestic flight to Jakarta to report back to Henrikson, or, more likely, go straight back to Amsterdam via Singapore. Job done.

The young man who had shown them the room handed Rita the key and left, closing the door behind him, and Harper advanced upon her. She backed towards the bed, smiling, mock-reluctant. 'I should make you wait another three days,' she said, 'wait until you've moved out of your old place, you know, finished with all that.'

'Should you?' he said, placing one hand on her chest and shoving her, neatly and gently, back onto the bed, and she grabbed the pillow and placed it over her face and he had to pull the pillow away and clear her hair from her face in order to be able to kiss her. He took her wrists and went to pin her arms above her head but she shoved him off, pushed him onto his back, rolled on top. 'Who has the upper hand now, John Harper?' she said.

'You,' he conceded, and yielded to her kiss.

In the early evening, they went out to eat and even though she refused to spend the night with him, he could not bring himself to return to the hut – he slept at the guesthouse alone. In the morning, she came by for breakfast.

The fine sun continued and they sat at a corner table in the restaurant upstairs: a view of the street rather than a valley, but fresh juice and eggs. This is going to be my life now, he thought, watching Rita as she scans a menu. Here we are, opposite each other at a table, and our primary task, our main responsibility, is to decide what sort of juice we feel like, how we want our eggs.

Rita checked her watch – she had work that morning but there was plenty of time. After she had gone, he would go back up to the hut for his last two nights. Now, he would be able to enjoy that small and finite solitude, now all that paranoia was behind him.

How ridiculous his fears seemed now. In his head, he listed all the things he realised were nonsense: the young men in the jeep as he sat drinking coffee and eating a cinnamon bun: they were just young men in a jeep, passing through town, off-duty soldiers or police cadets, perhaps. So what? The boys he thought were following him from the breakfast shack – why, exactly? Because they were sitting on a tree trunk near where he had chosen to sit down? Because they rose when he did? There had been no gathering of men in a brick-walled office or, if there had, their discussions had revolved around the appropriate size of his pay-off, how to avoid any public embarrassment for the company. And Joosten, poor Joosten – maybe it was the stuff he smoked that made him paranoid. Wrong place at the wrong time. Could happen to anybody.

The world is different now. Rita was right. He had allowed the things that had happened to him to colour his perspective far too much, sad but true. He would go back to the hut, enjoy his last couple of days there, and after that, his new life could begin.

'Will it take you long to pack?' Rita asked, and he spluttered into his coffee.

After they had eaten, she took out a map of the town and showed him how it was actually a series of adjoining villages and districts. She pointed at the areas on the edges that were being developed, talked him through the labyrinthine processes of leasing land locally; where they would have to register. At one point, while they were still scanning the map, heads bent towards each other, she lifted hers and looked at him and said, 'John . . .' thoughtfully. 'You know, I know you will think this is strange of me, but it's an odd name for you. It is a blank name, isn't it? There is a form of John in every language, isn't there? John for English, Jan or Hans in German, and Dutch, would it be Jan? Or Johan, is it Johan?'

In all the time he had been John Harper, hardly anyone had called him John. He was Harper at work. Francisca had known him as Nicolaas. He shrugged. 'Call me something else if you like. Anything you like. Just don't expect me to call you fluffy bunny or something in return.' It would be appropriate, after all, to shed John Harper now.

'Mmm,' she said, ignoring the bunny comment, 'I will have to give that some thought. What did your grandparents call you, the grandparents in California?'

'Nicolaas,' he said, 'or Nic, sometimes, that was mostly Nina. My grandfather, I don't know, most of the time he called me son.' And it came to him then, Poppa's deep tones, the ease with which he spoke the word, the same slow comfortableness with which he had called Nina *baby* or *hon*. *Son*. For a while, he had been a son. He thought then of Abang – call me Abang, he had said, *big brother*, as soon as Harper had arrived on the island, after taking just one look at him. *Adik*, he had called him in return: *little brother*. Abang had only called him that a handful of times, but it was enough: someone who cared enough to choose the right word for you, like Rita's students calling her *Ibu*. How important it was, to be named. Once, on the streets of Amsterdam, he had seen an elderly Indian man bending painfully to pick up a paper bag that he had dropped, and the youth of the Netherlands rushing past, none of them pausing, and he wasn't in a hurry that day himself so (uncharacteristically, he would concede) he had stopped and said, 'Uncle, please,' and bent and picked up the bag and handed it to the old man, who had given him a keen look and said, simply and without emotion, 'There should be more people like you in the world.' It was the only time anyone had ever said anything like that to him, and just because he had named the old man uncle.

Rita was looking at him. 'You had a father, for a while, there, didn't you?'

'Yes,' he said. 'You are right.'

She gave him a wide-eyed look then and made a small whooping sound. 'A miracle! Miracles will never cease!'

He pointed his spoon at her. 'Don't make a habit of it.' She rolled her eyes and he added, 'And it's wonders.'

'Wonders?'

'Wonders that will never cease, not miracles.'

'Okay, I will settle for wonders.'

He would have liked to turn it around then, to talk of her. He would have liked to say, *and what about you? What are you looking for? Your lost son?* But he knew that would make the light go from her eyes – and it wasn't the right time. She had to be at work soon and he had to go back to the hut.

But along with the fantasy house that they would build together in the rice fields, he pictured, then, a fantasy letter arriving from Belgium. He pictured Rita holding it with trembling hands, looking at him, as if for permission to open it, and him sitting her at the small table on their veranda and placing a supportive hand on her shoulder before leaving her to open it in private – she would know that he was just indoors, whenever she was ready. And after some time, she would come inside, her eyes brimful of tears, and hold the letter out to him and say, 'My son, he wants to come and visit.' And then there would be some months of wrangling with the father, during which he, Harper, would lose his cool once in a while and threaten to go over to Belgium and kick that idiot her ex-husband down the stairs, and Rita would cry at night or go silent – but eventually, it would all lead to this: one day, when the house was complete and the guest room furnished, they would be standing together at Denpasar airport, waiting for the boy to arrive. And he, Harper, would see him first amongst the many youths emerging from Arrivals, because Rita was looking for her child but he was looking for Rita. The son would be a strapping youth, well built, with Rita's soft features but dark hair. He would come over and he and Rita would embrace awkwardly, neither of them too emotional, not yet, and then he would turn and face Harper and shake his hand firmly and their eyes would meet in a moment of masculine recognition that, strange as this meeting might be for all of them, the one who would need protecting here would be Rita.

She hadn't told him her son's name yet: Viktor, perhaps, or Maxim? He would get the name eventually: she would tell him when she was ready to trust him with it. What does a man do when he is too old to look for father figures? Perhaps he finds a son.

Rita jumped up from the table. 'I have to go.' Her distracted, dreamy air was back, and he knew that, when they lived together, it would annoy him, that when her mind turned to her job, her responsibilities to her students, he would not be the focus of her attention any more. She would always switch off, just like that, say 'I have to go,' unexpectedly – he realised that he would have to quell his desire to become demanding at that stage. He would have to accept that she was still open to the world in a way that he was not. I'd better busy myself with building projects, he thought, otherwise I'll start to annoy her.

She bent her head and gave him a brief kiss on the lips. 'Next time I see you,' she said, 'two days' time, I'll have thought of a name to call you, then. Maybe I'll make something up.' She was gone.

He drove the car back to the top of the lane and left it there and walked up to the hut. Kadek might have been and gone already that morning, but if he was still there, maybe he would ask about buying the car. He wondered whether Kadek had been briefed about his departure yet or whether he would have to tell him himself. He would leave a handsome tip, in hard dollars. He hoped that Kadek would be sorry to see him go.

The doors to the hut were closed but the small silver padlock had not been attached to the metal loop that locked them shut: it was sitting on the table on the veranda, next to his washing bowl. That was unusual – Kadek was normally very thorough about locking up. Still, maybe things were different now, maybe Kadek knew he would be minding an empty building for a while, until the next incumbent that the Institute needed to squirrel away for a bit. Perhaps Kadek thought Harper wasn't returning at all after his meeting with the lawyer. He would be used to the arbitrary comings and goings of Institute staff by now.

Harper stood on the veranda, facing the door. Then he reached out, took hold of the iron circle that lifted the latch, twisted it slowly. The latch lifted with a squeak and a scrape. He pushed the door back.

Inside, the hut was clean and tidy. Kadek had remade the bed and smoothed it immaculately. The mosquito net was tied in a neat waterfall of cotton around each post, the white sheets tucked in tight. He had emptied the ashtray of the burnt shreds of Francisca's letter. The chair in front of the desk was inserted in its proper position neatly, not at the lazy diagonal that Harper always left it at. The hut could not have been more organised, more empty.

He stepped over the threshold. There was no breakfast waiting for him on the desk – that meant that Kadek had not been that morning, that the hut had been left tidy and emptied and unlocked all night while he had been at the guesthouse. He walked into the hut, leaving the door behind him pushed wide open, to admit the light. He went over to the shutters and opened them, pushing them back against the outside wall, and then all was filled with daylight inside, albeit still silent. He stood for a moment in the centre of the room.

Packing his few things wouldn't take long. Perhaps Kadek would come later.

He went down to the river for a walk.

He came back and made himself some powdered coffee.

He grew hungry, and found the remainder of a packet of biscuits that he had left in a cupboard, a dry remnant of one of his few trips to the mini-market in town.

He sat on the veranda for a bit, watching the view, then went back inside and, suddenly tired in the full heat of the day, lay down and took a nap on the immaculate bed. When he woke, he climbed off the bed, still a little sleepy, looked at the creased sheets and felt a sense of trespass – he never normally slept during the day. He tugged at the edges of the sheets and then neatened them with the flat of his hand, so that Kadek would not have to do it when he showed up later, and as he straightened, it came to him what was familiar about Johan. He stood for a moment in the middle of the room, then turned to the corner cupboard, where he kept the whisky and the cigarettes.

There was no trace of moon. He had to navigate by holding his hands out in front of him, feeling the tree trunks and then grasping them and hauling himself slowly round. Once he was through the trees, he stood at the edge of the rice field, in the pitch dark, the men with machetes only metres behind him, and watched as the red tail light of the motorcycle disappeared down the rise. That was all he saw, in the blackness, that one, small, round red light, his chance of escape, dropping down the track, disappearing as if into the earth – and then there was nothing but night, and he was alone in the rice field and the men were hunting him and they would have heard the sound of the motor for certain and be heading his way. Wayan had done more than leave him alone in the dark: he had drawn the men towards him.

He stepped carefully away from the trees, towards the rise, lifting his feet slowly so as not to make splashing sounds in the mud and water, although his breath sounded so loud in his own chest, he could scarcely believe it was not giving him away. The men were nearby, he knew it, perhaps standing still and listening for any sign of him, but every now and then, there was a shout or a scream from the burning house on the other side of the field. The men's companions were still killing Komang's family. The noises would distract the men, perhaps, and if he stayed motionless, invisible, they might return to the main task in hand.

He should have let Wayan use a light, even if it had risked him being discovered: to leave the man alone in the dark in a water field – how stupid of him, he only had himself to blame.

It was then he saw a movement, a shadow to his left, no more than the shift of something lighter in the dark, pale clothing perhaps, against the black wall of the treeline. The breath froze in his throat. In daytime, shadows were dark: in this pitch black, they were light. If Wayan had seen this ghost-shape moving around in the dark, of course he would have cracked.

The ghost flickered, whimpered, clutched his arm, thin fingers digging into his flesh. He grabbed at a bony shoulder and at that point a cloud above them must have shifted a little; there was a small amount of moonlight. He pulled the ghost towards him. It was Komang's wife. He looked down into her face, which was a rictus of fear. She must have been the fleeing shadow he had seen when he had watched the men murder Komang – she had been hoping to draw the men away from her home, her children. If so, she must know by now it was a strategy that had failed. He wondered how long she had been hiding in the trees, too terrified to return to her house, too terrified to run, perhaps hoping that one or two of the other household members had been able to flee in the chaos. And then she had realised that the tall figure she could just about see emerging from the trees was Harper, the stranger who had come to the house earlier that day, the man who her husband said was a friend.

He was holding her by the shoulder but she was also holding him, seizing his arm in a bony grip. They stood clutching at each other. For a moment or two they were both just clinging and breathing and he saw, mirrored in her petrified gaze, his own fear. He lifted a finger to his mouth, then, to indicate she should be silent, although his own breath was coming louder than hers.

He heard a scuffle in the undergrowth, turned, saw the glow of a flaming torch – and with no warning, the men were upon them. The ones holding the torch were further away than the ones who had come close in the dark, who had emerged from the trees behind Komang's wife. They must have been the party hunting her, not the one hunting him: the one hunting him was the more distant group. He felt a moment of fury that she had not only frightened Wayan away but led them to him. If she had stayed hidden in the trees, he would not have been discovered. He could have dropped down into an irrigation ditch while they were upon her.

These thoughts were swift – at once, several of the men grabbed her and she screamed and babbled in fear and they shouted back and the men with the torches came running, their feet splashing in the water.

They were surrounded then – between fifteen and twenty men, he estimated. It was hard to tell in the dark, with the shifting shadows thrown by the torches: each figure lit by orange had a shadow figure in black: in the dark, the men were doubled.

He knew he had one chance. He drew himself up to his full height and said loudly and firmly in Indonesian, 'I found her. She was hiding in the trees.'

The men on the edge of the group were talking excitedly but the two closest to Harper looked at him. One raised a paraffin lantern: Harper could see the oval of his face, questioning. 'I found her,' he repeated. 'She was trying to flee that way. There was a man waiting for her on a motorbike but he left.'

Komang's wife was still talking very fast, whimpering and

crying with a rise and fall, a rise into a small scream, a fall into a plea, the desperate sound of someone pleading for her life, her children – and one of the men, very small, very young-looking in the orange light, stepped forward and raised both his arms together, elbows bent, then struck her on the side of her head with an object Harper couldn't see. She gave a single, sharp cry and fell to the ground. The young man looked at Harper then, to see how he would react. Harper kept his face still.

The boy looked around and the other young men clapped him on the shoulder. Then the group turned back in on itself, began talking excitedly.

The older man with the oval face was still standing next to Harper. Harper folded his arms, said, 'What are they saying?'

The older man lifted his chin – his paraffin lantern swung to and fro, illuminating first one side of his face and one group of men, then the other side of his face and another. Komang's wife was just visible on the ground, a small heap, silent now, but alive, her breath heaving inside her, the curve of her back rising and falling. 'First we will put her face then her honour to the fire,' the man said, nodding towards the flaming torch held by a man on the other side of the group.

Harper stepped forward. Komang's wife was still bent in a heap. As he reached her, his feet sank in the mud and the irrigation water rose halfway up his calves. He grabbed the hair on the back of her head – it was loose and fell over his wrist – and she had only time for one final, inarticulate cry before he pushed her face down into the muddy water, put his other hand on the back of her head, and steeled every muscle in his arms to hold her there.

He was a young man. He was strong. His arms were like iron.

And yet, the strength of a woman desperate to live – she got one arm up and began clawing at his forearms. Her legs kicked out behind her, splashing in the water. She even managed to raise her back a little. Who would have thought such a small woman had that strength? One of the men had lifted a paraffin lantern high to illuminate the scene. Die quickly, Harper thought, for God's sake, die quickly, or they will stop me killing you. And yet, incredibly, she managed to shift her head a little and he had to use both hands to push her down again. And then one of the men dropped down to sit on her legs to stop them kicking out, and he knew that they would not stop him from killing her. Their own scheme was forgotten.

Strands of her hair clung across his wrist, the rest floating around her head; the ditch was illuminated black and orange; bubbles were rising through it. He began to count backwards from a hundred, softly, under his breath – he knew his lips were moving although there was no more than a whisper coming from them, *one hundred, ninety-nine, ninety-eight* . . . Her whole body shook and the hand, small and bony, continued to scrape at his arm . . . *eighty-four, eighty-three, eighty-two* . . . she dug her fingers into his arm . . . *seventy-two, seventy-one, seventy* . . . His counting was slow – more than a second per number, he thought: a slow count back from a hundred would be around three minutes. It took longer than that to drown but she was small and had already been face down for a minute or two before he started counting. She would surely lose consciousness soon. *Sixty-eight, sixty-seven, sixty-six* . . . He did not look up at the men who had gathered round him, watching. They had fallen silent. He concentrated all his effort on keeping the woman's head beneath the water. *Fifty-six, fifty-five, fifty-four* . . . he realised he was counting back in numerals but thinking in tens. *Forty-two, forty-one, forty* . . . The counting became everything. His arms were like rock now. It was the numbers in his head, the soft movements of his lips – that was what he concentrated on. *Thirty-three, thirty-two, thirty-one* . . . Time had no meaning any more. Only the numbers had meaning. *Twenty-eight, twenty-seven, twenty-six* . . . He was so nearly there. He just wanted to be there. *Fifteen, fourteen, thirteen* . . . The men around still said nothing, just stood, and the night insects were blaring and there was a crackle from one of the flaming torches but he could sense they were all motionless even though he didn't look up. And finally . . . *Three, two, ONE!*

Even after he had finished counting, he did not release her. He did not dare. If the job was not finished, she would be burnt to death, and he too, possibly. He stayed where he was, his breath heaving in his chest, waiting.

And then he realised that the small fingers digging into his arm had eased, some seconds ago, perhaps. The hand lost its grip, fell limp into the water with a tiny splash. He stayed motionless for a minute longer, to see if there were any more bubbles, then released her, took his hands away, but stayed kneeling. The woman lay still. The men around him remained motionless too, looking down.

Eventually, he looked around the group, got to his feet, unsteadily. He glanced at the older man who had been standing next to him and saw that the look on his face was one of shock. The man had seen not mercy in his actions but efficiency. The men's desire to torture her was born in heat, and all men understood that actions done in heat were excusable because they were men and that was what men did – but his ruthlessness in drowning Komang's wife seemed evil to them. Even though they would have taken her and done far worse to her than he had just done, they were, momentarily at least, afraid of him.

The men had stepped back but then the young one holding the torch moved forward, lifted Komang's wife up by her shirt. Her body was limp, her arms hanging down, water dripping from the ends of her fingers, her face hidden by the fall of her hair.

A murmur came from the men. One of them called something out and two of them laughed. Their moment of shocked silence was over. Denied the opportunity to torture her, they would now decide what to do with the body – a poor substitute for the person but one that would do. She would probably be hanging from a tree in the centre of the village in the morning. They would dismember her, perhaps, as they had her husband, her children. If he stayed with them, joined in, he would be safe: they would not question his allegiance now.

The excitement in the men's faces: the wide eyes, gritted teeth – you did not need to drink *arak* all day, like Benni's men, to have such an expression on your face. He had seen that same excitement on the faces of boys at school in Los Angeles or Amsterdam, on the young men of the Institute during training exercises. He began stepping backwards, into the dark. His feet sounded loud and splashy in the water to him but the men were intent on their conversation. He was halfway back across the field, moving slowly and carefully away from the men and the trees, when he heard a shout. The tone was unmistakeably hostile to his absence. He dropped down then, into the muddy water, took a deep breath, and pushed his own face into the mud.

Dawn is a promise. That is the mystery of it. It is as if you emerge from the swamp of night cell by cell yet in an instant. You are lying in an irrigation ditch, lying stretched flat in order to submerge yourself as much as possible, with only half your face turned upwards so that you can breathe, keeping your breath as shallow as possible while staying alive, knowing that each second of being alive may be your last because the men with flares and lanterns and machetes are only a few metres away and discovery is possible at any moment.

The birds announce it: the outlier birds, *cheep, cheep*, such a tiny, hopeful sound. The first hint of grey appears at the edges of the sky and, after a bit of tuning up, the whole chorus breaks out, the birds' triumphant orchestra, the musical holler of it, because however black the night has been they are still there and they cry out. The sky is grey and lightening by the minute, and you turn in the ditch, stiff and frozen to the core. You are still afraid but now it is light enough to see across the rice field, growing greener by the minute in the dawn light, that the men with machetes have gone – and you are still alive.

*

It took him four months to get to Los Angeles. Wayan may have abandoned him, but he had at least dropped his bag where the moped had been parked. Harper found it as soon as he rose from the irrigation ditch at dawn, snatched it up then headed off at a trotting run, away from the village. There was some money in a secret pocket on the inside of the bag, and his documents: the notes in his money belt had spent a night being soaked in mud and were unusable even after he rinsed them in fresh water and dried them on a rock. That was a week later, when he allowed himself to stop in the same place for more than a few hours.

He made it to the coast eventually, at one point hiding out on Lovina Beach in Singaraja, in the cabin of a very alcoholic and somewhat demented old Dutchman whose brain was pickled enough to think Harper was his house servant. After three weeks there, he stole the old man's moped – it hadn't been ridden in years – got it working and travelled along the coast until he met with a group of hippie dropouts who had been camping for a year, smoking dope and sleeping with each other. He told them his name was Leaf and he was on the run from the CIA, which was possibly, by that time, partly true. The group was only camping for another fortnight and then planning on taking the long route back to San Francisco on freight ships crossing the Pacific. Eventually, he hit Humboldt Bay, where he could access his Bank of America account for enough cash for a flight to Los Angeles.

He managed to call Nina from a payphone before he got on the flight. When she answered the phone, for a moment or two, he could not speak. She said, 'Hello . . . ? Hello . . . ? Who is this . . . ?' Then there was a pause. 'Hello . . . ?' He could tell by the tone of that last *hello* that she was about to hang up so forced himself to say, to spit out almost, 'Nina, it's me.' There was a shocked silence on the other end of the line.

At Los Angeles airport, he joined a line with three businessmen ahead of him and the occasional cab cruising to the kerb every five minutes or so. Eventually, it was his turn and he got into a battered vehicle driven by a fat white guy in a stained T-shirt who grunted when Harper gave him the address. There was something about the way the cab driver glanced in the rear-view mirror as he got in the back that he didn't like. While on the move, he had let his hair grow and adopted a soft, scrubby beard: he looked like the kind of young man other men hated. As they cruised down the slipway, he took a packet of cigarettes from his pocket and lit up, without offering one to the driver, who responded by fumbling for his own cigarettes on the dashboard. They both smoked their different brands in silence all the way.

'Want me to exit at Crenshaw?' the driver growled when they were on the Santa Monica Freeway, and Harper didn't know what he meant so he just nodded. This stretch of the freeway was new, had cut the Heights in two by the look of it.

When they pulled up outside Poppa and Nina's house, Harper saw the driver stare into the mirror again as he extracted a roll of bills from the side pocket of his holdall. He made a point of glancing at the notes rather than counting them out, then pushed a crumpled heap of them into the driver's outstretched hand, enjoying the brief look of confusion on his face as he worked out that this particular hippy dropout wasn't short of dough.

Harper stood on the pavement while the driver pulled away. After the sound of the engine and the smell of the cab's exhaust fumes had dissipated, he took a minute or two to breathe: the quiet, sloping street, the houses in an ascending row with their wooden facades painted in different pastel colours, the huge old cactus that was still in the front garden. The sunlight seemed so delicate here, in comparison with where he had come from. Standing on the empty street with the elegant droop of the vine that still twisted round the porch support and his bag at his feet, he realised he had wanted this homecoming so badly that he could not bring himself to mount the steps and knock on the door – the pleasure of this moment was so intense. What could be better than the seconds before you set eyes on someone you know will be overjoyed to see you?

He could have stood there for some time – but a shape passed the window and all at once, Nina flung the screen door wide.

In the kitchen, Nina said, 'I'll make tea, shall we take it out into the garden?' but he replied, 'Let's sit at the table,' because it reminded him of his first evening in the house and how he and Poppa had sat at the kitchen table drinking milkshakes and he had gazed longingly through the window at the garden and Jimmy the dog. Jimmy had died many years ago but there was still the iron stake dug into the grass at the bottom of the slope.

It was six years since his last visit: he had come for two weeks just before he began his military service in Holland. Nina's brown hair was stranded with white, she was stouter round the stomach and there was a certain stiffness in her movements. She fetched down the tea set he had brought from Amsterdam on that trip, the blue and white, standing on a chair to lift it down, refusing his help, holding it under the rattling tap for a few minutes to clean it of dust. When the kettle had come to the boil on the stovetop, she warmed the pot and the cups, set it on to boil again.

They were enjoying each other's presence so much that they talked of unimportant things until she wiped her hands on her light blue apron, joined him at the table and said, 'He will be so pleased to see you. I can't wait to see the look on his face.'

'How is he?'

Nina tried to prevent her smile from becoming effortful. She lifted the teapot. 'It's not good, Nic,' she said. 'A year, maybe, maybe less. Sometimes . . .' She did not finish the sentence but

Harper guessed she had been about to say, *sometimes I wish it would be a lot less*. The news that Poppa's condition was terminal had come just before Harper had left Holland for Jakarta. It had not stopped Harper taking the job.

It would be less than a year, as it turned out. Poppa would succumb to his illness five months later, and two years after that, while Harper was working as a labourer on a farm in the north-east of Holland, near the German border, Nina would be knocked down and killed by a Dodge pick-up that was speeding round the corner of Firestone Boulevard: and with Nina's death, his last link with America, those five years he had spent in California as part of a family, with grandparents and a little brother, would be gone. He would never return.

'Is the doctor good? Should I speak with him while I'm here? Do you have enough money?'

Nina smiled then. 'You were always trying to send us money.'

'What else am I going to spend it on?'

'Well you know what your Poppa would say, booze and women, son, booze and women.' This was a joke: Poppa had always been such an upright citizen.

'I like a bit of whisky, I guess. Drank a bit too much of it over there.' It was risky, mentioning his life in Europe. He wouldn't do it in front of his grandfather as it would be sure to prompt a question, but Nina was used to not-knowing things. She had not-known about Michael for year after year, not-known how Harper was getting on in Holland – never really known exactly how it had happened, losing Bud.

'And women?'

He shook his head slowly, grinning at her, already copying his grandfather's grin. 'Tryin' to marry me off?' He heard how his accent had aligned with hers. There had never been any Dutch in his English, not after those years here, but in Europe and Indonesia his English accent was completely blank – and here he was, in Nina's kitchen, drinking fine hot tea, already regaining his West Coast edge.

'You're a good-looking young man, mid-twenties, perfect age some would say.'

'I'm not sure marriage is for me.'

'Marriage is for everybody.' She had waited many years for it to be legal for her and Poppa to wed, just because she was Latina, him black.

'There's not a lot of women would want a husband does as much travelling as I do.' This, too, would be dangerous territory in front of Poppa.

He saw her glance at his forearms then. He was dressed in a loose T-shirt – the scratches had mostly faded during his time on the run but there were still some very fine white tracks on his brown forearm, unnoticeable but to anyone who really looked. If he had thought about it, he would have worn a long-sleeved shirt. Maybe he had wanted her to notice, wanted her to say, are you okay? What happened over there?

Nina raised her teacup to her lips, put it down.

He read the question in her face. 'I always meant to come back, but, you know, military service, and then this job, you know, and travel. I'm not saying never. I have to go back and straighten things out with work, then maybe, I don't know.'

Nina smiled delicately, to take the sting out of her reproach. 'We always kind of hoped for another child around the place one day, if you got married one day I mean. We always hoped you would come back here for good once you were old enough so's

Anika didn't have any say in the matter.' Quickly, she added, 'But we knew in our heart of hearts, once we lost you to Europe . . .' She shook her head. 'It's funny, you know, how when kids grow up, you can look back and see what they've grown into. You always wanted to go places. You once set off up the road when you'd only been living with us a month, taking a look around. Poppa and I came to the front of the house and just watched you head off along the pavement, up the hill. You didn't look back once. We were so amused, we just watched you, until you disappeared over the brow of the hill, that is, then Poppa got worried about you getting lost and came chasing after you. Don't know why, you were old enough to find your way back, it was just 'cos you were new to us. We worried about you as if you were an infant but you were six, after all.'

There was a long silence. Then Harper saw that a tear was making its way slowly down Nina's cheek, leaving a shining trail.

'Come on . . .' he whispered.

She fumbled with one hand for the handkerchief stuffed up the other sleeve, then whispered to herself, 'I'll never forgive her. I know that's wrong of me. But to take you away from us, when we'd already lost Bud. We were the only family you knew.'

'I know, I know.'

'We had to put you on a boat with a tag around your neck, send you off like a parcel, across that big ocean, all on your own, just a boy, to somewhere you couldn't even remember. Wasn't it enough, what we'd been through? Everything we had been through?'

'Well, she didn't quite see it that way, I guess.' His mother – the mother who had demanded him back, after what happened to Bud, only to make it clear that having a son living with her again was a mighty inconvenience when it came to her complicated love life.

'Don't go upsetting yourself because I've showed up.'

She lifted her head then, gave her face a final wipe, right and left, beamed at him resolutely. 'You showing up is always the best thing in the world, make no mistake about that.'

She looked up at the ceiling, then back at him. It was time.

The first thing he noticed as they mounted the stairs was the smell: a strong smell of antiseptic, something faintly rotten underneath. Then, as they paused on the landing, both of them listening to see if he was awake, the harsh rasp of Poppa's breathing, the effort in it, the sound of a man exhausted to be alive. The door was ajar; Nina pushed at it gently. Poppa was in the middle of the bed and on the other side of the room was a small cot that Nina must have been sleeping in at night. An oxygen cylinder stood upright on an iron support by the bed, the mask and tube hanging from the post of the bedstead. They still had the same flowered wallpaper, *dusty roses*, was how he had always thought of that pattern, faded now in the light through the net curtains.

They stopped just inside the door. Poppa looked asleep, his mouth open, his face tilted to the ceiling – even in repose, his brows were knitted in pain. Harper stared at him; the concave hollows of his cheeks, the white stubble on his chin.

He looked at his grandfather then and thought, you spent your whole life doing good, saving people, and now I need you to save me. I have done something that puts me beyond reach of forgiveness, and if you do not tell me how to find my way back into the world, I will never be able to do it.

A cough shook the old man then, and the sound of it was so deep and hollow: it came from the depths of his chest cavity in the same way that earthquake tremors come from the depths of the earth. It was hard to believe that such a cough could not shake his bones apart. From the knitting on his face, it was clear it was causing him great pain. They stepped forward into the room. Nina laid a hand on Poppa's arm and leaned down to him as he opened his eyes, saying with quiet joy, 'Look, Michael, look who is here to see you.' And Poppa looked past Nina and saw Harper, and his mouth opened in a huge if effortful grin and their gazes met, and Nina looked from one to the other, smiling with pleasure at the sight of them together.

They raised Poppa up a little in the bed and adjusted the cushions behind him to make him as comfortable as they could, then Nina left the room on the pretext of making more tea but they both knew it was to give them some time alone together. She would be downstairs while they talked, moving around her kitchen, maybe humming a little.

He drew up a wooden chair from the corner of the room and sat on it. Poppa had closed his eyes, briefly, pausing from the effort of being hoisted upright, but he opened them again, grimaced, and said, 'Well, son, look how tall and strong you are now. That's the good thing about not seeing you that often, you really get to appreciate the changes.' He coughed. 'Not too sure about that beard.'

'I'll shave while I'm here. How are you?' Harper said, a straight and simple question, to indicate that Poppa could speak the truth to him even if he was putting on a brave face when Nina was in the room.

Poppa grimaced again. 'Not so good, son, not so good at all.'

They talked then about the doctors who came and went, a nurse that Poppa had disliked who had to be dismissed, how helpful the neighbours had been. 'Take a look at all the good wishes downstairs.' He didn't know whether Nina had told Poppa about the money he had sent from Holland – Poppa was such a proud man, it was possible Nina had kept quiet. Poppa told him he had been relieved when the doctor had said there was no point in further surgery. He wasn't scared of dying, he said, but he was scared of mutilation. He had seen some terrible things done to people during some of his spells in hospital. It was a great relief to be allowed to die at home. There was a new drug on the market but it made him real sick.

After a while, Poppa reached out a hand, and Harper bent forward in his chair and took it, and then he leaned further forward still and rested his head on the stiff white sheets and Poppa stroked the back of his head and Harper wept a little. 'I'm sorry,' he snuffled after a while, his head still down, ashamed of crying and struggling against breaking down entirely.

'You've nothing to be sorry for . . .' Poppa said, his voice low and rattly. 'You'd be surprised, you know, son, just how many people come here to visit and end up crying on those bedcovers. When you have an illness and people know you won't live through it, well, it's strange, it's like you can offer them absolution.' He gave a chuckle then. 'Don't know why. All that training to be a lawyer, now it turns out I'm a priest. An awful lot of them cry. Say, did Nina tell you about the riots we've had here?' He shook his head. 'It's been bad.'

Harper was still and silent then, turned a little, let Poppa stroke his head. He could tell Poppa what he had done, that he had killed a woman, drowned her with his bare hands in an irrigation ditch. What would Poppa think of him then? The *son* he had raised when he had no reason to other than he was a good person? All those other people who came – he could just imagine the string of visitors Poppa must be getting after all the people he had worked for, over the years. He had expected to find the house full when he came; Nina must have got rid of them for his visit. Didn't he, Harper, deserve and need absolution more than any of them? All those people who had used and needed Poppa over the years, when Poppa should have belonged to him, to them: and they were still using him, coming to his deathbed wanting something. He realised that in the five years he had lived with this family, he had always wanted more of Poppa, always resented how much he had cared for other people, his standing in the community. He was a big man in every sense of the word but there had never been enough of him to go around.

Poor Poppa, always expected to have the answer, to be wise – but even as he thought this, and felt guilty for it, Harper could not prevent himself from craving it. Say the right thing, he pleaded, in his head.

Surely Poppa had intuited that all was not right with him? Surely now, he would ask Harper what was wrong, and fix it.

'What was it all for, Nicolaas?' Poppa said.

'What do you mean?' Harper asked, lifting his head.

'All that work. Young folk, smashing things, just wanting to be heard I guess.'

Harper looked at his grandfather, then rubbed the back of his hand across his face and drew breath. Poppa was dying. It wasn't about him.

'All that work,' Poppa repeated with a sigh. Nina had warned him of this downstairs, that Poppa had started to question his life, as any man in his position was entitled to do. She said he didn't even raise a smile about the Voting Rights Act.

He couldn't bear the thought that Poppa might be hard on himself: plenty of men had cause for that, not him. 'C'mon Poppa . . . You worked so hard.'

'Maybe if I'd worked a little less hard, I'd have taken better care of my own family.'

Was that really what Poppa thought? Here this man lay, a man who had worked so tirelessly for what he believed was right, and yet that very passion and tirelessness meant he could only see all the things that were still wrong. Harper thought of all the people he had met who were self-serving: the people in his line of work, who cared nothing for how their actions affected others as long as they earned a good living in an exciting way; the clean evil of the men with machetes and sickles for whom politics was no more than an excuse; himself – yes, himself. How many of those people would lie on their deathbeds excoriating themselves for what they had done or failed to do? The most evil would be the least self-questioning of all. And yet here, on this bed in this room smelling of antiseptic, lay a man who had worked all his life to do the right thing: a man who had done so much that he couldn't forgive himself for not doing enough.

Harper rested his hand on top of Poppa's where it lay on the bed sheet, lightly, because he didn't know if his skin would be sensitive – it felt as though it should be. It was hot and papery, the veins standing out in ropes. To see this man on his deathbed: it catapulted him backward and forward at once.

Poppa had his eyes closed now and for a few moments, Harper wondered if he had fallen asleep, then the hand beneath his moved, turned and grasped at Harper's with surprising strength, although he did not open his eyes. When he spoke, his voice was suddenly clear.

'When I die, Nicolaas, you're going to be the only one who saw what happened. I'm so sorry, son, so sorry to leave you with that.'

It was the only time Poppa had ever mentioned what happened to Bud, their joint complicity that day, their failure to save him.

'Can I ask you something?' Harper said then.

'Sure, ask away.'

'When Anika asked for me back, why didn't you try and stop her? Why didn't you fight it?'

Poppa looked at him then and the expression on his face was, if anything, amused rather than hurt. 'Is that what you think, son? We didn't fight? Oh, we fought. I was used to fighting.' He coughed again. 'Your mother wanted you back because of what happened to Bud. It happened when I was looking after you, too. It was my fault. You think there was a court in the land that would stop a child being sent back to his mother after that?' More coughing. 'We didn't tell you any of that because we didn't want you to go back to your mother hating her. We wanted to give you a chance.'

He thought, then, of the occasional card or letter he had sent to Nina and Poppa from Holland, during his teenage years. *I am well. It has been raining here all week. My favourite lesson at school is Geography. The maps are very interesting.* Staying in touch had never been his strong point.

Poppa had his eyes closed. Gradually, his breathing steadied, became slow and regular. On the branches of a tree outside the window, a bird was singing, out of sight.

*

Downstairs, Nina was wiping at the stovetop, more furiously than was strictly necessary. Harper saw how neat and clean the kitchen was – much tidier than he remembered it. He imagined Nina scrubbing the whole house, all of the time, in her impotent fury at Poppa's suffering.

'I'm afraid we have some folks coming round for supper later,' she said. 'Neighbours who moved in a couple of years ago, they're nice people. I told them our grandson was coming and hoped they'd take the hint but they said they're dying to meet you.'

'You shouldn't be cooking supper for anyone,' Harper said, 'you have enough to do.'

'Oh, they bring their own supper. You know how people are round here. Remember all that food they brought round after we lost Bud? I had to bring the dog in the house for the first time in his life and feed it to him in secret.'

They shared a smile.

'Your room is just the same. Want to take a look?'

'Maybe later. I want to know what I can do for you and Poppa while I'm here.'

She straightened up from where she had been wiping, shook the cloth over the sink, folded it once and laid it over the side. 'Like mending things? We have people lining up to do that.'

'Why can't he realise what a good man he was?'

'Because he was, I guess, too good to realise it. Neighbours won't stay long. How about you?'

'I could eat something.'

'Wasn't talking about tonight.'

He went over to her then, put his arms around her and held her against him, her small stout frame against his tall wiry one.

He felt the jolting of her body against him as she wept a little. He guessed that nobody had held her for a while.

Later, he would go up to his room and, before the neighbours came, he would shave off his beard and then sit on the back porch while Nina trimmed his hair with a pair of sharpened kitchen scissors and he would think about what he was going to say to Gregor at the Institute, how he was going to explain going off the radar for four months, and Nina would say, 'Sit still and look straight ahead now, Nic, or I'm going to take a slice off your ear.'

Dusk gathered, as if the valley was filling with smoke; deepening towards dark. He was sitting on the veranda, drinking whisky. For most of the afternoon, he had still expected Kadek, bringing something for dinner that he would place inside the hut, on the desk, coming back outside to the veranda and saying, with his customary politeness, 'Mr Harper, would you like me to light the lamps?'

Dusk gathered and grew. Kadek did not come with food. He did not come to light the lamps. Harper sat on the veranda for a while, drinking and smoking, then went back inside the hut and turned on the unreliable bedside lamp while he found the matches, lit the paraffin lamps himself, turned off the bedside lamp. He closed the shutters and pulled the door to behind him as he returned to the veranda, hanging one of the lamps from a hook on the inside of the roof. No sign of Kadek and it was too late for him to come now. So, Harper thought, tonight, then? It occurred to him to wonder, again, how implicated Kadek was. He had always wondered if, when Kadek said each morning, 'I hope you passed a peaceful night?' there was an element of derision in the question. But if Kadek was part of it, then he would not be risking warning Harper by failing to turn up for his duties. He would be here, as exquisitely polite as ever, keen to make sure that Harper was unaware. No, he thought, if it was tonight, then Kadek had been approached in the town earlier that day by a young man or woman he didn't know, who came up to him and said merely this: 'Don't go to the *bule*'s house tonight.' And after a momentary glance at the young man or woman's face, Kadek would have gone home. Or perhaps Johan's arrival was all the sign that Kadek needed. The Angel of Death didn't come roaring into town in red and black with a pitchfork in his hand, after all, not in the world that Harper worked in. He came smiling, in casual slacks and an open-necked shirt, reaching out his hand. He came carrying a briefcase. Or he turned up one evening, as the light was turning golden on the green fields, and one of the children came running into the house to tell you that there was a stranger standing outside in the yard.

If I was running the Institute, and I wanted a man to be unsuspecting, Harper thought as he sipped his whisky, I would give the man a large cheque, to lull him into a false sense of security and to provide a paper trail of my good intentions in the event of any investigation. I would hire local youths through a chain of command – each link knowing no more than the link either side of him – so that, ultimately, the act would be untraceable to me. That's what the men in suits did. The men in suits, on both sides of the equation, always kept their own hands clean. And he knew then that Abang had sent him up country to visit Komang that day not in order to warn him to escape with his family, but to give his murderers the signal that the time had come. He had not been sent to save Komang. He had been sent to kill him.

And when Johan stood on Harper's veranda yesterday, that was what was familiar about him. Harper had seen his own reflection.

The world is different now, Rita had said to him. They thought the world was different then.

There's a form of John in every language, isn't there? There certainly is.

His head was thick with whisky by the time he went back inside the hut. He pulled off his shirt and trousers and slung them over the back of the chair, flung back the sheets. There was no point in running. If he was right, they would find him; if he was wrong, then he would be sacrificing the possibility of happiness with Rita for nothing. There was only one way to find out if he was being paranoid or not. Two more nights in the hut: if they didn't come in that time, then he had been wrong about everything. It was that simple: two nights.

As he settled down, bunching up the pillow beneath his head with one arm, he thought, I wonder if, however ready you are, when the moment actually comes, you cannot help but fight. Even Poppa, he thought, ravaged with cancer, in pain: at the end, he fought, I'm sure he did. It would have been difficult for Nina to watch that fight, with its single possible outcome. He could just imagine the old man, skinny but large-boned in his bed, coughing ferociously, determined to hang on to those last scraps of life, the breath heaving inside him. And Bud. There must have been a split second when Bud realised what was happening to him – not while he was floating in the water, or even when he began to turn, but somewhere between hearing Harper scream his name and plummeting into the cascade of the fall. What would the mind of a five-year-old compute in that moment: would he have understood, or would the panic have been so raw, so unformed, that it was simply fear in its most concentrated form? Komang's wife: she would have understood. She fought, long beyond the point that Harper would have thought her capable of fighting. Perhaps every human being fought, in his or her final moments – fought inside their head, even if they were immobile, no matter what the tortures of remaining alive.

He lay awake, his eyes wide open in the dark, thinking all these thoughts and in the next minute thinking that he must not let paranoia take a grip of him again, not ever. He was completely certain he would never be able to sleep. That was the last thing he thought, three clear monosyllables. *I won't sleep*.

He dreamt of Rita. She was standing far away from him, on a road, looking out over a field. Then the field was a cliff, then she fell, and he woke with a start. The hut was dark and silent and he fell asleep again, immediately, dreamt of her again. This time, he dreamt she was being cut at by people he couldn't see, the way they had the corpulent I Gede Puger, the fat man famous for corruption. They had sliced the fat from his body, it was said, before they shot him in the head. He was standing on a bridge. Then she was beside him. They were cutting her but she didn't mind. He woke in panic, flailing, and realised dawn had already come and Kadek was on the veranda.

As he opened the doors, Kadek bowed good morning. 'I am sorry I did not come yesterday Mr Harper but my wife was sick.'

'I am sorry to hear that, Kadek, please pass on my good wishes.'

He could see, as he looked out over the valley, that it had not rained in the night: a dry night then, not a night to hide your tracks, not a night when the thunder of rain on the roof of the hut would have hidden any sounds on the veranda.

He splashed his face with the water Kadek had brought, lit a cigarette, sat on the veranda and listened to Kadek inside the hut tidying up, making the bed, smoothing the bed sheets with a swift motion of his hand so that they made a sound like the slowly flapping wing of some great bird, an albatross perhaps. So, that was why they hadn't come. They were waiting for rain. He wondered how much they would be paid. How much was he worth?

He wondered how Kadek lived: well, he hoped, if he was employed by a Western company, in a large compound with his extended family. He imagined Kadek's wife as young and pretty, two or three children, perhaps. Such lives were good lives as long as nothing went wrong – that was what he often thought when he passed through the villages; the slow pace of life, the communal living, the family ties. As long as there was enough food, and no one fell sick . . . he stared out at Gunung Agung, the holy mountain, floating above the trees . . . as long as the volcano didn't erupt or a tidal wave sweep away your fishing boat or pestilence destroy the rice harvest . . . as long as there wasn't a war or a devaluation of the rupiah or a coup. Rita and others like her could romanticise such lives, such islands, all they liked, but the people who lived here walked a tightrope every day of their lives.

After a few minutes, Kadek stepped over the threshold onto the veranda and, without speaking, placed a china cup of coffee next to his elbow. Kadek had intuited by his silence that it had not been a good night, he thought. Wearily, he relived his dream, sipping at the hot black coffee. He wondered if it really had been as long a dream as it had felt at the time, or if he had only remembered it as long. He had heard somewhere, back in Holland, that dreams occur in the second we rise from unconsciousness, in a flash – and that even if we think we have been dreaming for hours, it is only what we remember in a flash, time compressed. This thought had always fascinated him. Perhaps it was true of conscious memory too: decades could be remembered compressed into a moment, after all.

However horrible and odd the dream, it was at least a comfort that he had dreamt of Rita. He thought he would be pleased to dream of her in whatever form she might take: and surely that was something, whatever happened. How short a time he had known her and yet how large she loomed in his mind. Those who haunt us are not the most beautiful or most dear, he thought, far from it, merely those who arrive at a time in our lives when we are ready to be haunted.

Kadek came back out onto the veranda and said something. He was aware of Kadek's voice sounding in his ear, a small burst of noise to his left, but he did not register the words. Then Kadek said again, 'Mr Harper . . .'

'Yes?' Harper did not turn his head.

'Your breakfast. It is on the table but I could bring it to you?'

Harper turned his head, at last, and said, 'Oh, thank you, leave it, thank you.'

Kadek bowed.

He sat on the veranda for a while, then rose, slowly, wearily, from his seat, went and leaned his elbows on the rail, looking out over the valley. If he fulfilled his fantasy of the villa in the rice fields, building those bookshelves for Rita, how long would it be before he started sleeping badly again, crying out or disturbing her as he rose from the bed in the middle of the night? She would say, *what is it?* He would tell her, eventually, and so hand some of his memories to her. It would be like presenting her with a severed head wrapped in a bed sheet. Better to stay away than do that to her. He must strike a bargain with himself, and make it firm – once he left here, if he left here, he would put it behind him. Could he do that? Wasn't that the problem, always, not making a choice – but knowing whether you had a choice or not?

He became aware of Kadek standing next to him. The man had materialised soundlessly at his elbow. What was it now?

Kadek looked at him and said, 'It is all done now, Mr Harper.'

As they stood facing each other, it was as if all pretences had fallen away, and Kadek was saying, *you know the place you have come to now, all is finished*.

Then Kadek said, 'Will you be requiring a meal later today or perhaps you will eat in the town?'

'You don't need to come later, thank you.'

'Tomorrow morning, or will you be leaving before breakfast?'

Of course, Kadek had been informed of his departure. Perhaps Johan had gone to see him after his coffee with Harper in the smart restaurant, or perhaps there had been a phone call from whoever employed Kadek directly, probably an operative or an office in Denpasar.

'No, no, thank you, I won't require anything else . . .' Harper said. He hadn't realised this was the last time he would see him. He had assumed Kadek would be there on his final morning.

'And what of your transport requirements, Mr Harper?'

Again, this was something Harper had not considered. It didn't seem appropriate to enquire about buying the little battered car now. Kadek was clearly done with him.

'I will take the car into town in the morning, then leave it parked outside the Museum. I'll leave the keys at the entrance desk.'

Kadek bowed a little, said, 'It has been a pleasure to work for you, Mr Harper.' He straightened, gave a smile then, the smile of an equal, bidding goodbye.

Their goodbye was so peremptory, he could not think of a gesture. 'Thank you, thank you, yes, it's been a pleasure for me too.'

And then, as if the thought had only just come to him, Kadek added, 'Would you like me to fold and pack your clothes?'

'No thank you, I can do that myself, later today.' He had what, six shirts, three pairs of trousers, some T-shirts, his old boots, two pairs of shoes? He had a nice watch. He had an expensive leather bag with a zip that Francisca had bought him that was intended for toiletries. He used it for pens and pencils and disposable cigarette lighters and kept some of his cash folded and tucked into the lining where he had unpicked a seam. He had his notebook. He would tear out the pages, one by one, and burn them in the ashtray. That would take an hour or so.

And then, before he could think to extend his hand, thank Kadek again or mention a tip, Kadek had gone, leaving him alone on the veranda. Ostensibly, Harper had dismissed him, but Harper knew that it was he who had been dismissed.

As Harper settled down in his bed that night, his final night in the hut, he left the bedside lamp on for a while and watched the shadows of the insects dance against the thick mosquito net like his own *wayang* show. He understood that the whole of his life had been built upon the lie of logic. It was logic that relieved you of choice. If I don't do this job, someone else will. If my company doesn't invest in this mad and murderous regime, another will. If I don't kill this woman, then the men around me will and more slowly. All true: but there would always be one bad thing that was simply too bad to be justified in this way. If he had not drowned Komang's wife in the rice field then she would have been tortured to death over a period of several hours. But he had not drowned her to save her from being tortured. He had drowned her to show the men he was on their side. He had done it to save his own skin.

He lay, watching the insects dance. He thought of the pictures he had carried around in his head for so many years: Bud, disappearing over the fall; Komang's wife, the way her wet hair lay across his wrist as he pressed her face down; the moon over Jakarta that night, the yellow moon as he crouched by a canal and clutched a death list to his chest. And now, this moment now, watching the insects flick and flutter. What was any life but such moments, strung together, like beads on a necklace? Rita didn't wear any jewellery, just small gold stud earrings and a watch with a leather strap. An image came of her sitting in the bar on the night they met, her easy laugh, and the way that when she did it, she lifted a hand to place her fingers, briefly, against the bare flush of her throat. Moments like that: it was all a string of moments.

He lay there, calmly: such insights, lying there, such clarity, waiting for the moment when he would lean over, lift the net just enough to reach out and turn off the lamp, lie back in the dark, and eventually, despite it all, give way to sleep.

In the morning, he would rise, dress, go out onto the veranda – maybe even go for one last walk down to the river. He would extract some dollars from inside the lining of the toiletries bag and place them in the envelope from which he had taken the Institute's cheque. He would seal the envelope, write Kadek's name on it and leave it on the desk. After that, it would simply be a question of lifting his holdall over the threshold of the doorframe, descending the steps, taking the case down the path to the car. He had arranged with Rita that he would check into the guesthouse some time in the afternoon and she had said she would get there as soon as possible after work, so that they could have cocktails together to celebrate their plans. In a mirror image of their first meeting, he saw himself sitting at the table in the corner. He saw himself waiting for her, smoking, a little impatient, and how she would glance straight at that corner as she stepped into the bar. She would look at him and smile. Lying there in bed, he smiled back at her.

He woke a few hours later but not violently, merely with a sigh at the derisive note of victory in the ghekko's cry. Eh-*ur!* . . . the pause, then the continuing. So the goodwill of Kadek and the young woman who made the offering had proved fruitless. The ghekko had still come. He realised that although he had heard it almost every night, he had never seen it.

He lay awake in the dark, quite still, breathing gently and listening to the skittering of the creature's feet on the sloping wooden roof above his bed. It was nothing. It was only a ghekko. In the morning, it would be gone. In the morning, he would rise. Slowly, gently, he drifted back to sleep, a long fall into unconsciousness as unhurried as a man with a large parachute descending from a great height or a huge leaf detached from a tree on a still day: and as he drifted down, the sounds on the roof began to form a more regular pattern, *pit-pit*, pause, *pit-pit-pit*. It was just the ghekko, that was all, or some other creature, or his imagination – or maybe, yes, at last. It was the beginning of rain.

Acknowledgements

The idea for this novel came when I was a guest of the Ubud Writers and Readers Festival on the island of Bali, Indonesia, in 2012 and would not exist without the generous help of its Artistic Director, Janet De Neefe. My warmest thanks to her and Ketut Suardana for their kindness, hospitality and patience with my endless questions. I am also indebted to many others who helped with research or read the manuscript, in some cases both; in the Netherlands, Dr Revo Soekatno of Wikimedia Indonesia and Adriaan Van Dis; in Indonesia, the Tanjung Sari, Hotel Indonesia Kempinski, John H. McGlynn of the Lontar Foundation, Suzanty Santorius and Yosef Riadi; in the UK, Michael Arditti, Jacqui Lofthouse and Kevin Smullin Brown; and in the US, Dr Clayborne Carson of the King Research and Education Institute and Stanford University, for permission to quote him and for advice on the lives of the black middle classes in 1950s Los Angeles. Any errors in this novel remain entirely my responsibility.

The coup and counter-coup of 1965 led to the deaths of up to one million Indonesians, mostly members or suspected members of the Communist Party, the PKI. The violence included neighbour-on-neighbour killings at a time of great poverty and hardship but much of it was orchestrated by the military and aided by the provision of lists of names by the CIA, then engaged in a Cold War battle to prevent the spread of Communism throughout South East Asia. The existence of these lists is a matter of public record but the character of Harper and his role in the handover of one of them are both my invention, as is the institution he works for.

Private companies working as risk analysts or consultants for multinational corporations and governments have existed for decades and many are active worldwide today. Staff in London and Jakarta working for a long-established firm in this field gave me invaluable help with my research on the condition of anonymity for themselves and their employer. I'm very grateful for the insights they offered into a business that relies on discretion. There is no suggestion their activities are comparable with any of the events in this novel.

Heartfelt thanks as ever to my agent, Antony Harwood; to Sarah Savitt, to Hannah Griffiths and Lisa Baker of Faber & Faber UK and Sarah Crichton of Sarah Crichton Books / Farrar, Straus and Giroux, New York.